SPY WEDNESDAY

SPY WEDNESDAY

A Novel

Steven Sims

To order additional copies of this book, contact:
Xlibris Corporation
1-888-795-4274
www.Xlibris.com
Orders@Xlibris.com
27251

PROLOGUE

The summer sun still blazed as it began its descent into the Detroit skyline, and the thousands of fans were jubilant as they poured out of Tiger Stadium, buoyed by their double-header wins over the New York Yankees.

Making their way north from the main gate, three men walked abreast along the sidewalk between Michigan Avenue and the stadium's chalky blue wall. They laughed on the way to their parked car, and the weather was perfect for their drive back to Grand Rapids. The games had given them plenty to talk about on the three-hour trip.

They paused long enough for the tallest of the three to buy a cap from a street vendor, and he pulled it over his bald pate as they resumed their walk.

When it was over, it was curious to all involved that what happened next seemed to occur in slow motion.

Still shoulder to shoulder, the three were almost past the left field wall when the man in the center seemed to jerk in time with a distant pop, followed by another. His feet froze to the sidewalk as he wrenched both arms outward at shoulder level, then grabbed his chest with a gurgling gasp.

He rocked on buckling legs before he was slammed onto his back by two more shots from the street. The third bullet shattered both of his crossed hands on the way into his chest, and the last round gashed the right side of his neck.

The friend on his right dropped and ripped off his own shirt in futile attempts to stop the blood spurting from the dime-sized holes. The third man pointed into the street and screamed, "IT WAS THEM! THEY SHOT HIM, GODDAMN IT! IT WAS THEM!"

The driver floored the accelerator, sending the carload of laughing black teenage boys on a weave through the growing tangle of traffic and into a rubber-squealing turn onto Trumbull.

Several had already run to call for help, but it was obvious to anyone who could see that the felled man was really a corpse who just hadn't stopped breathing.

The man trying to stop the bleeding wondered how to administer CPR to someone with severe chest trauma. Finally, he and the man in the cap bent over their friend to assure him that help was on the way.

The thick circle of onlookers gasped as the wounded man grabbed the pair and tried to lift himself, gushing blood from the ragged exit wounds in his back.

"Tell Maureen I love her," he choked, sending a crimson cascade over his chin. "Tell Ken and Margaret I love them," he went on, his words moved by a combination of heroic effort and spasm.

Then, after a quick, shivering convulsion, he looked through his friends at what only the dying can see.

"The road never ends," he whispered.

And with the summer sun, he was gone.

CHAPTER ONE

It had happened again, just as he knew it would. Every night he spent at home during weekend visits from college they returned, just as they had since he was a boy. The somber recurrent dream seemed to be a phantom of his boyhood home, and the fingernail creases they put into his palms from nights spent with balled fists would stay sharp reminders well into his morning shower.

Even though the dreams had begun years before his father's death, they were a constant focus of the therapy he underwent for a couple of years after the murder. But they were never "resolved".

The nocturnal mind-play was always the same: the Perry family was all seated in the living room of their suburban Grand Rapids, Michigan home, silently watching television. Then the father, Walt Perry, stood and announced that he was leaving for work. Now a 22-year-old junior at Miami University, Ken was about eight in the dream, and sat silently between his mother, Maureen, and his 10-year-old sister Margaret, now a Chicago-based airline attendant.

Ken would be the only one to take notice as his tall, slender father stood, lifted his briefcase, turned his back to the front door and walked into the opposite wall, not against, but *into* the living room wall. Each dream would then end with Ken incredulous that no one but he noticed his father's surreal disappearance. The psychologist had connected Ken's dream with his father's untimely death in Detroit. But it had begun over a year *before* the murder. The dream never changed. No words were spoken, no face held expression, all was silent, unnoticed, unreal. Only Ken's father moved. Each time Ken wanted to alert his mother and sister to the bizarre departure, but he was gripped by frustrating paralysis . . . until he awoke to uncurl the fingers from his stinging palms. Sometimes they bled.

On this late summer morning the sunlight streaming into Ken's room soon roused him, and he pulled himself from the sheets with a long, yawning stretch. Squinting his blue eyes against the dresser's mirror, he patted his short brown bed-headed hair into shape, put his lean, six-foot-two frame through a quick set of stretches, and threw on his running gear.

The avid runner didn't usually work out in the morning, but he had found a good hard run an effective way to banish the dream, and the tension it brought, out through the soles of his feet. Clad in a Sierra Club Run T-shirt and red shorts, he steered his Brooks Beast running shoes for the stairway to the front door. Scheduled to run that fall's Detroit Free Press Marathon, he had already missed one day's training for the previous day's hitchhike home to Grand Rapids from his apartment in Oxford, Ohio. He had kept his small efficiency apartment there over the summer to take a class required for a double major in secondary education and philosophy at Miami, and he had thumbed home so he could pick up a few needed items and spend one last weekend with his mom and friends before the fall semester began. If he didn't run now he would miss three days in a row, since tonight would be spent with an old buddy, and all the next day he would be hitching back to school.

Ken always enjoyed visits back to his lifetime home at 2518 College Avenue, Southeast. The white, two-story, wood frame house had changed little during his lifetime, let alone in the last few months he'd been gone. The Early American furniture in the living and dining rooms was far from new, but looked as if it had never been used. Hearing his mother moving about below, he started down the staircase, straightening one of the family photos that peppered the floral print wallpaper.

"I was just putting in a load of laundry," the graying brunette said. "How about your favorite breakfast when you get back?"

"That'd be great, mom," Ken yelled over his pounding descent.

"I'll ready the usual," the slightly overweight 49-year-old answered, then leaned over the empty laundry basket she held.

Between his crashing plunge down the stairs and non-stop front door exit he pecked a kiss onto her waiting cheek. She crinkled her nose in disapproval of the trimmed brown beard and mustache he had grown, despite her vehement disapproval, over a year earlier. She repeatedly bemoaned the fact that the facial hair covered his deep, chiseled dimples, and made him look like a "hippie", although he kept his straight chestnut-brown hair above ears and collar.

A sunny, calm and warm morning greeted Ken as he set out on the six-mile course he had inherited from his father. Himself a runner, Walt Perry had charted the route with the odometer on the family car when he and his wife moved into their house twenty-three years earlier, just before Marg was born. The neighborhood remained suburban, although a bordering stretch of road had been converted into four-lane highway several years prior.

The mailboxes clipped by Ken at an easy nine-minute-mile pace, and his only interruption came at Garfield Park. There a woman in a van stopped him for what seemed like an hour as he repeated street directions over her load of screaming toddlers.

Ken compensated for the interruption by doubling his pace for the last eight blocks home, and a tall, sweaty glass of iced tea awaited him on the front porch. "You're the world's greatest mom!" he shouted as he grabbed the drink on the way inside.

"Put the glass in the kitchen sink," she echoed from somewhere upstairs. "It'll leave a ring on that table."

Ken lifted the tumbler from the living room coffee table and used a dry patch of T-shirt to wipe the wet circle from the mahogany.

"Are you psychic?" he asked as he approached Marg's room, where his mother sat sewing.

"No," she replied. "I'm a mother."

The longtime widow felt close to her absent daughter as she would work near the red and white cheerleader's pompoms that had hung from Marg's dresser mirror ever since she graduated from Catholic Central High School two years before Ken. The bed full of stuffed animals were moved only during Marg's frequent visits from Chicago.

Ken went into a long, soothing stretch as he entered his room, just past Marg's and across the hall from his mother's. It was there that his parents placed him in a bassinet when he was brought home from the maternity ward at Blodgett Hospital. The four-poster twin bed before him was the same one upon which he had faked illness to avoid school as a boy, and under which his mother had discovered the cache of Playboys accumulated during his adolescent hormonal awakening.

He fell onto his favorite chair, a huge, piano-legged, overstuffed leather beast of Salvation Army origin, and untied his shoes. A pilfered yellow, diamond-shaped "DIP" road sign clanged against the inside of his bedroom door as Ken kicked it shut and peeled off his clothes.

A minute later, wrapped in a Hotel Tuller towel, he dashed down the hall for a shower, scampered back and threw on gym shorts and a T-shirt from a long-forgotten road race. He took two stairs at a time to the living room, turned through the kitchen and then bounded down the twelve basement steps in four strides.

"One of these days you're going to collapse those stairs," his mother warned as she exited the laundry room. "We should've put in a firemen's pole for you."

Most of the Perry family's living, including informal meals, took place in the spacious, mahogany-paneled basement. One large room took up half of the basement and contained an old-fashioned brass and wood bar. A poker table rested between the bar and a high-backed wooden booth that had come from an old downtown Chicago pub. The large corner area opposite the booth held a billiard table, with cues, balls and other accessories hanging in racks on one wall. A large Tiffany lamp hung over the green felt playing surface.

The foot of the stairway rested between the billiards area and a smaller TV room where Ken had grown up alternating between tube-watching and homework. The time-worn but eminently comfortable Naugahyde couch, chair and recliner all huddled in their places around the large color television, and if Ken ever needed to relax, this was where he found himself. It was a haven, secure and calm (although it had seen some pretty rousing sleepovers and parties, usually thrown by Marg). The slightly sagging couch rested in the same place it had ever since it was purchased fifteen years earlier. Ken would often let his imagination float him back to the January night when, after a high school dance, he and classmate Hillary Stover both left their virginity on its smooth cushions. Mom and dad had been on a ski trip and Marg was away at flight attendants' training in Chicago.

A door across from the couch led to the unfinished, cement-block walled laundry and utility room that housed Ken's winery during his freshman year in high school. With a little training and a recipe provided by a friend, he had manufactured several batches of high-octane grape wine, keeping himself and his buddies considerably occupied for several summer afternoons. The enterprise came to a halt, however, when Mrs. Perry followed her nose to the source of the fermentation gasses, a five-gallon jug nestled under the stairway. Ken was immediately dispatched to sessions with a school counselor and Father Vince Gardner, his parish priest. They, in turn, soothed the illicit vintner's parents' fears with a consensus that their son's alcoholic adventures were typical adolescent exploration, not dipsomania.

They were right. Ken enjoyed an occasional drink with his friends, but he would never subject his body to real or sustained abuse. He was a runner. Anyway, he wouldn't need to seek refuge in a bottle because he had nothing from which to flee. His home life had been loving and supportive, his self-image and self-esteem high. The only phantom that taunted Ken had sporadically appeared during sleep, and disappeared into a wall.

"It's too nice to eat in here," Mrs. Perry said. "Let's go out to the picnic table."

Ken went up the stairs and out the back door onto the brick patio, where he took a damp cloth to the weathered redwood tabletop. His mother soon followed with a tray of his favored breakfast—several fresh bacon, lettuce and tomato sandwiches— along with cottage cheese and fruit, and a pitcher of iced tea.

"Are you settled in for the next semester?" she asked as they set their places.

"Yeah. I was pre-registered and got all the classes I requested, which is unusual," he said. "Usually, I get bumped from at least one because it's already filled or it conflicts with another class time. And staying in the same apartment as last year made it easier, too. I'm looking forward to seeing who else returns to my building," Ken said, lifting one of the sandwiches.

"What are your plans for tonight?" Mrs. Perry asked, pouring their drinks.

"Lyttle's going to pick me up and we're going to shoot some hoop at the school gym after dinner."

Steve Lyttle was Ken's best friend. A high school classmate, Lyttle had stayed in Grand Rapids after graduation and was a sociology major there at Grand Valley State College.

"After that we'll probably hang out somewhere until we're arrested," Ken told his mom with a grin. She handled his sense of humor well; after all, he had inherited it from the love of her life.

"You still owe me bail from last time," she countered.

"On Sunday," Ken went on, "it's an early morning departure to go back to Miami." He never used the word hitchhike when talking with his mother, who firmly denounced the practice. "After I take you to Sunday brunch," he quickly added, clapping the last of his sandwich crumbs onto his empty plate. "The usual, at the Sheraton." Sunday brunches had been a Perry family tradition since before he was born. They were livelier when Dad and Marg were there, but they still seemed present, even in their absence.

A rustling came from the shrubs next door, and the Perrys soon found themselves in idle conversation with Mrs. Doris Bilby, their next door neighbor and block gossip captain. Over the years, Ken had a lot of fun dropping incredible rumors into Mrs. Bilby's ear and watching them spread through the neighborhood like typhus. Once, he convinced the gray-haired gossip that Lyttle was wearing a cast on his leg not because of a football injury, but because he had been visited by Mafia leg breakers trying to collect a gambling debt. It took less than ninety minutes for the news to reach Lyttle's parents, twelve blocks away.

"It's a beautiful day, so I'll kill the two hours until Lyttle comes over by washing your car," Ken told his mother, wringing his hands on a paper towel. The Volvo wagon didn't really need a bath, but Ken wanted to do something more for his mom while he was home.

After hauling a bucket, hose and cleansers to the driveway, Ken vigorously assaulted the white Volvo as a Doors CD spun in its console.

"Hey, Ken!" came a velvety call.

He turned to spot Carol Hurley, a willowy beauty he hadn't seen for the three years since they had graduated together from Catholic Central High School. Leaning from the open driver's window of her parents' new, pearl-white Lincoln, Carol lived only two blocks away, although she and Ken had never really known each other. She was a society girl during their old high school days, dividing her time between being seen with the right people at the right places at the right fashionably late times, while joining all the right student clubs and activities to ensure that her 4.0-plus GPA would get her into the right Ivy League college. A well-placed phone call from her high-powered attorney father had helped.

"I thought you were at Princeton," Ken said, leaning against the soapy Volvo.

"I am," the tall, sexy-and-knows-it brunette said with a flourish. "This is all done with mirrors!

"Actually, our classes don't start for another two weeks," she explained. "So, I'm just killing time until I go back and time starts killing me."

"Princeton's rough, eh?"

"It's a bitch," she said. A gold bracelet dangled from her wrist as she waved a taxi around her idling car. "How are things at State?"

"I didn't go to Michigan State," Ken replied. "I picked up Miami of Ohio. Better choice for my majors, phil and secondary ed. What are you working on?"

"Business administration," she said. "I'll have my bachelor's degree next year and my MBA in under three if I'm a good girl and follow daddy's game plan."

A pause followed, the Ivy League vixen allowing Ken adequate time to pick up on her cues and make his move.

"I'm only in town for tonight," he said. "I go back tomorrow and have a week to prepare before classes start. I'm shooting hoop with Lyttle and some buddies this afternoon, then he and I are going downtown."

"I'm baby-sitting my three-year-old niece," Carol said dryly. "But if you get in early you're welcome to join us for pizza, a Peter Pan video and . . . whatever," she said with a grin.

I can't believe it, Ken thought as he smiled in return. *I'm being asked to bed by a business major. This is like Martha Stewart inviting Howard Stern to the prom.*

"Here's my sister's number," Carol said, pulling a pen and pad from above the visor. "It's nearby . . . in Ada."

Ken wondered why this distant preppie of his high school years was now showing obvious interest in him. For the fireworks and novelty of a one-night stand? A need for someone with more depth than that of her French perfume spritzer? His road-toned physique?

Yep, Ken thought with a laugh as he waved at the receding Lincoln. *It's gotta be my runner's buns!*

The Detroit luxury liner was hardly out of earshot when its purr was replaced by the hammering chaos of Lyttle's approaching

Volkswagen. He and Ken had spent many an hour cruising with friends in the dilapidated red Beetle.

"You're early!" Ken shouted as he coiled the green garden hose.

"Game's been moved up to 5 p.m. instead of 7," the short, sandy-haired driver said. "Damn volleyball players have the court tonight."

Ken had his friend run a chamois over the Volvo as he showered and changed clothes, and they pulled away in the Volkswagen at a quarter to five.

Saturday night pickup games were as much a part of Catholic Central High School as were the classes. More so, in fact, since nearly all of the players were alumni—some in their 40s. At least one, Mr. Pesetti, was a senior faculty member, and had taught all of the players in his speech or English classes at one time or another.

As the electric scoreboard ticked above the empty wooden stands, Ken's team lost by one point when Lyttle missed a last-second lay-up.

"I hate you!" Ken screamed, jerking up the rear of his friend's shorts.

"You can walk home then, you sonofabitch!" Lyttle shot back. "That'll leave more room in the Vee-Dub for babes!"

The horseplay continued into the locker room and out onto the parking lot, where rain began to fall as Lyttle conceded Ken a place in the Beetle.

Dinner was more subdued as they caught each other up on recent events over draft beer and cheddar double-cheeseburgers at Rosie O'Grady's Pub.

"You obviously haven't been practicing your lay-ups," Ken began. "So what's been occupying your time?"

"Mainly classes and Linda," he said, referring to Linda Martin, the girl he had dated since seventh grade. "She's halfway through her nursing program at Calvin College and pushing me harder and harder toward the altar."

"You're a fool if you let her get away," Ken said, a string of Bermuda onion hanging from his lip. "I don't know another female who'd tolerate you, let alone a fox like her!"

Linda had been on the same cheerleading squad with Ken's ex, so the topic of his love life was inevitable.

"Heard from Terri?" Lyttle asked, leaning back from his empty plate.

"No, and never will," Ken answered without looking up. "It was nice while it lasted, but she showed her stripes when she discovered life beyond Grand Rapids. She met 'Dr. Goodbar' during her first week in East Lansing and dropped me with a postage stamp."

Lyttle sipped his beer. He had heard some of the details from Linda, but was still unsure of what to tell his friend.

"It's okay," Ken said, wiping his mouth with a bar napkin. "Even though we didn't seem to have much in common, I felt we were connecting pretty well . . . But the way she broke up with me shows that she didn't take the relationship all that seriously."

"Women," Lyttle said, motioning for another pair of beers. "You can't live with 'em and you can't live with 'em.

"It's only 8:30," he continued. "What do you want to do?"

Ken glanced at his watch, silently weighing a night of bar-hopping with his best old high school buddy against several hours of horizontal calisthenics with a gorgeous old high school snob.

Two and a half hours and three pitchers later they were still talking—Ken about his lost love, and Lyttle about his, which was now, as he revealed several beers into the conversation, approaching a spring wedding. Ken accepted the offer to be best man. He only hoped that Terri wouldn't be asked to be a bridesmaid.

Still a little drained from the previous day's hitchhiking and that afternoon's basketball, Ken was obviously tired.

"Come on, amigo," Lyttle said with his trademark end-of-the-night phrase: "Let's get outta here before the cops come."

It was a quarter to 12 when Ken waved goodbye to the Volkswagen's taillights and unlocked his front door. He flipped on a light and saw a note his mother had left on the small table by the door.

> Kenny;
>
> I've gone to bed, but a Carol Hurley called and said she wasn't sure she gave you the right phone number. It is 555-9525. And she wanted me to be sure to tell you that "You can call late," Don Juan!
>
> Mom

Ken stood in the soft light that bathed the gold-on-blue wallpaper at the foot of the stairs. He knew the 20-minute drive to the neighboring town of Ada would hold no future beyond tonight, but oh, what a night it could be. He leaned against the banister, weighing the note. He wondered if he was losing his youth as his nearby bed beckoned louder than the baby-sitter's couch a short drive away.

All right, Ken thought. *I'll decide by midnight.*

He walked to the fridge, threw a handful of ice cubes into a glass of water and settled into the family room recliner at 11:50.

Ken Perry had always been a legs man, and Carol Hurley had a pair of the finest, joining at a truly world class derriere. Sitting alone in the silence, his thoughts drifted back to his junior year high school class picnic at Warren Dunes State Park, some 100 miles south on the Lake Michigan coastline. He was sitting with a group of about a dozen male and female classmates, and all went slack-jawed when, in one fluid, cross-armed motion, the nubile Miss Hurley pulled off her dark T-shirt and nonchalantly eased her boobs into a string bikini top. He wondered if they could possibly be as perfect as they had remained in his memory.

Twelve chimes sounded from the billiards room grandfather clock and Ken's decision was made.

He shifted to the couch, picked the telephone from the adjoining end table and dialed her number. Ken flipped the note across the room and lay on his back as Carol answered on the third ring.

"Hello, Carol, this is Ken . . . Yeah, I'm sorry, but I got together with Steve Lyttle, one beer turned into two, into three . . . I just got in and saw your message."

"Well, you missed Peter Pan," she said. "But my brother and sister-in-law don't fly back until tomorrow. I could rewind Peter Pan," she paused, "or maybe we could watch something from my brother's private collection . . .

"Bring some chardonnay," she urged.

"I don't think so," Ken replied, feeling like a fool. "I have an early morning commitment, and the rest of the day will be spent hitchhiking back to school. Drivers are hesitant to pick up a sleepwalking thumber," he quipped. Ken hoped the humor would help soften any sense of rejection or embarrassment she might feel.

"You know," he said, "I've often admired you from afar . . .
Remember Warren Dunes?"

"Yeah," she said with a laugh. "I guess I'd spent enough summers
in France with my cousins to feel less inhibited at public beaches."
Yeah, right, Ken thought. He never had bought the lifetime
flirt's excuse for her schoolgirl exhibitionism.

"I'll be up for another hour or so," she said. Then, hearing the
persistence in her own voice, the lonely brunette paused and wished
Ken well. He did the same, and asked for her home phone number.

"I'll give you a call during Thanksgiving break," he said. Two
minutes later they hung up on what both knew would probably
be their last conversation. Life had never brought them any closer
than they had just come, and it probably never again would.

Ken stood, crunched on a mouthful of ice, and moved to retrieve
the note he had flicked across the room.

Bending over, he grabbed a corner of the paper, but it slid
from his fingers as he stood. *Must've wedged under the paneling,* Ken
thought. On closer inspection, a full third of the four-by-six-inch
sheet of paper had disappeared at the edge of the green indoor-
outdoor carpeting.

Ken bent over again and noticed that the paper had slid over
the carpet and under the bottom of the wall. *That's not possible,* he
thought, since there was no space between the wood-veneer
paneling and the cement block wall to which it was glued.

"Great," he groaned aloud. "Must be a crack in the foundation."

His mother had mentioned no leakage in the basement, nor
was there evidence of any—no moisture or discoloration in the
carpet. And a light tapping on the baseboard sounded solid,
signaling no wood rot.

Moving a few inches above the baseboard to the paneling itself,
Ken tapped a few more times, checking to see if the adhesive used to
bond the wooden sheet was separating from its solid, 12-inch-thick
cement block backing. The strikes brought a deep, drumming echo,
not the sharper rapping he expected from thin wood over masonry.

Curious, Ken tapped farther up the panel to find the same
results at knee level, then waist height and, finally, just below the
seven-foot-high ceiling.

The dark mahogany panel appeared the same as the others
lining the basement walls. Ken tapped on those immediately left

and right of the one under which the paper had slid. He felt the hard sting of his knuckles against the thinly-veiled cement, and the crisp rapping sound was what he expected from such a surface.

Placing the paper back where it had slid under the baseboard, Ken noticed that there was no resistance to his sliding the whole sheet under the wall. Without removing it, Ken slid the paper carefully to the right and then the left to the adjacent panels. But it stopped there, and could be inserted beneath the bordering panels only as far as the width of the baseboard, about a half inch.

"This is no cracked foundation," Ken told himself, flipping on the recessed overhead lights.

With one well-placed stroke, he pounded the heel of his fist onto the center of the panel under scrutiny. The sound reminded him of that made when thumping watermelons to see if they're ripe, only it was amplified a hundred times.

It was definite. There was something other than just a cement wall behind that panel—the center panel on the north wall of the family room, directly between the television and a large brass floor lamp.

Ken went to the garage and returned with a flat steel yardstick. He found that it could be slid all the way under the panel, leaving only about a half inch so he could pull it back out. The same was true at the top, but the gap between the panel edges wasn't wide enough to insert the tool. The paper wouldn't fit there, either.

I can't believe this, Ken thought as he fell back into the recliner, staring at the brown, woodgrain panel. *I tell a beautiful woman I can't come over to ride her to nirvana because I'm tired, and then I stay up an hour pounding the basement walls.*

Well, he reasoned, *if that panel's not glued to a cement wall, it's got to be attached to something.*

Using one end of the heavy-gauge yardstick, Ken pried first at a corner of another panel to reveal dried black adhesive against gray cement.

He then took the device to the upper right corner of the panel in question and saw that it wouldn't separate, yielding barely enough to show the dull gray metal to which it was bonded.

Damn! he thought. *That looks like the edge of a steel fire door!* He could see what appeared to be a seam in the painted finish that insistently clung to the light brown backing of the panel.

This is getting spooky, Ken thought, staring at the panel as he backed into the recliner. "It's definitely a hidden door," he whispered, listening to each word as if it might make his discovery believable if he heard the phrase aloud.

If it is a door, then there has to be a way to open it, Ken reasoned. He considered another trip to the garage, for a crowbar, but mom would surely blow her stack at such spontaneous (if not insane) renovation. Besides, if the metal backing turned out to be a construction element with which he was unfamiliar—some sort of stress brace or something—then he would look pretty stupid trying to explain the demolished paneling. And there would be the cost and time he would have to invest in repairs.

What made the whole thing particularly weird was that Ken had watched the construction crew remodel the basement when he was age six, and he had seen the men place the panel directly over a very real, flat, gray cement block wall.

The chimes sounded 2 a.m.

"I'm not going to sleep until I solve this," Ken said, walking back to the five-by-seven-foot-square riddle.

Every door has to have hinges, he thought, *and at least one latch.* Without a knob, hidden release possibilities included a recessed latch in one or more of the edges, or a remote trip mechanism, such as those in old movies where someone would pull on a wall-mounted lamp and a panel would rotate open. *It could open inward or outward,* Ken thought, *slide on an inside track or pop straight forward or back . . .*

Ken grabbed the steel rule and probed for a hinge or latch, with no success.

Pressure, he thought, pushing hard at all four corners, then working his way to the center.

He pulled again with the metal yardstick at each corner as hard as he could, and noticed that each gave about a quarter inch. That wouldn't happen if any of them were close to a hinge or bolted latch.

Finally, as the clock struck three, Ken found himself climbing the stairs to fetch a crowbar and toolbox from the garage.

There has to be a clean way to do this, he thought, looking for a point of attempt that would cause minimal damage.

He decided to pry the lower right corner as much as he could, place a wedge inside and keep pulling until something, a latch or hinge, gave way.

Ken switched on the adjoining floor lamp and slipped a chisel blade beneath the panel's lower edge. Preparing to drive the blade further with a hammer, he leaned heavily against the panel.

Then he remembered.

Some fifteen years earlier his father had helped Ken build a tree house in the backyard. But it wasn't of the typical father-and-son construction. It was much more than the six plywood sheets that comprised its walls, floor and ceiling. A car battery powered a ceiling-mounted light bulb, and the one door had a special security feature . . . There was no outside knob or handle.

Ken's father had fastened a loose hook on the inside of the door next to a small ring on the doorjamb. To gain entry, one had to know where to place a magnet on the outside of the door and move it upward, lifting the steel hook on the other side from its place in the ring. The hook could be placed in such a way that it would fall back into the ring when the door was closed upon exit.

Through Ken's adolescent years, "the fort" proved a perfect place to hide dirty magazines, fireworks, cigarettes and other contraband.

Climbing the stairs yet another time, he yanked a large "I Love Chicago" magnet from a stack of clipped grocery coupons it held to the side of the refrigerator.

His heart quickened as he bounded back down the stairs, and it pounded beneath his T-shirt as he stopped and placed the magnet against the panel. Starting low on his right he moved the piece upward, his left ear against the cool, smooth surface.

Ken heard a distinct click about chest-high on his second upward sweep, but the panel would not budge. Three tries later the click was followed by a dull knock, and the right side of the panel was released by a spring and popped outward a half inch.

Ken stood, amazed, unconsciously holding his breath for so long that he finally gasped the musty air the door released. *This must be what they felt like when they opened Tut's tomb,* he thought, reaching to grasp the door's edge. It was a large variation of the gray fire doors common to schools, office buildings and other institutions; a painted steel shell filled with cork or wood. But this one was concealed behind a thin, but effective, wooden veil.

Pulling the panel outward, Ken saw a second door. Located at the end of a six-foot-long entryway little more than shoulder wide and giving him just enough head room to walk erect, the second door was the common wooden variety, with a regular knob and no lock or window.

His heart banging like a piston, Ken felt sweat on his hands as he retrieved a Coleman camping lantern from the laundry room and returned to the inside door.

Crouching, Ken held the lantern above his head, and its stark light was absorbed by the rough gray cement block walls as he turned the doorknob. The squeak that he expected from the faded door never came as it smoothly swung inward, and he held the lantern far ahead of himself, the same way a man might extend his hat on the end of a stick to check for gunfire.

Easing inside, the small cubicle reminded Ken of a crypt. The twelve-by-twelve-foot room's walls and low ceiling were lined with the same faded white, perforated, noise-eating acoustic panels that he had seen in a radio broadcasting booth. So was the inside of the door. The only thing in the room was a large gray-green Steelcase desk that occupied nearly half of the floor space. There was no chair.

"What the hell is this?" Ken asked aloud.

The room swallowed his question.

Ken placed the lantern on the bare desktop and sat next to it, facing the door. He slowly surveyed the room to the lantern's low, reassuring hiss.

Clipped wires sprouted from the ceiling where a light fixture once hung, and several large bolts protruded from the wall to the right of the desk. The bolts appeared to have previously held some sort of heavy electronic equipment, since they supported several scuttled gray circuit boxes and a jumble of severed wires.

A vertical row of the acoustic panels about five feet up on the wall behind the desk was badly scraped, with a couple of grooves suggesting that a file cabinet had once stood there.

The open end of a one-inch aluminum electrical conduit protruded from the same wall, just below the six and a half-foot high ceiling. Ken traced a line of screw holes from the conduit down to where the amputated multicolored spaghetti bristled at knee level on the adjoining wall.

Other screw holes in the same wall could have held shelving or some other wall-mounted item or items. Ken wondered why the place had been stripped so completely, down to the light fixtures, but the desk remained. It didn't take long to realize that it was too big to fit through the narrow entrance. It had to have been brought in during construction.

Ken decided that if there was only a desk to investigate, he would go over it with a microscope. He stood and saw that it held three drawers on either side and a shallow one in the center. The center drawer had a keyhole for the type of lock that secured all of the drawers. But they weren't locked, and Ken found each one empty of everything but dust—not even a staple or paper clip.

The low-pile blue carpeting was probably for sound reduction rather than comfort, Ken reasoned, since the rest of the room was so Spartan. He sank to all fours and found nothing in the carpet but four wear marks where the chair would have rested and a sharp, rectangular crease below the wall scratches that supported his file cabinet theory.

Ken sat on the floor with his back against the rear wall, again facing the doorway. "This is about as weird as finding a gun in your grandmother's purse," he whispered. He hoped the sound of his own voice would bring a hint of reassurance to the surreal situation.

It didn't.

"Where the hell did this place come from? And who used it? And for what?" Ken asked the room that absorbed his words like a sponge.

But this is the only place in the house where a secret room could be placed, he reasoned. There was nowhere on the first or second floors to conceal such a place, and no one could see the added room off of the basement because of its underground location. And while the bar and billiards rooms were highly visible to each other and the stairway, the television room could only be seen through its doorway. All windows in the basement were in window wells, set about eighteen inches into the ground, with panes of opaque amber glass.

"But how would someone in here know if it was safe to come out without being detected?" Ken wondered aloud as he moved back to its two doors.

Again, the wooden inside door appeared the same as any other door in the house. But on the inside of the heavy outer door Ken noticed a dark, four-inch-square piece at eye-level. He placed his right eye against it to find an inset fisheye lens. It afforded a view of the entire television room, wall to wall, floor to ceiling, including its entrance at the foot of the stairs.

Stepping to the outside of the door, Ken saw the dark brown mahogany knothole that camouflaged the peephole. Even though he knew the lens was there, Ken was unable to detect it through the ebony gnarl in the panel.

Feeling the edge of the door, he came to the magnetic release device which worked on basically the same principle as the one in his tree house, but was stronger and more sophisticated in design.

Leaving the outer door slightly ajar, Ken went to his sister's room and returned with her Polaroid camera to photograph his discovery. He painstakingly shot both sides of both doors, all four walls, floor, ceiling, and the desk's front, top, sides, empty drawers, and rear.

Backing almost reverently from the room, Ken pulled the inner door closed and then gingerly pushed the outer one shut. He heard a soft but solid double click as it latched.

By the time he replaced the tools, lantern and camera it was 6:15 a.m. He put the Polaroids face-down under the wallet on his dresser, pulled off his clothes and lay naked atop the cool, crisp sheets. With wake-up time approaching, Ken didn't set his alarm.

There was no chance he would fall asleep.

But tonight sleep wasn't necessary. Fate had finally taken him where the dreams had beckoned.

CHAPTER TWO

Due to his thick, monotoned Irish accent, Father Brendan Keough's sermons would remain an enigma to Ken. Exiting St. Paul the Apostle Catholic Church, Ken assured his mother that 8 a.m. Mass would be a lot easier to appreciate if he could understand the priest.

"Be nice, Kenny," she said as they approached the Volvo. "The poor man tries."

Given Ken's discovery of only hours earlier, he couldn't have focused his attention on the pope offering Mass with the Rolling Stones as altar boys.

"You look tired," Mrs. Perry said as her son steered the car into the Sheraton parking lot. "Didn't you sleep well?"

"No. I had a lot on my mind. You know . . . school starting, catching up on the local dirt with Steve last night . . . Did you know he's planning to marry Linda Martin? I'm best man."

"When?"

"Sometime this spring," he said with a smile, "barring cold feet or kidnappings."

The pair walked into the hotel's chrome-and-glass restaurant and a waiter led them past steaming casserole pans to a small table near the patio. Its French doors were open, letting in sunlight and the music of several birds in the manicured courtyard.

It was just after 9 a.m. when the Perrys returned from the buffet to place china plates full of scrambled eggs, hash browns, sausage and other trimmings on their white linen tablecloth.

"How long do I have with my only son before he abandons me once again for the debauchery of college life?" the impish matron asked, scowling over the rim of her coffee cup. She knew Ken would have to leave before noon to make it back to Oxford in one day.

"I've decided to head back tomorrow instead of today," he said, hoping he wasn't showing any emotion that might betray his bizarre discovery. He didn't quite know how or even if he should approach his mother about what was obviously a part of a huge secret that his father—her husband—had apparently not entrusted with them or Margaret. Ken also hoped his keenly intuitive mother would not see through his coming excuse to leave a day late.

"Last night after Lyttle dropped me off I went downstairs to call Carol and watch a little TV, and no sooner than I lay down I started having leg cramps," Ken said. His mother was all too familiar with his occasional runner's afflictions. "They finally let up at about dawn, and I figure I may have gotten a whopping 15 or 20 minutes' sleep. So, rather than head back in a walking coma, I thought I'd just leave early tomorrow."

"I thought I heard you in the hallway awfully late," she said. "If I'd known the trouble, I'd have given you a good massage. Anyway, I'm glad I'll have you an extra day."

"I'm going to do some work around the house for you," Ken gurgled through a mouthful of scrambled eggs. "The dimmer switch for the light over the pool table takes it to only about half the brightness it's supposed to," he lied. "And since we've had cable TV forever, I want to pull down that ancient rusty antenna from the roof before the winter wind does it for us, maybe taking half the shingles and a neighbor or two with it."

"It would be nice to check out the light switch and make sure the connection is safe," his mother said. "Just don't break your neck up on that roof! And watch the power lines," she was quick to add, waving her fruit cup at him. "You've seen those warnings on TV."

Ken gave her a "Don't worry, Mom," eye-roll and took a pull of black coffee, glad that the groundwork was set for his day of deeper investigation of the secret room. The billiard room light switch gave him an excuse to disappear into the basement for awhile, and the antenna removal would allow him to inspect the roof. All the wires sprouting in the small room must have once led to something equally interesting—a special antenna, coil, box or something. And the roof would be its most likely location.

Reaching into his right rear trouser pocket, Ken pulled out two of the Polaroids he shot in the mystery room—one of the desk front and rear wall, the other from inside the closed inner door and the adjacent wall with the clipped wires.

"Mom, I'm curious . . . Have you ever seen this place?"

"No," she said, holding the squares side-by-side. "It's an odd-looking place, so barren and cold-looking . . . Spooky . . . What is it?"

"I don't know," he carefully measured his words. "I found these in a seam of the trunk when I washed the Volvo yesterday. Probably something one of my or Marg's friends shot with her camera . . . Maybe in an abandoned farm we pulled over to explore during a road trip."

Ken and his sister had often used the car to drive groups of friends in camping trips to state forests and along the Lake Michigan coast, as well as weekenders in Chicago and Detroit for concerts or sporting events.

The excuse about where the photos came from made sense to Mrs. Perry. She sat them back in front of her son and began a casual conversation on Marg's newest boyfriend.

Ken slid the glossy photos back into his pocket as he and his mother rose from their meal. They then shared silence as he drove them home, she basking in the late summer warmth and he in a mental game of twenty questions.

So, he reasoned, the enigmatic room was his father's secret, shared now, through a late-night quirk, with his son alone. The only other person who could know about it, Ken reasoned, was Marg, and she was virtually incapable of keeping any kind of secret.

But what about his father's friends? At the time of his death, Walt Perry had two close and longtime buddies, Paul Cody and Dennis Truro, both fellow workers. They all were also teammates who regularly took turns driving each other to company or city league softball and basketball games and a bowling league. The trio would often bring their wives along on weekend trips, and the six of them even took several group vacations together.

Perry, Cody and Truro made a solid triad of friendship unlike any other that Ken had ever seen. It was as if their bond had been cemented in a leaking lifeboat or besieged foxhole.

But in the final analysis, Cody was his father's closest friend and *confidant*. He had joined father and son Perrys for at least a dozen road races. With square jaw and steely blue eyes, the Boston native could have been a Paul Newman clone, if not for his bald head. He refused to hide it with a "tarp", his derogatory term for a toupee.

Maybe Cody or Truro could offer a clue as to the room's function. Maybe not. Ken considered showing them the Polaroids.

But there had to be at least one other possible source of information on the secret chamber, he reasoned as he pulled the car into the driveway—*whoever built it.*

"Thank you for a lovely morning, Kenny," Mrs. Perry said as she unlocked the front door.

"It's gonna cost ya," he said as he walked the stairs to his room to change clothes. "I'll expect grilled cheese at noon, sharp! In the meantime, I'll fix that rheostat."

"You'd better be careful, mister. You're no electrician!"

"Don't worry, Mom," Ken kidded. "It's a simple job. And if I die now I'll make a lot of mean-spirited profs very unhappy!"

Mrs. Perry spent every Sunday afternoon the same way, oil painting near the picture window in the living room. So, Ken reasoned, he was free until lunch time, about two hours away, to give the hidden room another once-over.

Toolbox in hand and clad in a Detroit Pistons T-shirt, cutoff blue jeans and old tennies, he moved back down to the basement just after 10 a.m.

He threw a cloth over the green felt of the billiard table, quickly spread a few wrenches, pliers, nuts and bolts over it and removed the faceplate from the rheostat switch on the wall by the stairs.

Easing toward the secret panel in the adjoining room, Ken decided that if his mother came down while he was in the hidden room, he would just wait until she left, work his way up the stairs and out the back door. The he would re-enter the house with an alibi that he had been in the garage looking for a tool.

The magnet touched the woodgrain surface, the clicks sounded and the panel popped open an inch on Ken's first try. Holding a flashlight (he couldn't risk being seen hauling the Coleman around) he pulled the panel shut behind him, then passed through and closed the second door.

The spongy, time-yellowed acoustic tiles lining the walls and ceiling gave the room a heavy, tomblike silence. The strong beam from the flashlight was also sucked into them like ink into a blotter.

Ken wondered how much of his father's life had been swallowed by the room, and how much he could wring back out.

He pulled a small magnifying glass from his back pocket and began to go over the dusty blue carpet an inch at a time, left wall to right, front to back. Three staples had been ground into it between the desk and where the file cabinet had stood. That was all.

Next Ken knelt and scrutinized the wall-mounted boxes and their clipped wires. An outline on the cement showed that they had been attached to another box just above them, which was now gone. Two half-inch aluminum electrical conduits had been sawed off just above the spot where the box, about a foot square, had been removed. One of the conduits held a wire that Ken decided must have carried electricity into the room, probably through a now-disconnected tap into the line serving the nearest basement outlet. The other cool metal pipe was empty, extended into the entryway between the two doors, and rose into the ceiling. If it extended in a straight line upward from there, Ken thought, the conduit would come out of the ground somewhere near the rear left side of the house.

"So these clipped wires were go-between lines for something above and something in here," he murmured, "something so freaking important that it had its own freaking room in our own freaking house!"

Ken's emotions were beginning to alternate between confusion and disbelief from his "through the looking glass" experience and a growing resentment that his father had not trusted his own family— his only son—enough to share what was obviously a massive secret.

One by one, Ken removed all seven desk drawers, placed them on the desktop and studied them top and bottom. He even shone the flashlight into the empty desk cavities before replacing the drawers.

Nothing.

The acoustic wall tiles were clean, except for scrape marks from the now-gone file cabinet and where two framed pieces had hung— one behind the desk and one on the right wall about five feet from the clipped wires. The acoustic tiles to the left of the desk showed punctures and smudges indicating that they had probably doubled as a bulletin board.

Just as he was ready to leave, satisfied that he had gleaned what little evidence that hadn't been scoured from the cubicle, Ken noticed something else. What he had earlier dismissed as a dirty smudge on the wall next to the desktop was, in fact, printing.

The word HOLYSTONE was lightly inked on the wall, upside down, at desktop height. Apparently, Ken reasoned, the word had been accidentally placed there when someone bumped a rubber stamp against it from the desktop. He didn't recall ever seeing or hearing the word before, and it held no meaning for him.

Other than that, the room was a testament to silence.

Then, as his father had probably done many times, Ken eased up to the eyepiece, made sure his exit would be undetected, and quickly closed the door behind him.

After replacing the dimmer switch plate and gathering his tools, Ken went up the stairway and straight out through the back door. Dropping the toolbox onto the poured cement patio, he tried not to run as he rounded the rear left corner of the house.

There, behind some low bushes his mother had planted just after they had moved into the house, rose the metal conduit. Even without the bushes, the dull gray aluminum rod would hardly be noticeable alongside the building's cement foundation. But the vertical tube was visible for only about 18 inches before it again disappeared, up and behind the white aluminum siding.

"Time to tackle that TV antenna," Ken said with a grunt as he stood. Minutes later he raised an old wood extension ladder from the same spot.

Nearly at the top, Ken almost lost his footing as a shout came.

"Kenny, it's almost 12:30 . . . Aren't you coming in for lunch?"

"Oh, yeah," he called back. "I lost track of the time. I'll be right there."

Ken again nearly fell as he descended the ladder, then caught himself running around the back of the house for the kitchen door.

"Get a grip, Ken," he warned himself, stopping to catch his breath. "If mom senses that something's wrong, how the hell will you explain this to her?"

Beyond the immediate shock and confusion the mystery room would elicit, Mrs. Perry would also suffer pain and resentment that her husband had not entrusted her with something very important in his life. Ken would not risk hurting her. He decided to resist the impulse to hurry through lunch in order to speed back up to the roof for more clues regarding the room. To avoid suspicion, he would spend at least thirty minutes eating the two grilled cheese sandwiches and salad his mother had waiting on the dining room table.

"The dimmer switch downstairs just needed adjusting," he lied as he took a seat next to his mother. "And that rusty scarecrow on the roof should be a quick job, too."

"Well, you just make sure you don't fall down or touch any power lines. We don't want to replace one scarecrow with another," she warned.

"Kenny," she paused, "is something the matter? Something about you seems different this weekend, as if your mind is somewhere else. Is there a problem at school?"

A part of Ken groaned to share the discovery with her. It was like finding a time capsule that their beloved husband and father had left, inexplicably hidden and empty. What if the room turned out to hold an invisible skeleton from his father's past? If Ken did share this new find with his mother and Marg, and they never figured out the puzzle's final shape, the scattered pieces could haunt them forever.

No, Ken reasoned as he finished his first sandwich. *I can't say a word until I know the whole story.*

"Actually, I've been thinking about the breakup with Terri."

"Well, Kenny, I'm sure you'll meet someone who interests you. Just be open to new friends," came her ever-wise advice. "If you begin with that, you won't have to wonder about wherever it leads you. It's the best foundation for any relationship."

"Do you write cards for Hallmark when I'm not around?" Ken teased his mother.

She responded with a turned-up nose, and the lightened atmosphere convinced Ken that his mother had bought his excuse for his preoccupied state of mind.

He spent another ten minutes sharing iced tea with his mother as she filled him in on "Margnews."

"Your sister's buying her first house," she said. "It's a little two-bedroom bungalow in a cute neighborhood about a half-hour from O'Hare. She's going to rent the second bedroom to Janice."

Janice Copley was a raving beauty who had been Marg's best friend ever since they completed flight attendant training together in Chicago. They had been roommates in a rented flat in the city's Old Town district ever since, and it was one of Ken's fantasies that the five-foot-eleven-inch Natalie Wood look-alike would silently slip into the sofa bed with him on one of his weekend visits to see Marg. But like his sister, Janice flitted from Porsche-driving doctor to Ferrari-driving CEO to any of the various libido-driven pro athletes they met in the sky.

"I'm going for a week to help Marg straighten things around her new place when the paperwork's done and her stuff's moved in," Mrs. Perry said, "probably in several weeks."

"Sounds like a good idea," Ken said. "It'll be a good excuse for you three to send out for pizza, drink too much wine and act like sorority girls!"

She swatted Ken's face with her napkin as he pushed out his chair and headed for the back door.

"Watch for falling TV antennas," he shouted as the screen door slammed behind him.

Again atop the ladder, Ken noticed that the electrical conduit with roots in the secret room emerged from behind the top of the siding, between the rain gutter and roof.

But the tube's contents, like the guts of the cryptic room, had been scuttled. The pipe had been cut, any wires pulled out. A row of small marks, two feet apart, showed where a smaller line or wire had been anchored from the now empty pipe to a spot on that rear side of the gabled roof, just below its peak.

There, just behind the attic ventilation fan, were four quarter-inch steel bolts. They were left in the roof after whatever they once held in place had been removed. To take out the bolts themselves would have possibly caused a leak in the roof, Ken reasoned. That would have drawn attention to the fact that something had been there.

The bolts formed a square about six inches across, and the adjacent low, circular, wind-driven fan on one side and the roof peak on the other would have hidden something less than six inches tall.

Everything—the conduit, nuts and bolts, existing wires in the basement—were either aluminum, stainless steel or copper, so there was no telltale rust to help discern how long they had been in place. The whole setup was obviously a base for an antenna of some kind. Whether it was for two-way communication or sending or receiving only, Ken could not know. He had learned, however, that the room's existence implicated at least three factors: his father, someone at the other end of the radio link, and whatever it was that moved through the airwaves between them.

Ken hauled the toolbox up the ladder. Still less than twenty-four hours old, his accidental discovery had already taken him literally from the bottom to the top of the one building in the world that he thought he knew best. He didn't yet know what to think about what it said of the man who had raised him and was his best friend. The numb shock of Ken's discovery was giving way to a feeling he wanted to fight, but was not sure he should—a haunting sense of betrayal.

Standing straight, Ken took a long, deep breath and stared at the dilapidated tree house in the elm some 40 feet across the backyard. A blue jay's song called him back from a childhood memory and he bent over, pulled his sister's camera from the toolbox and took a quick shot of the section of roof holding the four bolts.

Then, after snipping some guy wires and wrenching the old television antenna from its rusty bolts, Ken heaved the eight-foot, 1950s-era beast over the edge. It looked like a falling satellite as it clattered onto the grassy back yard. Another thirty-five minutes of hack-sawing later the skeletal beast was hauled to the curb in pieces manageable for the maw of a Grand Rapids municipal garbage truck.

Filthy from his day's work, Ken entered the house and trudged up to a hot shower. While removing his cutoffs he saw blood glisten on his right knee, probably from kneeling on the rough roofing shingles.

Passing his mom's room en route to the bathroom, he jerked a double take toward the open bedroom door, imagining that he had glimpsed his father. That had happened to Ken often in the first year or so following his father's death, but never in those since.

Pausing, Ken took two deep breaths, entered the white-tiled bathroom, hung his robe on a towel bar and cranked the shower's hot water faucet. Parting the plastic curtain to step into the stream, he once again jerked his gaze toward what had seemed a flash of his father's form in the steamy mirror behind him. Ken saw his own reflection, paused, raised both hands over his face and slowly but firmly massaged it.

Stepping into the shower, he let the hot water pelt his face and he tried to relax. Within seconds he started to tremble, first his legs, then hands, arms and head. His chest tightened and his labored breathing grew shallow.

My God, he thought. *What's going on here? Am I having a heart attack, nervous breakdown or what?*

He knew that a discovery like the one he had made that weekend would bring massive emotional pressure. And there was no question that he was confused, exhausted, and more than a little afraid of what the mystery was all about.

There was no one emotion that guided his mind. Instead, the confusing whirl of feelings encircled Ken like a pack of snarling dogs. He hadn't yet realized that he needed to focus on one of them in order to fight his way out.

Maybe that's it, he reasoned. *This whole thing is just overwhelming you, Ken. Get a grip. Look at this logically . . . Pull together what you've found. Piece together what you can and you'll have to find out something. Just get a grip!*

He felt like going to bed and just turning everything off until the next day, but it was only 3 p.m.

If sleeping the tension away wasn't an option, trying to run it out was. Ken toweled off, suited up and offered a quick "See ya in a few" to his mother on his way out of the house.

About twenty minutes later he was back at his old high school, where he followed the driveway through the vacant parking lot back to the track.

Loosened up by his run to get there, Ken set his wrist stopwatch and did three hard one-mile runs, back-to-back, with two minutes' rest between each. His times were 5:45, 6:12 and 6:58.

If this doesn't knock the heebie-jeebies out of me, nothing will, he thought as he bent over and grasped both ankles, sucking air.

For the next three hours he alternated several easy laps on the quarter-mile oval with one or two hard, fast ones, stopping only to stretch or take water from the fountain.

When Ken realized that his determination to run off his anxiety was about to bring him to heat exhaustion, he stripped off his tank top, tucked it into the back of his shorts and walked to the nearby bleachers. He lay on the first aluminum bench, and the cool metal felt good on his sweat-slickened back.

Eggshell-white cumulus clouds seemed to call Ken upward as they sailed eastward across the sky. He felt like lying in them and drifting away, wherever. And yet, he knew that soon the serene giants would turn black, become too heavy for the sky and cry themselves to the earth.

Then a bird lilted in song, and Ken recalled a dead robin he had seen on the street during his run to the track.

"Okay, Ken," he said aloud, with determination. "You're going to have to either pull yourself out of this funk or look for a good shrink!

"Where's Carol Hurley when you need her?" he shouted upward, followed by an exhausted laugh.

The reality check motivated Ken to sit up and look at his watch. Just after 7 p.m. After a few more easy laps, he began a loose, easy gait home.

After a second, more relaxed shower, Ken joined his mother for a barbecued chicken dinner on their candle-lit patio, and he explained that he would begin his hitchhike back to Miami at dawn.

They then shared small talk in the kitchen as he did the dishes and she put together a bag lunch for his journey back to school.

Kissing her on the cheek, Ken returned to his bedroom just before nine. He grabbed his backpack and threw in the Polaroids of the basement and roof, and a manila envelope full of old family photographs he had always planned to sort and place in an album. Then, almost as an afterthought, he deposited the two reference books and cross country spikes he had come home for in the first place.

Sleep didn't come easily. And when it did, Ken again dreamed he saw his father. But this time he was sitting upright behind the desk in the dark basement chamber, wearing a mask.

CHAPTER THREE

Maureen Perry hummed along with a song on the radio and stirred waffle batter as Ken dragged himself through a groggy, pre-dawn wake-up. After a shave and shower he threw on his newest pair of blue jeans and a red number 16 Miami football jersey (looking All-American was good for snagging rides), and pocketed his wallet that held a twenty and two fives.

Despite his cold shower, he was still half asleep as he trudged his full backpack downstairs and into the dining room.

"Black stay-awake juice for the king of the road," the matron lilted as she filled his coffee cup. "And a nice stack of strawberry waffles."

"Mom, I didn't want you to get up early for me, let alone go through all this trouble . . . But I'm glad you did!" Ken admitted as he poured syrup over the steaming stack.

"I've decided to drive you to Lansing," she announced. "And I don't want any argument. If you insist on this foolish hitchhiking, then I, as a mother, have the right to see you safely that far."

Ken groaned, but deep down he was thankful for his mother's concern, and the quick first leg of the trip would put him on the southbound shoulder of I-69 by 8 a.m. That meant, with good rides, that he could be back in Oxford by late afternoon.

"I'm ready to leave when you are, Kenny," she said. "I'll run upstairs and get my keys."

"Take your time, mom. I'll need at least one more cup of coffee before I'm really awake."

Mrs. Perry munched a banana muffin as she left the table, and Ken wondered how she always looked so fresh so early in the morning. While she had always been a 'morning glory,' Ken, Marg and their father were always at their best at night.

Ken turned in his chair, peered through the window and saw low, ragged clouds scouring the rosy purple dawn.

"It's supposed to rain by noon," Mrs. Perry said as she breezed back into the room. "But it should stay north of the Indiana line. At least that's what the guy on the radio said. So instead of having thieves, drunks, murderers *and* rain to worry about, you'll only have to watch for the thieves, drunks and murderers."

"I have my poncho just in case," Ken replied as he stood with his stuffed knapsack. "And," he growled, "it makes me look *reeaaal* tough!"

Both laughed as he slung the bag over one shoulder, set his cup in the sink and again yawned.

"We'd better get out of here before you go back to bed, son. You can catch another forty winks during the ride to Lansing . . . But you'd better never let me hear of you falling asleep in a car with a stranger!"

"Never . . . until *at least* the second date," he said with a grin.

She reacted with a sharp jab of her keys to the seat of Ken's blue jeans as they left the house.

Ken threw his pack onto the Volvo's back seat, reclined the front passenger's seat and yawned again. Mrs. Perry slid her seat forward, adjusted the rearview mirror and backed the car into the street.

Eyes closed, Ken heard the radio click on, and after a few minutes of news, a weather report affirmed the forecast his mother had heard earlier. Then, as Paul Harvey punctuated a UFO sighting report and congratulations to a couple on their seventy-fifth wedding anniversary with an ad for some kind of miracle laxative, Ken tried to doze off.

As the wagon droned eastward along I-96, Ken felt his face warm and cool and warm again as clouds drifted across the sun. An all-too-short time later, he heard gravel crunch under the tires as his mom guided the car onto the shoulder of the Interstate 69 interchange for Ken's southward journey.

"Ohh," he groaned. "Slap me or something . . . I can't wake up!"

"I should slap you," his mother said. "Maybe that would knock some sense into you to stop this hitchhiking."

Ken leaned over and kissed her cheek. "You know," he said, "we college students are supposed to rebel against our parents' common sense . . . And besides," he added, "if I get picked up by just one more psychopath, that will be one thousand on the nose and I'll qualify for my 'Lucky Thumber' merit badge."

The flustered mother growled at the steering wheel, but Ken's humor did make her feel less nervous. *Again, like his father,* she thought. *He could talk his way into or out of anything.*

Ken opened his door, pulled his bag from the back seat and again reached across the front seat to hug and kiss his mother.

"Don't worry, mom. I've never had a problem with this. I'm a big boy."

"I know. I love you, Kenny."

"I love you, too, mom. I'll call when I get in, as always."

"You'd better," she answered, then waved as her son turned and walked to the I-69 south on-ramp.

He offered another wave as the white car disappeared west in the growing morning traffic.

Ken yawned as he reached into his pack and retrieved a cardboard sign. On one side, the blue Magic Marker letters read "Ohio." He would flip it over to the "Miami U" side after he crossed the state line.

Friday's hitch home to Grand Rapids had gone smoothly. Leaving his apartment just after dawn, he got a quick ride from a fellow Miami student for the seven miles to College Corner, resting smack on the Ohio-Indiana line. He then continued to ride 27 north in a van that made the quiet hopscotch past cornfields and small towns and more cornfields. The two-lane blacktop glided first through Richmond, a hilly home to a large Quaker college. Ken stood in the late summer morning listening to a blue jay's song as he waited for another ride at a lonely stretch somewhere between Richmond and Lynn. No breeze had stirred, and he could hear the oncoming traffic almost as soon as it was visible on the rolling horizon and, sadly, for about the same distance after the non-stoppers cruised past him. Several rides later he was home in time for his mother's Yankee pot roast dinner.

The whole trip usually took an average of six to eight rides, during which Ken and his chauffeurs would agree or argue on the Cubs' pennant chances, nuclear energy, why the corn's too short, abortion, whether country music is a contradiction in terms, and the usual politics and religion. Ken had only been bounced from one ride for his differing opinions. (One should never question a man with an NRA decal on his FRONT windshield as to his right to own an assault weapon.) It was one of Ken's persistent roadside daydreams that maybe he would be picked up and find a quick if not meaningful "relationship" with a firm, young, errant farmer's daughter.

Now standing in the early dawn mist of Lansing's rural southern outskirts, Ken liked how the feelings of exposure, dependence and vulnerability that come with hitchhiking triggered and sharpened his body's senses. The smell of wildflowers, diesel exhaust and roadside restaurants always came through as strongly as if experiencing them for the first time. The sun was always brighter and warmer. And when forced to seek refuge from the rain, he always noticed its temperature—warm or cool in the summer, with a cold bite in the early spring or fall.

While throwing on his poncho during a downpour the previous summer, Ken realized that he had never really given much thought to the fluid, vigorous sensuality of rain before it had seduced him on that country two-lane.

The rain's a lot like love, he thought. *It comes, complicates life for awhile and leaves, all on its own terms.*

But he hoped for clear weather as he pulled the 'Ohio' sign upward and, right thumb extended, assumed the position.

A part in the clouds brought a blaze of sunlight that turned the surrounding dew-covered fields of Queen Anne's Lace to shimmering diamonds on green felt.

Ken began walking slowly backward, his pack slung over his left shoulder. After what seemed a long time, he looked at his watch to see that it was only 8:19. Traffic had picked up, and he hoped for a ride with a salesman or trucker making a long drive south.

He felt a spray of cool, misty raindrops fleck his face, arms and neck. While pondering whether he would need the poncho, a gray Ford Taurus veered onto the shoulder about forty yards ahead of him. Brake lights shone, and it backed up for Ken.

A black driver about his age leaned over to unlock the passenger's door, and Ken saw that he was wearing a brown U.S. Army uniform.

"Thanks," Ken said. "I was bracing myself for some rain."

"That's all right," the driver said. "Where in Ohio are you headed?"

"Going back to school at Miami University, in Oxford. It's about a half hour northwest of Cincinnati," Ken explained, sliding his cardboard sign under the pack between his feet.

"I'm headed for Fort Knox, Kentucky," the soldier said. "So I'll be passing fairly close to your destination. I'll be going due west of Cinci. Just let me know where you need to get out."

The water dots hitting the windshield grew rounder, started to streak, and the wipers began a steady cadence.

"Fantastic," Ken said. "I appreciate the lift. Let me know if I can give you a hand with the driving."

The driver nodded. It turned out that Corporal Robert "Crump" Crumpton had been visiting his home that weekend too, in Lansing. He had flown in from Fort Knox and was now returning with his wife's car. He said she had to leave it in Lansing when the starter died during a visit several weeks earlier.

The sky grew fair, and relaxed conversation came naturally to the pair as the Taurus cut through the Midwestern farmland.

Crump had been a sprinter and hurdler in high school, but football was his passion. In addition to his speed, the wide receiver had the frame of a bank vault, a combination that brought him regional acclaim and a football scholarship to Notre Dame.

A weight room accident had left him with a ruptured disc that robbed him of the scholarship. But the Army had made good on a promised "full-ride" to Fort Leonard Wood Boot Camp U. And now the helicopter mechanic was making "a passable life" for his wife and twin two-year-old daughters.

With each pause in the conversation, Ken considered sharing his surreal discovery of two days earlier with his fellow traveler. He desperately needed to tell someone about it. And this would be a relatively risk-free disclosure, he reasoned. Crump knew him only as a college student from Ohio, and when they said their goodbyes later that day, they would undoubtedly never again meet.

Just inside the Indiana border, Ken offered Crump one of his two sandwiches and the driver wheeled the car onto the next exit. The corporal took the Ford through a McDonald's drive-through for two sodas, then pulled the car into a parking space and the pair sat at a nearby picnic table.

It was 10:45, and Ken was halfway home.

"Chopper mechanic, eh?" Ken asked as they sat at the table. "Planning a military career or are you looking at a future in civilian life?"

"Not sure," the easy-going soldier answered. He exchanged a soda, straw and napkins with Ken for a large whole wheat pita stuffed with tuna salad, tomatoes and alfalfa sprouts.

"I'm a good mechanic, and Army life comes easy to me. The retirement plan looks good too," Crump said. "But I've always had a strong desire to study sociology."

Crump turned, sat with his back against the edge of the tabletop and watched two young boys trying to coax a kite into the nearly calm sky.

"I think education made the difference in my family. My dad was the only black MD in Niles, Michigan until we moved to Lansing when I was a boy. He's retired now. After thirty-five years of doctoring in a low-rent neighborhood for mostly non-paying patients, he couldn't afford to help me with college tuition. The frustration on my father's face because he couldn't send me hurt worse than my realization I couldn't go," he sighed. "I think he may have also blamed himself in some way for being helpless to fix my back after the lifting injury took my football scholarship.

"Anyway, my back wasn't bad enough to keep me out of the Army. And I may go to college on my G.I. benefits when my hitch is up. My wife is supportive of the idea. We'll see what happens."

Crump pulled the plastic lid from his empty cup and his ice glistened as he shook it onto the grass.

"Yeah," Ken replied, and like a leaf falling from a tree, his thoughts returned to his own father and the secret room.

"Better hit the road," Crump said. They were back on I-69 south before his ice melted.

It would be about two more hours before they reached Indianapolis, where Ken would take I-70 east. He excused himself for a rest, closed his eyes and thought about his father.

The lunch conversation had momentarily distracted him from trying to find a hole in his father's life that the puzzle piece basement room might fill.

Walt Perry had been a model husband and father to his wife and two children. The Perry household made Beaver Cleaver's family look dysfunctional. Walt and Maureen shared intense devotion for Ken and his sister who returned the same, bonding the family with love and trust. The confidence, independence and high self-esteem that made Ken and Margaret brats in adolescence helped them mature into secure and well adjusted, if not high-spirited, adults. Trust was total and respect assured, so parent-child communication was natural and complete. Ken and Margaret wouldn't tell their parents everything they did on a night out with friends, but they knew they could.

Ken remembered one of his father's favorite sayings: "Your conscience is your best friend or your jailer." And he wondered if it was the friend or the jailer that had kept his dad from sharing the secret room with his family.

Shifting in the vinyl seat, Ken rested both hands on his left leg and leaned his head against the side window. A jet from a dashboard air conditioner vent nearly numbed his right arm, and he listened as Crump adjusted the volume on a George Benson CD.

Forty-two years before his death, Ken's dad was born to high school math teacher Chester Perry and his artist wife Dinah in Springfield, Massachusetts. An only child, Walt (no one—not parents, not even his wife—called him Walter) shared his father's fascination for numbers and physics. He had also inherited his mother's artist's temperament, dimpled smile and, curiously, her photographic memory. As she would paint a ship, landscape or portrait from nothing more than a passing glimpse, her son Walt would work at mathematical quizzes his father had thought up for him. They might involve finding the number of beach balls that could fit in their swimming pool, how many postage stamps could be applied to the surface of the Green Monster in Fenway Park's left field, or how fast he would have to pedal to ride his bicycle to any given destination his father would assign.

Then, as Walt grew older, it was on to algebra, advanced calculus, statistics and, finally, theoretical physics—all before high school graduation.

Ken remembered playing croquet with his grandpa on the wide, flat lawn behind their three-story Victorian house in Springfield. The tall, thin man always wore suspenders—braces, he called them. His straight white hair looked soft and never needed combing, and his handlebar mustache made his ever-present smile seem bigger than it was.

Ken was seven when his grandpa died of a heart attack. His was the first funeral Ken ever attended. And it was only the fifth time he had ever seen the old man. Their visits had been confined to four week-long vacations Ken's family had made from Grand Rapids to Springfield during his young life. So his grandpa was the first 'lifelong' friend Ken would lose. Ten years later, his father would be the second.

Without warning, an sharp blow crushed the air from Ken's lungs as he slammed into the Ford's dashboard. He gasped air full of burned rubber from the car's locked, screaming tires as an azure blur swerved wildly before them.

"JESUS CHRIST!" Crump screamed. He fought for control of the car with his left arm, kept Ken from going through the windshield with his right, and stomped the brakes to avoid the tumbling van.

The Taurus came to a 200-yard sliding stop on outside shoulder gravel, and the smell of asphalt-fried tires stuck to the sweat on Ken's upper lip.

Crump slipped the transmission into park, hit the flashers, turned off the ignition and his chest swelled with a deep breath. He leaned back his head, closed his eyes and exhaled.

Ken silently placed his forehead and both palms on the dash.

"If I wanted to fly," Crump said slowly, "I would've joined the fucking Air Force."

"Ho-lee shit," Ken groaned into the dashboard.

A few silent seconds later they left the car and ran back to the van. Several other witnesses had already used cellphones to call for help and were waving traffic around the old blue Volkswagen minibus. Three men and a woman staggered around the rolled heap that rested half in the right lane, half on the shoulder. The obviously drunken quartet weaved and bobbed around the battered van, nursing their wounds and bumming smokes from the gathering crowd.

"Let's get outta here," Crump sneered. "It's all over for them until their arraignment hangovers."

Both snapped on their seat belts before Crump nosed his car back into the slowed traffic.

"I felt like laying into those bastards," Crump growled. "You had your eyes closed when that van passed us. They were doing at least 90. They got blocked behind two 18-wheelers and tried to pass on the left shoulder, hit gravel and started spinning back over the highway like a top before slamming onto their side on the opposite shoulder. Assholes were so loaded they probably won't remember any of it."

"Where are we?" Ken asked.

"Just passed Alexandria. Be coming up on Indianapolis soon. I'll take a swing around the eastern side of the city so you can get onto I-70 east."

"Thanks," Ken said with a nod. He paused, watched the heat volatiles rise from the distant asphalt and cleared his throat.

"You know, the damnedest thing happened to me while I was home this weekend . . ."

Ken's trailing voice hooked Crump's attention.

"I got together with my best friend for a couple of beers after he said he had something heavy to tell me. I was afraid he was in some kind of trouble, but it turns out the guy found *a hidden room* in *his own house* . . . an empty basement chamber complete with trick door and electrical wiring. The poor guy's father died a few years ago, and up until my buddy stumbled onto it last month, no one knew it was there, not even his mom."

"Wild," Crump said. "What did he do for a living?"

"He was a number-cruncher for a consulting firm."

Actually, Ken's father was a statistician and systems analyst with Knoblock Systems. Based in Baltimore, the company had regional offices in Grand Rapids, Miami, Denver and San Diego. It was a pool of computer experts available for consultation or troubleshooting for government and private sector groups needing the best in high-tech savvy.

"Well, you know, I did hear about something like that once," the driver said. "A boot camp buddy of mine is an MP at Fort Knox, and he's a spy buff, always reading espionage novels and like that. Anyway, once he told me about an article he saw in some newspaper or magazine about a high-level US intelligence operative in London who disappeared. He was feared kidnapped, killed or defected.

"While the search was on for this guy, a smell forced his wife to call a pest control company to come and remove what she thought was probably a dead mouse or rat inside a wall. Turns out it was her husband. He apparently died of natural causes while working in a hidden room she knew nothing about in their home. I guess it was a sort of top secret home office. Must've really blown the old lady's mind."

A chill swept Ken, and his hand felt numb as he wiped sweat from his brow. His body was responding to the overload of confusion and stress.

"Comin' up on '70," Crump said, tapping his right turn signal. "I'll take the exit ramp so I won't have to stop and start again on the interstate . . . Don't want to risk a brush with another alcohol-guided missile."

"I appreciate it," Ken said. He readied his pack and sign for departure. "After the long ride and brush with death I feel like we're old friends."

Crump stopped the car on the eastbound side of I-70 at the foot of the on-ramp for his return to I-69.

"Hey, I hope you catch that sociology degree somewhere down the road," Ken said, shaking Crump's hand.

"Yeah, I hope so too . . . And I hope your friend finds peace to go with his discovery."

Crump's voice was low and sympathetic as he looked Ken in the eye. He knew Ken had been talking about himself.

A final wave and Ken walked to the head of the ramp, dropped his bag and held the Miami sign chest-high with both hands. About one hundred miles from Oxford, his watch showed 2:10 p.m. With two or three good rides he could be back on campus early enough to get his student ID photo taken before the office in Roudebush Hall closed at 4:30.

A red-winged blackbird chattered and dive-bombed the intruder who stood too close to the roadside tree that held her young. In no mood for a turf dispute, Ken grabbed his pack and darted up onto the interstate's shoulder.

A column of about twenty motorcycles, two abreast, approached in the far distance. Ken lifted his pack, crossed the shoulder and sat on the guardrail, waiting for the bikers to pass.

As they thundered by, Ken could read the gang's colors on several of the armless denim jackets—Mellow Pirates.

As the Harleys rapped over the horizon, Ken ambled back to his place by the highway's white stripe edging. Seconds later, what initially looked like an attempt to run him down turned out to be his final ride.

Just as he was ready to dive out of its path, a beat-up, candy-apple red Camaro skidded to a stop less than ten feet before Ken. It looked like the lone driver collapsed onto the front seat, but it turned out that he was trying, unsuccessfully, to open the passenger's door for Ken.

"Wah' happnin', bud?" the phenomenally loaded man boomed.

"It's all happnin'!" Ken returned with a laugh. The wheel-man wore cutoff Miami U sweat pants, a Chi Omega Big Brother T-shirt and looked no more than 18 years old.

Before Ken could slam the door shut and return to his thumbing, the drunk piped up.

"Hey! You goin' to Miami?"

"I'm tryin'," Ken said.

"Me too, but I'm really drunk," the driver howled. "Hey bud, I know . . . Why don't *you* drive and *I'll sleep?*"

"Are you sure?" Ken asked.

"You gay?"

"No."

"Then I'm sure," the driver matter-of-factly slurred.

By the time Ken had walked around to the driver's door, the pilot had crawled over the front seat, dropped onto the back seat and buried his face in a TKE pillow.

"I sure hope this thing's not stolen," Ken sighed. Adjusting the rearview mirror, he caught another look at his newest traveling companion, who was already unconscious.

Ken saw the name Chaz and Tau Kappa Epsilon on the wooden key fob dangling from the ignition. Throwing the car into gear, he snapped an Ozzy Osborne CD from the stereo, dropped it onto the floor mat and looked for a jazz station.

"This is a better trade-off than you realize, Chaz," Ken shouted over his shoulder at the comatose teen. "I get a ride the rest of the way home, and you're spared the indignity of having your ass vaporized against the side of a bridge abutment."

An hour and forty minutes later Ken passed the entrance to Hueston Woods. With only seven miles of Route 27 to Oxford, he hoped his backseat passenger was still alive. The wasted wassailer hadn't so much as groaned during the whole ride.

As Oxford's green water tower came into view, Ken fought the impulse to park the Greek's car behind Bonham House, the campus police station.

"I guess I owe you this much," Ken mumbled, pulling the Camaro to a stop outside the TKE house. Leaving the keys in the ignition and his window open, Ken grabbed his pack and blew the booze-mummified Chaz a goodbye kiss.

"Hey!" Ken yelled to a couple of Tekes talking near their front porch. "Special delivery," he said, pointing toward the Camaro. "Daddy's home from rehab!"

Ken shook his head as he moved toward the edge of campus. *It's so damn unfair,* he thought. *Guys like Crump end up in boot camp while idiots like Chaz skate through four or five drunken years of toga parties, skipping classes and buying term papers.*

The Westminster chimes from Miami's Beta Bell Tower signaled 3:45 p.m. as Ken negotiated the heavy student traffic on High Street and crossed the wide green lawn to Roudebush Hall. Entering the long, three-story building through a side door, he followed a series of photocopied 'University ID' signs to a long line in the basement.

At 4 p.m. he was one of the last students that day to have his visage, student number and address sealed in plastic.

As usual, Ken was unhappy with the picture. Beside the fact that he didn't consider himself photogenic, the fatigue of that day's hitching and the deeper wear of his discovery at home had brought a heaviness to his face.

Ken slid the card into a plastic wallet-window and tucked it into his rear pocket as he left through the same door he'd entered.

Pack in hand, he moved westward over the length of the campus, looking forward to his apartment and dinner.

A steady flow of students were arriving on campus anew or returning from their summer away. They toted books, supplies and latex-lettered T-shirts and sweats from the bookstores, stopping to clog doorways, corners and benches under the random, ancient oaks. The exhilaration of a new school year and socializing had not yet been tempered homework by the pound, term paper and exam all-nighters, pompous profs or nightmare roommates.

Ken pondered how everything comes alive in a college town in late summer, not spring. Most would find what they would later refer back to as the best days of their lives; others would be forced from that exciting new life by debt, illness or simple failure.

But for the time being, the newly revived coed community rode an almost palpable wave of enthusiasm.

Ken caught a whiff of perfume as a ponytailed freshman bobbed past him and through the propped-open doors of King Library.

Anxious to research the story Crump had told him of the spy who'd been found dead in a secret room, Ken stopped and thought about doing some quick digging through the reference section.

But the library would be open until midnight, so he kept walking, planning to return after a shower and some food.

A quick left down some cement steps and past McGuffey Hall, and Ken was off campus and moving west on Spring Street. Three and a half blocks later he entered the second doorway of 402 Heather Lane and plodded up the stairs.

At the top, Ken unlocked his door and walked into his apartment. He tapped the wall-mounted air conditioner on, tossed his pack onto the sofa bed and walked to the kitchen wall phone to call his mother.

"Mom, I made it," he told her answering machine. "It was pretty smooth sailing; I even got back in time to get my student ID. Take care, and I'll be checking in later. Love ya, Mom."

Ken pulled a jar of Gatorade from the fridge and didn't bother with a glass as he carried the quart into the bathroom. One shave, shower and half-quart of drink later he wrapped a towel around himself and returned to the kitchen. Midway through construction of a sliced turkey, provolone and tomato sandwich a sudden, writhing emptiness seized his gut. He stuffed the food into a resealable plastic bag and tossed it into the fridge.

"What the hell am I looking for?" he asked aloud as he gazed from the kitchen window overlooking the tangled green overgrowth of the woods behind his building. Even with its refrigerator, stove, two-seat dinette set, sink and cupboards, Ken's kitchen was still smaller than the hidden room he had found. As he realized that it was just as quiet, too, the refrigerator motor kicked on, spinning Ken from the window.

"What am I looking for?" he repeated as his heart pounded.

"Answers," he ran a hand over his beard. "Answers."

He dressed, stuck a small pad of paper and a pen in his back pocket and headed for King Library.

Walking between King's wide, square concrete pillars, he strode toward the reference section and leaned back against a wall.

"Where the hell do I begin?" he asked himself. "An American spy drops dead in a secret room in his London residence . . . Where do I find something like that?"

He did recall that Crump's friend had seen the story in a newspaper or magazine article. Did that mean television or radio had aired it? Maybe it was just a rumor someone had attributed to a print article that never existed, or it could be based on fiction—something Crump's MP friend had seen in a movie, TV program or read in a novel and later recalled as fact.

Ken decided his best bet was to begin with a newspaper and magazine search. So he retrieved his pen and pad and dropped into a chair before a computer to crank some search engines.

He jotted a list of key words that might lead to the information: national security, espionage, spying, CIA, FBI, MI5, MI6, disappearances, missing persons, discoveries, mysteries, secret, hidden . . .

As the key words grew more and more general, Ken felt more and more fatigued. Leaning heavily against the wooden chair back, he closed his eyes and took a deep breath.

I'll find a thesaurus, he thought. *Then I can cross-check the words on my list against it and find more possible leads.*

But his eyes wouldn't open and his legs resisted his brain's order to stand. Drained by the day's physical and emotional strain, Ken was succumbing to involuntary sleep.

"Get up and walk around or nod out," he muttered as he finally stood, stashed his pen and notes and headed for the exit. Not yet 7 p.m., he decided to take a walk to unwind, then hit the hay early. He needed sleep more than he realized.

Thumbs jammed into his front belt loops, Ken walked south into the lengthening shadows of Harrison, Irvin and Elliott halls and onto the expansive green Hub, or sidewalk-spoked center of campus.

What did Ken really know of his father? The question hurt, because it was now obvious that whomever or whatever he believed his model parent to have been was not based on the full story.

"How about a best-case/worst-case scenario?" Ken asked himself, turning south onto Spring Street.

Best case: he was a high-level security, intelligence or defense worker with a need for 24-hour access to his work or peers. Or maybe he was involved in top-clearance statistical or computer research or development for Knoblock or a client company.

"Worst case scenario?" he asked himself aloud, now away from the mid-campus crowds as he moved closer to Patterson Avenue and the wooded Western Campus area. "Industrial espionage? Could dad have been ripping off his employer or a client?

Or, he pondered, returning to silence with a swallow, *could it be the absolutely worst possibility? Could Walt Perry's secret basement chamber have been financed by some foreign power?*

That's crazy! Ken thought, banishing the idea as if he'd caught himself in some incestuous fantasy.

This is all just too weird, he continued, a little unnerved by the extremes he was allowing his imagination to breach. If all families were like his, he had reasoned so many times, there would be no drug addiction, gangs, prisons or wars. Love, honesty and respect ruled the home that Walt Perry had built with his wife, and any kind of dark secret—let alone a gray subterranean chamber—was unimaginable.

But it was real.

Ken crossed Patterson Avenue and saw the sidewalk lampposts flicker on in the gathering darkness. He passed Patterson Place and walked onto the first of two stone arch supported bridges that loomed twenty feet above a grassy Western Campus valley.

Spotting a pair of rabbits, he paused and sat on the wide, sun-warmed cement ledge. Try as he could, Ken could think of nothing but the hidden room that cast his father in a suspicious light.

How could that damned basement room go undiscovered by the occupant's wife and two children? After all, they had spent at least half of their time as a family in that basement watching TV, playing pool, listening to music, playing cards . . .

But then again, Ken reasoned as he lowered himself back onto the walkway, maybe the hidden room was used only once or twice per month. Or per year. Or even more infrequently, a contingency room kept at hand for emergency use.

But the worn carpet, the pinholes in the wall tiles, and other clues suggested that his father had spent a good deal of time there.

When Ken was nine, he had spent nearly two weeks in and out of consciousness with a severe strain of flu. Had he witnessed his father's entry or exit from the secret room while in that twilight world? Was that what had spawned the "walking into the wall" dreams?

Passing the rough-cut granite blocks of Kumler Chapel, Ken headed down the long walkway back towards Patterson and the dorm-smothered south side of campus.

The sun had fallen and the lights of Tappan Hall glowed softly as he approached.

The Perrys didn't enjoy the kind of wealth that Ken understood to accompany either industrial or foreign-funded spying. Anyway, his dad would never betray his company or country. So the secret room must have been an extension of his father's job in the nearly windowless seven-story Knoblock building in downtown Grand Rapids.

"That leaves three options," Ken told himself as he passed Tappan, successfully fighting the urge to stop and ogle a bra-wearing coed who lolled past a second floor window.

If placed by his father's employer, the room was for company work, corporate work contracted by Knoblock, or for another third-party concern. No matter how hard Ken searched for a more likely client, he kept returning to one Uncle Sam.

And that brought Ken back to Crump's second-hand story about the American spy in England. His wife knew nothing of the secret room in her own home which would steal her husband's last living moments. Who did this American work for? Did the West or East engineer the chamber? Friend or foe? Whatever the details, Ken hoped the story was authentic, and that he could find it.

Ken ambled past Dodds and Scott halls, slowly reviewing his father's life like a movie editor—frame by frame.

Walt Perry's growing up in Massachusetts was typical and carefree, judging by the tons of happy family snapshots Ken had seen at home and on his grandpa's knee in Springfield. Walt had played army as a boy, owned a BB gun, and loved but didn't excel in sports, except running. In high school he chased the girls, ran with the guys and got average grades in all but math, where, under his father's tutelage, he shone like the baby moon hubcaps on his first car, a '50 Chevy Belair.

Stellar SAT scores in math and his father's firm standing in MIT's old boys' network breezed Walt into classes there in 1968. He went on for a year and a half of 4.0 honors classes.

Then, in a move that Ken had never understood, the man who would be his father—the MIT up-and-comer on a fast track to a glowing career—walked off campus, rode the subway to Boston's central Army recruiting station and raised his right hand.

As the Vietnam conflict raged, Walt Perry enlisted himself into the service of his country—noble and understandable enough— and just as predictably he was attached to the Army Corps of Engineers.

So why, after boot camp and six months of extended training did the math whiz spend the rest of his four-year hitch managing an officers club golf course in Puerto Rico? Ken could have understood his father's involvement in design or construction of the 18-hole San Juan facility, but it had been completed for nearly two years when he arrived in early 1971.

Other past anomalies now looming larger in Ken's whirling mind were that his dad had no photos from Puerto Rico—unheard of for a serviceman pulling overseas duty. And, most interesting to Ken, his father didn't even like, let alone play, golf.

Whenever asked about his Puerto Rico duty, Ken's father would shrug and insist, "That's the Army for ya."

Ken wished that at least once he had pressed a little beyond that.

Rounding a low hedge, Ken began his westward walk along Spring Street toward Heather Lane, four blocks distant.

After the Army, his father returned to MIT to finish his bachelor's degree in statistics, picking up a second major in linguistics.

While remaining there for master's degrees in both disciplines, Walt met clerk Maureen Fennell as he was browsing the shelves of her father's book shop in Cambridge. A local girl with a love for the arts and literature, she would mix with poets and artists, spend late nights singing along with the Harvard Square street musicians and debate religion, politics and philosophy in student garrets until dawn.

Walt's wry, dimpled smile, sharp wit and underlying old-school, chivalric charm enthralled the anything-but-naive twenty-year-old.

Despite Walt's study areas, which Maureen described as "boredom as a blunt instrument," the pair continued to date through his year and a half of grad school. The lithe, red-mopped woman then waited faithfully for her fiancé as he spent six months of job training at Knoblock Systems' headquarters in Baltimore. He remained with the company from the time he was recruited at MIT until his death.

After convert classes at St. Paul Catholic Church in Cambridge (he had been baptized Episcopalian), Walt and Maureen were wed there in 1975. Marg was born about a year after they moved to Grand Rapids, where Knoblock had placed Walt in their research and development division.

Tight work restrictions designed to protect the company and its clients meant that Walt couldn't talk about his work outside the lab, and Maureen couldn't have cared less.

But Walt never stopped loving his job, wife or children. In fact, it was a real "Father Knows Best" household—no spouse or child abuse, no drunken screams at dinner, no scandal, tragedy, hits, runs or serious errors—until one early July evening outside Tiger Stadium.

Was it really a random killing? Ken thought as he kept walking. If his father had been enmeshed in some clandestine activity or organization—if he was a *spy*—then there was a good chance someone would want him dead. It comes with the job description.

Ken didn't know who his father's allies were, but whoever they were, they would have enemies. Like everyone else, Ken had seen scores of spy movies that all wove betrayal through trust through betrayal, and on and on and on. All too often they left an acrid aftertaste for the nation's trusted, if not always familiar, security agencies. Disenchanted operatives either "crossed over," dashed into the cold or simply disappeared. Anonymous agencies of intrigue would smoothly and silently go about their work like an octopus, watching unseen from murky depths, always ready to strike and retreat into an inky cloud.

Did coincidence put Truro and Cody with Walt Perry at his 'random killing'? Or were they caught helpless at their friend's calculated assassination? Or did they walk him into it?

Ken stopped in front of Bishop Hall, sat on the cement steps leading to the dorm and dropped his head onto folded arms.

Again he felt himself losing his mental focus, his concentration fading as possibilities he could accept clashed with others too fantastic or repugnant to consider. He had to find a point of reference that would keep the centrifugal force of his imagination from spinning out of control.

Ken called his father's image before his mind's eye, carefully scanning each detail—the glittering eyes, light smile wrinkles at the corners of those eyes and mouth, the deep dimples. He silently stared into the eyes of that mental hologram, but he could not make it speak.

Drawing a long breath, Ken looked up at the reassuring glow from one of the old lampposts. Wondering if he was being unfair in the suspicious eye he was casting over his father's past, he pulled out his wallet and retrieved his dad's picture.

The wrinkles were barely discernible, but the dimples and gleaming eyes seemed 3-D. Ken stared long, deep and hard into the blue-green eyes, but found no deception, fear or betrayal.

Ken's new Miami ID fell from the wallet and landed face down on the steps. He picked it up, turned it over and saw his own image.

He held the two pictures side-by-side.

Then, with the photos pressed between his praying palms, Ken again closed his eyes.

"God help me," he moaned towards the stairs. "I'm sorry, dad."

Standing, Ken glimpsed King Library, where his walk began. Nudging the photos back into his wallet, he recalled a saying:

Every time a person dies, it's like a library burns.

CHAPTER FOUR

Just about where the red brick streets melt into two-lane blacktop, Ken was one mile into a fourteen-mile workout. There he settled into his cruising pace, soaking in the mid-August sun that hugged the rolling farm country between Oxford and Hueston Woods State Park, the turnaround point on his run.

The yellow block M on his blue nylon running shorts was already sticking to his right leg, wet from perspiration. Sweat channeled down his washboard abdomen and the small of his back.

After four miles his red bandanna headband was soaked, but still channeled the sweat from his eyes.

Besides training for that fall's Detroit Free Press Marathon, today's long run would help Ken deal with the emotional aftershocks of his weekend discovery. More than a hobby, running was his mantra. Each silent stride held his mind in a place where he could distance himself from and examine the rest of his life or none of it, pondering such deep mysteries as Stonehenge, or why the drop-dead beauty in the music store refused to shave her legs. But all that had been shoved from his mind by the consuming discovery of last Saturday.

He approached a covered wooden bridge that seemed an anachronism, even amidst the 19th century saltbox homes skirting the picture-postcard southwestern Ohio campus town. He wondered how long the structure would last before it, like his lost high school love or his father's memory, would come apart and fall into the stream of time.

The span's worn planks thumped a deep, giant's heartbeat with each gliding bounce of Ken's running shoes, and its brief shade tempted him to stop for a rest as the still, cool air kissed his bare chest. But that was a reward awaiting him at the state park, where he would allow himself a quick water break before his return run.

Back in the sunlight of Brown Road, Ken braced himself for the yammering fur streaks that would assail him from the ramshackle farmhouse he approached. Just as the bridge was always there, so too were the pair of mutts that seemed to find a singular delight in harassing runners, cyclists or anything else with ankles. The smaller one looked more like a worn-out dust mop, and was roused into a frenzy of bravado (which it would certainly otherwise lack) by a larger, stupid-looking animal that probably slept when not eating or being a pain in the ass.

Experience had shown Ken that the canine duo was best dealt with by ignoring them and running straight ahead. The dogs would have the satisfaction of chasing a foe, but they sensed too much confidence in this one to challenge it with more than half-hearted nips amidst their torrent of barks and snarls.

Two miles from the park where he would turn around at the beach and sailing slips on Acton Lake, Ken followed the blacktop ribbon down a long, steep valley. Holding his seven-minute-mile pace, he cruised down one side of the incline and pushed up the other. Sweat dripped from his nose and saturated beard, and he looked forward to the park water fountain.

The side road into the large state park and marina wound through thick woods dotted with grassy, sunlight-dappled picnic areas that reminded Ken of impressionist art. The final quarter-mile before the marina consisted of an almost vertical descent into its parking lot, boat slips, beach and concession stand.

As Ken drew long, steady swallows of lukewarm water from the concession building's wall-mounted fountain, a yellow, competition model Frisbee soared against the bricks inches above his head.

"Sorry, dude," panted a drunk in a Sigma Chi T-shirt.

"Fer sher, dude," Ken replied, correct in his assumption that the frat boy wouldn't catch his sarcasm.

Taking a moment to sit on the grass and stretch his leg muscles, the runner surveyed the pre-semester antics of his fellow student arrivals. The airspace not occupied by Frisbees, footballs and an occasional beer can was saturated with the scent of suntan oil and barbecue. A discordant symphony blared from the fleet of boom-boxes sprinkled over the beach, usually positioned next to a picnic cooler where the tanning students would turn faithfully every half hour. About three-quarters of the crowd were Greeks. They sported their fraternity or sorority letters on everything from flags hung on makeshift tree branch standards to one particularly fetching "Kappa Tau" stitched over the left cheek of a red bikini bottom.

Ken and most of his friends were in the minority at Miami University, also known as 'the North American mother of fraternities and sororities'. Many had originated there since the red brick and ivy school was founded in 1809. Ken felt that the palatial charter houses that dotted the school's perimeter were shrines to snobbery, and he was quite at home with his GDI (God-Damned Independent) peers at student ghetto keggers.

Midway into the first stride of the seven-mile run back to his apartment, Ken spotted two friends sunning from lounge chairs on the beach between the docks and parking lot.

"Tom! Chloe!" he yelled, glad to see familiar faces. Ken had met the pair two years before in an Introduction to Philosophy class, and given the sense of isolation that had come with his surreal discovery, he was eager to reconnect with friends. Besides, since the recent loss of his girl friend, he found it heartening that this couple remained together.

Tom Porter and Chloe Bach ("No relation," she would automatically offer during introductions) would blend in easily in Greenwich Village or Berkeley, but in the wash of preppies in the park, they were as conspicuous as a clown at a funeral.

As Ken approached, Tom threw down a pen and pad and reached into a Styrofoam cooler between his and Chloe's chairs. Their purloined McDonald's flag hung limply from a broomstick fastened to their cooler, which was painted olive drab with a Red Cross insignia.

"Have some fuel, Mister Marathon," Tom shouted, and he lobbed a bottle of Little Kings Cream Ale in a perfect arc to his approaching friend.

"Damn, it's good to see you guys," Ken panted as he stooped for the bottle opener that hung by a string from the cooler. "How was your summer?"

"Not bad," Tom replied. "Chloe and I worked in Sandusky, at Cedar Point Amusement Park."

"We made a fair amount of cash doing street entertaining there," his strawberry blonde partner added. "And we stayed at my folks' place in Cleveland. I don't know what was more fun," she said with a smile, "seeing all those Technicolor yawns coming from the beer-and-weenie-stuffed *touristas* as they came off the park rides, or watching my dad sneak around the house each night trying to catch us."

"I know where I felt safer," Tom quipped. "So, did you bid a tearful summer farewell to your retired high school cheerleader?"

Ken shook his head. "It was a permanent farewell. I think her first year in college taught her that there are other options besides old high school flames. She found a nice pre-med boy at Michigan State. I guess I can't blame her," he said with a shrug, keeping the atmosphere light. "For what that myopic, lab coat-wearing twerp will make in medicine, maybe I should go out with him!"

All three laughed, and Ken realized that the sound was more medicine for his concealed confusion than for his wounded heart as he downed the last of his Little Kings.

"Gotta hit the pavement before my muscles start to tighten up," he said, tossing the empty green bottle to Chloe. "I'm still in Heather Lane Apartments. I'll stop by the Stables to see you two later."

The three-story house Tom, Chloe and several other students occupied in the student ghetto west of the old green water tower in the town square had been dubbed the Aegean Stables. It was probably a misnomer, however, because unlike its namesake from Greek mythology, Hercules certainly couldn't clean it in one day, no matter how large the shovel.

Ordinarily, a workout interruption as long as he had just experienced irritated Ken, but seeing his friends had helped pull him from what had become incessant rumination on the hidden room. The cloudless electric blue sky, the musky scent from the damp, tree-covered earth near the lake, and one well-executed wolf-whistle from a passing carload of coeds all came through more clearly now.

Ken exited Hueston Woods and veered back onto humpy Brown Road for his "return flight," ruminating on how fourteen miles of hot, dusty Midwestern road can make a cold shower a very appealing finish line. His heart squeezed water and salt through every pore in his body and he felt strong.

A growling Little Kings-induced belch tore from Ken's throat, punctuating the 'poc, poc, poc' of his shoes against the asphalt, and he pondered how primal scream therapy couldn't rival the therapeutic value of one good beer burp.

His strong pace, the rolling countryside and reuniting with old friends over cold libation breathed a renewed feeling in him that things would be good again, that the mystery now dogging him would be resolved.

Reentering the downhill slope of the half-mile-long valley, Ken reminded himself not to allow the pull of gravity to break his pace, and he gave special attention to the proper bend of his knees to avoid locking, jarring and injury.

Keeping his pace on the up-side was more a matter of a quarter-mile of grit than of balance. Then the remaining five miles home would all be level to slightly downhill.

Leaning forward and lowering his head, Ken was several strides into the climb when he heard what sounded like a spinning revolver cylinder coming up fast behind him. Without breaking his stride he turned to see that it came from the whirling derailleur of a coasting 10-speed bike, piloted by a woman who could have been built according to his specifications.

A sly grin came to her high-cheeked face, framed to the chin by a jet black page boy haircut. Her mirrored sunglasses reflected the white line along the road's shoulder that separated them by inches.

Hers was the smile, Ken imagined, of a non-runner who hoped the steep stretch of road would bring him the pedestrian humbling all "joggers" so richly deserve.

A breeze clipped Ken as the willowy cyclist cruised past his left side, and she smiled as if to ask, "Don't you feel silly doing that to yourself?"

But the hill was slowing her quickly, and she leaned forward to downshift, showing the back of the white, ribbed tank-top that narrowed to her lean waist. It was tucked into the most nicely packed pair of khaki hiking shorts that Ken had ever seen, and he wished he could shake hands with whoever invented the 10-speed bicycle seat.

"I like your smile," Ken half shouted. "If I help you to the top will you buy me a beer?"

"Oh, you joggers are so cute," she cooed, still smiling but steadily putting more effort into each push of the pedals.

"I may be cute," he conceded, "but I'm a *runner,* not a *jogger.* Joggers wear Dayglo green polyester Dior warm-ups," he took a breath, "spend more time talking about running than attempting to actually do it," he gulped another breath, "and they have the uncanny ability to run slower than most people walk."

"So, what's a runner then?" the raven-haired beauty called over her shoulder. Her handlebars began a slight weave, and Ken heard a 'shunk' as she slipped the gears into first.

"I am," came his reply, whispered into her ear as he reached her side. Ken slowed his pace to keep even with the cyclist, whose knees were now rising and falling at about twice the rate of his.

"That looks like a lot of work," he observed. "Maybe you should take up jogging."

Fifty yards from the summit, Ken placed his sweaty left hand onto the small of the woman's back and began to push, rubbing in the turn their spontaneous contest had taken. He hoped for more than just a free drink as he began pushing her toward the top.

"This is one brew you'll have to earn," the cyclist said. She stopped pedaling, pushed her sunglasses to the end of her nose and looked over them and directly into his blue-green eyes.

The ragged runner was transfixed. Her eyes were the purest, deepest blue he had ever seen. He felt almost like he could fall headlong into them and never be heard from again—or care to be.

Turning her gaze straight ahead, she realized that the last time she felt the strong, even push of a man's hand guiding her along on a bike it was that of her father. She turned back to the runner, subconsciously hoping to see once again that steadfast parent. He had died less than a year after teaching the little girl how to balance a two-wheeler. She wondered how much more smoothly her life would have gone had he been around long enough to help her learn how to balance it, too.

"Get thee to a brewery!" Ken yelled as they reached the top, giving the rested biker a final push along the level pavement. "I'll drink nearly any brand, but I prefer imports. When and where do I collect?"

She laughed. "You'll have to take a shower first!"

"Not during?" he groaned.

The seductive cyclist leaned forward again, a little slower this time, and eased the gears into fifth. Giving the pedals a half-turn she coasted slowly, offering another view of perfect female form.

"Tonight. Eight o'clock. The Balcony," she said, looking straight ahead. She then turned and again unabashedly peered deeply into his sweat-framed eyes.

A beautiful woman's eyes invite men to a place where they can never go, Ken thought. Where had the eyes of his last love taken him?

The cyclist glided away, making the long, smooth turn that would send her onto a straightway past the old farmhouse with the dogs and into Oxford. By the time Ken cleared the turn, she was gone.

Coming up on the farmhouse, the bedraggled runner now began to notice the deep, heavy ache that the hillside encounter had visited upon his lungs and legs. The dogs must have been diverted by some unlucky cat or rabbit, because neither appeared as he passed their turf. Soon he thumped back through the covered bridge, and a little later the familiar herringbone-pattern red bricks—one of the town's trademarks—vibrated at his feet as he re-entered Oxford.

Brown Road turned into College Avenue, and as Ken came to the High Street intersection he passed the forest green, two-story wood frame house belonging to his philosophy advisor, Dr. Jim Arsenault, and his wife Francoise. Several girls watched Ken from the front porch of the Oxford College women's dorm on the opposite corner. They and the realization that he was only a half-mile from his apartment moved Ken to quicken his pace.

He dashed east on Spring Street, and two blocks later turned right, onto the gravel-surfaced Heather Lane, where his apartment building was nestled in the wood-shrouded elbow of the L-shaped secondary road.

Bounding to a stop on his building's parking lot, the exhausted runner eased along the sidewalk towards the second of the two stairwell entrances. He was greeted by the whoops, hollers and applause of his neighbors from the eight-apartment building who were well into an impromptu volleyball game and back-to-school barbecue on the rear lawn.

"Thank you, my loyal fans," Ken said with a bow, and he dropped onto the tree-enclosed lawn and went into his stretches.

"Why don't you join us for some V-ball, beers and bee-cue?" invited one of the organizers. He was Todd Blakely, Ken's downstairs neighbor and a pre-law student who looked more like a bodyguard or fullback than a briefcase-and-pinstripes type.

Ken bent over and touched his forehead to his right knee. "Have to take a rain check," he said, catching a shy young blonde's smile as he again sat upright. "I'd like to be a better neighbor and get to know the new arrivals, but I have to get cleaned up and meet someone uptown by eight."

"Allow me to introduce you to the new tenants of 'Heathen Lane'," Blakely said. "On the winning team," he announced with a flourish toward the four teammates on his side of the net, "we have returning occupants and not-too-shabby lawn athletes Anne Mallory and Linda Kent." Ken was glad to see they had returned. Anne, an anthropology major, was a little plain in appearance, but had the bright-eyed smile that had helped to recruit the pair's large circle of friends. Linda was returning to studies in English literature and looked like the rich daddy's daughter that she was. Even now, her poise was that of a countess as she wore faded Levi's cutoffs and a Duke University basketball jersey she got from her boyfriend, a classics major at the school.

Anne and Linda had joined the rest of the tenants for the picnic and volleyball, accompanied by the Best of ZZ Top, jamming from Blakely's open living room window. But Ken knew that when the studious pair re-entered their one-bedroom apartment across from Blakely's studio, they would go back to Perrier, primates, Chaucer and National Public Radio.

Their teammates were Barry Buchman and Michael Tierney, who shared an apartment adjoining Mallory and Kent. They were returning sophomores and official "little brothers" to the building's established community of upperclassmen and women.

Slim, petite and deceptively shy-looking Jan Siegel once again occupied the ground-level studio apartment on the red brick building's east end. Ken wondered if the pretty, bedroom-eyed journalism major would still be in the habit of making love with her boyfriend du jour in her living room with the drapes open. It was an especially curious practice when one considered its location— on the well-traveled walkway between the building's wall-mounted mailboxes and the parking lot.

Rooming again across the hall from Ken's place and above Kent and Mallory were the official building party beasts, Brian Resnick and Jim Heavner, known to all as "Black and Blue," respectively. The pair were definitely Miami University students, but their majors

were anybody's guess—themselves included. Taxidermy fascinated
Jim, or Blue, and he was renowned for stuffing fresh roadkills of
every genus and size native to southwestern Ohio. Brian, a.k.a.
Black, was engaged in the eternal overhaul of his red 1976 Mustang
convertible, which was said to be responsible for the demise of
most of his roommate's furry menagerie.

"Rochelle DeLeeuw and Diane Bettis moved in yesterday,"
Blakely said. The blonde, freshmanesque teammates smiled and
nodded in unison. The closer of the two, Rochelle, was the girl
Ken had caught glimpsing his stretches earlier. The ponytailed
blonde bit her lip and seemed coy as a high school freshman as she
watched the runner stand.

"I ran high school track in Dayton," she offered. The lowering
sun struck a spark from her emerald-green eyes. "Sprints, relays
and hurdles. More speed than stamina. I've never been much good
at anything longer than the half-mile."

"Well," Ken said with a laugh, "living in the same building
with Black, Blue and Blakely, you'll need that speed!"

The group laughed and Ken dodged a barrage of beer cans
and rib bones as he rounded the building and ducked into its rear
entrance. Pulling his key from a hidden groove in the railing on
the way up to his second floor studio apartment, Ken checked his
watch as he opened the door. It was 5:30, leaving plenty of time to
shower, kill a slab of ribs and walk the seven blocks to meet the
cycle goddess at The Balcony.

Ken draped his socks and shorts over a towel bar, stepped into
the shower and shivered as he unleashed a torrent of icy water
against his chest. He stood motionless in the pelting stream, then
slowly began to move the soap over his body, thinking about those
he had seen during his run, especially the cyclist.

As the sweat and grime of fourteen miles flowed from his body,
it felt renewed. Then, as if by default, his mind drifted back to the
damp, dark chamber his father had maintained in secrecy, and the
questions it begged. It was a mocking enigma he couldn't wash
away.

CHAPTER FIVE

The Balcony had the distinction of being the most conveniently located of the several student bars in Oxford, a block west of the school on the east end of High Street, the town's main drag. It was a good meeting spot offering a laid-back, peanut shell-littered atmosphere with a classic rock-stocked jukebox. On the weekends it showcased high-energy live bands from the Cincinnati-Indianapolis-Columbus area.

Ken entered the small foyer the bar shared with its downstairs neighbor, Ozzie's, a semiformal beanery catering to parents in town to visit their student children.

Turning left past the Chamber of Commerce pamphlet rack, Ken entered the red brick-walled stairway, thick with a heavy bass jukebox echo. Midway up, he recognized it as the Rolling Stones' "Jumpin' Jack Flash."

Walking through the propped-open doorway, Ken was greeted by the smell of beer, smoke, popcorn and suntan oil. The latter would be replaced in a month or so by whatever aftershave and perfume had the biggest ads in Men's Health and Cosmo.

It was a busy Thursday night in the bar, with returning students taking up about half of the booths and tables. The barn wood walls soaked up much of the light from the simple hanging fixtures, and a gentle stir came through the row of open windows overlooking High Street.

Moving toward a small table at one of the windows, Ken's new, white tennis shoes glowed like two bouncing rabbits in the dim light as he walked across the vacant dance floor. The group was fairly subdued, and the only noise between songs came from a group of drunk fraternity boys jeering passing women from the roof of their nearby Phi Gamma house.

Turning his gaze through the window, Ken saw a shock of pink-and-green-clad sorority femmes giggle their way out of the

Baskin-Robbins across the street. A couple of them pointed in opposite directions, probably offering suggestions for their next stop on a return-to-campus tour. They squealed, jumped up and down and disappeared into a Jeep with Rhode Island license plates.

Turning to survey the bar's clientele, Ken was fascinated by a most unlikely combinations of persons. The two couples standing at the far end of the bar looked like the result of a software glitch at a computerized dating service.

The men appeared to be in their early 30s and were decked out with full black leather biker regalia, complete with their club's colors, the Mellow Pirates. He recalled seeing that same logo on the jackets worn by the gang that had passed him on the highway. The portentous pair had managed to connect with two freshmanesque girls who could not yet have seen year 19. Dressed in pastel shorts, Madras blouses and Espadrilles, the coeds looked ready for Parents' Weekend or a sorority mixer.

It was obvious to Ken and everyone else that the girls were being pursued by leather-clad predators. And all four were engaged in some of the most vigorous slammer-tossing he had ever seen.

The girls would twitter and the men guffaw as they slammed shot glasses onto the drink-splotched bar. The foaming mix of club soda and liquor was then tossed down the hatch, minus what had sprayed through their fingers during the slamming process.

The girls giggled like idiots as they gulped and burped and gulped again. Their suitors stood expressionless and silent, beer-bellies protruding while they drained their glasses like park bears going at honey jars.

Just as Ken was beginning to seriously worry about the fate in store for the blithering, color-coordinated girls, a similarly dressed coed of about twenty stormed into the bar.

"Dammit Kirsten! What is this shit?" she screamed, moving across the room like a Marine drill instructor. She pulled one of the girls aside and shot her the high-eyebrowed, stiff-lipped, tilted-head expression that women use to convey pure fury. The third girl was now laughing so hard she had to hold onto the bar to keep from falling. The bikers shot each other a disappointed look and slid to a nearby table, realizing that their investment in the price of a good number of slammers would not bring them libidinal release, at least not from this sweet young pair.

Ken heard the older girl say something about "Mom and Dad" and "eight in the morning," then witnessed their less-than-graceful exit. The laugher lost her slammers—and lunch—at the doorway.

"Bullshit!" barked the bartender, turning for a closet door. He flung it open, grabbed a bucket and mop and went to work.

At eight sharp Ken saw his dark-haired date approaching from across the street. A red nylon gym bag was slung over her shoulder, both hands jammed into the back pockets of her straightleg jeans.

Seconds later she emerged from the stairway, sporting a broad smile as she glanced over her shoulder at Big Sister and the descending drunks.

The early-20ish woman looked to be nearly six feet tall, Ken thought as she leaned to say something to the balding, potbellied barkeep. He wheeled, turned two bottles from a cooler and popped the caps as she fished her wallet from the gym bag. She handed the bartender a ten as he clinked two glasses over the bottlenecks and shoved them, two napkins and change into her hands.

She showed a slight, close-mouthed smile as she neared the table, and Ken was sure she must be some sort of athlete. She was firm and lean, and Ken knew she had to be involved in something beside cycling to give her the perfect blend of curve and tone, stature and poise.

Gymnastics, he thought. *Maybe beamwork or floor routines.*

Ken stood as she approached, and she motioned him to sit as she put the bottles of St. Pauli Girl Dark on the center of the rough-finished, initial-carved table, then dropped the gym bag between her chair and the wall.

Her faded jeans and loose-fitting, pearl-white T-shirt looked soft against her taut, tan skin. She sat, pulled her chair close to the table and leaned forward on crossed arms. Then, for the third time that day, she looked directly and unabashedly into Ken's eyes. Crystal clear and forever blue, her gaze transfixed him so completely that he didn't realize he was staring back.

"Are you going to make me pour them, too?" she asked, cocking her head.

He half-filled both glasses from one of the amber bottles and handed her one. Drinks raised, their eyes met again in a silent toast as their glasses sounded a dull 'clack'. The drinks went down like liquid night, smooth and cool.

"Your taste in beer is admirable," Ken said, topping off their glasses with the remainder of the bottle. "I remember telling you of my fondness for imports, but I'm surprised you got one for yourself. I've never before met a woman who drank anything heavier than Weight Watchers Lite."

"It's something I picked up in Europe," she said, crossing her legs and leaning back. "I spent last year studying at Miami's Luxembourg campus.

"My friends and I spent more than a few weekends in a VW minibus on road trips to French, Belgian, German and Swiss bistros. The Belgian abbey beer is the best I've ever had," she said with a sigh. "Can't get that in here, though."

"I'm not as well traveled as you," Ken said. "I've done most of my sampling here or at Rosie O'Grady's Pub in Grand Rapids."

She smiled. "That explains the Michigan block M on your shorts today. Did you grow up in Grand Rapids?"

"Yeah. Born and raised. I left there three years ago for classes here. I go back for holidays and an occasional weekend. How about you?"

"I'm a fellow Michigander," she said with a smile. "Born in a summer cottage near Traverse City and raised just north of Motown in Birmingham. I'm just returning to Miami from the year in Europe I told you about. I'm beginning my junior year here in liberal arts."

Ken's interest grew.

"What's your major?" he asked.

"Art photography major with a minor in dance."

The dance minor explained her physical shape. Next Ken decided to test her sense of humor.

"Art photography? What are you going to do with that, take baby pictures at Kmart?"

"I suppose I could," she countered. "But the fast lane has always scared me. I'll probably just continue to show and sell my pieces."

"Show and sell?"

"I have work on display in a couple of galleries in the Detroit area," she purred. "And my occasional sales have given me enough to pay for three years of college, one of them abroad.

"But the Kmart idea shows imagination," she said. "I'll keep it in mind in case things dry up.

"So, what's your major?"

"Philosophy," Ken answered, straining to keep a straight face after the jab he had just given the practicality of her choice.

"*Philosophy!?!*" she squealed, her voice rivaling David Bowie's as his "Suffragette City" bounced from the jukebox. "Are you kidding? You can't even sell *that* at *Kmart!*"

She saw him smile broadly for the first time, his beard showing light creases where those dimples hid.

Ken noticed he didn't feel lonely anymore. He didn't yet know this curious blend of beauty, brains and sass, but he knew he wanted to.

"My name's Ken Perry."

"Well, Ken Perry," the coal-haired woman responded, "I'm Jill Mangan, and now that I've successfully defended my impractical major, what have you to say for the love of wisdom as an inroad to the Great American Dream?"

"Not much really. I'm not interested in the little white house, cum or sans picket fence, station wagon, St. Bernard dog and/or 1.5 children." He slid his right palm onto the window sill and looked into the street.

"So what is your dream, then?"

"I'm not sure," he answered. "Maybe that's why I read philosophy; I'm trying to figure it all out."

For the first time since Ken had entered the bar, he thought of the hidden room.

"So how does Plato plan to pay his rent?"

"The same way Plato paid his," Ken said. "By teaching. I've already met my academic requirements for a minor in secondary education, and depending on how my phil workload is this year, I could pull teaching into a second major."

"You're a real grab bag," the woman said. "I don't think I've ever met a philosopher/teacher/jock before."

"You still haven't. I'm studying to become the first two, and I don't know that being a serious runner makes me a jock."

"Why do you run?" she asked. "I can't think of anything else, with the possible exception of a few classes, that could be so boring and painful at the same time."

"You've never really tried it, have you?"

"I prefer dancing," she answered.

"Why do you dance?" Ken countered.

"It's spontaneous, uninhibited, flowing and beautiful . . . like entering into and becoming one with the music."

"Sounds a lot like sex," Ken said.

"Maybe," she replied. "But you still haven't given me a good reason for getting out and frying the soles of your feet on miles of August blacktop."

"I can't give you any one good reason why you or anyone else should," he said, pouring the remainder of the second bottle into their glasses. "I can only tell you why I do it."

"That was my original question," she replied.

"Everything else changes," Ken said. His mind returned to his family basement as he again leveled his gaze on the street below. "The road stays the same, and running gives me a sense of stability. Everything else is uncertain, unreliable."

"I hope you don't think that playing the part of the cynic is romantic," she replied, "because I think it's corny and depressing. Besides, that wasn't a cynic I saw greeting two friends at Hueston Woods today. Why, you even interrupted your run to swap smiles and sillies over what looked like a Little Kings. That doesn't smack of cynical withdrawal or a brooding devotion to 'the road'."

Ken was surprised and pleased that she had not only noticed him at the park earlier that day, but that she had paid him such close attention.

"My friends and family are more important than the road," he assured. "Like I said, what makes the road, running, so important to me is that it is constant. It helps me to tie all the other random, beautiful, ugly and absurd stuff together. So, if you want to give me a label, I suppose the best you could do is call me an 'existential runner' . . . Certainly not *jock,* and *anything* but *jogger.*"

"It's good to know that you place friends and family above running," Jill said.

"I like to think we all cheer each other on," Ken said, "in running and everything else."

A bluish-silver dart scooped up the two empty bottles, followed by the voice of a tall, thin waitress. "Have another?" she blurted in the automatic half-scream that kept her a decibel above the jukebox. Silver-and-turquoise jewelry bobbled from both of her wrists and earlobes and most of her fingers.

"Yeah," Ken said. "Two more."

She nodded and moved on.

"Friends cheer each other on," Ken repeated. "They give you that edge that just might be enough to keep you on pace, to kick that much harder, to make it first to the finish line or at least know you gave it your best effort. Friends are a part of the race."

Two fresh beers were placed on the table, and Ken peeled a ten from his wallet. He gave it to the waitress and then reached in again to retrieve a worn, faded color photo.

"This is a picture of my dad," he said, handing it to Jill across the table. "He was a runner back in the days before it was urban chic. He was on his high school and college cross country and track teams in the late fifties and early sixties. And a wife, two kids and getting established in a good business consulting firm still couldn't keep him from finding time for his running.

"My older sister, Margaret, was a femme fatale from day one. The only running she ever did was after or away from boys.

"Some of my earliest memories are of standing at the living room window, waiting for my dad to round the corner on the home stretch of his daily run. Snow, rain, heat, cold—it didn't matter—he always went into his kick at the corner and hugged me when he came in.

A flashing image of the hidden room tainted the beloved memory like venom through a fang.

"Then, when I was five, he let me start running with him. Not his regular route or pace, of course," Ken said with a smile, "but he'd go one or two laps around the block with me, always encouraging me: 'Nice pace, Mister Perry!' or 'Okay, Mister Perry, let's see that kick!' He never let me win, like a lot of other fathers would. He wanted that experience to be genuine."

The brunette held the photo in both hands, finding similarities and differences between the man across the table and the clean-shaven image of the one who shared his eyes, smile and dimples.

"We always called each other Mister Perry when we ran," Ken recalled, and it was then that Jill realized that all references to his father were in the past tense.

"In fact," he looked at her and laughed, "dad even had some T-shirts printed up for us to wear during training runs and races. His said MISTER PERRY in capital letters, and mine said the same, all in lower case.

"The next summer, when I was six, we ran our first road race together," Ken said. "It was a five-kilometer St. Patrick's Day run in Grand Rapids, to benefit a local hospital. Dad ran my pace so we could enjoy the race together—and we did, my dad and I both feeling so proud of each other. I would've rather run that short, three-point-one-mile local event with my father than to have done a record-setting Boston Marathon without him."

Ken looked at her again. "I'm sorry, I didn't mean to go into a long monologue."

"That's all right," she said a little too softly for him to hear over the music. He saw that she understood, and the way she held the photograph mirrored the way she seemed to be holding his words. He felt that she was truly, totally there with him.

"As I got older I had a pretty typical life," he continued, "hanging out with the guys, chasing the cheerleaders, and dragging into the house past curfew on more than a few weekend nights, trying to sneak past my folks to bed.

"But dad and I always managed to find time to get in at least one five-mile run per week, and we ran in lots of races, too. We'd throw our gear into the car, often bringing along my high school buddies or his work pals. Sometimes we'd drive overnight for a race.

"When I was seven, dad took me to my first 10-kilometer run. Six-point-two miles is a long way for a kid that age to run," Ken said. "And I felt like I was about to run a marathon when the starting horn blew. It was the Old Midland River Race, following beautiful, old logging trails along the Tittabawasee River, ending with a lap on the track in the Northwood Institute stadium. 'This is our day, Mister Perry,' he yelled to me as we found our pace. I was scared to death that I'd cramp up or something and have to stop and walk, ruining the race. But the opposite happened. It was my dad who had the tough break.

"We had gone about half the distance when he suddenly dropped to the dirt road as if he'd been tackled or something. I didn't know it then, but he had tripped over the top of a large rock sticking out of the road, and when he came down he broke his right wrist and tore his left quadricep. He grabbed his leg with his one good arm and I could see he was in agony."

As Jill listened she saw that Ken was reliving the experience, not merely describing it. His voice and expressions were totally present to what had occurred some fifteen years before.

"He looked up at me and said, 'Keep running, Mister Perry! You're running this one for both of us. I'll see you at the finish line.' So I went on.

"The sag wagon picked him up and would have taken him to the hospital," Ken said, catching her questioning look. "That's slang for the van on hand for injured or dropped-out runners," he explained. "Anyway, dad had the guys splint his wrist, wind his leg in about forty yards of Ace bandages and prop him between mom and a crutch at the finish line.

"When I got within earshot, they screamed like I was neck-and-neck with Jessie Owens. I felt and looked like a wet dishrag, but I was glad to be so sweaty, because I thought that might hide the tears I'd been shedding for my poor dad. He didn't have nature's camouflage, and the tears rolled down his face as he yelled, *Attaway, Mister Perry! That's my boy!* Mom had more than a little trouble holding him up as he waved his crutch in the air while I stumbled over the finish line."

Once again Ken paused in a little embarrassment as he realized how long he had rambled on.

"I'm sorry," he said. "I really didn't intend to talk about myself so much."

"I could show you the best spots in Luxembourg or Brussels for a bite to eat after a few drinks," Jill said, shifting the topic. "But I'm starving and I have no idea where the good munchie joints are in Alma Materville."

"You like subs?"

"Love a good one."

"Allow me," Ken said. He grabbed her gym bag and ushered her down the stairs. Back outside, they rounded Poplar Street and walked into the brightly lit Philadelphia Sub Shop.

"These guys make the best veggie sub in the world," Ken said, leading her past the white Formica tables to the ordering counter.

"Veggie sounds good to me too," Jill said, "with vinegar and oil."

A teenager came through a side doorway, wringing wet hands on his tomato-splotched apron.

"Two veggies with V and O," Ken said. "To go."

The sandwich architect disappeared into the kitchen, and the pair walked to the shop's front windows. "The night's too pretty to sit in here," Ken said. "We could eat while I walk you home. Where do you live?"

"I'm a resident assistant in Minnich Hall, in charge of second floor south, where I lived as a freshman," Jill explained. "When I got home from Luxembourg the university offered me the position. They said my academic, athletic and extracurricular record here in Miami and on the Luxembourg campus made me a good candidate to head-up a floor of girls. At first I thought it would be glorified babysitting, but really it's a lot of fun. And yes," she finally answered, "I'd like that walk."

Ken paid for the brown, football-shaped bag and grabbed a few napkins from a dispenser on the counter.

The couple turned back onto High Street, unwrapped their subs and began to eat as they passed The Balcony.

"Mmmm, you were right," Jill moaned. "This is great!"

"How often do you get home?" she asked.

"Usually one weekend a month during the warm weather," Ken replied. "And for Christmas and other holidays. I like Oxford, so I don't mind spending most of my time here. I used to go back home mainly to visit my girlfriend, but we split up this summer."

He threw his sub wrapper into a waste barrel as they entered the university grounds, walking under the red brick arch at the corner of Campus and High streets.

"I like to see mom once in a while, too," he added. "She gets kinda lonesome without Margaret and me. Marg's a flight attendant with United, based out of Chicago. My dad died when I was a senior in high school."

He said it calmly and matter-of-factly. Too much so, she thought.

The pair walked past Irvin Hall, where Ken's philosophy classes met. They glanced through a window that had probably been left open by accident, and Ken shivered from the aura projected by the dark, lifeless room.

"It was a Saturday," he said, dropping the butt of his sandwich into another trash barrel. "Dad and I had planned to see a Tigers-Yankees double-header in Detroit, but I got the flu and couldn't go."

He slid both hands into his rear pockets, and her gym bag gently bounced on his back as they walked.

"So he called a couple of his friends from work and they drove to Detroit for the games. About eight that night, the three of them were walking back to their car and somebody shot my dad, in the chest, from a passing car, for no reason.

Or so he had always believed.

"The cops got a good description of the car, but they never found it or the black teenagers inside . . . Probably a bunch of drunk assholes looking to take their boredom, frustration or hatred out on the first warm target they came across."

There was another silence, and Jill stopped Ken, placing one hand on his chest while holding the remnants of her sandwich in the other. Without speaking, she turned him around, unzipped the gym bag and slid the white-paper-wrapped portion inside. She closed the bag and plucked an oak leaf from a low branch as they continued walking. They stopped at a ten-foot-tall spherical bronze sundial which had been erected as a gift from one of the school's sororities. It rested on a low terrace overlooking a broad, flat and nearly treeless courtyard bordered on the other three sides by dormitories, including Minnich Hall, where Jill was staying.

Instead of turning left for the weathered black slate steps down to the sidewalk and her dorm, Jill took Ken's hand and pulled him straight ahead to the low wall behind the sundial. Light and music filtered through dorm windows and over the broad courtyard.

"I didn't know my dad as well as you knew yours," she said, easing onto the stone wall. Ken sat beside her.

"I was only eight when he died in a car accident. He went out to get milk," she continued. "Mom had made a typical Tuesday dinner, tuna casserole, and she ran out of milk. Nothing about that day was unusual at all . . . totally and perfectly typical, status quo," she said with more than a touch of irony. "It was like, 'Well, I'm going to the store now' one minute, and the next minute I'm watching my mother bury her face in her hands as a Michigan State trooper tells her something too quietly for me to hear.

"It was as if the world had come to an end in some strange way that still left dinner steaming on the stove. The lights were on, but they only seemed to highlight his absence. The light became a mockery, saying 'He's gone, and there is no dark place in which to place any hope of finding him.'

"Mom just sat there, and I was so frightened because she wasn't crying; she just stared into the middle of the room. Finally, I couldn't take it anymore. I started crying and ran over and we put our arms around each other. That's when she began to cry, too. That's how we stayed until the video that we hadn't paid any attention to finally ended.

"My helping mom clear the unused dishes from the table was more of a silent rite of passage than anything else, driving home the realization that it was just us now."

Jill lay on her back and cupped her hands under her head as she watched the stars vibrate in the moonless sky.

"Harry Mangan was a good dad," she said wistfully. "He never missed a single dance recital I was ever in, from my age four debut as a dancing rabbit to some of my first efforts in toe shoes just before he died. He was always Santa on Christmas and the Knight in Shining Armor in the bedtime stories he read me most nights. Mom would sit on the bed and listen, too, the expression on her face probably not much different from mine. They were very much in love, and he was her real-life Prince Charming.

"He didn't teach me dance, photography or any of the other things I 'do'. But he taught me how to love," the beauty said with a smile. "And how to ride a bike."

She wanted to tell Ken how strongly he had brought back the memory of her father earlier that day when he pushed her up that country road hill. But she felt that the heavy summer night with its stars and sentiment had already caused her to wax a little too melancholy. She sat up, and they shared a deep closeness as they watched several students play Frisbee under a lamppost at the far end of the courtyard.

Ken eased an arm around his newfound friend, and she folded both of hers around his waist and lay her head on his chest. A lone cricket offered a rhythmic reminder of the here and now, that the past is gone.

The Westminster chimes of the campus bell tower echoed over the couple, and both counted aloud the eleven rings that followed.

Jill slowly lifted her head, brushed her hair from her cheek and stretched, arching her back.

"Come on," she said, tugging his left pants pocket. "I'll introduce you to my roommates. I told them I'd be back by eleven. It's the first night we're all here and we're supposed to get the room straightened around."

"Sure," Ken replied, once again shouldering her bag. "By the way," he said as they descended the five slate steps, "Why do you have me carting this bag around? Coming from the gym?"

"Yeah," she said. "Racquetball. I had a game with one of my friends from the art department. I was going home to prepare for it when we met on the road."

"Who won?"

"Let's just say I'm glad there was no wager," she said with a pretend scowl.

The couple turned into the lobby of Minnich Hall, one of the five three-story, red brick dorms lining the courtyard.

"Brace yourself," Jill warned, leading Ken past the front desk and up the stairs toward her second floor suite. "Both of my roommates arrived today, and when I left this afternoon for my racquetball match they were already revved into party mode. They're both sophomores with the back-to-school crazies."

Ken pulled open the heavy gray stairwell door and they entered a hallway strewn with cardboard boxes and packing paper.

"The halls of academia?" Ken shouted over blaring stereo music.

"The halls of Montezuma!" Jill yelled back.

Most of the doors in the hallway were open. Ken thought about how single women living in private homes or apartments would never go about their daily routine with the front door open and unattended. But in a dormitory they are rarely closed (with the exceptions of amorous activity, kegger convocations or the sharing of other controlled substances).

In the spirit of floor unity, the girls all had their radios tuned to the same station, Cincinnati's WKRC-FM, as they settled into their rooms, sharing popcorn and summer gossip.

Ken and Jill navigated the hall as they would a jungle, stepping around luggage, boxes and other moving-in debris while dodging hyperactive coeds darting room to room.

About two-thirds of the way down the south end of the hall, Jill rounded an open door bearing a small *RESIDENT ASSISTANT* plaque and Ken followed.

"Welcome home, mom!" they screamed. "You're just in time!"

Jill's roommates stood in the center of the large off-white room all three shared. The shorter, dark-haired of the two wore a full-length raccoon coat over a tank top T-shirt and gym shorts. The taller one was clad in plaid Bahamas and a Hawaiian shirt, with bright red-framed sunglasses that matched her Miami U visor.

Both were in the midst of a frenzied, barefooted dance to "The Time Warp," roaring from the Rocky Horror Picture Show soundtrack in their CD player.

"*It's just a jump to the left, and then a slip to the ri-i-ight. Put your hands on your hips, and everything's all ri-i-ight . . .* ," they sang along, jumping and weaving with the tune as Ken and Jill watched.

Ken waved as Jill moved past a desk in one corner and sat her gym bag on a nearby bed. She unzipped it, retrieved the remnants of her sub and placed it in the trio's mini-refrigerator, tucked under a bookshelf against the opposite wall.

She motioned Ken toward an array of black-and-white photos that hung on the two walls that joined at the desk in her corner of the room. The trio shared an adjoining bath with the next suite.

The two sophomores railed into the song's chorus, stiffened arms and legs jerking in time, as Jill hung her racquetball racquet next to a sorority paddle on the wall. Then she disappeared into the bathroom and Ken focused on her photos.

The roughly thirty photographs varied in size, and all were unceremoniously taped or pinned to the wall, save for one. Stark close-ups of weathered, chipped, gray statues' faces with haunting, unseeing eyes were interspersed with shots of deserted farm houses, burned-out Detroit storefronts, snow-burdened park benches and a series on an overgrown, tumbling ruin that was once a lively rural train station.

The one framed photo was an eight-by-ten-inch print of the face of a very old black man, his wrinkled but spotless white shirt buttoned to the top. A momentarily forgotten, half-eaten apple hung inches from his parchment lips, his selfless gaze fixed on the photographer. Ken pondered the infinite depth that shone through the man's cataract-dulled eyes.

Jill reappeared and joined him in silently scanning what she had frozen in time.

The music blared to a crescendo as the 'Rocky Sisters' went into a finale that would have meant a slipped disc for most aerobics instructors. When the music stopped, the shorter of the two shed her raccoon coat and threw it over a bedpost. Her stocking-footed partner glided to the stereo and spun the volume knob to zero before the next track began.

"Gearing up for 'Rocky Horror Picture Show' tomorrow," explained the taller girl, pulling the dark glasses from her sparkling light-green eyes. "It's playing in Withrow's small gym."

"Okay ladies," Jill broke in. "Slow down and let me introduce you to a friend, before you scare him away.

"This is Ken Perry. I think I told you earlier today about how we met. He's a fellow Michigander, as well as a philosopher, runner, and beer connoisseur.

"Ken," Jill said, moving between the two roommates who were catching their breath, "this is Kaaren O'Reilly, the most un-Irish Irishwoman ever to escape Canton, Ohio."

An impish grin came to the coed as she pulled off her visor and swept reddish-brown hair from her perspiring neck. "I don't get into the Irish thing," she explained. "And with a name like mine, the first thing people expect is a drunken brogue and leprechaun shoes."

"And this," Jill continued, "is Chris Phillips, from Dayton."

"Nice fur coat," Ken said.

"Thanks," she chirped. "I trapped it myself."

"Sure," O'Reilly jeered. "Make fun of slaughtering a couple of hundred cute little raccoons for your feminine vanity."

"At least they never suffered," Chris reassured in a smooth but equally sarcastic tone. "I got the little guys drunk before I skinned 'em!"

They all laughed and Chris pulled the "Rocky Horror" CD from the stereo and switched the machine off. Even so, the rock 'n' roll booming through the hallway still competed with their getting-acquainted conversation.

"Care for something to drink, Ken?" O'Reilly asked, pulling a Diet Coke from the refrigerator.

"No, thanks."

"How about a sandwich, then?" Chris piped up. "We've got plenty of fresh raccoon meat."

"Tryin' to quit," he apologized.

Kaaren and Chris returned to work unloading boxes stacked in the eighteen-by-twenty-foot room while Ken and Jill watched, leaning against a windowsill.

Ken noticed two more sorority paddles, a pennant and Greek letter decals scattered about the room. When Kaaren pulled what appeared to be a sorority pledge book from a suitcase, he had to speak up.

"Kaaren, for someone so averse to traditional stereotypes, I'd think that you, and the rest of you, for that matter, would be the last ones on campus—no, make that all the earth—to be sorority girls."

The girls laughed, jumped into the middle of the room and put their arms around each other's shoulders, as if preparing for some sort of ritual.

"We're not Greeks," Jill announced. "WE'RE BOZOS!" all three shouted, then shook their hands, palms forward, next to their heads in imitation of the famed clown's electrical-shock hairdo.

Ken looked more closely at the paddle hanging nearest to him and noticed that its Greek letters—beta, theta, zeta, theta—did indeed resemble the word BOZO.

"Wanna join?" Chris asked.

"I'm not sure," he replied. "Does BOZO promote the exclusive, elitist, prep, white bread, conservative, Lacoste and Topsiders credo that guides the rest of Pan-Hellenia?"

"Come to our Rush Week kickoff on Saturday and you'll find out," Jill said. "I think you'll fit in quite nicely. Your friends from Hueston Woods said they'll be there."

"Tom and Chloe?"

"Yeah," she nodded. "Chloe and I both lived in Boyd Hall our freshman year. I was on my way to talk with them just as you were leaving."

"In the meantime," Kaaren interrupted, "why don't you join us tomorrow night for 'Rocky Horror Picture Show?' It's showing at 9 p.m., then we're going to pillage Taco Bell."

"Sounds like fun," Ken said. "But I have to get some . . . research done. I didn't get any school prep done today, and most of yesterday was spent coming back from a weekend home, in Grand Rapids.

"Did you drive or run the whole distance?" Jill quipped.

"Neither. I don't have wheels of my own, so I hitch."

"That sounds dangerous," Chris said.

"Not really," he said. "I get to see some of the prettiest country in the Midwest while meeting some interesting folks along the way."

"Aren't you worried that one of those interesting people might decide to turn you into a *National Enquirer* headline?" Jill asked. "You know, something like 'Indy pig farmer turns college hitcher into pair of hunting boots'?"

"I'm a big boy," Ken replied. "I could just as well be hurt in an accidental crash with a well-intentioned driver. And besides, a nut could just as easily do one in at a public place as he could on a country road."

His father's face again flashed across his mind.

"I do know a couple of other guys from Michigan who I catch rides with sometimes during the winter months," Ken said. "But during the good weather I prefer the country air, scenery and free feeling that traveling with a backpack brings. The solitude and silence of the anonymous two-lane blacktop helps me to see life from a different perspective. I've found that when I get out of my comfort zone and ditch a timetable, I can hear that 'still small voice' people talk about. The distractions are gone.

"The first time I hitchhiked home was about two months after I got here my freshman year," he recalled. "It was purely out of necessity, since the only other folks from Michigan I had met here either didn't have cars or weren't going home that weekend. I took US 27 north into Indiana, and after standing for over an hour next to a plowed-under cornfield on a lonely, flat stretch just north of Richmond, I began to worry, alternating between staring at my wristwatch and amending my estimated time of arrival.

"Finally, it dawned on me," he said, his voice lowering, "I turned from the road and looked around me. It was beautiful. I realized the cobalt blue sky, musky aroma of the freshly plowed topsoil and rattling chafe of the withered, parchment cornstalks had been with me all along, but unacknowledged. A ramshackle, weather-faded red barn stood alone on a dirt road that wound into the pasture. At first it symbolized desolation, appearing abandoned and forgotten among the sea of lifeless stalks.

"Then something amazing happened," Ken went on, his voice rising the way someone's does when sharing good news. "All of a

sudden I . . . like . . . *emptied into* the . . . place . . . the *moment.* It
was like I was absorbed in the present. God! It was wonderful!

"Then a ride pulled over and *it* was over," he said. "*It's* never
happened to me again since."

"I can see why you're in philosophy," Jill said.

Ken leaned up from the windowsill and looked at his watch.

"I should get going," he said. "It's almost 1 a.m."

Jill held out both hands and Ken pulled her to her feet. As
they walked toward the hallway, he turned. "I'm glad I met you
guys. I can't make tomorrow's movie, but I wouldn't miss that
BOZO Rush."

"Great!" Chris said, raising her head from a box. "You have the
makings of an A-1 BOZO, and I see you already have a Big Sister
to sponsor you."

Ken waved at Chris and Kaaren as he and Jill turned into the
hall and weaved through the debris to the stairwell.

"You know," she said, "thumbing north sounds like it would
be fun. Maybe I could tag along some weekend and get a few shots
of that barn."

"They say a male-female couple is the best combination for
hitchhiking," Ken said. "The man offers security for the woman,
and the woman gives drivers the sense that they are picking up a
normal couple, and not some lone social deviant."

They left the stairway and walked through the lobby, where a
student was sleeping at the front desk, and stopped at the main
entrance. After a brief silence, Ken opened the white wooden door
and they stepped across the wide sidewalk and onto the edge of
the courtyard. A cricket fled their approach and a large, lone moth
fluttered around the humming globe of a nearby lamppost.

"I'm glad we met," Ken said, his silhouette steady against the
starry background. "I think we'd both have fun if you joined me
for a hitch. Until then, we'll have to get acquainted as fellow Greeks,
or Geeks, or whatever Beta Theta Zeta Theta members call
themselves."

"We're just BOZOs," Jill said, taking his hand.

"Ain't it the truth," Ken answered with a smile, and they kissed.

Ken turned and started toward the sundial and Spring Street
for his five-block walk home.

"Oh!" Jill called. "I almost forgot." She reached into a rear pocket and pulled out a piece of paper as she ran the few steps to him.

She took Ken's right hand in hers, placed his father's picture on his palm, kissed his cheek and hurried back to the dorm.

The familiar image was a gray blur under the faint lamplight, and Ken ran a hand over his own face, searching for that trace of his father in his own features.

"Tomorrow maybe I can start bringing you a little more into focus," he told the photo, then slid it back into his billfold and turned for home.

CHAPTER SIX

Ken walked into the first of his third year German classes hoping to see one or two friends to help take sleepy edge off the 8 a.m. sessions. The hour of class would be followed by another sixty minutes of lesson and exam tapes in the adjoining language lab on the second floor of Irvin Hall.

Most of the fourteen in the class, Ken included, had been together through the previous two years of German courses. But Ken had gotten to know only two—Holly Vining and Mike Johnson. All three had adjoining lab cubicles in German 101 and their mutual sense of humor and dislike for the computerized lessons had quickly brought them together. But it was purely a classroom relationship for Ken, who had never exchanged phone numbers or otherwise socialized with Holly, a petite blonde of Finnish descent, or her boyfriend Mike, a baby-faced, five-foot-ten geology major.

A picture-perfect Bavarian schoolmaster, the tall, thin and bespectacled Professor Topinka wore an unseasonably heavy three-piece tweed suit and included the formal Herr or Fraulein before each name he recited from the class roster. After distributing the course outline and posting his office hours on the chalkboard, he led the group in a half hour of light discussion—all in German.

After class Ken shared small talk with Holly and Mike, quickly labeled three blank tapes, stashed them in his cubbyhole in the cubicle-rowed lab and left to buy his textbooks. But first he had to dash back home to retrieve the class schedule he'd forgotten when he left earlier. Arriving at his door, he pulled out his keys and noticed a folded note stuck in the crack above the latch.

Ken,
    Just stopped by on the way home from a trip to the store. Gimme a call.

                                   Tom

Ken punched the speed dial option for the man who had become his best friend at the school.

"Stables," a throaty female voice answered.

"Annette, this is Ken. How's it goin'?"

"Hey!" came the cheerful response. "It's great to hear from you! How was your summer?"

"All right," Ken told Annette Heid, a lithe, high-cheeked blonde who reminded him of Diana Rigg, the seductive Emma Peel character in the classic TV show "The Avengers". He had considered striking up a dating relationship with her ever since Tom had introduced her as one of his housemates several years earlier. But Ken had always been sidelined by his old high school girl friend, and now by Jill Mangan.

"What will this make," Ken asked, "your third or fourth year in the Stables?"

"Fourth," the geology grad student sighed. "They have to keep me as a housemate here—I'm the only one who can figure out the phone bills!"

"Hey," Ken said with a laugh, "is Tom around? I just ducked in for a minute and he left me a note."

"Sorry, Ken. He's out with Earl and Jan (two more of the Stables residents). They went out to buy odds and ends for the house. I'll tell him you called."

"Thanks."

Class schedule in hand, Ken strode up Heather Lane's gravel to High Street and entered the mayhem of the Co-op Bookstore, a half-block west of Ozzie's and The Balcony.

First came the German text and two lab workbooks. Then he found the four texts required for his other Tuesday/Thursday class—a graduate Religion Department course in Taoism, a Chinese tradition viewed as a religion and philosophical system.

Then, bumping and bouncing through several waves of book-laden students, Ken set about unshelving the texts for his Monday/Wednesday/Friday classes in Developmental Psych (mandatory for his teaching certificate), and two philosophy courses—Existentialism and its precursor, Phenomenological Method.

Existentialism intrigued Ken. From the rabid atheism and absurd universe of Sartre and Nietzche to the self-annihilation of Zen to the desolate "dark night of the soul" of St. John of the

Cross, all centered on the imminent mystery of being. Ken read about it through the writings of philosophers and saints, but he tasted it while lost in the strides of a long, hard run, or hitching along a remote country road.

Methodically stacking biggest at bottom to smallest on top, Ken hauled his nearly thirty pounds of books towards a checkout lane, grabbing several notebooks and an extra-large Miami University football jersey along the way. Earlier that summer Marg had put in a special request for another jersey to replace the one she had ruptured on a coffee table corner. The roomy red and white garment had become her favorite nightshirt.

Waiting behind a short Asian freshman holding half his weight in business administration books, Ken glanced through the store's front windows to see Jill's roommates, Chris and Kaaren, as they bounded into the Dairy Queen across the street.

Five minutes and a $425 check later, Ken lugged his backpack and a pair of large, bulging Co-op Bookstore bags over to the pair.

"Hey, Ken!" Chris yelled from the counter. She licked the circumference of a mint chocolate chip cone, gingerly holding it a safe distance from her white blouse and culottes. Kaaren bit her lip in concentration as she stared through the glass countertop, unable to pick a flavor.

"You should've come to 'Rocky Horror Picture Show' with us," Chris told the approaching Ken. "It was a riot!"

"Yeah," Kaaren agreed, pointing out her choice to the man behind the counter. "We had the Time Warp down perfect. And look," she said, crinkling her nose as she lifted her Ray-Bans to expose a mildly blackened eye. "Got hit by a guy throwing charred bread during the 'I propose a toast' scene," she said proudly.

Ken grinned. "I admire your tenacity. Did you get a Purple Heart?"

"Better than that, she's getting a date out of it," Chris slurred as she licked dribbled ice cream from her wrist. "The guy asked her out for this Friday."

"Ready for classes?" Kaaren asked, pointing her cone at Ken's new books.

"Yeah. I had German this morning," he said. "Tonight's Chinese philosophy, and tomorrow I have my first set of Monday/Wednesday/Fridays.

"In the meantime, I go back to my place to drop this stuff off and make a U-turn for the library . . . for some research."

"We have to be going, too," Kaaren said. "We have one o'clocks to get ready for. Hey, why don't you come by later on tonight after your class? Jill can fill you in on this weekend's BOZO Rush."

Ken knew he wouldn't feel much like partying until some of the mystery surrounding his dad's secret had been cleared up. He said he'd try to stop by their room after class, but was careful to promise nothing.

Kaaren and Chris turned for campus and their dorm, while Ken's next stop would be the bank. The money from his weekend trip was spent, his apartment cupboards were nearly bare, and he might want to ask Jill someplace for a lunch or dinner.

He strode along High Street to the century-old, solidly Midwestern-looking Ohio Dime Savings Bank. The gray granite-block structure held the marble tables and counters common to most banks during the early 1900s, as was the faded mural on the length of the wall behind the tellers, depicting scenes from Oxford's history. The staunch building was as warm and reassuring as a grandparent's lap.

Ken stood behind what appeared to be several Miami football players, each toting a huge equipment bag. When his turn came for a teller, he felt a slap on his back.

"Ken, what's happnin'?"

Ken hadn't seen Tom enter the bank just behind him.

"Hey, forget your ski mask?" Ken quipped.

"Nah, making a deposit. My last paycheck from my summer job at Cedar Point just came in the mail, and I wanted to get it behind bars before Chloe saw it.

"Annette told me you called about my note," he said as the teller urged Ken forward. "Wanna grab lunch?"

"Sure," Ken replied, and they headed for Bailey's Diner. The small greasy spoon sat tucked between a bicycle shop and a shoe store in the shadow of the water tower on the town green.

Ken felt like a pack mule as he lugged his bulky white Coop bags into the crowded eatery.

"Over there!" Tom yelled, motioning toward a group of businessmen vacating a booth along the rear wall.

The pair ordered sodas and cheeseburger baskets, and Ken weighed whether or not he should confide in Tom the bizarre news from his latest trip home. It was a load he desperately needed help in carrying, but he didn't want to drag a friend into something he himself still couldn't believe, let alone understand.

On the other hand, his mind was reeling from conjecture on the secret. What consequences could knowledge of the room hold for Ken, his mother, or anyone else he told? Ken's father had always closely guarded the corporate secrets entrusted to him in his research and development work, and Ken wouldn't want to compromise anything his father would've wanted to remain concealed. What if others in his father's business had secret rooms for their work that could then be compromised if word got out of his dad's?

Ironically, loyalty to his father was now a factor in deciding what to do regarding investigation or disclosure of the cryptic chamber.

Imagination and fatigue spun and mangled anything Ken fed into the blender of his mind. As their drinks arrived, he realized he didn't know exactly what happened to someone experiencing a nervous breakdown. But whatever the clinical symptoms, his body and mind told him that he needed to find a pressure valve, and soon.

Tom pulled a scrap of paper from his notebook and scribbled a note. "I've gotta pick up a few things from the store tonight, and I'll forget unless I write them down.

"Hey, what's this I hear about you and Jill?" he asked, stuffing the note into his shirt pocket. "Chloe tells me you two really hit it off."

"Yeah, I met her on the run back from Hueston Woods, then we had a couple of drinks at The Balcony, shared some Philly subs, and I walked her to her dorm."

"Well, you don't sound too excited about her," Tom observed.

"Oh, I am," Ken was quick to respond. He paused, searching for words to obliquely describe the conundrum that had consumed him.

Tom immediately sensed his friend's distraction.

"Hey Ken," he said, making eye contact as he lowered his burger. "What's up?"

"Ever been to the Twilight Zone, Tommy?"

"I have a feeling you're not talking about my favorite brand of cigarette, are you?"

"No. I rode my thumb to this one, not a cloud," Ken said. He was known to share a few puffs from a joint with friends at a party, but that was rare. And he never used anything stronger.

"On my last hitch home I think Rod Serling picked me up and drove me to my doorstep, where Alice and I promptly danced through the looking glass."

Tom just looked at Ken. Unsure what to say, he hoped his silence would prod his friend to continue.

"I know this isn't fair, but being the buddy that you are, I'm sure you'll understand that I don't feel right in sharing anything more right now," Ken said in slow, measured words. "Something heavy's pushing me—hard, and when I know a little more and can share some of this, I'm really going to need someone to listen. I trust you like a brother, Tom, but the fact is, I'll have to get some kind of handle on this before I know what to say."

"Fair enough," Tom said with a nod. "I'm here, bro. But I wouldn't be a real friend if I didn't ask you one thing . . . Are you okay? Are you safe?"

"So far, the only heat I'm feeling is from the gears grinding inside my skull. But our talk is going to make things a little easier to manage, so long as I know somebody's there if the dam breaks."

"Whatever you need," Tom assured.

"Thanks," Ken said. He looked at his watch and picked up the check. "I'll pay. You leave the tip," he said as he gathered his bags.

"Hey," Tom called as Ken started for the cashier. "Maybe you should call on Jill. She's a great lady, and there's no smoother salve for the troubled soul."

"Yeah, maybe."

Tom stayed behind to finish his fries as Ken hauled his backpack and Co-op bags the few blocks to his apartment.

After dumping them onto his bed and grabbing his notes from the previous night, he headed back down the stairs. The newly emerged sun greeted him as he left for the library and Taoism class.

"Hello Ken," a schoolgirl voice sang from the back yard. Ken backed up a step and spotted Rochelle, the Sweet Sixteen sprinter from Dayton. The petite freshman's red bikini-clad form lay spread-eagle on a yellow blanket, and her blonde tresses were braided into long pigtails that danced as she rested her chin atop crossed arms. A pitcher of iced tea and a suntan oil-smeared French lit text glistened at her side.

"Hey, it's the Dayton speedster—studying hard, I see."

"I have only one Tuesday/Thursday class, from 8 a.m. to 9:30," she said, raising onto her elbows. "So I'm done for the rest of the day. The bad news is that I have four Monday/Wednesday/Fridays."

"Well, catch a few rays for me," Ken sighed, waving farewell with his notebook. "I have to spend the rest of the day in King's dark, damp halls."

"You going to Brian's funeral on Thursday?" Rochelle yelled in afterthought.

Ken froze, then turned slowly. "What are you talking about?"

"Nobody told you?" she giggled, eyes squinting against the glaring sun. "Black's going to make his first ROTC parachute jump on Friday morning, so Blue's throwing a funeral party for him Thursday night."

"Outstanding!" Ken said with a smile. "I'll get the particulars from Blue.

"Well, Miss Coppertone, I'd better get to the library. Thanks for the party tip, and don't forget to turn every fifteen minutes!"

If there had been any doubt in Ken's mind that school was officially back in session, it was now gone; within the past several hours he'd been invited to two parties.

"Too bad I can't loosen up and look forward to them," he told himself. In the absence of the secret room mystery he would have relished the thought of cultivating his relationship with Jill and whatever mayhem this BOZO Rush held in store. It didn't hurt that the firm, young, braided sprite from his apartment building was either too innocent or too horny to bother concealing her interest in him.

Crossing the edge of campus, Ken saw Boofus, the campus dog, chase a squirrel up an oak. The huge black Labrador retriever wore a red bandanna around his neck and was well fed and otherwise cared for by the entire Miami University student body. No one knew where the dog had come came from, but he was welcome at every frat house, dorm and student apartment building, and one hell of a Frisbee catcher.

Boofus' barks gave way to shuffling footsteps and muffled conversation as Ken entered the library and settled in at one of the heavy wooden tables in the reference section.

The task before him made the proverbial needle in a haystack look like a beach ball on a putting green. Not only did he have about a dozen equally viable or useless key words to research, but just scanning the sites the Internet gave him for any one of them could take all day, let alone actually visiting them. Should he look up every entry for 'espionage' and the other words from every volume of the Reader's Guide to Periodical Literature for the past five years? Ten? Twenty? Or maybe going back over even or odd years, to cover a longer time span more quickly? Or, he thought, should he instead take his list of words to the *New York Times* Index, since the cloak-and-dagger story should have attracted wide newspaper coverage?

Ken felt resentment that the time spent on his new obsession would compound his already weighty study demands, and he dug past his textbooks to retrieve a note pad from his pack. He logged onto a computer, sat a pen on his pad and cracked his knuckles loud enough to bring an annoyed stare from the reference librarian.

Opening the previous year's Reader's Guide, Ken began with keywords 'spies' and 'intelligence'. Two o'clock crawled into 4 as he gulped waves of information, but not a drop that spoke to his needs. The glut of entries under 'espionage' quickly brought him to 6:30, and he realized he had worked past dinnertime when a gnawing hunger joined the frustration smoldering in his gut.

His combinations of "espionage", "London" and "England" along with "secret room", "hidden room", "secret chamber", "hidden chamber", and several other keyword combinations all brought a flood of information—some mundane, some kinky—but none led to the story Crump had recounted of the dead spy in London. Or had it been another city?

A half hour later Ken stuffed his smattering of uninspired notes back into his pack and trudged for the exit.

The humid late summer night carried the heavy smell of freshly cut grass as Ken cut across the lawn to High Street and walked two blocks to his 7 p.m. Taoism seminar. It met in the Old Manse, a two-story whitewashed brick structure named for its original function as a local pastor's residence. More than 100 years old, the small building now housed Miami's Department of Religious Studies. The university's American Studies offices were also tucked into a corner of its basement.

Ken walked through the front doorway, straight ahead past a worn but polished wooden staircase, and up a second set of three carpeted steps into the building's sole classroom. The cozy library extended from the rear of the building and contained a long, broad and ancient conference table with matching, padded-leather chairs. A red brick fireplace, book cases crammed with dusty, obscure texts, and portraits of former department heads punctuated the windows, which wrapped around the room. It was softly but evenly lit by two small chandeliers and several wall-mounted lamps, and it smelled of leather, wood polish and Windex. A year earlier Ken had a philosophy class here, and it remained his favorite place on campus.

Arriving just before the 90-minute class was to begin, he took a seat near the darkened fireplace at the far end of the mahogany table. This would be Ken's first graduate-level class, but he would have to settle for undergraduate credit. His strong philosophy background and the recommendation of that department's chairman had opened the door for him.

The seven classmates began to share introductions while waiting for their prof. Ken knew three of the four Religion Department graduate assistants taking the class. The others were a department-approved religious studies underclassmen and a Chinese pulp and paper technology student who had been granted entry to the class because of his native familiarity with the subject.

Adjunct professor Wayne Higgins flipped on the light switch with his free hand as he carried a large, steaming cup of tea, tag fluttering, in the other. The cup hugged several books and a bulging, slightly ruptured manila folder tucked under his arm.

"Good evening, everyone," the bearded and balding prof offered in a nasal, Midwestern voice. "I thought we should begin by introducing ourselves. My name's Wayne Higgins, and I'll be leading this seminar on Taoism this semester here at Miami, and stay on next semester with other Chinese course offerings as a visiting faculty member. I've spent the past eight years teaching at the University of Hawaii, most recently doing eighteen months in China, where I conducted research in countryside villages while being based in Beijing. After a lot of groveling before Chinese officials, I was granted a little look at popular Taoism as it has survived the Maoist Revolution of the 1940s and Cultural Revolution of twenty years later.

"Before packing off for the Orient," he continued with a wry smile, "I was raised amidst the corn and sleet of Keokuk, Iowa. There I faithfully observed the Midwestern rites of passage, such as standing with other men in the street, one foot on the Ford pickup's bumper, drinking beer, talking baseball and spitting.

"I have an enduring love for the American heartland, and that's why I'm here—offering one class this semester and next, allowing me the freedom to prepare the findings from my Asian expedition.

"I see one of you, a Mr. Chen Li Fen, is Chinese?" he asked, turning to the paper tech major.

"Yes, Dr. Higgins," the slight man answered in a soft, but clipped voice. "I am from Hong Kong. During the Cultural Revolution of which you spoke, my family fled there from our home in Honan, where my father taught mathematics in secondary school."

"Welcome," the professor said. "We are fortunate to have you with us, especially since you are from the same Chinese province as Taoism's founder, Lao Tzu. We'll be interested in your observations."

The wood-paneled, den-like seminar room went well with Dr. Higgins' teaching style, and Ken looked forward to what promised to be an interesting course. The remainder of the 90-minute class was spent in individual introductions and small talk, but the darkened hall outside the entrance periodically reminded Ken of the basement chamber some five hundred miles away.

Dr. Higgins told the class to read the first half of Arthur Waley's "A Study of the Tao Te Ching and Its Place in Chinese Thought" for their next class, on Thursday. After a little more light conversation, the small group adjourned into the cool, starry night.

Ken headed south across campus in the direction of Minnich Hall and pondered whether he should drop in on Jill or turn west at Spring Street for home and a late night run. His mystery-coiled tension would be lessened, if not released, by a good, hard run. Then again, it might be better yet to let that stress be absorbed by the passion he had glimpsed in Jill's sharp blue eyes. But the couple hadn't yet come that far.

The perfume of a row of magnolia trees enveloped Ken as he walked past McGuffey Hall and off campus. With only two and a half blocks to Heather Lane, he saw the outline of a tall woman approaching under the streetlights. They came together in the light cast onto the corner of Poplar and Spring streets.

"Ken? Is that you?"

"Jill! I was just thinking of stopping in to see you, but I'm bushed . . . Just got out of a long night class that followed hours spinning my wheels in tedious, futile research."

"I didn't think you used wheels, being the romantic runner and all," she teased. "Anyway, I'm just coming from your place. I stopped by on my way from one of my study groups. It meets in Fox and Hounds Apartments for a poli sci class. I knocked a couple of times and left a note on your door."

Ken was glad they had met.

"How 'bout a toddy for my troubles?" Jill said, inviting herself to his apartment. "It's less than two blocks away. And besides, I'm curious to see what a runner/teacher/philosopher's digs look like."

"Ever seen Times Square after New Year's Eve?" Ken asked with a smile. Jill stood in silence, arms crossed over her book bag.

"Okay," he conceded, "You are welcome to join me for an after dinner aperitif, but I'm afraid my stock is limited to Gatorade, generic colas and iced tea on this no-notice basis."

"Fair enough."

The brunette turned and walked close enough that her left arm and hip brushed and bumped against Ken's, and he felt like a high school freshman as he wondered if he should take her hand.

A sudden breeze flitted Jill's dark hair against Ken's cheek and seized him with its subtle yet musky, intoxicating scent.

He shifted his backpack to the opposite shoulder and slipped his hand into hers. Turning from the Spring Street sidewalk onto the gravel of Heather Lane, they left the glaring streetlights and walked in silent darkness toward the lone parking lot light at the end of Ken's building.

Holding hands with Jill felt natural, soothing, and Ken didn't want to let go as he opened the stairwell door. Jill hurried up the steps before him and plucked her folded note from his door frame.

"Can't I read it?" Ken asked.

"I'm a woman of mystery," she said in a whisper. "Keep 'em guessing; that's what my momma says."

"If you're not careful, you're going to blow your chances for a Gatorade daiquiri," Ken countered. Then he turned the key, threw open the door and jumped aside.

"Welcome to my castle," he beckoned, bowing and waving her into the spacious combination living room-bedroom. It looked much as Jill thought it would, books and papers jumbled on the large, built-in corner desk, walls scattered with posters of runners, racing greats, and Albert Einstein. A portable color television rested atop the two large black trunks in which he'd shipped his stuff from Grand Rapids. Next to the TV was an eight-by-ten color photo of Ken's mother hugging him as a young boy and his dad, both grinning and wearing Old Kent River Run race numbers pinned to their sweaty Mister Perry T-shirts.

"Where are your trophies, Medals of Honor, orthopedic X-rays, et cetera?" Jill asked, stooping to scrutinize the photo.

"I don't have that many; they're at home in my room, along with a string of about 200 race numbers I've saved over the years."

Ken motioned for Jill to follow him the several steps past the hall closet and bathroom to the tiny kitchen. He opened the refrigerator, removed a pitcher and poured a glass.

"Sun tea?" he offered. "I add cloves, a little star anise and no sugar. It's great. Want to try some?"

"Sure, but just a half glass. I don't want the caffeine to keep me up all night. Doesn't it mess with your sleep?"

"I have other things that do that these days," he said, sounding more fatigued than mysterious.

"Like what?"

"Come on," he said, shifting both them and the topic. "Let's sit down in the other room." On the way to the couch, Ken picked up Carly Simon's "Come Upstairs" CD and popped it into his stereo.

"Is this music okay?"

"Sure," Jill answered. "What did you mean when you said other things keep you awake at night?"

Joining her on the ancient brown sofa, Ken looked tired.

"Well, what with the situation in Lower Botswana, or is it the Upper Volta . . . Oh well, one of my philosophy profs is trying to convince me that I don't exist anyway, so I guess it really doesn't matter . . .

"I propose a toast," he announced, hoping to seal his verbal diversion. "To us, on our first time together in my apartment, on my bed."

"Whoa, big guy," Jill said with a good-natured groan. "I can't be that big a misjudger of human nature. Hey, where is your bed, anyway? I've seen the whole place and . . . Ohh," she said, patting the front of her cushion. "This must be a sofa bed."

"Bingo!" Ken said with a wink. "So, you see, even if I don't unfold Starship Whoopee, we were undeniably on it together . . . during your first visit, no less!"

"I can see why you're not getting any sleep," Jill observed. "You are one frustrated camper!"

Beneath all their humor, Ken wished Jill could see the hidden truth of her jest.

"All kidding aside, I'm glad you came over," he said. "As I mentioned earlier, I almost stopped by your place tonight."

"Why didn't you?"

"It was getting late," Ken repeated. He wondered if she was buying his fatigue as an excuse for his general uneasiness.

"Also, I wanted to ask you more about this BOZO business."

"That's one of the reasons I stopped by," Jill said. "I hope you're caught up enough to make our BOZO Rush this Saturday.

"Essentially, it's an all-day picnic/kegger that starts at noon at the BOZO House, a great two-story party palace occupied by eight BOZOs on College Avenue. Prospective members arrive with their sponsors and then party all day and get to know the BOZOs, who then vote on allowing the newcomers' membership."

"Sounds like a solemn occasion," Ken said.

"The mystical swearing-in takes place at midnight. That's when we humiliate, embarrass and welcome you in, share the secret handshake, dress you up funny and give you your official BOZO paddle and other great stuff. It's definitely a rite of passage."

"What does it cost?" Ken asked.

"A little humility," she replied. "And probably a pretty good hangover."

"Noon, huh?"

"Yeah, what do you say? It's really a great group. Mostly humanities and lib arts folks able to carry on a good conversation or just carry on in general. I'm sure you'll know a good number of them already, like Tom and Chloe."

"How many BOZOs are there?"

"Probably forty or fifty. We get together every second or third weekend for some kind of party, attend concerts and tailgaters at games and other stuff together. Since we're not an officially chartered campus organization, we don't have to fret the scruples of administration oversight.

"We're planning a bus trip this Saturday to see a Who concert. It'll be a great time."

"I'm not sure," Ken said. It definitely sounded like his kind of group, but he was beginning to wonder about what kind of time it would take from his research of the hidden basement room. And he'd almost forgotten that he now had homework for classes, as well.

"I may have to spend a good piece of Saturday on a research assignment that I can't get out of," he said. "How about if I let you know later?"

Jill rolled her eyes. "I need to know now, because if you join I'll have to prepare some things as your sponsor. Come on, you can do your homework on Sunday. Or if you have *that* much to do, I'll help you on Friday or Sunday. What do you say?"

"Okay, okay," Ken conceded. "But I'm afraid you can't help me with that research. You'd have to have background information in order to know what you'd be looking for, and it's pretty involved. I'll just take a few extra hours in King on Sunday."

"All right!" she said, jumping from the couch. "I'm proud of you. You are *undeniably* BOZO material."

Jill handed Ken her empty glass and picked up her backpack.

"I'd better get back to Minnich," she said, moving toward the door. Ken rose, sat the glasses on his desktop and joined her at the open doorway.

"I'll walk you," he said.

"No. It's been a long day and I think I'll just enjoy the quiet night. There's no point in you spending the better part of an hour just to see me home.

"Anyway," she said, "I may stop in at King myself to pick up a book I'll need for one of my classes. So I'm only going a few blocks."

Even though the night had gone well, and Ken knew Jill enjoyed his company as much as he did hers, he sensed that there was some concern on her mind, too.

"If you insist," Ken said. "But just for the record, I *did offer*, so I don't lose my perfect gentleman status."

"Aren't we forgetting the foldaway bed crack?" Jill said with a raised eyebrow.

"Even so," he said, "there are relatively few of even we 'nearly perfect' gentlemen."

Jill smiled, and Ken again took her hand. She dropped her backpack with her other hand and took a half step back inside the doorway. Moving his cheek against her forehead, Ken slid both arms around her waist, and she around his. Silently, gently and firmly they embraced, and Jill felt the slow, steady runner's heartbeat beneath his warm rugby jersey.

Brushing a tress of shining black hair from Jill's left ear, Ken kissed her temple, then moved to her cheek. Her eyelids drifted closed as she moved her hands up Ken's back and over his shoulders, and once again her fragrance stirred his senses.

Jill's perfect lips parted slowly at the touch of Ken's tongue, and he wasn't sure if she tottered or leaned back intentionally as she bumped against the cement block wall.

Cupping the back of Ken's head with both hands, Jill's tongue flitted and danced with his as their breath fell heavier on each other's faces. Tugging her from the wall, Ken slid one hand over her left breast and felt a knotted nipple under her cotton blouse.

For the first time since his last trip home, his mind was freed from the buzzing swirl of questions. He leaned back and again placed his cheek on Jill's. The intoxication of her embrace was pushing him to move farther and faster than was now right for them. And he didn't want to scare her away, either with accelerated affection or news he didn't know how to share with her . . . or anyone.

Jill stared out the living room window. She sensed that something that had been holding Ken back had eased its grip, but would not allow him to open fully.

"I want to walk you to King," Ken insisted.

She nodded, squeezed his hand and picked up her bag.

They said nothing the whole four blocks to the library, and when they arrived, Ken let go of her hand and kissed her cheek.

"I'll call you tomorrow about Saturday," he promised.

Jill smiled, nodded and headed for the glass doors.

Turning abruptly, she called Ken's name and rushed to stop him near one of the pillars.

"If something's wrong, I'd like to help you . . . if I can."

It was all Ken could do to keep from pulling her aside to lay out his whole weird, confusing, frustrating story. But he was determined that until he understood at least something about his father's mystery room, he must keep it to himself.

"Maybe later, when we can have a BOZO-to-BOZO talk about it," he said, coaxing a smile. "Meeting you was the best thing that's happened to me in a long time, Jill. I want you to know that."

"Thanks," she said, squeezing his hand and pecking him on the lips. "Me, too."

Again she turned for the library doors.

Ken felt as if his head had been ventilated of a heavy fog, and walking home he decided to go for that night run.

After 90 minutes of sprints on the Tallawanda High School track, Ken showered and dropped into bed near midnight.

He fell asleep quickly, his breath searching for a trace of Jill's perfume.

CHAPTER SEVEN

Ken's Wednesday classes dragged by as he sought a coherent plan to research the hidden room. That way, when he got to King after his philosophy and psych lectures, he wouldn't just blindly attack the reference section, as he had the previous two days.

Following his morning and midday philosophy classes, an Einstein-haired, monotoned Dr. Max Clark didn't do much to rivet Ken to the wonders of developmental psych. After concentrating long enough to remember the prof's name, grab a syllabus and jot down the first assignment, it was 3:30 and the end of that day's classes.

Ken thought about going home for a bite and to freshen up. Instead, he grabbed a bottled water from a vending machine in the library basement and headed for the reference stacks with the few leads he'd scribbled down. He'd take a dinner study break later.

A group of four from Ken's phenomenology class sat at a table across the large room, and he moved to avoid their seeing him. Earlier that day they had asked him to join a study group they were forming, and Ken told them he had an appointment he couldn't break. He did plan to join the group later, since the class was renowned for its difficulty and he knew he could use the help.

Ken had enough leads from his short list to keep him busy until seven, when he decided on the Philadelphia Sub Shop for his dinner break. A light rain hurried his three-block trip to the restaurant, and he reviewed his research notes while waiting for his heated cheese veggie.

Several articles from scientific journals had piqued Ken's interest, but that was about all he had to show for another three hours of book-burrowing. Articles from popular magazines such as The Reader's Digest's "Spy Who Vanished," Time's "Where Was Our Man in Havana?" and Art News's "Two Lives of Anthony

Blunt" offered hopeful titles, but nothing on the dead spy in London, secret rooms in spying, or any other connection Ken could link to his father. A New Republic story titled "Most Secret Agents: NSA Spying" introduced him to the National Security Agency, a super-secret organization of which he, like most Americans, knew next to nothing.

Ken's father had been a Department of Defense employee prior to his company work in Grand Rapids. But Knoblock Systems did have its home base in Baltimore, on the edge the nation's intelligence hub of FBI, CIA and NSA headquarters clustered in Washington, Virginia and Maryland.

Ken realized that just about any person could be imagined into a position with just about any organization if he worked at it long enough. His father could've been with the FBI, IBM, NSA or ASPCA. The empty speculation was beginning to ring more and more hollow.

The only other information Ken could find regarding the NSA was a couple of several-year-old Aviation Week & Space Technology stories, one on an NSA "Jumpseat" program's wind-down "as Soviets shift to newer satellites," the other titled "STU-3 secure telephones offered to U.S. defense contractors."

Now, this is interesting, he thought, since the subject matter was well within his father's realm of expertise. After all, there were a lot of wires snipped from that dark room after his dad's demise. After spending the last of his three hours scouring the Internet for more on the NSA, all he found was the usual crackpot conspiracy theory stuff. No primary or credible source material on the organization at all, except for James Bamford's book "The Puzzle Palace." The library's computer showed the book lost or stolen. Ken ordered a copy via the Inter-Library Loan service.

Still, Ken was not excited about any of the information. He knew he could very well be chasing mere shadows of something real or imagined.

What could he do? Call an agency that doesn't even exist on official government listings and ask for the department in charge of secret home bases and questionable killings?

Ken knew that approaching any agency would be ridiculous. His father could have worked for any number of known or covert security, intelligence, defense or corporate organizations. He was a genius in mathematics—the fundamental language of code, computer and electronics applications—the intelligence playing field.

The library research made for interesting reading, but yielded no trace of a link or similarity to the scenario he'd discovered back in his basement.

"Hot veggie and cheese," the waiter said, placing the order on the table.

Ken walked to the cooler for his drink, picked up a pepper shaker and noticed that it was still raining.

This is sheer futility, he thought, pausing over his meal. He stared at the pile of notes, realizing how useless they were, and a wave of discouragement pushed him back in his chair.

Any fishing trips back in the reference section would be aimless, a waste of time. School wasn't a week old and he was already behind in one of his classes. Assignments were left undone and his presence in the classroom was that of a cardboard cut-out, taking up space while his mind raced around his father's past.

The sub steamed before Ken as he stared out the window and mumbled in a low but deliberate voice; "No. No more." There would be no more scrabbling through the Internet, reference books, magazines and microfilm for a "silver bullet" that he probably wouldn't recognize if it was shot between his eyes.

If you want water, he thought in silence, *you have to go to the well.*

The well—the hidden room, his father's friends, job and memories—was in Grand Rapids, Michigan. Walt Perry was gone, Ken reasoned, but Cody and Truro were still alive and well, and still working for Knoblock Systems. Cody was the closer of the two to his father, and whether the hidden room was related to the senior Perry's work or not, Paul Cody must have known about it. Was there one like it in his basement?

"Someone built it," Ken told himself. "Someone, most probably but not definitely my dad, used it, and someone else had to be involved with its functioning," he continued. "And someone has the answer.

"Present tense," he said over the now-cold sub. "Someone *has* the answer."

Ken scooped up the uneaten food and pile of notes and dropped them into the trash. It felt good. Tossing the papers represented a shift he knew was necessary if he was serious about finding answers.

Just as important, maybe more so, was the possibility that the hidden room could provide an explanation for what everyone had accepted as the random, senseless killing of his father.

Now a steady rain fell, and Ken asked the waiter for a piece of cardboard from the kitchen to use as an umbrella during his walk home. A two-foot-square section of a waxed lettuce box appeared, and Ken used it to manage a relatively dry walk back to his place, where he arrived just before 9 p.m.

He decided to devote himself to homework until 10:30, then go for a half-hour run, raining or not.

After reading the first third of Waley's commentary on the *Tao Te Ching*, Ken worked on several pages of German translation, then looked outside.

The rain had stopped, and the oak branches by his living room window held large drops, hanging silently in the evening calm. Ken collected his running gear from the shower rod, drank a quick glass of iced tea and grabbed a pen. He turned to the wall phone and punched three digits.

"Information for what city and state, please?"

"Grand Rapids, Michigan."

"Go ahead, sir."

"Yes. I need two numbers. The first is for a Paul Cody, on Saginaw Road; the other is for Dennis Truro, and I don't recall his address."

The operator read Cody's number, then disappeared as a monotone electronic voice offered Truro's.

Ken scrawled the numbers on a note pad and hung up.

This is the only way to start, he thought. *I just have to remember to go about this in the right way.*

Pretty tall order, he considered, since he was clueless about what that was.

Ken would just feel the pair out, leading conversation to a place where they would either acknowledge some sort of guarded information, or satisfy him that they knew nothing about his father's secret.

He would leave more direct confrontation to a time and place dictated by common sense and whatever solid information he could glean. Ken would also heed his gut instincts. He had inherited his father's keen intuition.

If you listen to your conscience it can be your closest friend, he again recalled his father's words. *Ignore it, and it will be your jailer.*

Several minutes later Ken found himself running in a cool, light mist that gave the streetlights an amber aura.

The Beta Bells chimed 10 p.m. as he ran a 10-K route he had charted along Chestnut Street, weaving through the grassy Western Campus, around the main campus and back home along the red bricks of High and Main streets.

It took him forty-three minutes.

The combination of finding direction and focus for his investigation and forcing himself to address his neglected homework were giving Ken a sense of renewed control. After his shower, he felt rested for the first time since his trip home.

Early the next morning, Ken began the day with a hard speed workout on the high school track. He hoped it would help him carry the previous night's positive plan and feelings into the new day. Gasping air between 220-yard sprints, he found himself recalling the dream where his father sat silently in the secret room, his face covered by a mask. It had returned last night.

Ken punctuated the wind sprints with mental activity just as intense.

When should he call Cody and Truro? Should he phone both, or only Cody? Cody had been his father's best friend and therefore more likely to know something.

Should he telephone, or make a trip home for a face-to-face encounter?

Ken leaned on a drinking fountain and considered that it would be a more level playing field if he confronted one rather than both of his father's old friends. He should keep communication simple, between himself and only one other, taking group dynamics out of the equation.

It should be Cody, he thought. He had definitely been closer to Ken's father than Truro, who was often a third party addition to their activities.

Truro was nearly always asked to join the senior Perry and
Cody for pickup basketball games, fishing trips and several summer
helicopter camping forays into northern Ontario.

But it was always and exclusively Cody who, after sharing dinner
with the Perry family, would accompany Walt Perry to the basement
bar for late-night shop talk, peppered with project names and
numbers. His wife, Jeanette, would join Mrs. Perry for coffee and
cards in the TV room.

One whole evening for Walt and Paul could be spent in a low,
meandering discussion about "Sweetwater-23" or "Nessie-9." Their
conversation was always saturated with electronic jargon and the
pair reminded Ken of two brain surgeons or physicists as they
rehashed lingo that he couldn't remotely understand. That's why
they had let him listen.

As Ken grew older, he realized that his father was in a cutting-
edge field with powerful, influential clientele. Had someone from
that client base engineered Walt Perry's death?

"That's it," Ken concluded. "My only hope for some kind of
direct answer or clue for further leads rests in Cody or Truro."

Decisiveness. With each solid decision, Ken felt a renewed
sense of control, direction and hope. But he also knew that without
a plan, he would look like some sort of fool—at best.

It would be Cody. Contact, initial contact, anyway, would be
by phone. Popping up at his door would be too abrupt, and after
one or two casual, "feeler" calls, Ken could initiate a meeting, if
things went well.

Okay, but when? When should he call this old friend of the
family whom he hadn't seen in more than a year?

*Hello . . . Mr. Cody, this is Ken . . . Yeah, I was just wondering . . .
Wouldn't know anything about a secret room I found late one night in
my basement, would you?*

Yeah, right.

No, this would be more like verbal surgery than casual
reminiscence. If Ken was successful, he would bring the clam to
spit out a pearl without any noticeable prying.

Could that really be possible? Would someone in a business
that calls for something like in-home secret chambers be susceptible
to the subtle probings of a college junior? But Ken's father had

been Cody's best friend . . . Shouldn't that count for something in the confidence department?

A couple of dozen teenagers in shorts and T-shirts took to the track's infield for phys ed class, and Ken realized he was behind schedule.

He missed his 8 a.m. German class and arrived at the following language lab twenty minutes late. After doing his best to focus on a recorded lesson, he abandoned the task to exchange small talk with Holly and Mike, then left for the student union.

Ken bought a large coffee and doughnut in the Shriver Center cafeteria, commonly known as 'the Zebra Room' because of its black-and-white-striped wallpaper.

Ken would make up his missed German assignment and prepare for Friday's classes. He knew there would be no time for studying that night, with his evening Taoism class to be followed by Black's mock funeral party.

Ken broke from his studies only twice during the next seven hours—for the noon pizza lunch he took outside onto the Student Union terrace, and a half-hour of conversation after bumping into Annette Heid while on his way home for a shower at five.

He entered his stairway to find two guys helping Blue carry an old, battered casket into his living room. "Can't have a proper funeral without a body-box," Heavner said with a grin. He explained that the oak coffin was secured through a friend in one of the frats. It was property of the Greeks for use in their perennial Paddy Murphy parties, in which the first to fall unconscious during the drunken revels was placed inside the box, dubbed Paddy Murphy and, as such, became the centerpiece for the duration of the festivities.

"Mighty fine looking model," Ken replied. "How does Black feel about all this?"

"He's in his glory," Blue said. He has no problem being the main attraction, and if I hadn't planned this gig he probably would have done it for himself!"

"But isn't he afraid it will jinx his ROTC jump?"

"Are you kidding?" Heavner said as the coffin was lowered onto a large coffee table. "The only things that scare Resnick are study and hard work. He's the perfect roommate," he said with a laugh.

"Next to Jessica Simpson," Ken said over his shoulder as he unlocked his own door. "I've got a 7 o'clock, but I'll be back for the wake ASAP."

"Grieving starts at 9 sharp."

Ken switched on the local news on his television and sipped sun tea until the weather came on. Then he took a shower, collected his text and notebook and left with a half hour to make the eight-block walk to the Old Manse.

Ken had a real love for the writings of Taoism, with their combination of haunting mystery and bedrock common sense. The soft lighting over the time-scarred wooden bookcases stuffed with yellowing tomes, portraits of past department heads and cocoa-hued wood trimming of the lecture room fostered a secure, cozy feeling.

As the class drew to a close, the group discussed Waley's commentary on chapter twelve of the *Tao Te Ching*, and one verse stuck in Ken's mind as he walked home:

> *Excess of hunting and chasing*
> *Makes minds go mad.*

True enough. But could the madness born of hunting and chasing be any more agonizing than that of seeing your father, your best friend, slip into the darkness as a stranger? If, it turned out, he didn't really know his own father, of what else could he be sure?

Save it for tomorrow, he thought as he left for home.

Moments later he walked between the cars that jammed his apartment building parking lot.

"Hey!" a voice called to Ken. "Need a date for a funeral?"

The cry came from Jan Siegel, who left her apartment just after Ken had passed her door.

"Where's Brad?" he asked, referring to Jan's longtime on-again, off-again boyfriend.

"Oh, he's got the flu. Besides, his folks are bringing some of his stuff down from Jersey this weekend and he has to make sure his apartment is squared away for their visit. Last time he had a hell of a time convincing them that a pair of my monogrammed panties his little sister found under a couch cushion had dropped out of my laundry basket.

Ken opened the stairway door for Jan and he caught a whiff of pot that clung to her black evening dress.

The roar of more than fifty partyers came from Black and Blue's open door, and one couple sat talking on the stairwell railing. A second pair was engaged in early-phase foreplay in a shadowy corner of the second floor landing.

"I'll be over in a minute," Ken said as he unlocked his door. Jan entered the party as he dropped off his books, splashed his face with water and Tuscany cologne and changed his shirt. He snatched a six-pack of Rolling Rock from his refrigerator and crossed the hall.

Black waved a greeting to Ken from the casket, where he sat with one arm over the edge as if he were riding in a sports car. "Ken! Glad you could make it," he yelled, waving a nearly empty champagne bottle. He wore a green ROTC uniform, a white silk scarf around his neck.

"Wouldn't miss it!" Ken called back, offering the thumbs-up sign. He weaved his way back to the kitchen, wedged five of the beers into the packed refrigerator and twisted the cap off the sixth.

Everyone from the building was there, in addition to dozens of Black and Blue's friends. Most of the guys were dressed casually, but nearly all of the women had taken the opportunity to dress in theme for the occasion, as Jan had done, decked in black dresses, one complete with gloves and veiled hat.

"Okay everyone!" Heavner bellowed above the crowd's low roar. "Hey, quiet!"

"All right, ladies and gentlemen," Blue said from a makeshift TV-tray podium next to the casket. "Given that our guest of honor has only a few hours left before he makes his first 'big splash' in his military career, I think it is appropriate that I, as his faithful roommate, offer a few kind words in his memory . . . er, honor."

Resnick tilted a dribble of champagne onto Heavner's shoes as he continued to read the eulogy.

"Known to most of you as 'Black,' I will always remember Brian Paul Resnick simply as a crazy sumbitch," he said, faking a tear. "You have all proven that you are dear friends and loved ones of the nearly departed, who now rests before you in a semi-conscious state as his moment of glory approaches."

A girl on the couch slid from her boyfriend's lap to the floor with a loud thump.

"Well, Black," Heavner said, turning to Resnick. "That's the worst that can happen to you tomorrow, except you'll have a lot farther to fall."

The room erupted with laughter and Black stretched from his coffin to grab an unattended bottle of beer from an end table.

"Isn't he an inspiration, ladies and gentlemen?" Heavner continued, patting Resnick's head. "Only hours from hurtling through space with a crushing hangover, our hero still wears the facade of a man undaunted.

"It was truly great knowin' ya," he said, shaking Black's hand. "I know you'll make all of us in the will very proud."

Resnick again trickled his drink onto Heavner's shoes.

"I'm going to ignore that, given the brief amount of quality time we may have left together," Blue told his roommate. "And now, I would encourage all of you to file by and view the body, be that as it may, and pay any potentially final respects."

"Ladies first!" Resnick yelled. "This may be your last chance to make your move!"

Blue signaled a friend at the stereo and she pressed a button that began the haunting strains of Elton John's "Funeral for a Friend." A line formed next to Black's casket and Blue shook the liquid from his shoes as he made his way to the kitchen for another drink.

"Hey Blue, if Black creams out tomorrow, are you going to stuff him?" Barry Buchman asked the amateur taxidermist.

"No," Heavner replied with a grin, pointing to a blonde near the door. "But if she plays her cards right, I just may mount her."

"Oh, puhleeze," Anne Mallory groaned from behind Heavner.

"Sorry, Anne . . . Animal instincts, you know . . . ," and he continued to the kitchen.

Blue grabbed the first bottle that his hand touched in the refrigerator, and he joined Ken and several others talking around the small kitchen table.

The group of mostly ROTC members first focused on parachute-jumping which, it turned out, all in the group had done, since they were senior cadets. Ken enjoyed his first encounter with the ROTC crowd. He found their straight-on, no bullshit, military attitude honest, if not a little too macho for his more casual approach to life.

Leaning against the kitchen stove, Ken mostly listened as the talk meandered from jump stories to how Miami's football team could take the MAC conference title that fall if it had learned from the past season's mistakes, to the inevitable focus on women and non-military conquest.

As the topics shifted, so did Ken's attention, floating back and forth from his indecision on when and how to handle the phone call to Cody.

"Aren't you going to mingle?" a timid voice came from his right. It was Rochelle, the blonde freshman from Dayton. Her black mini-dress was in striking contrast to her shining golden hair, pulled tight and fixed at the back of her head by an ebony clasp. She looked like a little girl as she carried a large red plastic cup to the refrigerator and half-filled it with white wine.

"This is actually pretty interesting," Ken told her. "I'm learning how to invade countries and interrogate sorority girls."

"Don't you dance?" Rochelle asked, motioning toward the crowd in the living room. About half of them, Black included, were dancing to the Pointer Sisters' "Jump," one of the theme selections Blue had chosen for the party.

"Sounds like a good idea," Ken said. "Just what the doctor ordered, in fact." He took Rochelle's hand, led her into the living room and placed both of their drinks on a windowsill.

Ken had never been much of a dancer, with a sense of rhythm geared more toward the road than the dance floor. But the energy and connection with someone else helped pull his mind from its tortuous treadmill. As "Jump" gave way to the Rolling Stones' "Get Off of My Cloud," they had made eye contact several times, and Ken was aroused by the earthy sensuality that pulsed just beneath his partner's innocent smile.

The song ended and Ken reached for their drinks and handed Rochelle her wine.

"Thanks, that was fun," he said. "I'm glad I didn't break either of our feet . . . I'm a much better runner than a dancer."

"No, you did really good," she said, squeezing his arm. "I enjoyed dancing with you." Her voice was slightly slurred, and

Ken knew that the several ounces of wine left in her glass, combined with what she had already taken into her petite body, would equate into a pretty good drunk. He was glad she lived in the building and wouldn't have far to go home. And her roommate, Diane, was talking with two couples in the doorway.

There was an awkward silence as Rochelle held her cup in both hands and stared at Ken.

Apart from running, he and the freshman shared no other interests, and even if he weren't predisposed with a consuming mystery, and a real fascination with Jill, Ken would be hesitant, at best, to get involved with a love interest who lived only yards from his door.

The moment was broken when Todd Blakely stepped forward and asked Ken to help him haul a beer keg from his car.

"Sure," Ken said. "Excuse me, Rochelle, but duty calls."

"Looks like you two were getting cozy," Todd said as they shuffled down the stairs.

"I didn't know zinfandel was such a good aphrodisiac. But I don't believe in dating the neighbors," Ken said as he helped Blakely pull the aluminum keg from his hatchback. "Where's Roberta?" he asked, referring to Blakely's girl friend.

"She couldn't make it tonight because she has to baby-sit for one of her profs," he answered as they hauled the keg across the parking lot. "That's okay. I kind of like flying solo once in awhile. It feels good to spend a night or two off the leash."

The pair re-entered Black and Blue's apartment, took the keg to a waiting tub of ice in a corner of the living room, next to the casket, and Blakely set about tapping it.

Rochelle had joined Diane in talking with the two couples, and Ken asked Anne Mallory to dance. She was a good friend, and they held a light conversation through three songs before taking freshly vacated space on the couch.

"I'm glad we're finally getting some time together," she said. "I've wanted to ask you if everything's all right. You've seemed so . . . preoccupied . . . not your usual self. Is everything okay?"

The question could have been considered as prying, if it had come from someone else. But, as with Tom, Ken knew Anne's query was motivated by true, friendly concern.

"I've been trying to deal with something that has hit me pretty hard, but I really can't tell anyone about it yet," he said. "You're one of my best friends down here, and if I could tell anyone, I would tell you," he stressed. "But right now all I can do is work on it myself."

"Well, you know that if you need anything, you can depend on me, and Diane, too," Anne said. "For that matter, I know Blakely, Black and Blue and everyone else in the building cares about you."

"Thanks," Ken said. "I can tell you that it's not my health, and nobody's after me or anything like that . . . I guess you could say it's a family problem."

Family problem . . . There was a term Ken never thought he would be connected with.

"Anne, have you ever been blindsided by something that someone in your family either did or said that you felt was completely impossible? Has anyone in your family ever been discovered in something that seemed like it couldn't have possibly happened?"

She hesitated, and brushed her hair from her forehead. "Once. Yeah, once, a few years ago.

"You've met my family several times," Anne said. "In fact, I recall your mentioning that we have such a fun time when they come up from New Mexico for visits."

Ken nodded. Anne's parents and two younger brothers had made several visits to Oxford from their home in Albuquerque. "You guys always seem to have such great times together," he said.

"We do. But it's not because we haven't had to work at it for awhile. See, my mom went to the mailbox one morning five years ago and pulled out a letter from a woman who turned out to be my dad's on-the-side lover. It hit mom and the rest of us like a sniper's bullet—not only unexpected but, as you said, *impossible.*

"Well, it turned out to be not only possible, but very much the fact, and my folks separated for six months. Dad was sincerely and completely repentant, mom had the wisdom and patience to understand and forgive him, and we kids followed her advice to remember the good times and that none of us were perfect.

"We're all human," Anne said in a slow, deliberate voice. "Remembering our love for each other and that we are all human, that's what healed our family."

"Hey Ken!" Blakely screamed. "Do you know how to tap a damn beer keg?"

Before Ken could answer no, Black jumped from the casket, grabbed the tapper and drove it into the keg with a spray of foam as the room erupted with cheers.

"Who's going to take care of all of you when I'm gone?" Black yelled, wiping suds from his face.

"Don't worry," one of his ROTC buddies shouted. "If you cream-out tomorrow, we'll just switch to buying it by the case!"

Someone cranked the Grundig's volume to 10 and Ken motioned Anne toward the door.

"Just wanted to thank you for your listening ear," he said, "and for the kind words."

"I'd like to tell you that everything will work out," she said. "But since you're a phil major, I'll just say that I'm sure that everything will be as it will be. I've always found a sort of comfort in fatalism, I guess."

"Sounds more positive to me," Ken said. "I mean, if you feel bummed about whatever will be, then it's fatalism; on the other hand, if you feel good about it, then it's faith . . . Am I preaching now, boring you, or both?"

"Whatever you said, it makes sense to me," she answered. "I just don't know if that means I've had too much to drink or too little . . ."

"Concerning my situation, I guess its a moot point," Ken explained, "since my conundrum springs from the past . . . Although I'm trying to figure out how to take it into the future. No," he said with a pause, "I guess I'm trying to bring it into the present. If you haven't noticed, I'm just plain boggled."

"Remember," Anne said, leaning against the stairwell wall, "I'm just downstairs if you want to talk."

"Thanks. I know," Ken replied. He kissed Anne's cheek and took her empty cup. "Let me get you another . . . What are you drinking?"

"Thanks anyway," she answered, turning for the stairs. "I'm just about funeraled-out. Please give my regards to the aspiring human asteroid."

"I need some air," Ken said, setting their empties along the wall. "Let me walk you down."

After waving a farewell at Anne's door, Ken turned and stepped outside. He headed toward town and walked, intent on thinking of nothing except the sights, smells and sounds of the night. There was an electric locust hum from the trees near Heather Lane, and the low drone of car tires along Spring Street's bricks. The outdoors always smelled sweeter after leaving the smoke and beer-laden air of a bar or party, and someone's open window offered a static-laced radio chronicle of an extra-innings Reds-Cubs baseball game.

Ken paused, closed his eyes and drew a long, deep sigh before meandering towards campus. Midway into his return home, he was seized by a loneliness so deep that it halted him. It wasn't the loneliness that a good friend like Tom or a woman could cure. It was the punishing type of despair that temporarily saps all energy. It came from the empty corner of his being where the image of his father, the very model for his own life, had once been.

My God, Ken thought. *Have I lost my father* again?

Ken Perry had never been too concerned with heaven or hell. His father had lived on in his memories, in his heart. But now those memories were being called onto the witness stand, and his heart was feeling more and more like the dark room he had discovered.

He looked at his watch. It was just before midnight. *Tomorrow,* he decided. *I call Cody tomorrow.*

Ken walked up his building's stairway, gave a quick wave to a couple coming from Black's funeral and entered his apartment. He thought about going back to the party, but the walk had dulled his desire for socializing.

He kicked off his shoes, pulled his shirttail from his blue jeans and went into the bathroom. While brushing his teeth, he heard a light knock at his door.

"Yeah!" he yelled, thinking it would be Black or Blue in need of ice or some other party necessity.

"Hello, Ken?"

Ken recognized Rochelle's meek half-whisper, rinsed the toothpaste from his mouth and opened the door. Still holding her cup, the blonde was flushed and shoeless, her toes curling in her black nylons.

"Aren't you coming back to the party?" she asked in the sing-song voice of too much wine.

"Well, I have a long day planned tomorrow, and I figured I'd get a good start on my sleep."

"I really enjoyed talking with you earlier," she said. "I thought we were going to talk some more."

"Would you like to come in?" Ken asked.

"Sure, thanks," Rochelle replied, walking unsteadily to the couch. "Did you go for a run today?"

"Uh-huh," he said, "early this morning, some speed work on the high school track."

The golden-haired sprite was all the more alluring as she knelt on the sofa and sat upright atop the soles of her crossed feet. The bottom of her condensation-beaded cup brought a glistening sheen to where she balanced it on her upper thighs, just beneath the taut hem of her dress.

"Hold on and I'll get a drink, too," Ken said, and he rose to fetch whatever was left in his refrigerator.

"No, wait!" the freshman said anxiously, setting her cup on an end table. "Too much alcohol's bad for you." Reaching gingerly between her breasts, she retrieved a marijuana cigarette.

"I hope I'm not shocking you," she said with a serious look. "I don't usually drink, because I try to take care of my body. And I think smoking a little pot just at parties or with a friend, is better . . . No hangover, and it's not the same as smoking cigarettes . . . Only one or two a weekend isn't going to give you cancer . . . And . . ."

Ken touched a finger to her lips. Too tired to battle temptation, he reached next to several candles on an end table and pulled open a book of matches. Rochelle climbed onto his lap and licked her lips, working one end of the twisted cigarette paper as Ken held a match to the other.

She took a few easy breaths and offered a deep, dreamy moan as she exhaled. She moaned again as she held the stick to Ken's lips, her tongue dancing along his neck.

Ken looked down at the spreading legs that made the dress hem flirt with the coed's crotch. He realized it was the marijuana euphoria, and not necessarily the saucy teenager, that had seduced him with the promise of escape from his cryptic obsession.

Leaving Ken's neck for her turn at the joint, Rochelle saw that he had noticed her legs. She took a long drag and held it as she leaned back, the black hem rising to expose the garters that pinched her dark nylons.

Ken slowly ran his right hand along the inside of her left thigh, and gently pushed the dress up to her waist. A tuft of blonde hair lie matted between her legs under her sheer black panties, and she guided his palm over the smooth, warm mound.

Rochelle flipped down both of her gown's spaghetti straps, pulled the clasp from her hair and fumbled with the zipper behind her back. Ken drew it down for her as she leaned forward to pull at his shirt, and her hair brushed his cheek.

Rochelle stood quickly, opened her bra from the front and kicked the dress from around her feet in one remarkably fluid motion, given her inebriated state. With another low moan, the blonde straddled Ken and leaned upward. He took one small but perfectly sculpted breast into his mouth, slipped both palms under her panties to grip her bottom and pulled her tight.

Rochelle could clearly feel Ken's erect penis under his heavy denim jeans as she picked the nearly spent joint from the edge of the end table, took a quick hit and handed it to him. She grappled with his pants as he finished the cigarette, dropping the roach into what was left of his drink.

The pot made Ken feel as if he were falling as Rochelle breathed heavily onto his neck. His excitement skyrocketed when he noticed the reflection of her ass on the black television screen, jiggling as she fumbled with his belt buckle.

Finally, in a fit of conscience, Ken placed both hands beneath Rochelle's arms and stood, pulling her to her feet. Even with all the pressure brought by the continuing days of frustration and confusion, he would not be able to live with himself if he took advantage of a drunk freshman.

Ken stroked Rochelle's hair and kissed her cheek as he prepared to suggest that he walk her home. Suddenly she flinched, and a gurgle came from her throat as she jerked away. "Oh no!" she sputtered as she sprang from the couch.

Tripping over her own clothing, she crashed onto the coffee table and vomited a stream of wine and pizza onto the floor.

Ken pulled a handkerchief from his blue jeans and dabbed the crying girl's mouth and chin. "There, there," he said. "It's okay. Are you all right?"

"I'm so sorry," she said in gasping sobs. "I came over here when you were home for the night and I just acted stupid and now look . . ."

Gently pulling her once again to her feet, Ken embraced Rochelle and held her as he would a child. There was something genuine in their embrace that was missing from their passion of moments earlier. He had no idea of the demons or empty corners that lay in Rochelle's wine-and-smoke wake, but her trembling sobs helped him to remember that he was not alone. *Everyone,* he thought, *has a secret room in their life.*

Ken wrapped Rochelle's shoulders with a blanket and walked her into the kitchen for a glass of water. She stopped crying.

Both were silent as they dressed, cleaned up the mess and walked to Rochelle's apartment.

"One nice thing about alcohol," Ken said with a consoling smile. "You don't remember a thing the next morning."

"Thanks," Rochelle said, and kissed his cheek. As she opened her door, they could hear her roommate, Diane, in the shower.

"You're a sweetheart," Ken said, and the door closed.

"He looked at his wrist for the time, but he hadn't put his watch back on. Black and Blue's apartment was nearly quiet, and Ken estimated the time at 3 a.m. Looking upward, the cloudless sky was full of stars, and they made him feel peaceful.

Ken passed the entrance for his apartment and walked across the back lawn and through the narrow, sleeping woods to the Stewart Middle School athletic field. He climbed onto the top bench of an aluminum bleachers and lay on his back. He looked for familiar constellations and listened to the crickets, an occasional car, and the last of the partygoers as they laughed their way from Heather Lane Apartments.

Ken didn't want to think about anything. He concentrated on the stars. And later, after sliding into a deep sleep he dreamed that Jill appeared, took him by the hand and led him home.

CHAPTER EIGHT

Dew had started to dampen Ken's clothes by the time the early morning chill roused him from sleep. He crawled into his own bed just before dawn, sparing him what could have been a rude awakening by a local cop or a group of junior high kids.

Now, along with everything else, he was starting to wonder about his drinking. He'd always liked hoisting a beer or two with friends at a party or after a game, but he rarely got drunk. And it had certainly never before caused him to crash for the night in a public place.

The fact that Ken did make it to his 9 a.m. phenomenology class on time helped him feel less guilty about his week-night revel. Besides, he reasoned, falling asleep on the bleachers came less from drink than it did from a combination of fatigue, silence and a hypnotic tapestry of stars.

He was red-eyed and tired, but not hungover. The whole incident did raise a red flag that he was glad he had spotted before it was brought up to him by someone else. Taking up drinking as a hobby would not only screw up his studies, it could kill his running in general, let alone a hoped-for personal best finishing time at the Detroit Free Press Marathon, coming up quick in mid-October.

Ken had run the "Freep" ever since he was a senior in high school. He had also finished a half-dozen other marathons, and even though they all outclassed the Detroit race in terms of scenery, it remained his favorite. Beginning across the Detroit River in Windsor, Canada's MacArthur Park, the race included road running's only underwater mile, through the tunnel that arches under the river to open in downtown Motown. The runners then passed Tiger Stadium on their way south along Michigan Avenue, and again on their return north. Winding through the shadows of the central business district they finally approached the gleaming

Renaissance Center towers and the finish line in the adjoining Hart Plaza.

Ken had run his first Freep only several weeks after his father's death. About a block after he strode across Trumbull Avenue, he stopped on the Michigan Avenue sidewalk where his father had been felled outside Tiger Stadium's left field wall.

During that first Free Press marathon, and in each of the three he had run since, Ken always stopped there long enough to drop to one knee and press a palm to the cement.

"For you, Dad."

After promising classmates he would take part in the next phenomenology study group the following Sunday, Ken left Irvin Hall and headed uptown. He ducked into the Philly for a veggie and cheese sub to go, then moved on to the Oxford General Store for a quart of cold cranberry juice. He brought his lunch back to campus and took a seat outside King Library on the round cement bench centered with an inlaid, manhole-size bronze Kappa Kappa Gamma seal.

Ken unwrapped the sandwich, unzipped his backpack and twisted the lid from his drink. A natural diuretic, the cranberry juice would help flush any party poisons out of his system. He looked forward to sweating out the rest in a run after his afternoon developmental psych lecture.

After a long, throat-numbing drink of the icy, tart juice, Ken pulled the psych text from his pack and opened it on his lap, hoping to at least skim the first three chapters that had been assigned at the previous class.

Munching on the sandwich in his right hand, his eyes skimmed the pages as he occasionally stopped to highlight a few words with the marker in his left.

A shadow came over the book and Ken looked up to see Rochelle. Once again the young blonde had assumed an air of innocence, crossed arms cradling her books against faded coverall jeans.

"Hi," she said through a remorseful smile.

"Hi back," Ken replied. "Have a seat . . . Want part of my sandwich?"

"Thanks," she said. "But I'm on my way home. I'm having lunch with Diane."

"You know, I'm really sorry about last night," she said, lowering her books. "I hope you don't think I'm a bad person. I'm kind of new to the college party thing and I think I just overdid it. I'm really not that way."

"No apology necessary. I consider it an honor anytime a beautiful young woman pays me a visit," he said with a smile. "If we hadn't had too much wine and smoke, I'm sure we would've had fun getting to know each other . . . Maybe we could get together for a run and one of my famous 'pasta del Perry' dinners some afternoon."

"Yeah," Rochelle said. "That sounds like fun. Are you a good cook?"

"Not really. I mostly open cans and boil macaroni and cheese and instant rice. But my dad taught me how to make an excellent four-alarm chili, and mom passed on the pasta dish—shrimp, scallops and tuna in a creamy garlic sauce over bowtie pasta."

"That sure sounds better than the canned ravioli I have waiting for me, but if I don't hurry I'll miss that," Rochelle said as she turned for the street. "I'm looking forward to our pasta del Perry."

"We'll make it happen," Ken called with a wave, and he watched her walk away, ponytail swaying.

As she left, Ken noticed Jill and Kaaren talking with each other as they watched him from near the library arches. Kaaren walked in the direction of their dorm, and Jill smiled as she approached Ken.

"So," she said with a hint of sarcasm, "will that blonde be buying you a beer tonight?"

"We had our drinks last night," he said. "But despite all the pressure, I'm saving myself for you."

"Yeah, right!" Jill said, rolling her eyes as she sat next to him. She picked up the cranberry juice, took a drink and paused.

"Will the 'Big Man on Campus' be able to clear his events calendar for tonight's BOZO rush?"

Ken had forgotten about the party, still feeling the aftermath of the one the night before.

"You're not backing out are you?" she said, cooling her neck with the juice bottle. "These are great folks and you'll have a wonderful time. Come on, say yes."

Why not? Ken thought. After all, the previous night's party had helped him to pry away from his obsession with his new, sinister mystery. And more and more he was captivated by Jill, too.

"When and where?" he said.

"Eight p.m., corner of College and Church. You won't be able to miss it," she said, standing with the juice. "There'll be a sign in the front, and a crowd. Why don't you meet me at my room at 7:30 and we can walk over together? Right now I have to get to class," she said, starting for Western Campus.

"Seven-thirty it is," Ken called back.

With no time left to review his psych book, he guzzled the rest of his cranberry juice, trashed the rest of his sub and headed for class.

Ken managed to stay at least semi-focused on Dr. Clark's hour-long treatment of the psychic repercussions of post-infantile toilet training. He decided that he'd better get used to the prof's plodding monotone delivery, since the academic displayed no apparent capacity for emotion or enthusiasm.

Back home, Ken hurried into his running gear for a quick five miles before the party. He already noticed that today had been much easier on him than the previous few. He hadn't obsessed on the matter of the basement room.

Yet, like the room itself, the mystery behind it remained a dark question mark . . . hidden for the time being, but not forgotten. Not now, anyway.

The sun was low in the west as Ken ran over the railroad tracks crossing Main Street, and he turned to pass the large, old student apartment houses lining Chestnut.

As much as he was drawn to Jill, Ken wished he had the night free to ponder his next move in unraveling the mystery behind the secret room.

Sure, he had decided to call Cody, but how could he be certain that wasn't a mistake?

In the final analysis—at least with what he had to go on—Ken saw no better plan of action. And action, he concluded, was the only way to find an answer. If he didn't seek a solution, none was likely to drop into his lap.

Ken wheeled about-face at a tree that marked the midway point of his five-mile route, and he felt the sun warm his sweaty back.

He tried to remember the last time he'd seen or spoken with Paul Cody. Cody and his wife came over to the Perrys' house at least once every couple of weeks for about a year after his dad died. They would play pool or card games with Ken and his mother, share conversation over an evening meal, and sometimes join them for after-dinner walks along the neighborhood's oak-lined streets.

But by the time Ken left for college, the visits had dwindled to holidays, his mother's birthday, wedding anniversary or other times she might need a pick-me-up.

Several blocks away from the Chessie System railroad tracks, Ken saw a freight train wobbling over the Chestnut Street crossing, so he detoured onto Locust. He finally figured that the last time he had seen Cody was the previous Christmas. Even though the Codys were Episcopalian, they always joined the Perrys for Midnight Mass at St. Paul's.

Paul Cody always said the only real difference between the two faiths was that Episcopalian priests are allowed to marry, while their Catholic counterparts could only have girlfriends or altar boys.

Ken's father would then counter with a barb about the Episcopalian Church being "Catholicism Lite," or that the church had served as a handy way to make an honest man out of Henry VIII.

Anyway, the previous Christmas Eve, Paul and Jeanette Cody had joined Ken and his mother for Midnight Mass. It was followed by an exchange of gifts and mugs of buttered rum before the Perrys' fireplace. Ken got the Codys a duck decoy for their extensive collection, and they gave him an electric shaver.

"Your mother told us she was tired of you using all the toilet paper in the house to stop the bleeding on your razor-ravaged neck and cheeks," Paul Cody said as Ken opened the box. "And she's afraid someday you'll use that as an excuse to grow a beard."

That turned out to be prophetic, since Ken grew his first full beard several months later. And unlike his fuzzy attempts during high school, this one came in thick enough that he decided to keep it . . . to his mother's chagrin.

By the time Ken got to where the railroad tracks cross Spring Street, the train had passed and he sprinted hard the last few blocks home.

The swollen sun blazed cherry-red on the horizon as Ken cruised into his back yard and dropped for his stretches. His sweat-slickened legs squeaked with each lunge against the warm grass until he stood and entered the building.

"Is this man or spirit that I behold before me?" Ken asked, peering through Black and Blue's opened doorway. Black lay on the sofa, still wearing his camouflage ROTC fatigues as he ate a bowl of cereal.

"It was great! Outstanding!" Black babbled through a mouthful of Cocoa Puffs. "Got scared shitless and flew like a bird! Talk about feeling *alive!* . . . I got to go *twice!*"

"You're nuts, Black."

"Yeah," he said with a grin. "Freakin' *crazy!* It was *great!*"

"Well, I'm glad that A: you enjoyed it, and B: that you lived through it," Ken said as he untucked his T-shirt. "Maybe next week they'll let you jump without a chute. That should really light your fuse!"

"I'm ready when you are," Black replied, crossing his combat boots atop the coffee table.

"I think I'll stick to flying coach," Ken said as he turned toward his door and peeled off his shirt. "Anyway, I'm glad you're still with us."

"I appreciate that," Black said. "You're beautiful, man!"

"Right back at ya, Superman," Ken replied.

Unlocking his door, he entered to see a folded piece of paper that had been slipped underneath.

> *Ken,*
> *Forgot to tell you; bring a change of clothes.*
>
> *Jill*

Oh great, Ken thought. *This can only mean some sort of mud-slinging ritual, baptism by beer, or another contrived humiliation.*

But what the hell. Maybe a good, all-out, unbridled debacle was just what he needed. Anything from a mystic hazing to garden-variety foolishness would provide a great way to blow off some steam. And Jill wouldn't be involved with anything truly ludicrous.

Yeah, Ken thought. *What the hell.* And he stuffed a pair of Levi's and a shirt into his pack.

A quick shower later he found himself dressed, spare clothes in hand and ready to leave.

Sitting at the kitchen table, he lowered his pack to the floor and eyed the wall phone. Even though he hadn't given much thought to what he would say, the urge to call Paul Cody had steadily built in Ken. If he was to find out anything, that would be the only way.

Ken's left knee bounced with nervous energy and he breathed a deep sigh of frustration as he stared at the phone.

Suddenly it rang, and Ken jumped as if it had exploded.

"Ken, I'm running late, so don't come by to pick me up," Jill's voice came through the receiver. "You know where it is, right?"

"Yeah, sure. Is everything okay?"

"Kaaren got stung by a bee in our room and freaked because she's allergic to them. By the time we ran across the courtyard to the health center she was in anaphylactic shock. I spent all afternoon there with her and making calls to her family. She'll be okay, but I just got back and I have to change. I may be a little late, but I'll be there."

"Don't worry," Ken told her. "I know Tom and Chloe will be there, and I should run into at least one or two others I know, so I won't be going in cold turkey."

"Okay," she said. "See you at eight, or just a little after."

"See you then," Ken replied, and they hung up.

Good, he thought. *I can use the time I would've spent walking to Jill's to think of what to say to Cody.*

He turned his gaze outside the kitchen window to a brown squirrel that leaped from branch to branch in the woods behind the building.

Suddenly he turned, seized the handset and dialed the numbers.

Straightforward, he thought as the connection completed. *I'll just be as straightforward as I can without giving him the particulars.*

The phone rang three times before Jeanette Cody answered.

"Hello, Cody residence."

"Hi, Mrs. Cody. This is Ken, Ken Perry . . ."

"Oh, Kenny!" she chimed. "I'm so glad to hear from you! How are you doing at school? You are in Ohio, aren't you?"

"Yeah. I'm doing great. Classes are all going well and I'm going to get together with a group of friends tonight . . ."

"Well this sure is a surprise," Mrs. Cody repeated, sounding thrilled that he would call. "We haven't heard from you in so long. What's the occasion?"

Ken hesitated, fearing that saying the wrong thing would make him sound silly or strange. He was sure that she had picked up on his hesitation as a sign that something was not quite right, and she had already noted that it was unusual to hear from him in the first place.

"I was wondering if Mr. Cody was in," he said. "I have a question or two I'd like to ask him."

"Sure," she said. "We just finished dinner and he's in the den. Can you hold on?"

"Oh yeah, fine, thanks," Ken answered, and he felt his chest tighten over his drumming heart.

Leaning on the wall, Ken rested his head against a forearm as he pressed the phone to his ear.

Finally picking up his receiver, Paul Cody was just as cheerful as his wife had been.

"Hey, Ken! How you been doin', buddy?"

"Great, Mr. Cody. I hope I didn't interrupt anything."

"No, just catching up on some reading. Jeanette said you wanted to ask me something."

"Yeah," Ken said, backing into a kitchen chair. "Yeah . . . It's about something I sort of . . . came across . . . and am having a little trouble understanding."

"I'll help if I can," Cody said. His voice dropped an octave as he read the concern in Ken's.

Ken wanted to get it over with, to describe the hidden room he'd found and ask if Cody knew anything about it.

But he couldn't do that. If Cody knew nothing of it, Ken would feel like a fool asking the question, even though he could bring Cody to the room to prove its existence. But that would mean Ken's mother would have to know, too, and he wasn't sure she was ready for that. Her husband's death had devastated her, and without good reason, Ken wouldn't reopen that agonizing wound.

Besides, if Cody *did* know about it, would he be willing, or even able, to admit that, or to share anything more on the matter?

"I went home last weekend to see mom and pick up a few things before classes began, and I came across something that I can't quite understand."

"What was it?"

"Well," Ken said, measuring and weighing each word as he answered. "I'm not sure. I was hoping you could help me figure it out."

"I'll do my best," Cody replied.

"Well, I, uh . . . I found something that I think dad left, but I'm not sure. And, well, it would've been unlike him, but . . . What I mean is, it's something I hadn't known about—none of us did—mom, Marg or me, and I don't understand it."

"Of course," Cody repeated. "I'll do whatever I can to help. What is it? What did you find?"

Ken had painted himself into a very uncomfortable corner. Barely into his exchange with Cody, Ken felt that he needed more time to figure out what he was going to tell him, how he would proceed. He needed time.

"I'll tell you what," Ken said after the awkward silence. "I'll be coming home again soon. Maybe we could set up a meeting?"

"When?"

"It would have to be during a weekend," Ken said. "Anytime on a weekend."

"Sure, Ken. I'd be glad to . . . Are you all right?"

"Oh, yeah," he answered with a nervous laugh. "I'm just trying to understand something dad left behind."

Ken wished he hadn't repeated that.

"Well, I'm going to be traveling a lot on business from now until Christmas, but if you give me a minute, I'll get my schedule."

"Thanks, Mr. Cody."

Suddenly, Ken was feeling incredibly foolish. He could imagine the conversation the Codys would have after his call:

I sure hope Ken's okay. He certainly sounded strange . . . I hope there's nothing wrong at school or at home . . .

At home . . . Ken would have to be sure the Codys didn't say anything to his mother.

"Okay, I'm back," Mr. Cody's deep, strong voice came through the line. "I leave this weekend for a series of meetings the coming week in Denver, but I'll be back here next weekend."

"That sounds good," Ken said. "By the way, if you don't mind, could you keep this quiet if you see my mom? It's kind of personal."

"No problem," Cody assured. "Give me a call when you get into town and I'd be glad to sit down with you about whatever's on your mind."

"Thanks, Mr. Cody," Ken said. "I will."

Both hung up together, without a goodbye. It was as if the unfinished nature of the call made words of closure unnecessary.

Ken picked up the bag of clothes and left for the party, feeling awkward about the way the call had gone but glad that he had made it. He had crossed the Rubicon. He would set the meeting, and something would come of it. It had to.

A full-blown three-keg cookout greeted Ken when he came upon the BOZO house. Music blasted from speakers on the elevated front porch, and an oversized beach ball bounced from group to group scattered across the front yard talking, dancing and eating from food spread over two joined picnic tables. Groups were clotted around the beer kegs on both sides of the lawn and atop a deck on the flat roof over the garage attached to the white, two-story wood frame house.

Tom slipped away from Chloe and several others who were in animated discussion.

"Hey Ken, glad you could make it," he said. "I hope you're hungry."

"Smells good," Ken said, looking while a short, fat guy in cutoff overalls dealt cheese slices onto sizzling burgers.

"That's our prez, Dave Pung," Tom said. "He and several other architecture majors live here and founded the BOZOs a few years ago.

"Throw your pack over there," Tom said, motioning to a pile of bags inside the front door. "I'll introduce you to Dave."

"Who's his helper?" Ken asked, referring to the gorgeous blonde in shorts and halter top who stood at Pung's side.

"That's Fonda Madden, his girlfriend, roommate and BOZO vice president."

"Forget it," Chloe said from behind Ken. "They're irretrievably in love. And besides, you don't want to blow your chances with Jill, do you? She'll be here anytime, and if you're really interested in her, you shouldn't pay too much attention to the assistant chef's buns."

"Spoken like a woman who really knows how to train a man," Ken said with a doleful glance at Tom.

"That hurt, man," Tom said. "That was cold, very cold."

"Speaking of cold, I've been here ten minutes and I don't have a beer," Ken said. "Come on, we can hit a keg on the way to meeting the royal couple."

Ken instantly liked Dave and Fonda. During Tom's brief introduction Ken learned that both were architecture students and, like him, Fonda was a Michigan transplant, from Traverse City. Dave was a local, having grown up in a house less than a mile away.

Waiting for Jill, Ken watched Tom pile potato salad and cole slaw next to the two grilled hot dogs on his paper plate, and Dave stood on a folding chair to address the crowd.

"Greetings, my children!" he shouted, waving a spatula in one hand and a barbecue fork in the other. "Once again we come together in the spirit of the Great Orange-Haired One to share food, drink and friendship very seriously, and most everything else not so much so.

"Those of you who are new should know by now that we are a fratority of fun and we avoid the self-important, quasi-religious lifestyles of the *Alpha Beta Whoozits* and *Gamma Gamma Globulins*.

"However, recognizing that a degree of ritual is essential to any group's sense of identity, existing members will be asked to rededicate themselves as BOZOs at tonight's initiation ceremony when we swear in the fresh recruits.

"The solemnities will begin just after sundown and will be ushered-in by a report from la pistola pyrotechnica," he said, holding up a boater's flare gun.

"Oh, wonderful," came a voice from the crowd. "Watch where you park your cars!"

The remark was in reference to the previous year's party, when Dave's errant flare landed on a neighbor's convertible top, burning through it and the front seat.

"Not to worry," Dave said, twirling the pistol several times before holstering it in one of his coverall pockets. "This year I feel lucky!"

"Meanwhile, eat, drink and be merry!" Pung yelled, and a perfectly thrown football grazed him as he jumped from the chair.

"Well, Jill was right," Ken told Tom. "I like this group already."

"Of course I was," Jill said as she took his arm from behind. "And I believe it's your turn to get *me* a drink."

Tom returned to Chloe and the rest of the group he was with when Ken arrived, and found that Chris and Kaaren had joined them.

Ken walked with Jill to one of the kegs.

"Well, are you ready to become a BOZO?" she asked.

"So far I'm not too scared," Ken answered, filling two plastic cups from the tapper. He handed Jill one and they walked to the grill, where they pointed out burger choices to Dave. He flipped two onto buns and dropped them onto their waiting paper plates.

"Well you should be," she told Ken. "Have you had all your shots?"

"I went through high school dating a drama-queen cheerleader," he answered. "I can handle anything."

As the sun accelerated its dusky slide toward night, the pair took their meal around to the backyard, away from the music and party noise, where several small groups lazed in conversation.

Jill and Ken sat in the shade of a large elm, plates balanced on their crossed legs.

"How did your first week of classes go?" she asked.

Ken set his plate aside and stretched stomach-down on the warm grass, then leaned atop both elbows.

"Oh, sort of the usual," he said. "You know, getting to know classmates, sizing up profs who are sizing us up . . ."

"But I think it's going to be a good year," he said, forcing some enthusiasm. "I have a good variety of classes to keep me interested, even if one or two of the profs do their best to put us to sleep.

"How about you?"

"I got all the classes I applied for, and so far everything's under control there," Jill said. "The only thing that's been a little stressing is that Chris and Kaaren haven't let up . . . All week long they've been so fired-up that I've considered force-feeding them tranquilizers. But we all get along great, and anytime now the reality of reading requirements, term papers and cramming for exams should slow them down a little."

Finishing her food, Jill picked up her cup and sat with her back against the tree trunk.

"You're a new friend, but I feel like you're my oldest, like I've known you forever," Ken said, his voice trailing off as he heard himself lapsing into clichés.

He heaved another sigh and watched the house's shadow creep closer.

Jill closed her eyes and together they listened to the sounds of the party, the occasional car that drove along the alley behind the yard, a couple of distant barking dogs.

They were sharing the language of trust—silence.

Quickly the sky went from blue to dark purple until finally, unannounced, a cheer rose from the front yard as a red flare hissed toward the emerging stars.

"It's time," Jill said in a menacing tone. "Are you ready?"

Ken stood and helped her to her feet.

"Let's do it," he said.

They held hands as they walked around the house to the front door and followed the last of the group into the foyer that connected the living room on one side and the equally large dining area on the other. The house was darkened, and each person received a lit candle on the way inside.

"All right, listen up!" Fonda shouted from her position a few steps up the stairway between the two rooms. "Let's have all the initiated BOZOs in a big circle, with the prospective members forming an inner circle."

"Just remember," Ken said as he left Jill's side, "if this is *particularly* humiliating, I know where you sleep."

"No guts, no glory," she whispered back.

Ken joined about a dozen other male and female students in the center of the ring, and the tape-recorded roar of a gong filled the room. Someone switched on a flashlight and focused the beam on Dave, who appeared at the top of the stairs in full Bozo the Clown regalia.

Holding a huge, tattered, leather-bound book, he solemnly proceeded down the stairs, floppy red shoes snapping with each step. Arriving at the landing, he handed the book to Fonda, who held it open for him.

Then, raising his arms high, Dave yelled, *"HI KIDS!"*

"HI BOZO!" the initiated screamed in return.

"So who are these I see before me?" he read from the book in ritual formality.

"They are noble friends who wish to join our number," those in the outer ring responded.

"Repeat after me," Bozo-Dave instructed Ken and the others in the inner circle. "I *state your name,* wish to join the illustrious, secret and ignominious Fratoricus Bozobicus."

All did.

"Okay," he said, snapping the book shut. "That's it. You're in."

Everyone blew out their candles as Dave began his climb back up the stairs. Then, pausing, as in afterthought, he turned back to the group.

"Oh yeah," Dave said. "There's one more thing."

Again he raised his arms. "May the sweet taste of this moment remain with you always!" he proclaimed. At that signal the senior BOZOs released a torrent of cream pies at the unsuspecting initiates as Dave fled down the upstairs hall.

As the screaming settled the lights returned, the stereo blared to life and most of the group migrated back out to the beer, food and clear summer night.

"That was very moving," Jill said as she handed Ken his change of clothes.

"I'm all misty," he said, wiping whipped cream from his eyes.

"There's a shower in the upstairs bathroom and another in the garage," she said, handing Ken a white beach towel. He opened it to see that large red cloth BOZO letters had been sewn onto it, and it had been signed by all the members.

"Want to help me break it in?" he asked.

She licked some of the sticky foam from his neck. "Maybe later."

Members of the group washed pie from the walls and hardwood floor as Ken walked to the end of the line for the garage shower. Chloe hugged him and gave him an ice cream bar.

"I'm so proud of you," she gushed.

"Yeah," he said, crunching into the treat. "I guess it makes everything in my life up until now seem inconsequential."

"Well, we have a lot of fun during the year, and hey," Chloe urged, leaning close to his ear, "I think Jill's your *perfect* match."

"We'll see," Ken said, and took his turn at the shower.

Jill joined several of the others by the red brick fireplace where Christmas stockings for Dave, Fonda and their housemates hung year-round.

When Jill saw Ken re-enter through the door attaching the garage to the kitchen, she approached him with a brown paper bag.

"Here's your membership kit," she said, opening the bag. "First, like any self-respecting, pretentious secret society member, you'll be expected to display these in a conspicuous place," Jill instructed, handing him a set of Greek-letter BOZO decals.

"Next, a certificate of membership, signed by Grand Bozo Dave, with myself as your sponsor . . .

"And finally," she said, "a copy of our rules and regulations."

Ken took the small black book with "BOZO Bylaws, Rules and Regulations" embossed on the cover. Opening it, he found all of its pages blank except for the last, which read:

> *Did you really think we would have*
> *any bylaws, rules or regulations?*

"And last but not least," Jill said, pulling a wooden paddle from the bag, "I present you with your memorial BOZO induction paddle."

"Oh, no! I knew it," Ken groaned. "The pie escapade was bad enough, but please don't tell me I'm going to have to go through a frat-style ass-paddling."

"Oh, no," Jill assured. "It's just for decoration. You know, on a wall or bookshelf at home."

"Good," he said.

"Here," Jill said, reaching for the varnished, cricket bat-shaped piece. "Let me show you where I signed it.

"Hey!" she said, looking over Ken's shoulder. "Who's she?"

"Who?" Ken asked as he turned to look.

Jill wheeled at Ken with the paddle, connecting with a sharp crack, and he grabbed his ass as if he'd been shot with a stun-gun.

DAMN! he screamed, and leaped from the tile floor.

OH! DAMN! Ken repeated, leaning against his knees to catch his breath. "Just when I was beginning to *like* you!"

"Oh, come on," Jill said. "That wasn't so bad, was it?"

Before he could answer, another scream came from the front yard, followed by another in the living room.

"You went from awfully sweet to ruthlessly sadistic in a mighty brief time-span," Ken said, standing and massaging his violated region with both hands.

Jill moved forward, placed her arms around Ken and slid her hands under his.

"Well, I guess you just owe me a spanking," she said, and their eyes closed as they entered a long kiss.

"If that's the way it works, then hit me again," Ken said, brushing a dark strand of hair from her cheek. He nuzzled her neck just behind the jaw and drank in her scent. Jill's breasts heaved into him as she drew a sudden gasp, and she ran her fingertips up through the hair at the back of his head.

Ken felt the same rush of physical signals that had been tripped by Rochelle the night before, but this time with a different edge. He knew the passion—the connection he and Jill wanted to share—was grounded in a desire that encompassed much more than bedroom gymnastics. Unlike the episode with the blonde freshman, Ken and Jill shared a growing intoxication born of passion, and not a passion triggered by intoxication.

Jill released Ken, replaced his things into the bag, took his hand and led him back to the living room. They walked over to Dave, who was dancing with Fonda in a small group near the stereo.

"We have to get going," Jill yelled through cupped hands into Dave's ear. "It's getting late and I promised to help Ken with something after the meeting."

"Okay, but wait just a minute," Dave yelled back, motioning for Fonda to turn down the music. "I have to make some announcements to the group."

After calling everyone to the living room from the rest of the house and yard, Pung explained that a list of members' names, addresses and phone numbers would be available at the next meeting.

"And don't forget that this weekend we're having our first road trip of the year," Dave said, "Saturday we make our first overnighter to Detroit for the Who concert at Joe Louis Arena. We're doing it on a Sixties retro theme."

Over the years, the BOZOs had collected enough in membership dues to buy an old yellow school bus they used for group outings, and had taken it as far as Florida for spring break.

"An even hundred bucks each covers concert tickets, as well as 'champagne flight' transportation to and from the venue aboard the BOZO bus," Dave said. "And remember, it's a Sixties theme, so dust off your grandparents' bell bottoms and love beads and brace yourself for a trip you can tell your illegitimate grandchildren about. See me or Fonda for sign-up."

Dave hopped off the chair and someone cranked the music back up as Ken and Jill bid their goodbyes and left.

"By the way," Ken said as he slipped an arm around her waist. "Just what did you promise to help me with, anyway?"

"Remember that shower request?" Jill asked. "You mentioned it twice, once when we met and again tonight . . . I've arranged for another RA to cover for me tonight."

They walked slowly until they got to Ken's door, where Jill took his key and opened it.

He dropped the bags of wet clothes and BOZO gear onto the carpet and she tossed his keys onto the desk.

Again Ken ran both hands through her silken ebony hair as their tongues met, flickered and probed. Jill kissed his ears and breathed heavy as she pulled his shirt from his pants, and their fingers intertwined as they fell back onto the couch.

Jill unbuttoned his shirt from bottom to top, stopping briefly so he could pull her T-shirt over her head and shoulders.

Jill massaged Ken's temples with her fingertips as she leaned forward and lowered her firm breasts to his lips. Cupping them in both hands, he pushed his face between the mounds and kissed the smooth, drumhead-tight skin over her breastbone. Jill's tan lines excited Ken, her vanilla breasts and pale, hard nipples in erotic contrast to the rest of her cinnamon-tanned skin.

Her breasts lowered onto the dark hair of Ken's chest as their lips again met, and he pulled hard against the small of her back.

Jill lay astride Ken and felt him flinch as her body pressed against the swollen member between his legs.

Ken helped her to an upright sitting position and undid her belt. Just as he unzipped her shorts, she stood, knelt next to the couch and opened Ken's jeans. Pulling his zipper wide, she freed his penis, kissed one side and then slowly took its full length between her lips.

Tingling rushes shot up Ken's sides as Jill stroked them with her fingertips, and after less than a minute he stood and pulled her up and into his arms. He bent to remove his pants and underwear, and she placed her hands on his shoulders, signaling him to remove hers.

Nibbling her neck, then breasts and stomach, Ken lowered himself to a kneeling position before Jill, her hands trembling on his lean, strong shoulders. He eased down her already unfastened denim shorts, then offered an open-mouthed kiss to the small white triangle of cotton at the front of her bikini briefs.

Quickly flipping her panties downward with her thumbs, Jill breathed loudly as she laced her fingers behind Ken's head. He placed one hand on the inside of her thighs and the other over her derriere as his breaths fell long and heavy over the matting of tight black curls he slowly parted with his tongue.

Jill shuddered and Ken thought she was falling as she leaned hard against his shoulders.

Ken stood, took her hand and led her to the bathroom door, where he paused to retrieve a candle from the darkened kitchen. The match he struck roared like a flaming arrow in the tiny, dark bathroom, and Ken lit the white candle he then placed atop the sink.

Turning on the shower, Ken tested the water and then helped Jill into the warm, pelting stream.

Embraced from behind, Jill felt the water flow over her chest and stomach as Ken's erection nuzzled between her buttocks. It then slid through the space between her legs on its way up inside her.

Jill issued a low, almost wailing moan as she leaned back hard against Ken, her fingernails digging the outside of his hips.

Ken's arms enfolded Jill to embrace her stomach and breasts as the couple moved in long, slow, rhythmic pumps. Turning back, Jill tried to kiss his rasping lips, but could reach only his cheek. So he withdrew, wheeled her around and channeled his passion from his opened mouth to hers.

Jill reinserted his penis, then reached behind and above her to steady herself against a chrome towel bar. Her back arched in passion as they continued, rising and falling in and out of the shimmering spray of water. The shower looked like a Roman candle in the darkness as its torrent of drops reflected the candle flame.

Ken's lips and tongue traced the curve of Jill's neck, and he hugged her legs as he bent to place a stopper in the drain. When the tub was half filled with water he lay on his back, she stretched atop him, and they continued to make love, fixed on the flame dancing in each other's eyes.

CHAPTER NINE

Waking with the dawn, Ken and Jill made love again in his sofa bed, and he fixed a pancake breakfast as she lingered between the crisp, clean sheets.

"I really wish I didn't have to leave so early," she said, wrapping her arms around his waist as he reached into a cupboard for syrup. "But as an RA, I have to be back by 8:30 to take the rest of my floor to join in the annual Miami River cleanup. It's a community service project my dorm takes part in each year," she explained. "Want to join us?"

"Thanks anyway," Ken said, pouring their coffee. "But I need to get in a good weekend distance run, and I promised to help Tom, Chloe and the gang with some house painting."

The consuming passion of last night and again this morning now gave way to a deeper connection Ken and Jill shared in silence as they prepared for the coming day. Wrapped in a towel, Ken was shaving as Jill stole a sip of his coffee on her dash into the shower. Before he could finish she emerged from the steamy chamber, snatched his towel and pinched his ass on her way to the living room.

After Ken's turn in the shower he grabbed clothes from his closet and chest of drawers as the already dressed Jill applied makeup. She stuffed a tortoise shell compact into her purse and pulled out a round blue item about the same size. She opened it and picked a tiny white pill from its numbered wheel.

"I want you to know something," she told Ken as he brought her water. "I don't take these routinely. I don't need to. But I started yesterday," she went on, showing him the two empty spaces in her birth control pill case, "because I knew I wanted to be with you . . ."

Ken embraced Jill and kissed her forehead. Again, their silence surpassed words.

Leaving the building hand in hand, they noticed Ken's neighbors Anne, Linda, Barry and Michael, sitting at a card table in the shade of an ancient, gnarled oak. They shared bagels and cream cheese along with a pot of tea Anne had brought from her apartment. Each sat quietly with a section of Linda's *New York Times.*

"Good morning, guys," Ken said, holding Jill's hand. "This is my friend, Jill.

"Jill," he continued, snatching a freshly prepared bagel from Barry's plate, "these are some of my neighbors—roommates Anne Mallory and Linda Kent, and Michael Tierney and Barry 'No Bagel' Buchman."

"This is so nice," Jill said of the outdoor breakfast. "Do you do this often?"

"As long as the weather allows," Barry said. "During the week we're out a little earlier in order to finish by class time."

"If Ken wasn't such as sleepy-head, he'd join us," Anne added.

"Hey, listen," Ken defended himself, "out of all eight apartments in this building, yours are the only ones stirring early enough to do this each morning.

"When you get a brunch going, let me know."

They bid their goodbyes, and as Jill turned away, all four at the table gave Ken a "we know what you've been up to" look. Linda scowled as Tierney flashed Ken the thumbs-up sign.

Ken and Jill held hands all the way back to Minnich Hall. Their conversation shifted from the party the night before to more bits and pieces on their families back home to how beautiful the morning was.

After walking Jill up the stairs to her room, Ken kissed her in the quiet hallway.

"The weekend is young," she said, leaning back against her door. "Have any plans?"

"After my run I'm supposed to help Tom, Chloe and some of their housemates paint the outside of the Aegean Stables," he said. "Their landlord agreed to give them a month's rent if they painted the outside of the building, and another free month when they do the inside.

"We're going to paint until dark, then send out for pizza and hang out there. Why don't you come by whenever you get done saving the Miami River?"

"I might do that," Jill said, and she nearly fell backward as the door opened from the inside.

"Well, look who's here, Kaaren," Chris said with a sly grin. "It's Jill and her *friend*, Ken.

"I'm glad you're finally home," she continued. "We were just on our way to the campus police with your photo and a description of what you were wearing when you disappeared last night."

"Your concern touches me deeply," Jill countered, and her hair brushed Ken's cheek as she turned to enter the doorway. "But you knew Emily was covering for me . . . I just had to help Ken with a project," she explained, shooting him a smile.

"Must've been one exhausting *project*," Kaaren said.

"Give us a second," Jill answered.

Stepping back into the hall, she pulled the door shut behind her. "It was one project I'll never forget," Ken said as they embraced. A short kiss later he turned, walked to the stairwell and stopped.

"You don't know how much I needed to meet you, especially now," he said. "Maybe next time I can tell you a little more about what's been going on with me, and I'd like to know a lot more about you."

Jill smiled as Ken opened the stairwell door. "Oh yeah," he said in afterthought. "Thanks for bringing me into the BOZOs . . . And for helping me with that 'project.'"

"It was my pleasure," Jill said with a wave, and she watched as the door hissed closed behind him.

For awhile, Ken felt almost as if he could be free of the haunting discovery back home. But the liberating joy that Jill had brought him was drowned by a wave of realization. No matter how great things went with Jill, no matter how well or badly anything else in his life fared, the dark, yawning emptiness of that room would plague his heart and mind.

He could lose himself for a while in Jill, or a long run, the pages of a textbook, or a party. But the room would always reemerge to prod him like the missing dot to an immense question mark.

He wished he hadn't found it.

The early time combined with scattered clouds would mean cool running conditions for the next hour or so, and a light western breeze had stirred since he and Jill left his apartment.

Walking back onto his buildings' parking lot, Ken noticed that the breakfast group was gone, but Rochelle and Diane were already sunning on the rear lawn. He wondered how many bikinis Rochelle had, since the red one she wore the previous day had been replaced by another of blue-green plaid. She was busy applying suntan oil to Diane's back, and neither noticed as Ken slipped inside the building.

After changing into his running gear, Ken took a quart of ice water from the refrigerator and opted for a timed run rather than a set distance. He decided to see how far east he could run along State Road 73 in one hour, then try to cover the distance back in the same amount of time.

The workout would help him focus on both speed and distance, and with the Detroit Free Press Marathon just over two months away, he felt a need to start concentrating on both. Up until now his workouts had alternated between long road runs and short speedwork on the high school track.

If Ken drank the whole quart of water, he would be hydrated enough for the first five or six miles. He didn't know of any public water sources along that route, and he couldn't count on coming upon any lawn sprinklers or friendly car-washers, so he filled two plastic bottles from the tap and loaded them into his runner's belt.

After a toilet stop Ken dropped the water belt on his desk, sprawled on the carpet to stretch and a knock came at the door.

He rose with a grunt, twisted the doorknob and his eyes widened as the door swung open.

"Well good morning, Ken. I'll bet you didn't expect to see me this soon!"

Paul Cody reached out to shake Ken's hand, and he was speechless as the smiling man in the blue suit offered him a small package with the other.

"Chocolate chip," Cody said as Ken took the white cardboard box. "Jeanette sent them along with her love."

"I don't believe this," Ken said as he backed up for Cody to enter. "I felt like I was looking at a ghost . . . . It seems like we just hung up from our interstate phone conversation."

"I know," Cody said, sitting on the edge of Ken's unmade sofa bed. "I couldn't believe it myself; a real stroke of good luck. I told you I was traveling over the coming week," he continued. "Well, I was supposed to fly out tomorrow for Denver on a flight from Grand Rapids with a change of planes in Detroit. But I called and found out that if I left this morning instead, I could get a stopover in Cincinnati, so I rented a car and here I am.

"It's not much time," he went on. "But you sounded like whatever was on your mind was important, and I figured we could discuss it over a bite to eat—on me."

"You didn't have to do that," Ken said, feeling humbled by all the trouble the old family friend had gone through for him. "I mean, you went so far out of your way, and I really could've waited until next week . . ."

"Nonsense," Cody said, eyeing the pile of books on Ken's desk. "It looks like you're the busy one."

"Now *that's* nonsense," Ken countered, and they both laughed.

"Looks like I caught you heading out for a run," Cody said.

"Yeah, but that's okay. I can go later. Have you had breakfast?"

"Just coffee and a Danish on the plane, and more coffee on the drive here," Cody answered.

"Let me change and I'll buy you breakfast uptown," Ken said. He grabbed an armload of clothes and headed for the bathroom.

"Only if I buy," Cody said. "And we can talk about that surprise you were telling me about last night."

Ken closed the bathroom door and wished he could just stay there until Cody left. *Damn!* he thought as he pulled on his pants. *How did I get into this? What am I going to tell this guy? . . . 'Thanks for the cookies and scrambled eggs . . . You wouldn't know anything about a small, hidden room in my family's basement, would you?'*

Ken thought he would have at least a week to figure out how to put the question to Cody, and whether or not he wanted to actually take him to the hidden room.

But now, with no preparation, he would have only the time between a quick clothing change and the short drive to Bailey's Diner to put together some kind of sane-sounding delivery.

Emerging in blue jeans and a plain white T-shirt, Ken slipped on his shoes and joined Cody, who was already holding the front door for him.

"When do you have to be back for your flight out of Cincinnati?" Ken asked as they got into Cody's rental car.

That's the only bad thing," Cody said, seat belts sliding into place as he turned the key. "I fly out at three, so I should leave here by one."

Not yet 10 a.m., that sounded like more than enough time to Ken, and he just hoped he could maneuver for three hours without sounding or seeming crazy.

"Oh, wait a second. I forgot something," Ken said, and he dashed back to his apartment.

Returning empty-handed, Ken got into the waiting Buick Regal and directed Cody to Bailey's.

"Oxford looks like a great little town," Cody said as they walked from the car to the diner. "I love that old water tower on the town square."

"Yeah," Ken responded as they sat in a corner booth. "Even though it's in the center of town, climbers still manage to give it a pretty good dose of graffiti each year."

Cody ordered steak and eggs and urged Ken to do the same. But he declined, opting instead for only black coffee.

"I have my long run of the week today, and I can't eat anything this soon before," he explained. "I'm training for the Detroit Free Press Marathon."

"I'm glad to see you're still running," Cody said as their coffee arrived. "Whenever I see a runner it reminds me of you and your dad, racing around the neighborhood together. Are you on Miami's track or cross country team?"

"No. I thought about it, but I'd rather run for fun, when and how I want to," Ken said. "Classes and study bring enough structure to my schedule. I prefer to race on my own clock and calendar. I get enough competition with the occasional 5 or 10-K road race, and besides the Freep in the fall, I try to run another marathon somewhere each spring. Last March I did the Los Angeles Marathon with a three-hour-two-minute time that qualified me for the Boston Marathon next March."

"Not too shabby," Cody said, and he stretched his arms behind him along the top of the booth. "I'm kind of anxious to hear more on what you called me about," he said. "Whatever you," he hesitated, "came across . . . Well, it sounds like it really surprised you."

"Yeah," Ken said. "Yeah, it did."

The middle-aged, cheerful waitress brought Cody's food, and he was careful to pick up and pocket the check before touching his knife and fork.

"Are you sure you don't want a good breakfast?" Cody asked.

"It does look tempting," Ken said, "but I gotta do that long run. I have plans for tonight, so it can't wait.

"I've hooked up with a group from the Miami Running Club who want to make the trip to the Free Press marathon together in a van owned by one of the track coaches. And he has a buddy in Detroit, at Wayne State University, who's setting us up with overnight dorm space."

"Sounds like a good time," Cody said, and he moved his empty coffee cup to the edge of the table for a refill. He continued to talk as he shook ketchup onto his hash browns.

"You know, Ken, every time I see someone running through the neighborhood or my car gets stopped in traffic for runners in a road race, I still look to see if I can find you and, by force of habit, sometimes I'll imagine I see your dad. It was always uplifting to see you two running together, even if it did make me feel all the more like a couch potato."

"Yeah," Ken reflected. "He was my best friend."

"I know," Cody said, and he stopped slicing his steak to look Ken in the eye.

"What's wrong, Ken?"

Ken leaned back against the padded plastic booth and watched as an Oxford police car pull over an old couple whose van had rolled through a red light.

Okay, Ken thought as he looked into his chipped cup. *Here goes.*

He leaned forward and pulled a Polaroid print from his back pocket. It was what he had dashed back to his apartment for from Cody's car. Ken set it on the table and slid it next to Cody's plate.

"What's this?" Cody asked. He took his napkin to his mouth with one hand as he reached into his suit for his reading glasses with the other. His piercing eyes narrowed as he studied the picture. After several seconds he returned it to the table.

"What is it?" he asked again.

"I was hoping you might know," Ken said. "I was looking through one of dad's old books and it fell out of the pages. There were several more, apparently of the same room, tucked inside the back cover. I thought maybe they were of someplace where you guys had worked, or something like that."

"I have no idea what it is," Cody said, again picking up and studying the photograph.

"Just a desk in a bare room . . . where some kind of electronic equipment was apparently yanked out . . . Are you sure this was your dad's?" he asked, holding the picture up between them.

"The book was his . . . some computer technology title . . . and they were stuck inside. I was looking through some of dad's old stuff, picked the book up out of curiosity and found the pictures . . . I suppose someone else could have put them there, but it's not the kind of book mom, Marg or I would read. And since the title dealt with dad's field of work I figured maybe you, as a colleague . . ."

"No," Cody interrupted. "I don't have a clue. Could they be from one of his other friends' hunting camps or something? That might account for the stark, no-frills cement block construction."

"Then why would it have a desk . . . and no windows?" Ken pressed.

"I don't know. But this photo looks pretty new. Couldn't your mom or Marg or someone your dad had loaned the book to have slipped the photos inside and forgot them?"

"It is in good condition, but I attributed that to its being pressed tight between the pages, away from light and air," Ken countered. He felt almost smug about how well his hastily fabricated story was holding up.

"Well I'll tell you what, Ken. I'm going to see a few of the guys at work who knew your dad, and one of them might know. Why don't I show it to them?"

Before Ken could answer, Cody had slipped the Polaroid into his coat pocket along with his glasses.

"Yeah, sure. Thanks," Ken said, and he felt a wave of cold, electric anxiety wash through him. Did that photo have a small date stamp, lot number or other marking he hadn't noticed that could prove it was recently shot?

"I'd appreciate your returning it . . . having belonged to dad and all . . ."

"Of course, Ken, as soon as the guys have a look."

"Thanks, Mr. Cody," Ken said. "Just mail it back to me whenever you've finished . . . I appreciate it . . . I'm just curious to know what kind of place dad would think enough of to keep several pictures of it," he once again lied.

What really burned inside Ken at the moment was an intense desire to go home to the other Polaroids and see if they bore any tell-tale manufacturer's markings. If there were, he thought, he could cook up some excuse like discovering that the book had been borrowed just before his father's death, or that it was from a box of books his mother had recently bought at a garage sale.

"I guess I still don't understand, Ken," Cody's voice was soft but insistent. "Why would a photograph like this unsettle you so?"

"I'm not sure myself, Ken said. He drew from his deeper, genuine uncertainty to give substance to his explanation.

"It's just that when it fell into my lap, it seemed so . . . *weird*, so unlike anyplace I've ever seen or heard of. It must have meant something to my father; otherwise, why the pictures? Maybe I called you because I was hoping the you could tell me something about the picture that could share something of importance from my dad's life.

"I guess it's the starkness, the anonymity, the mystery," he continued. "It's almost like it's a picture of *nowhere* . . . like a frame hanging somewhere with nothing inside."

Cody pulled the photo out to look at it again, studying it at arm's length.

"Well, Ken," Knoblock Systems is a big outfit, but I've never seen anything there resembling this—at headquarters in Baltimore, back in Grand Rapids or any of the other branches I've been to.

"It almost looks like a bomb shelter or a bunker of some sort," Cody said. His forehead creased deeply as his squint seemed to sear through the print. "Could it be from his old army days?"

"Yeah, that's possible. It does have that sterile, military look. Too bad I don't know any of his old army buddies."

"Maybe if no one from work recognizes it, I can help you locate somebody from his old unit," Cody suggested, and again he pocketed the picture.

"Oh, you wouldn't have to take that kind of time or effort," Ken said. You have better things to do. Besides, I'm sure it's not that important."

"No problem," Cody said as he returned to eating his steak and eggs. "Now you've got me curious," he said with a smile. "We'll get to the bottom of this."

Ken wanted to be consoled by the understanding and cooperation extended by Cody. But several things stood in the way.

The picture in Cody's pocket could contradict Ken's story if it proved to be recent. Even if Cody accepted it as old and well-preserved, Ken had not offered a truly sound reason why it should have unsettled him enough to call Cody about it.

"I guess I just felt it was something from my dad's past I wanted to somehow share, to take part in," Ken said with a sigh of false resignation. "That's why I was going through his books and things . . . sort of reminiscing, taking a stroll down memory lane. And when I came across something I didn't recognize, I guess I felt there was something missing, that I had been left out of something in dad's life."

"I can understand that," Cody said. "He was taken too soon. You . . . ," he hesitated, "we . . . should have had him with us much longer."

The silence that followed seemed more comfortable to Ken as both reflected on the loss of his father. Ken was sure the sentimental curiosity excuse would explain his interest in the pictures.

It was almost noon, and the cafe began to fill with a noisy lunch crowd.

"I could use a walk after that meal," Cody said. "Do you have time to give me a quick tour of the campus before I catch my flight out?"

"Sure," Ken said, and he wasn't allowed to leave the tip as Cody lay several dollar bills on the table.

"I told you this was on me," he said, and after paying the cashier he followed Ken out the door onto High Street.

Their conversation drifted from Ken's classes to fraternity life (Cody was a Sigma Chi) to whom Ken was dating to Cody's own days at the University of Illinois.

By the time they made their ranging loop south to the Western Campus and back to the Buick it was 12:40.

"Just enough time to drop you off at your apartment and head back to the airport," Cody said, checking his watch.

Moments later they wheeled up to Heather Lane Apartments, and Cody sat with the engine running as he reached for Ken's hand.

"It was a quick visit, but I'm glad we reconnected," Cody said as they shook hands.

"I really appreciate your time and your concern," Ken said. "You really didn't have to . . ."

"I know, I know," Cody said as he returned his grip to the steering wheel. "When someone you love is gone, and their memory is all you have, little things can become enormous. Anything unfamiliar to that past relationship can be . . . unsettling.

"Don't let insecurity threaten or distort what you know you shared with your father."

"Thanks," Ken said, and he exited the car. "Thanks a lot."

"I'll be in touch."

There came a quick, reassuring wave from the driver and the flash of brake lights as the Buick turned toward Main Street, and Ken was alone.

He didn't know why, but he didn't want to return to his apartment—not right away. Instead he headed back up Heather Lane and along the short block past several student apartment houses towards Stewart Middle School. Realizing he had no destination, he stopped and sat on one of the playground swings that hung motionless in the midday calm. A lot had just happened, and Ken sat bent over, elbows on his knees as he stared at the brown earthen rut beneath the swing.

Yes, he thought, *a lot had happened.* But just what? This, he deduced, was where he had to do his best to put his imagination into neutral and process the new developments as objectively as possible. Until he did that, speculation about anything else had too much potential to mislead, embarrass or get him into some kind of trouble.

A group of boys with baseball gear crossed College Avenue on their way to the school's ball field, and Ken moved to the aluminum bleachers to watch as they chose sides and began play.

A fat, red-haired boy of about twelve strained as he took the catcher's stance. Ken felt sorry for him and hoped his team would win.

The game stopped as the sound of a long, screaming skid, followed by a grinding crash, came from about a block away, and the kids dropped their equipment as they scrambled to investigate.

"Hey mister, will you watch our stuff a coupla minutes?" the pitcher yelled.

"Sure, no problem," Ken said, and they were gone.

He leaned back and looked at the baseball on the mound, the bats and gloves strewn around the chain-link backstop.

Two minutes ago the field was abuzz with the beginnings of a sandlot battle. Twenty minutes earlier Ken was tap dancing a tightrope between what he wanted to tell Cody and what he felt safe enough to share.

The boys would soon return to their game. Ken pondered his next move in learning more about the hidden room, possible connections between it and his father's job, and whether either or both pointed to another reason for his father's "random" murder.

The first thing to do would be to look at those other Polaroids to see if they had any dates, serial or lot numbers on them, Ken thought. Then he would force himself to take his mind off the matter as best he could during his long run out State Route 73 and back.

Ken was swatting at a cloud of gnats when the ballplayers returned.

"Thanks for watching our stuff," the sandy-haired pitcher shouted as they retook their positions. "Some old man and old lady in a van crashed into a pizza man. Nobody got hurt, though."

"Thanks for the news report," Ken said, and he wondered if it was the same old couple he saw being ticketed earlier that day.

"Have fun, guys," Ken said, and the kids waved as he left.

Back in his apartment, Ken pulled the rest of the Polaroids from his desk drawer. He was relieved to see no telltale printing of any kind on them, front or back.

Midway into replacing them he stopped. Whether it stemmed from paranoia or just being careful, he thought it would hurt nothing to find a place outside his apartment to keep the photos. In the meantime, he pulled up a loose carpet corner and slid them underneath. *They'll be okay there for now,* he thought.

Ken threw on the running gear he had ready when Cody showed up earlier, and after a quick, long drink of water he was on his way. Cutting through the center of campus, Ken passed Shideler Hall, crossed Patterson Avenue and strode east on Route 73.

The marching band practiced on Cook Field as he ran by on the two-lane blacktop. And after passing Miami's riding stables and crossing Four Mile Creek, he was officially out of Oxford.

Ken spent most of his mental energy watching for traffic or dogs as he ran on the shoulder of the westbound lane, and he still felt strong when his watch alarm signaled that an hour had passed.

Turning, he pulled a water bottle from his belt and kept running as he drained and replaced it.

It was curious, Ken thought, that while Cody's unannounced visit had somewhat panicked him, it had also left him more mentally focused and with an increased sense of control. He had time to process what had gone on in their meeting and felt sure he hadn't made any blunders. He did wish he hadn't let Cody keep the photo. But it didn't show anything that wasn't pictured on any of the several he had kept.

After his run, Ken would go to Tom and Chloe's and help paint their house and then maybe do something with Jill, if she showed up.

Ken wished he'd worn his shades as he ran into the sun on his return, and the marching band was gone as he passed Cook Field.

The alarm again sounded from his wrist, and Ken felt pretty good about making all but the last mile or so back within the same time the hard outbound run had taken. He made up for the return deficit by nearly doubling his pace through campus and back to his apartment. He arrived just after 5 p.m.

"I didn't forget you guys. I had a surprise house guest and the time ran away from me," Ken told Chloe on his kitchen phone. "I'll be there in a half hour. I just need to shower and get dressed."

"Okay," Chloe said, "but bringing something from the Party Store would go a long way in proving your remorse."

"Hey, listen, it doesn't get dark until after nine, so I can still put in a few good hours with a brush."

"We saved the top part of the house just for you," she responded. "I don't want to say our ladder sucks, but how well do you bounce?"

"Very funny," Ken said. "You know I fear nothing . . . But just in case, I will pick up some of that liquid courage from the Party Store."

"Thirty minutes, not more!" Chloe admonished.

"I'm on my way," Ken assured, and he hung up.

There was only one thing he felt there was left to do before ending the day. Ken was concerned that Cody or his wife might say something to his mother about his calling them, or about Cody's visit. He felt he had successfully deflected his mother's suspicions the weekend he found the room, but a phone call or visit from one or both of the Codys could revive her concerns about what he had been up to during his last trip home.

The phone rang several times before Ken's mother answered.

"Hi, mom. How's it goin' up there?"

"Oh, pretty much the same, just watching TV and getting ready to go play bridge with the Thompsons and a few other friends. What's up with you? Is everything all right down there?"

"Yeah, fine," Ken said. "I was just thinking of you and decided to check in."

"I hope your studies are off to a good start. You know, Marg and Janice got their paperwork pushed through, and I'm helping them move into her house next weekend. If you're not busy, I'm sure they could use your help and we'd all appreciate seeing you again. I know you *always* enjoy seeing *Miss Copley*," she teased.

"I'd love to help you out and see Marg's new place, *and Miss Copley*," he replied. "But I'm committed to joining a group of friends for a concert in Detroit. The plans are all made."

"Well, after she's moved in maybe you can make it to her housewarming. Marg hasn't scheduled it, but I'm sure she'll need at least two or three weeks to settle in first."

"Yeah," Ken said. "That would be fun." He thought a moment and continued. "So you're going over to the Thompsons . . . How are they?"

"Pretty good, I guess. Our bridge club circulates its meetings between their place, ours, and the dozen or so others in the group."

"Are the Cody's in the bridge club?" he asked.

"No, not for the past few years. Why do you ask?"

"Well, remember that picture I showed you at last week's brunch?" He didn't wait for her reply. "I called to ask Mr. Cody if he could help me identify it. I figured maybe it was from an old hunting camp they used or something," Ken lied. "And son-of-a-gun if he didn't show up here today for a quick visit between flights at Cincinnati International."

"You're kidding!"

"No. It was real nice. Turns out he didn't know what the picture was of either, but he took me to breakfast and I showed him around the campus. We had a good visit."

"Well, I haven't seen Paul or Jeanette in ages," Mrs. Perry said. "How are they doing?"

"All right, I guess. He's still working hard for old Knoblock, and he said Mrs. Cody is fine, too."

"Well I'm glad you told me. I hope you gave them my best."

"Of course," Ken said. "Well, I wish I could talk longer, but I have to go help some friends paint their house. Enjoy your cards, and DON'T CHEAT!"

"Fifty million comedians in the world and I have to give birth to another!" she groaned. "I love you, son."

"I love you too, mom," Ken answered, and they hung up.

He watched the drapes stir at the opened living room windows. Ken felt confident that the call he had just made had prepared his mother for any mention Paul Cody or his wife might make to her about the call he had made to the Codys in Grand Rapids, or of Paul's visit to Ken in Oxford.

It took just over a half hour for Ken to shower, throw on an old shirt and jeans, pick up a case of Little Kings at the Party Store and appear at the Aegean Stables. A small army of friends had joined Tom and his housemates in applying white paint and green trim to the aging three-story structure. Plastic plates and cups from a picnic lunch overflowed a trash can, and a clutch of paper towels fluttered from where they clung to a puddle of paint on the lawn.

"I don't know what you were so concerned about," Ken said as he sat the beer next to where Chloe was painting on the porch. "You already have enough people here to coat the Golden Gate Bridge."

A damp rag smelling of turpentine landed on Ken's shoulder, followed by a shout from atop a nearby ladder.

"Hey, you lazy bastard! I said we were gonna start at 9 a.m., *not p.m.*," Tom drawled over his dripping brush. "Where the hell have you been, working on another *project*?"

"You're lucky to have enough friends to help you paint a bird house," Ken called as he threw the rag back. "And even those of us who claim to like you have other things we sometimes have to tend to. I'll have you know I was visited by an out-of-town brunch guest."

"No shit," Tom said as he dabbed at a window shutter. "Your probation officer?"

"Close," Ken answered. "A friend of the family. He said he was just passing through, but I think my mom hired him to make sure I'm actually a student here."

"Well don't just stand there. Grab a brush and have at it! Better yet, hand me one of those Little Kings, then grab a brush."

Ken threw Tom a bottle, picked up an unattended brush, poured some paint into a coffee can and took a position near Chloe and Annette on the old building's wide, wrap-around porch.

"I thought maybe you'd bring Jill," Chloe said.

"She took her floor from Minnich Hall to the river clean-up, but she told me she might stop by later."

"Who was your visitor?" Annette asked. Ken wondered what it was about dressing-down that often made some women all the more attractive. Already a striking beauty, something about Annette's loosely gathered blonde mane, paint-smeared and spattered shorts, T-shirt and cheap canvas tennis shoes heightened her already considerable appeal.

"It was a friend of my dad's, from Grand Rapids," Ken said. "I called him recently to ask a question and he decided to stop by and say hello between flights on a business trip. He had a stopover at Cincinnati International."

"What a nice thing to do," she cooed.

"Yeah. I didn't even know he was coming. He surprised me, just showed up at my door this morning."

"No kidding? That's kind of weird," Chloe said as she dragged her drop cloth to another section of the porch. "I mean, do you really want people dropping in like that? Don't you like some notice?"

No shit! Ken thought before answering.

"Like I said, it was during a break in his flight from Michigan to Denver. I think any inconvenience to me was more than offset by what he went through to rent a car and drive it to and from Oxford in time for his flight out.

"He left at about one, then I did a run I had planned for this morning."

Conversation between Ken, Chloe and Annette faded as they painted their way in different directions, and soon Ken was finding relaxation in the simple brush strokes, smoothing fresh white paint over the dull, faded blue.

The number of painters slowly grew as dusk descended, and by the time they had to stop due to darkness, the transition from house-painting to house party was seamless. Beer, pizza and napkins replaced paint brushes and rags, but the heavy smell of latex paint and turpentine hung in the air.

Ken helped Tom carry the last of the painting supplies and drop cloths into a shed behind the house and returned in time to see Jill, Chris and Kaaren arrive. Kaaren carried a grocery sack with a large bag of cheese curls sticking out the top.

"We knew you'd need good, wholesome nourishment after a long day's work," Kaaren said, setting the bag on the porch steps. "Cheetos, Doritos, Fritos, Tostitos . . . If it ends in O's, we've got it," Chris said, emptying the bag item by item. She pulled a six-pack of beer from the bottom and popped one open.

"*Schlitz?*" Tom said with a groan. "My god, girl, did you find that during the river clean-up?"

"The guy Chris met at Rocky Horror left it in our refrigerator," Jill explained. "I told him I didn't know what made me madder, the fact that he brought alcohol into the dorm or that it was such awful stuff."

"He has other, more redeeming qualities," Chris said with a smile.

"So why didn't you bring him along?" Ken asked. "Is he under house arrest or something?"

"Worse," Chris said. "Mono. He's sick as a dog. So far, other than the river clean-up, my weekend's been spent playing nurse and watching him sleep."

"Sounds like you're ready for marriage," Tom said as he tore open a bag of chips. "That's what my mom's been doing for the past 20 years—watching dad sleep on the couch."

Conversation shifted to the BOZO party of the night before, and Chloe asked if Ken planned to go on the road trip to the Who concert that weekend.

"Sure he is," Tom said. "And don't try to back out on me . . . They were down to the last 10 tickets last week when I picked one up for you along with mine and Chloe's."

"Don't worry, I plan on going," Ken said. "But a hundred bucks?"

"Hey," Tom answered, "that includes the concert ticket, bus transportation to and from Detroit with a keg and munchies—all-inclusive, as we say in the travel industry. Come on . . . Jill's going. We're all going."

"Well it would have been nice if you'd checked with me first," Ken said. "I mean, $100 is a tidy chunk of change for a struggling student."

"Don't worry about it," Jill said, tossing him a bag of Fritos. "You'll never starve as long as you have us."

The stereo that had supplied music for the painters all day now served up the soundtrack for a subdued lazing away of what would probably be one of the few warm-weather weekend nights left for southwest Ohio. Soon the balmy evenings would give way to autumn chill, then culminate in the cold winters that alternated thick snow with freezing rains.

For now, though, Ken and Jill were comfortable as they found an empty corner on the old wooden porch.

"I see you lived through another 'long run,'" she said.

"And you the river clean-up . . . I guess that makes us both survivors," he answered, and with a clink of their Little Kings bottles they toasted the accomplishment.

"Actually, the run was the easy part."

"Is Chloe that hard a taskmaster?" Jill asked.

"No, I mean before the painting," Ken explained. "When I returned from walking you home one of my dad's old friends surprised me with a visit."

"Uh oh," Jill moaned. "Nothing worse than having to entertain a friend of the folks. Not too much of a wet blanket, I hope."

"No. Actually, he's a good old friend of the family, and we've always gotten along well, although I hadn't seen him for over a year. "But he didn't just show up without reason. I recently called him for something," Ken said, remaining vague. "Then, while he was between flights in Cincinnati he decided to make a side trip here to see if he could help me out."

"Sounds like a nice guy, willing to go out of his way like that and all," Jill said. "What made the experience uncomfortable?"

It was happening again. Still unable to let go of his secret, Ken would have to maneuver around it. Or would he? With each meeting he trusted Jill more. But it was more than that. After all, he trusted his mother and sister, of course, and Tom was totally trustworthy, as were Chloe, Lyttle and all of his friends.

The problem was that Ken didn't know how to share with others what he didn't understand himself, or what repercussions that could bring down on them . . .

But the meeting with Cody had to have brought him at least a little closer to some degree of understanding, if not a definitive answer.

"Remember my sharing with you that I'm trying to understand something?"

Jill nodded.

"Well," he hesitated, "it has to do with that. I called him because I felt he might be able to help me understand something a little more clearly, but I didn't go into details.

"When he showed up at my doorstep I wasn't ready to talk it out, and I was in kind of a delicate situation, trying to tell him what I needed to without misspeaking myself or talking too much.

"I'm sorry if this is confusing or vague, I just can't help it . . . I'm doing my best."

"I can see that," Jill said. "So how did it all come out?"

"I think it went well. We agreed to keep in touch . . . He's checking into something for me."

A pizza delivery car pulled up to the curb and was met with whoops from the group.

"Only the very best for my people," Tom said as he paid for five large pizzas. "*And* one helluva lot cheaper than paying professional painters!"

Jill and Ken were forced away as the porch became an impromptu pizzeria. They picked a couple of slices from the boxes Chloe had opened on a porch swing-turned picnic table, grabbed their drinks and moved to a bench at the bus stop in front of the house.

The change in setting offered Ken the perfect opportunity to switch their topic of discussion, as well.

"So, did you and your ladies restore the Miami River to its primordial splendor?"

"I don't know about that, but it's shy about a ton of fast food trash, bottles and cans, old tires and other debris that called it home this morning. We even found a Kroger shopping cart, in the *middle* of the river, no less than five miles from the store!

"The best part was watching Kaaren get attacked by a goose," Jill said with a laugh. "There was an old plastic antifreeze bottle stuck in the brush at the shore and it must have been near the bird's nest or something, because it wouldn't budge for Kaaren to pass.

"I didn't think those things could move so fast. Apparently, neither did Kaaren, because it beaked her ass pretty good several times as she tried to scramble up the bank to safety. Between all the honking and screaming, I nearly wet my pants!"

There was a long pause as Ken and Jill laughed. Then Jill spoke again.

"You look tired," she told Ken. "That visit from your father's friend took a lot out of you, didn't it?"

"Maybe. But two hours of hard running, followed by at least that long in grueling house-painting may account for any shortage of energy, too."

Jill just smiled.

"All right," he conceded. "Even though it went well it *was* hard, stressful. But as I said, I'm doing my best."

Ken didn't know about Jill, but he was becoming increasingly aware that he apparently hadn't convinced himself that all stood so well after his meeting with Cody.

And what was Cody thinking about all this? What was he thinking about Ken? Did he think his old dead friend's son was going loony? Did Ken know something he shouldn't? Was it all really *nothing* at all?

So far, the secret Ken had discovered had been shared with only one other person, Cody, and only a small, anonymous portion of it, at that.

Was that good? Would the emotional or practical benefit of telling a trusted friend—Lyttle, Tom, or maybe Jill—outweigh any jeopardy the disclosure could bring upon any or all of them?

"Hey!" Jill said, snapping her fingers. "I'm over here."

"Sorry. I guess I'm more tired than I thought. I think I need to call it a night. I apologize if I'm a little out of it."

"That's okay. I'm going to hang out awhile and walk back to the dorm with Chris and Kaaren."

"What are you doing tomorrow?" Ken asked.

"I was thinking of riding my bike out to Hueston Woods for some reading by the water. Want to join me? You could borrow a bike at my dorm, and I plan on coming back in time for dinner at five. Then I need to spend a little time at King, return to the dorm for a floor meeting at eight, and get my laundry done before bed."

"You know, I am behind in my homework, and Hueston's a much better setting for that than my place or the library, so I will join you. You're sure you can get me a bike?"

"Yeah," Jill said. "We have one that someone left chained to the rack at Minnich last fall. When we returned this semester no one had claimed it, so we cut the lock, put on our own and keep it available for residents to sign out until the owner returns.

"I was planning to leave at about nine a.m. Is that a good time for you?"

It was, Ken said, and he promised to bring a Thermos of iced sun tea if she would pack sandwiches.

Their plans set, Ken offered his goodbyes to Tom and his housemates, then returned to Jill at the bench for a long goodnight kiss. She raised one leg slowly up the inside of Ken's thigh, and he tightened his hug enough to lift her out of the street light and into the shadow of a tree. Then, arms draped around Ken's shoulders and lips against his neck, she hung limp in his embrace.

"I'm surprised you didn't decline the bicycle idea and prefer to run alongside me again tomorrow," Jill said, their foreheads now touching.

"I considered it. But not only am I a great runner, I'm a fantastic sweater, as well. If I were to run to the park, the 'male scent' would probably drive you too mad to leave much concentration for the books."

"I think that's probably the most egotistical description of body odor that I've ever heard," Jill said.

"Exactly," Ken replied, and pecked her on the lips. "I'll see you at nine sharp, ready to roll."

One more long kiss later, he headed home.

CHAPTER TEN

Morning came early for Ken as the whistling of Linda's *New York Times* delivery man came through his open window.

Getting up to go to the bathroom he felt rested and ready to start the day, so he dressed and left for an early run. Covering his five-mile route across campus and back, the streets were empty and a heavy dew covered the grass like a sheet of silk.

The morning church traffic began to stir as Ken ran back home, and by the time he showered and fixed breakfast it was only 7:30.

As Ken buttered some toast, he remembered the reassuring feeling he had as he saw students walking to Kumler Chapel on the Western Campus and the Sesquicentennial Chapel on Spring Street. Couples and families in cars were destined for other churches in town and it gave him a sense of comfort to be reminded that a lot of people still answer a call to prayer, faith and goodness.

In a snap decision, Ken tore off the shorts and T-shirt he had put on for his trip to Hueston Woods with Jill. Instead he threw on khakis and a knit shirt, gulped down the rest of his coffee and left for the 8 a.m. Mass at St. Mary's. Located almost directly across the street from The Balcony, St. Mary's was the only Catholic church serving Oxford and its university population. Ken had been inside the old red brick church only a couple of times in his three years at Miami. The first was just to check it out when he arrived as a freshman, and the other was when he stopped in for prayer one year on his father's birthday.

Ken still went to Mass each Sunday with his mother during the summer and at Christmas, Easter and on other trips home.

He entered the church and sat in an empty pew near the rear of the scattered gathering just before Father Jack Kreiter began Mass. The group looked like they were almost all "townies," or local families, and that didn't surprise Ken since the hour was much too early for most self-respecting Catholic student weekend partyers. He knew that most of the practicing Catholic students came for the 10 a.m. and noon Masses offered for them in the student chapel on the second floor of the parish hall across the alley behind the main church and rectory.

As a couple of lay people Ken didn't recognize offered the Scripture readings, he again was swept with positive emotion, a feeling that he was in a good place, with good people, for a good reason. And he listened closely as Father Kreiter read the Gospel passage for that day, relating how Christ told his disciples to "Render unto Caesar what is Caesar's, and unto God what is God's."

"I've always felt this would be a more appropriate message on April 15," Father Kreiter said. "Of course, in rendering to God what is God's, we would be rendering everything, since everything we have comes from him. In paying taxes for the betterment of our community through their proper use, unless that violates God's law, we are rendering to God. As long as those taxes we give to the government build roads, help educate, empower and raise up the poor and suffering in our midst, it would be a sin not to render unto Caesar.

"But if Caesar oppresses the people of his own or another land, bloats with corruption, injustice, arrogance or any other evil, then we serve God by rejecting Caesar.

"Let us all thank God that we live in a land which, although far from perfect, allows us to be free and in a position to help bring or preserve freedom for others less blessed.

"Inevitably, I'm going to make somebody angry if I preach on politics," the young priest said, looking up and pushing his glasses back with one finger. "So let me conclude with one irrefutable point—to us Catholics, anyway.

"Ultimately, our faith, our hope, our salvation rest in God and are brought to us in and through his son, Jesus Christ. When you or I die, no matter what our bumper stickers say, we will no longer be Democrats, Republicans, liberals, conservatives, Greens, Whigs or whatever. What we decided, believed and *did* will go with us for judgment.

"In conclusion," Father Kreiter said with a sigh, "let's rise for prayer, thankful that our judge will be a loving God, and not Teddy Kennedy or Rush Limbaugh."

Several minutes later, despite having not gone to confession for over a year, Ken took communion with the rest of the group, returned to his pew, knelt, and closed his eyes in silence. He thought about the sermon he just heard and about how it related to what he was going through. Did his father work for Caesar? Was his father part of the good, faithful work of a government responding to the needs of its people? Or maybe he was a good man caught up in a bad situation? Or by a bad employer? Had Caesar killed his father?

Ken opened his eyes and looked at the tortured Christ on the cross above the altar. Jesus was given up by a friend and knew he was going to die. Was it the same for Ken's father? Was Detroit Walt Perry's Jerusalem? Was Cody, Truro, Knoblock Systems, or something they were all a part of his father's Judas?

Or was he just the unfortunate target of a random act, the same way that God "causes the rain to fall upon the just and the unjust?"

For most in that small church, Father Kreiter's sermon would probably stay with them about as far as the parking lot. For Ken, it had become input for a mental program that could spin on forever.

Leaving the church at 8:45, Ken used a pay phone at the Campus Center store next door to let Jill know he would be a little late. He hurried home, changed clothes, packed his books and tea and arrived at her room in Minnich at 9:20.

"I'm sorry I'm late," Ken said as Jill opened her door, and she leaned forward in mid-sentence to give him a peck on the lips.

"Mmm," he said. "Glad to see you're the forgiving type."

"Don't take it for granted," she answered, and turned for her backpack.

After a quick pre-flight checkup that included adjustment of the borrowed 10-speed's handlebars and seat, Ken fell in behind Jill for their pedal to Hueston Woods. The morning traffic had become busier as they rode single file through Oxford, remaining silent until they were out of town and past the farmhouse with the yapping dogs.

"You'd think that by now somebody would have run down those obnoxious bastards," Ken said as the barking faded behind them.

"I don't think they go after anything motorized," Jill said. "Just live prey."

"Maybe so, but one of these days they're going to take off after the wrong runner and get a Nike enema."

Huge white cumulus clouds sailed overhead as they rode into the park and past the camping and picnic areas and down to the beach parking lot. They locked their bikes to a rack by the rest rooms and walked to the wooden docks by the boat ramp and swimming area.

Ken and Jill picked a deserted dock near the end of the pier, walked about twenty feet to its end and dropped their packs on the brown, weathered planks. The dock gently bobbed as floats kept it atop the water, and it rose and fell with the wakes of passing boats. Some hauled fishermen, others pulled water-skiers, and Miami's sailing club was getting familiar with several new skiffs in the light breeze.

There was a line of cars and trucks waiting to use the boat launch, and the beach was just as busy as it was the day Ken and Jill met. But they were far enough away from the noise to concentrate on their reading.

Ken pulled two cups and a Thermos from his pack and Jill spread a blanket, sat, put on her sunglasses and opened a copy of Cosmopolitan.

"You came out here to study Cosmo?" Ken asked, handing her a cup of tea.

"Of course not," she said, waving a textbook she pulled from her pack. "It's just easier to study if you kind of 'ease into it.'"

Jill reached back into her bag, pulled out some sunscreen and handed it to Ken. "Don't miss anyplace," she said as she pulled off her T-shirt to expose a red bikini top. "I burn easily."

"I can see why," Ken replied. "I'm getting hot just sitting next to you."

Standing, she kicked off her cutoff shorts to reveal the bottom half of the suit, then reached down and pulled Ken's T-shirt over his head.

"Before this goes any further, I think I should tell you I'm a virgin," he said, batting his eyes.

"If that's true, your evil twin or alter ego must really know how to show a girl a good time," she answered, taking back the bottle.

"Here . . . I'll do you first, then you do me."

Ken sat facing the passing boats as Jill smoothed the cold lotion across his back and shoulders.

"Didn't you bring anything for swimming?"

"Sure," he replied. "I guess I'm just not as anxious to get out of my pants as you are."

"Yeah, right," she groaned, and dropped the lotion bottle in his lap. "My turn."

Jill went back to her magazine as Ken rubbed the lotion on her.

"What did you bring to work on, I mean besides me," she asked.

"A couple of things. A book on Chinese philosophy," he said, pulling Waley's text from his bag. "And a little German translation and some notes from a research project I'm working on." The green notebook that followed Waley's book from the bag held the "research project," bits and pieces on his quest to explain the hidden room. But it read more like a diary than study findings, detailing more about his questions and feelings than facts and answers.

The German seemed the best choice. The translation would be more engaging than simple reading. And he just didn't want to deal with any more tail-chasing speculation on the dark room. Not now, anyway.

Ken finished massaging the oil onto Jill's shoulders and lay with his head resting on the small of her back. Then, listening to the chattering birds and other beach and boating sounds, they went about their tasks silently until lunchtime.

Jill shared the fresh deli bread, cheese and Granny Smith apples she had brought and they washed it down with Ken's iced sun tea.

"Time for a swim," Jill said, and she slid feet-first from the end of the dock. "Oh, God, the water's perfect. Come on in."

"But what about cramps," Ken protested sarcastically. "My mom said to always wait an hour."

"Come on, 'Sonny,' let's live on the edge!"

They took a long swim, away from the beach crowd, laughing, splashing and holding hands as they floated side-by-side. Refreshed and energized by the cool water, they climbed back onto the dock and gathered their things. Leaving their packs with a cheerful old lady running the concession stand, they took a walk to dry off in the sun, first along the beach and then up a trail into the woods.

Coming upon a bright, grassy clearing, Jill sat with her back against an old oak tree and stretched her arms towards Ken.

He lowered into her embrace, his head on her breast, and together they looked for faces, animals and other shapes in the clouds.

Jill's top came off as their attention quickly moved from the imaginative to the amorous, but the mood was shattered with the sudden appearance of about a dozen Cub Scouts and their overweight Den Mother. Jill tied the strap on her bikini top as she and Ken rose together, and the Den Mother went slack-jawed, abruptly ending her field trip narrative.

"Me Tarzan, she Jill," Ken said. He then bent over, threw Jill over his shoulder and headed back down the path to the beach.

"Do you think we traumatized those poor children?" he asked as she waved the group goodbye.

"Nah," Jill answered. "A Scout is brave . . . But I'm not sure Momma Bear will ever be the same."

Back at the beach, Ken gave the woman at the concession stand a couple of dollars for watching their packs, and Jill talked him into another long, lazy swim back at the dock. They were several hundred feet from the mob of swimmers at the sandy beach, and the bathlike water and forest-scented breeze were enthralling, bringing them to a depth of relaxation Ken could not previously recall. Floating, turning, gently paddling and treading to keep their position in the water, the creaking wood of the dock, their breath and light splashes were all they heard.

"We have to leave here sooner or later," Jill moaned.

"Later," Ken said without opening his eyes.

"I have *got* to be back by dinner time."

"No way," Ken answered. "I'm staying forever. If the snack shop lady wasn't so nice we could kill her, hide the body and run it ourselves."

"Sounds like a fulfilling life," Jill said as she pushed his floating body toward the dock. "But I think our destiny lies elsewhere."

Ken boosted himself onto the end of the planks, pulled Jill up and they gathered their things for the ride back to town.

Back at Minnich Hall, Ken and Jill nosed their bikes into the rack and she gave him a quick kiss.

"I'd better get upstairs and drop this stuff off so I can join Chris and Kaaren in the dining hall," she said, darting for the entrance. "Thanks for a great day . . . Call me!"

Ken snapped the bike lock closed, picked up his pack and began his walk home. He went a couple of blocks out of his way so he could spend more time in the cool night creeping over the calm of dinnertime.

After a soup and sandwich supper with the evening news, he grabbed the same pack he had taken to the Hueston Woods and headed back to campus and King Library.

Phenomenology was proving to be a lot more challenging than Ken had imagined, so he appreciated that he had access to a study group outside of class time. Professor Jim Delacroix was an expert on the subject and congenial in his lecturing, even using humor from time to time. But he still spoke way above the heads of Ken and the rest of the dozen in the class.

The texts were not much help either, as Husserl's complex and stratospheric jargon-studded books read like a cross between calculus and Mandarin Chinese.

Ken exited an elevator at King's third floor and found nearly everyone from the class gathered around a table outside the study carrel of Mike Tatro.

"Glad you could make it, Ken," Tatro said as Ken pulled a chair up to the large oak table. As a graduate assistant in the Department of Religious Studies and an adept of phenomenology, Tatro had offered to lead the study group.

"Well, I guess we might as well start," the tall, thin and black-haired graduate assistant said. Rising from his place at the head of the table he backed up a couple of steps and leaned into the open doorway of his study carrel. The outside walls of the second and third floors of the library were lined with the small private study rooms which were provided for masters and doctoral candidates. No bigger than a walk-in closet, each came with a simple desk and chair, lamp, small bookcase against the outer wall, an air vent in the ceiling and heat vent near the floor. Depending on the occupant's creativity and emotional makeup the cubicles could range from sterile to crazy, claustrophobic to cozy. Tatro's fell somewhere in-between. A couple of World War I biplane models hung by fishing line from the ceiling, and photos of family, girl friends and his two Persian cats were taped to the cream-white wall over his desk. There was also a small electric pot to heat water for his stash of teas, which more than one visitor had mistaken for pot as they were

kept in baggies on the window sill. Tatro was grateful for the key
to his personal carrel, which was his base for reference work as he
prepared his master's thesis. Otherwise he would have to constantly
shuttle armloads of books to and from his apartment across town.

"Okay," he said, returning with a handful of papers. "Those of
you who weren't here last time should put your name and phone
number on this list," he said, handing it to Ken. "And these are
copies of an outline I did on the first week's lectures. I thought we
could each take turns preparing a summary of the previous week's
material and then spend these sessions discussing them."

The group agreed, and Ken was glad he had decided to join
them. The arcane language of phenomenology was hard enough to
digest with a clear mind, and given what Ken was going through,
the necessary concentration was nearly impossible. He found that
when he did open Husserl's "Cartesian Mediations: An Introduction
to Phenomenology," the sentences were so technically abstract and
long that he rarely got the message between the capital letter and
the period on the first try. While reading sections including "The
Ego as substrate of habitualities," and "The noematic-ontic mode of
givenness of the Other, as transcendental clue for the constitutional
theory of the experience of someone else," Ken had to dissect some
sentences word by word, as he did in his German translation.

"Does anybody feel like they really understand this shit?" Tatro
asked as he pulled a metal tea ball from his steaming mug.

"Thank God," one of the less talkative women from the class
responded. "I was afraid I was the only one not getting it."

"If anyone here is 'getting it,' please step forward and take the
bridge now," Tatro said. The group offered a collective laugh of
relief, reassured that they were hoeing a tough intellectual row
together.

"Barring the appearance of a Phenomenology 101 Messiah to
lead us, I will ask you all to join me at the top of handout page
one," Tatro instructed.

"Roman numeral one: 'What is phenomenology?' Any takers?"

A shy-looking anthropology major found the definition
provided on page 19 of another of their texts, Maurice Nathanson's
"Edmund Husserl: Philosopher of Infinite Tasks."

"Phenomenology is a presuppositionless philosophy which
holds consciousness to be the matrix of all phenomena, considers

phenomena to be objects of intentional acts and treats them as essences, demands its own method, concerns itself with pre predicative experience, offers itself as the foundation of science, and comprises a philosophy of the life-world, a defense of Reason, and ultimately a critique of philosophy."

She closed the book, looked up, removed her glasses and just smiled.

"Okay," Tatro said. "Thanks, Sherry . . . So that should clear it up for everyone, right? I mean, on your next trip home, when your mom or little brother asks you what 'that book' is about," he continued, raising "Cartesian Meditations" overhead, "They'll understand when you tell them it's a yada-yada presuppositionless philosophy which holds consciousness to be the matrix of all yada-yada-yada . . . Right?

"My guess is that you're probably where I was, and the rest of my Intro to Phenom class was when we were halfway through our first semester . . . without a study group like this, in the unenviable position of spending hours of reading and note-taking and *still* not being quite sure what the hell the subject was really all about."

He stopped for a sip of tea. It was star anise, and the subtle licorice smell had a calming effect as it settled over the table.

"So let's start by putting what we're supposed to have learned into our own words. That way, we should learn a little more about what we don't understand, and understand a little more about what we already know."

Beginning with Sherry and going around the table, each in the group offered his or her understanding of phenomenology. They ranged from Sherry's comparison of it to "the way an unbiased person, like someone in a trance, would experience reality," to Tatro's more seasoned description. He explained that phenomenology investigates the ways consciousness processes what it perceives, and explores if and how it is possible to grasp experience as it truly is, free of all subjective bias and presupposition.

"You look across the room and see a guy sleeping over his homework," Tatro said, motioning toward his subject, a slack-jawed student draped in a chair.

"But how much of what we see is *as it is in itself*, and how much is what we imply per our intentionality, or what our mind tells us to see?"

"That's easy," Ken said. "It's a student, in the library, at night, looking somewhere between asleep and flat-line dead. It's got to be just as we see it."

A laugh went through the group, and Tatro conceded that it probably wasn't the best example.

"Okay," he tried again. "You're sitting on a beach and looking out over water. You see something and know it's a sailboat in the distance. Is it possible to take away all presuppositions of what you see? Is it possible to see the whiteness of the sails, the shape of the hull, and not take for granted that the other side of the boat is as you expect it to be . . . How do you really know what it is?"

"Because it's a freakin' sailboat," whined Jerry, one of the grad students.

"That's the point," Tatro said. "Based on all that you know, and have experienced, it must be a sailboat. What else could it be?"

"But how much of our experience at other levels is based on what we bring to the experience rather than what it *really* is? And how do we ever directly and fully experience something without coloring it by our presuppositions if we must use them to process experience?

"The bottom line is, do we know reality as it is in itself, or is it projected from within, as colored by our presuppositions, wishes, fears or desires?"

All were absorbed in the ensuing discussion until flashing overhead lights signaled that the library would close in fifteen minutes, at midnight.

"Oh, man, I forgot," Ken said, shoving his papers into his pack. "I have to hit the reference desk before it closes. I'll see you in class."

Flying down the stairs, Ken caught the reference librarian as she was locking her desk.

"I'm sorry, but I was wondering if a book I ordered came in. It's "The Puzzle Palace," by James Bamford . . . Have it?"

"Hold on," she said, and fingered the books on a nearby shelf. "Yes, here it is. Came in today." She looked at Ken's student ID and handed him the paperback. "You'd better hurry," she said. "It's just about time to lock up."

Ken hustled to the check-out desk, again presented his ID and stuffed the date-stamped book in his pack. He looked forward to reading what was the only popular book he could find on the super-secret National Security Agency. And although he had no reason to believe his father was involved with it or any such organization, the book might offer him clues to help account for the discovery he had made at home.

Back in his apartment, Ken settled into bed with Bamford's book. Flipping through the pages he read about the NSA's vast intelligence gathering system of satellites, computers, technological "platforms" or listening posts, code-makers and code-breakers. The appendix offered a list of acronyms in the super-spook lexicon: HUMINT, for human intelligence, ELINT, for electronic intelligence, SIGINT for signals intelligence, and even UGB for underground building.

Or maybe UGR for underground room? he wondered.

Ken found the book interesting, and some of its players had career and educational profiles similar to his father's. But there was nothing he could find that seemed to link his father's work, the secret room or anything else to anything in the book. Sure, he thought, his dad could have worked for an NSA cover company, but he could just as easily have been undercover with the FBI or CIA, or, for that matter, the KGB. He could have been a corporate spy for a rival computer firm, or he might even have had some deep dark personal interest that he entertained in the basement's veiled cubicle.

No, Ken thought as he dropped the closed book on his chest. This was not the secluded hideaway of a man harboring some lurid or deviant sin of the flesh or other excess. This wasn't an opium den or bondage pit. File cabinets, desks and electronic fittings aren't necessary for anything like that.

At 2:30 a.m. Ken rose, brushed his teeth and flopped back into bed. Turning off the lamp, he decided to return the book the next afternoon. Sure, it would be an interesting read, but it would not help him answer the question for which he ordered it, and he already had more than enough required reading for his classes.

No, the best way to find out more would be through talking with Cody. He was sure Cody knew something. He was too close to Ken's father at work and play not to have known something. Ken was disappointed that his father's old friend hadn't recognized the room from the photos, but he still had a gut feeling that Cody knew more than he had admitted.

The next morning, Ken rose early and vowed that he would spend that second full school week devoting himself to his studies, making up for the half-hearted start of the previous week.

During the break between his phenomenology and existentialism classes, he stopped by Jill's room. But she, Chris and Kaaren were all out.

"Jill," he scribbled on a notebook page, "I just stopped by to say hi between classes . . . Will call or stop by again later."

After hesitating, he decided against "love," as a sign-off, jotted "See you then," signed and folded the paper and slid it under the door.

Ken's existentialism class ended at 11:30 and he made it back to Minnich Hall just before noon. This time Jill's door was open.

"Anyone home?" he yelled as he leaned inside. The sheer, white cotton drapes stirred at an open window, and Ken moved inside to take a seat at Jill's desk.

A couple of minutes later Chris came in carrying a basket of fresh laundry.

"Hey, Ken, you're here just in time to help me fold sheets," she said, dumping the load onto her bed. "Jill got your note and said to tell you she can't make lunch because of a meeting with one of her profs. But she'll be here later this afternoon."

"Thanks," Ken said, standing to shoulder his backpack. "It's nothing important. I just wanted to say hello. I'll call later tonight, sometime after dinner."

"Sure, I'll be glad to tell her. But wait!" Chris said, blocking his exit. "I was serious. You've got to help me fold these."

She pulled two white, twin-size bed sheets from the pile of clothes. "Here, take two corners."

"No problem," Ken said, helping her first with the bottom, then the top sheet. "Need any help with those tricky-to-fold, lacy undies?"

"I'll tell Jill you stopped by and will call her," Chris said, shoving him out the still-open door.

Ken's afternoon developmental psych class went by quickly, and after dinner he fell asleep on his couch while watching the news. Waking at about 8 p.m. he called Jill and they spent the next hour in small talk. They ended by setting a lunch date for Wednesday, where they would firm up plans for that weekend's BOZO bus trip to the concert in Detroit.

Tuesday's day and night classes were punctuated by a good, hard, 38-minute 10K run, and by Wednesday morning Ken was finding that the focus on his studies was helping relieve his anxiety about the secret room.

Joining Jill at the Zebra Room for lunch, he suggested that they take their trays out onto the patio.

"Heard any more from your dad's friend?" she asked.

"No," Ken said as they moved to a vacant bench. Jill took the foil from her grilled chicken sandwich and used it to push her French fries onto the pile by Ken's cheeseburger.

"Do you think you will?"

"Oh, I don't know," Ken answered, watching the reflection of those walking by the large pool between the performing arts building and Hiestand Hall. "You know how it is, people say I'll see you later, or I'll be in touch, because it's easier than goodbye. It has an uncomfortable finality to it, I guess . . . Anyway, I'm sure I'll see him and his wife again sooner or later, since they're friends of the family."

"Well, I've been thinking it's about time we took another nature hike," Jill said. She dipped a fry in catsup and stuck it in his mouth. "What do you say we blow off our afternoon classes and go scare some more Cub Scouts?"

"Why, what are you proposing?" Ken asked, looking over the top of his sunglasses.

"Well, it's a little late for a ride out to Hueston Woods, but it's such a beautiful day, and we don't have that many left before fall. Why don't we stop by my room, grab a blanket and take some reading out to Western Campus?"

"I don't know," Ken said. "That would mean my missing one of Dr. Max Clarke's stimulating developmental psych lectures . . ."

Jill took off his sunglasses, smiled and squeezed his arm.

"Oh, all right," he said. "But we *are* going out there to study, right?"

"Absolutely," Jill said, jumping to her feet. "And we still have to make sure we're on-course for our trip to Detroit this weekend, too."

As Jill began the short walk back to her dorm, Ken hurried home to put on shorts and grab some homework. On the way back to meet Jill, he stopped by King and dropped "The Puzzle Palace" into the book return. It was just before 2 p.m. when he returned to find Jill waiting for him outside Minnich Hall, and they immediately left its front porch.

Following the sidewalk past Patterson Place and through some woods they came to the first of two weathered stone and mortar bridges which arched about 20 feet above the rolling green meadow. Jill and Ken joined hands as they moved down and under the bridge, through one of its arches onto the expansive, manicured lawn that shone electric green under the bright midday sun. They walked about 100 yards and stretched their blanket onto a patch of lawn hidden from the bridge by an outcropping of trees and brush.

"You know," Ken said as he picked Waley's book from his pack, "the more I get to know you, the more I like you, including your study habits."

Jill was quiet as she settled onto her side and opened a faded red book with a French title. Ken sat cross-legged next to her and found his place in Waley's study of the *Tao Te Ching*.

Shadows from the surrounding trees moved over and beyond the pair as afternoon became early evening. Neither spoke a word from the time they settled on the blanket until the Beta Bells chimed 6 p.m.

"I have to meet the girls for dinner," Jill said, doing a long, slow stretch as she sat up.

"I'm too relaxed to move," Ken said. "I think I'll just catch a few Z's here. Think you could stop by and wake me up on the way to your morning classes?"

"That's where I draw the line," she said, helping him to his feet. "I don't date men who sleep on lawns or live out of shopping carts."

Ken wondered what she would think if she knew he had spent a drunken night sleeping outdoors just days before.

"Really, though, that's the most studying I've done in one sitting since classes began," he said. "And I know I haven't felt this relaxed in ages. I think a good dose of Mother Nature was just what the doctor ordered."

"Does that mean you're having a better time dealing with the problem you told me about? I didn't want to bring it up, but . . ."

"Not really," Ken answered as he helped Jill fold the blanket. "I guess maybe I'm learning to let go or distance myself from it a little. Maybe then I can see and handle it better."

The conversation shifted as they joined hands and made their way back to Minnich Hall.

"Wait a minute!" Ken said. "Just when and where do we meet Saturday, and what do I bring?"

"The bus leaves the BOZO house at ten a.m. Dave Pung has our tickets and there will be coolers of beer, wine and soda on board. We'll stop for an early dinner somewhere along the way, and then after the concert we'll spend the night on the bus before heading back Sunday morning. So all you really need to bring is enough money to eat a couple of meals on the road, and for any souvenirs or other stuff at the concert or along the way."

"Doesn't your mom still live in Detroit? Are you going to see her?"

"She does, but there won't be any free time for us to get together. That's okay though, because I didn't leave all that long ago, and I'll be going home again for Thanksgiving. So it's no big deal," Jill continued. "Mom called me earlier today just to talk and I didn't tell her about the trip because I knew I'd feel guilty if she knew I was coming up without stopping at home."

"Don't feel too guilty," Ken said, stroking her hair. "How many people would want a busload of BOZOs in their driveway?"

After another kiss, Ken ambled back to his building, where Black and Blue were leaving their apartment. They were in a hurry, and Blue tapped the cement block walls and stairway railing with drumsticks as they bounded down the steps.

"Big Ken! We were looking for you," Black said, nearly colliding with him at the entrance. "Wednesday's open mike night at the Roadhouse, and Blue here's gonna sit in with one of the bands. Want to join us?"

Apparently, besides auto restoration, taxidermy and parachute-jumping, Blue was also a pretty fair drummer. Even so, Ken and the rest of the Heather Lane residents were glad he had no set to practice on in his apartment.

"I don't know . . ."

"Aw, come on," Blue said, poking Ken's gut with a drumstick.
"All right," Ken said. "But I can't stay long."

Halfway down the stairs Ken's phone rang and Black and Blue
groaned as he spun back to answer it.

"Come on, man!" Black shouted. "We're supposed to be there
by seven."

"Hang on, dammit!" Ken yelled back. He left the key in his
door as he ran to the phone.

"Yeah, hello."

"Kenny, this is your mother. I hope I didn't interrupt anything."

"No, I was just heading out with a couple of friends from next
door. What's up?"

"I just wanted to call to make sure we're all up to speed on
what's happening this weekend," Mrs. Perry said, and Ken
wondered if she could hear Blue's drumming on Linda's bike spokes
downstairs.

"What do you mean?"

"I wanted to remind you that I'm going to Margaret's on Friday
and I'll be there the following week to help her, Janice and their
friends move her into her new house. I didn't think you were
planning to come home this soon again, but if you were, I didn't
want you to wonder where I went."

"This Saturday I'm joining a group from campus that's going
on an overnight trip to Detroit for a concert. Remember the girl I
told you about . . . Jill?"

"Uh huh."

"Well, she and I are going with a group I met through her, and
we should have a pretty good time. Do you think you have enough
hands for Marg's move, or should I feel guilty about not being
there to help?"

"Yes, we have plenty of help, and yes, you should feel guilty," his
mother said. "It's the least you can do in lieu of some heavy lifting."

"Yeah, like you're going to need me," Ken said with a laugh.
"Marg and Janice will probably have every eligible bachelor in
Chicago there to help."

Black and Blue began chanting "PER-RY, PER-RY, PER-RY,"
loud enough for Ken's mother to hear.

"Well, Kenny, I'd better let you go. It sounds like the natives are restless."

"Sorry, Mom. I've fallen in with a bad crowd."

"I just hope you stop sometime during your fun this weekend and say a prayer for your poor old mother as she helps your sister move."

"Yeah, right. I know better than that! Marg and Janice will have more male help running around than it took to build the pyramids."

"Anyway," she said, "you be a good boy on your trip . . . And when are you going to bring this wonderful Jill home to meet me?"

"I won't be able to introduce you to anybody if these guys kill me," Ken said over the yet louder chanting. "I have to run. I'll try to call you in Chicago."

"No, I'll call you. Jill's phone will be disconnected."

"Okay. I should be back from Detroit sometime Sunday night."

"Talk with you then, son."

"All right, Mom. I love you."

"I love you, too."

Ken thought for a second, walked back to the stairwell and waved his friends on.

"Go ahead," he called to the pair. "I just got some news from home, and I have to make some plans."

The following week Ken remained faithful to his classes and study schedule, slipping runs of varying distances into each day. Despite long hours in the library researching the hidden room, he also kept himself socially active to prevent self-isolation, dividing lunches and after-school study breaks among Jill, Tom and Chloe.

But something else began to trouble Ken. When he returned to his apartment for lunch after his German studies on Thursday, he noticed a couple of oddities. The books and papers in his study corner seemed to have been moved, and two tacks were missing from the bottom corners of a poster hanging above his dresser.

Later that night when he returned from his Taoism class everything was in place, but there was a small streak of sugar on the counter next to the canister. Ken was always good about cleaning up in the kitchen so as to keep ants and other insects out.

I haven't had cereal in days, he thought. And that was about the only time he used sugar.

The day's minor curiosities were pushed from Ken's mind when his rumbling stomach reminded him that he hadn't had dinner, so he scanned the cork bulletin board next to the phone and spotted a half-off coupon for a Philadelphia Sub Shop sandwich. When he pulled at its push-pin, the bulletin board crashed to the floor.

"Shit!" Ken yelled as its frame splintered. He picked up the corkboard, looked at the holes where it had been screwed into the drywall and saw that they had apparently worked themselves loose.

But I just put that damn thing up a few weeks ago and it was solid, he recalled. The only way those screws would loosen that quickly was if they were removed and replaced, weakening the settings.

Ken wouldn't have given the disturbed study nook, missing poster tacks, spilled sugar or loosened bulletin board a second thought, independent of each other. But their simultaneous occurrence made him wonder. Had someone searched his apartment? What would they be seeking in his books, behind a poster or bulletin board, in a sugar canister?

He knew.

He hoped he was wrong, that someone had instead been looking for drugs, money or other valuables. But anyone who knew him or his lifestyle would also know he had none of that. And an anonymous thief who broke into his place as an act of opportunity would have taken the eight dollars and change that rested on his end table, or his CD player.

How could he know for sure whether someone had broken in and moved things around, or he had made the changes himself without giving them further thought. Maybe his recollection about how he left his study area was simply wrong. Perhaps he never noticed a sugar spill from the last bowl of raisin bran he ate. Or that Tom, Jill or another visitor pinched a couple of poster tacks to use at their place, or that he may have inadvertently botched the job when he mounted the bulletin board.

"Wait a minute," Ken said, snapping his fingers. "I know!"

He walked to his closet and reached up to the single overhead shelf. If anyone had searched his apartment, this should tell him for sure. Atop several boxes, well above his head, Ken gingerly retrieved a large peanut butter jar. When he had set up his computer earlier in the month, he broke the plastic top to a toner cartridge for his printer, and put the cartridge in the glass jar so it would not make a mess if disturbed. After replacing the lid he placed the jar high on the closet shelf to remain out of the way until needed.

If someone grabbed the container from below, not aware of its contents, the toner should have spilled inside the jar. As soon as Ken lowered the glass from its place he saw that the inside of the jar was coated with the black powder. It was something an intruder could not leave as it had been found. Shaking the jar yet more, the swirling ink became a smoking gun. Ken's place had been searched. Someone had systematically gone through it, probably at least twice.

And he knew what they were looking for.

Ken closed his drapes, pulled a kitchen chair over to the bathroom doorway and stood on it. He pulled the door toward him and peered at the top edge, where a small brass thumbtack was embedded next to a short groove in the wood. He carefully lifted plastic fishing line and a small envelope slid from the groove he had carved into the top of the hollow door. It was a trick he had learned from a pot-smoker he once dated. She had cut a hole in the top of her bathroom door, filled a test tube from the science lab with marijuana, tied it to a string and dropped it into the door, tacking the end of the string next to the hole. A tissue covering kept the stash from sounding against the inside of the door as it opened or closed.

Ken removed the taped fishing line from the brown envelope and slipped it into a notebook that he then placed in his book bag.

That night, after leaving his Taoism class, Ken entered King Library and took the stairs to the third floor. Looking across the room he saw Tatro seated at the table outside his carrel, its door open.

Turning his back towards Tatro, who had not seen him, Ken sat his backpack on a table and retrieved the brown envelope and a small roll of tape. He stuck them in his rear pocket, shouldered his pack and moved toward Tatro. He was absorbed in the book resting open in his lap as his bare feet lay crossed on the table before him.

A pool had formed around the soggy tea bag next to his empty cup.

"Hey, Mike!" Ken said, sitting on the edge of the table. "Workin' hard, man?"

"Nah, just going over a few pages before they turn off the lights and kick me out. What's up with you?"

"Just wanted to know if I could ask you a favor," Ken said, pulling a book from under his arm. "I'm working on a paper and I really need this book to do the job. But it's from the reference section, so I can't check it out of the building, and it's embedded with a magnetic security strip, so if I try to just walk out with it the alarm will sound."

"So what's the problem? If you can't remove it neither can anyone else, so it should be there when you need it."

"Yeah, it should be," Ken said. "But tonight was the first time in four tries on separate days that I finally found it where it should be. Apparently, somebody else hid it for their use and took their time to replace it. Or maybe a library staffer just recently found and reshelved it.

"I can't risk its disappearing again," he continued. "The report's due next week and I'm doing it as a special project, so there shouldn't be a big demand for it by a class or other group now anyway. Would you mind if I stashed it in your carrel until next Wednesday?"

"But if I'm not here to let you in how will you work on your report?"

"You're *always* here, Mike."

"Sad but true," the grad student conceded with a sigh. "Go ahead," he waved his pencil's eraser at the tiny room behind him. "You can put it anywhere."

"Thanks," Ken said. "You don't know how much this will help me!"

Tatro went back to his book while Ken swung the carrel door closed behind him, dropped the book on a rear corner of the desk and fell to his knees. He quickly pulled the single drawer out, double-taped the envelope to the bottom, pushed the drawer back in and returned to Tatro.

"Thanks again, Mike. I was admiring your tea collection. Where do you get that stuff?"

"Place in Richmond called Mother Nature's Pantry. Why? You trying to find some?"

"No, I'm your basic Lipton or Tetley's man. I was just curious. Anyway, thanks again for the help. See you and the rest of the phenom group Sunday, if not before."

"De nada," Tatro said, and the overhead lights flickered, signaling quarter to twelve.

By nature, Ken was neither nervous nor suspicious. But knowing that someone had searched his apartment, and probably more than once, kicked his emotional state back into overdrive.

The intrusion so soon after showing Cody the secret room photos could not be coincidence. Ken's only credit card, his TV, CD player and other high-theft items were all left intact. Cody, or someone who received word from him, had to have been searching for those Polaroids.

But now, thanks to Ken's unwitting accomplice in King Library, they were safe.

Still, if "they" had combed his residence, what else had they done, or would do? Was his apartment, telephone or both tapped? Was he being watched? Followed? Would friends, family, neighbors, professors or others fall under scrutiny? What about his safety? Would someone want him silenced, either through intimidation or violence? Could that be what happened to his father?"

It always came back to that.

Ken felt as if ice water was rushing into his stomach as he realized that the turmoil was no longer all between his ears. He was concerned that Cody knew something, had by now reported to someone else, and at the very least Ken had been the target of a secret investigation.

Ken had been reviewing his father's past under a microscope. Now someone had pulled a lens over him. He wondered if this was what a frog felt like before being dissected.

CHAPTER ELEVEN

A thundering crash against his door vaulted Ken from a sound sleep. He was halfway to the golf club he kept in his closet when he identified the commotion as Black and Blue scuffling in the hall.

"Sorry 'bout that, Ken. Didn't mean to wake you," Black grunted from his end of the sofa he and Blue were wrestling down the stairs. "Had a little accident last night and thought we'd replace it before our good friends at Collegiate Rentals, Inc., got wind of it and assessed a fee."

Ken saw that the center cushions, back and rear of the couch were scorched, and water dribbled from its hemorrhaged upholstery.

"You guys have a hot date?" Ken asked, rubbing his eyes.

"Doofus here dozed off and dropped a Marlboro behind the cushions," Blue explained. "Smoke alarm woke us up about fifteen minutes after we turned in last night, and it took us a good hour to get all the smoldering guts doused.

"So now we're going to give it a proper burial and hit the yard sales to find a replacement."

"Good luck," Ken said. "I hope you can find something to match your discriminating decor."

"Want to join us?" Blue asked. "Maybe you can make an acquisition for your place."

"Thanks anyway, but I have plans . . . I'm going to a concert in Detroit with Jill and a bunch of friends," Ken said. "We leave at ten this morning, and I want to get a run in first." His clock radio showed that it was just after eight.

Black shrugged as he and Blue re-shouldered the burnt couch. "Okay, but it's your missed opportunity . . .

"Oh yeah," Blue continued, stopping at the foot of the stairs. "We'll keep an eye on the place while you're gone. Ann and Linda said they saw a couple of suspicious looking older guys in suits coming upstairs one day last week. Said they stayed about a half-hour or so before coming back down and leaving, but never heard them knock or talk with anyone. Our place is fine. Had any trouble with yours?"

"No, not that I know of," Ken said.

After a hurried check to make sure the Polaroids were safe, Ken changed and took off for a fast three-miler, passing Black and Blue as they used a hammer and crowbar to break down the couch for the Dumpster.

When he returned, Black was sweeping the smaller pieces into a pile as Blue sat in his car scouring *The Oxford Press* for garage sales.

By the time Ken showered, changed into his jeans, tie-dyed T-shirt and sandals and started for the BOZO house, they had left.

As Ken walked up College Avenue, he saw a faded yellow school bus parked along the curb before the BOZO house. He moved towards Tom, Chloe and Jill, who were speaking together on the outside edge of a group of about forty gathered on the lawn between the bus and house. Tom and Chloe wore matching bell-bottom jeans and loose-fitting African dashiki shirts. Jill's cutoff shorts had a large white peace sign embroidered over the right thigh, and several strands of love beads danced over her tie-dyed tank top. She wore one bright red silk scarf as a headband and a yellow one as a belt. Chloe's wire-rimmed sunglasses had round, rose-colored lenses, and Tom wore an old top hat.

"Greetings, my brother," Tom called to Ken, his hand raised in a peace sign.

"Right back at ya, oh great flower child," Ken replied, and the two exchanged an elaborate, '60s-style handshake that would have made any hippie-era stalwart proud.

Ken greeted Chloe with a hug and gave Jill a quick kiss.

"Where are Chris and Kaaren?"

Jill pointed to the pair, who were also dressed in retro-fashion, busily helping Dave and Fonda load the bus with plastic trash cans, bags of ice and cases of beer, wine and soda.

Though they had been painted over, the words Butler County Schools remained legible on either side of the retired canary behemoth. Otherwise it looked about the same as it did when in use ferrying schoolchildren.

But when Ken joined the others in boarding it for the trip, he saw that only the first four rows of seats remained intact. The rest had been removed to leave the majority of the space open, and several dozen cushions of various sizes and shapes, and an occasional neatly folded blanket lined the outside edges of its clean, carpeted floor. Two large speakers were bolted to the floor on either side of the rear escape door, and several smaller speakers were mounted along the ceiling. A round table about four feet in diameter sat in the middle of the open space, and though all the windows were open, the bus was hot from sitting in the morning sun.

Ken, Jill, Chloe and Tom settled behind the seats on the left side, and when all had boarded, Dave stood next to his driver's seat and called the names of all who had registered for the trip. A miniskirted blonde on one of the front seats said the only two not present had to back out at the last minute, and another girl, whose name was not called, explained to Dave that she heard about the trip from friends and asked if she could tag along. She said she had already bought her own concert ticket through the campus Ticketmaster outlet, and would be glad to pay for the ride.

"My friends told me this looked like a really fun group," the tall and very attractive brunette told Dave. "I'm willing to pay the full $100, even though I have a ticket."

"Listen, we have plenty of room, and if you're not a BOZO but thinking of joining, consider this a welcome gesture," he said. "No charge."

"Thanks," she said. "That's great!" And she hurried to a cushion near the back.

"All right, listen up!" Dave said as he raised his arms. "Looks like we're ready to roll. If anybody needs to use the john, please do so now. Fonda's still in the house and you have a minute till she comes out and we go.

"Item two: This trip is for fun, but remember not to throw anything out the windows, press any indiscreet body parts against same, or perpetrate any other foolishness that will cause the cops to pull us over and rain on our parade. I'm the designated driver up and back, so you can relax and enjoy the ride. We'll stop about halfway there for a bite to eat, and we should get into Detroit one to two hours before show time. I'll drop everybody off at the arena, go park the bus and join you. We'll handle the return the same

way. After the concert I'll go get the bus and return for you. We'll
then go to a friend of mine's in Ann Arbor, sleep in the bus there
and leave for home Sunday morning. Any questions?"

"What's the in-flight movie?" someone yelled.

"How to deal with a smartass," Dave shot back, and he turned
the key as Fonda skipped from the house to board the bus.

The bus pulled from the curb and all applauded as Dave ground
the transmission from first into second, then third gear. After a few
stop signs and traffic lights, they were cruising east on Route 73
with The Who's "Magic Bus" booming from the speakers.

Tom and Ken opened beers while Jill and Chloe paced
themselves with sodas, and the smell of marijuana came and went
in the breezy vehicle.

By the time they merged onto the northbound lanes of I-75,
there was a card game in one rear corner, another group singing
along with a guitarist in the other, and Chris and Kaaren were
among the half dozen playing the '60s classic "Twister" on a plastic
sheet spread by the round table.

"How often do the BOZOs take road trips like this?" Ken asked.

"Only one overnight or long distance trip per semester," Jill
said. "And every couple of months or so we go for short hops to
clubs in Cincinnati, Dayton, Indianapolis, somewhere like that."

"Well this is great," Ken said. "You should do it more often."

"*We* should," she corrected him. "Remember? You're one of *us*
now . . . I'm going to talk with Tina for awhile," she said, pointing
to a girl seated behind Dave. "Why don't you mix a little and get
to know the group?"

"Good idea," Ken said, and he moved toward the card game,
leaving Tom and Chloe to each other.

"What are they playing?" the tall brunette newcomer to the
group asked Ken from behind. Her glass beads brushed his shoulder
and she smelled of patchouli. Earlier he hadn't noticed her striking
beauty, with large, brown almond-shaped eyes set between high
cheekbones, her shiny straight chestnut hair pulled back into long,
flowing pigtails. Either she was unaware of the 60s theme dress or
ignored it, because she wore a regular pair of old, faded blue jean
shorts, a red cotton Miami T-shirt and sandals.

"Looks like hearts," he replied. "My name's Ken."

"I'm Crystal."

"So, you're thinking about joining the BOZOs?"

"Yeah," she said. "I heard about the group from friends and it sounds like fun. Is it?"

"So far so good," Ken told her. "I just joined, but I've had a lot of fun with them already. It turns out that several of my friends were already members."

The card game ended and a girl holding the deck asked if there were any new players.

"Yes, you have two more here," Crystal said, and she pulled Ken with her into the circle as the dealer flicked them cards.

The players got to know each other during the game, and Ken got up between hands to get another beer.

"Would you be sweet and get me a glass of that white wine?" Crystal asked, stroking his calf.

"No problem," Ken said, and he stopped to see Jill as he went for the drinks.

"Are you having fun?" she asked.

"Yeah. Got into a card game and now I know a few more people. Why don't you join us?"

"Maybe later, Ken. This is Tina. She and I were freshman roommates," Jill said, nodding at the thin redhead next to her. "We're catching up on old times."

"Actually, Jill's telling me all about you," Tina said in her Alabama drawl. "I understand you're good at *projects*."

"You can't believe everything you hear," Ken demurred.

"Oh, I trust Jill," Tina assured. "Besides being roommates, we once got food poisoning together from undercooked hamburgers we ate in town, then spent nearly a week in adjoining beds in the health center."

"Yup," Jill added. "We found out the hard way that there's no dieting plan in the world more effective than a few days of diarrhea and projectile vomiting."

"I'm going back to play cards," Ken said. "If I keep talking with you two I won't be able to eat lunch."

They agreed to get together when the bus stopped for their meal, and Ken returned to the back of the bus, where he handed Crystal her wine and she gave him a handful of cards.

"I was playing for you while you were gone," she said with a smile. "It was some of your best so far!"

"Thanks . . . I think," he said, and the vibration of road through the bus floor and the music from the speakers droned on until the bus veered off the interstate at Piqua. Dave brought them to a stop in a lot between a McDonald's and Long John Silver restaurants.

"Okay, it's chow time," he shouted over the chatter. "We've got fish on one side, beef on the other and exactly one hour until blast-off for Detroit."

It was two p.m. and Crystal followed Ken as he joined Jill, Tom and Chloe outside the bus.

"What'll it be, surf or turf?" Chloe asked as they eyed both eateries.

"I feel like a good ol' pre-concert cheeseburger and fries," Tom said. "How about you guys?"

"Sounds good to me," Ken answered.

"Me too," Crystal chimed from outside their small circle. "Sorry," she said as the group looked her way, unaware she had joined them. "I just met Ken on the bus and when lunch broke up our card game I thought I'd tag along. Is that okay?"

"Of course," Jill said, sending a subtle message as she took Ken's hand. "We'd better get in the food line before it stretches back to Oxford."

Already busy with their typical midday crowd from the adjacent interstate, the influx of "hippies" sent the McDonald's staff into overdrive. The revelers also served as entertainment or annoyance to other customers of varying temperament.

Tom and Ken ordered for the girls as they used the bathroom. When they returned, the guys took their turn at the plumbing as Jill, Chloe and Crystal carried their food outside the packed restaurant to find a picnic spot.

They settled in the shade of a willow near a neighboring gas station, and when the guys joined them, Ken was reminded of his lunch with Crump.

"I can't wait!" Crystal said, unwrapping a burger. "I haven't been to a concert in years, and I love The Who."

"Crystal's thinking of joining the BOZOs," Ken said. "I told her how I just did, and how great the group's been."

"It is a wonderful group," Chloe said. "I hope you join. Maybe I can sponsor you. What are you studying?"

"I'm a junior majoring in English, and if I look older, it's because I am," Crystal explained. "I dropped out of my sophomore year to help my husband through law school. But as soon as he passed the bar he kept going, straight to divorce court. So now, five years later, I'm back in school full time. I just thank God we never had children.

"I grew up in Cincinnati and that's where Ted, my ex, got his degree. Anybody else from Cinci?"

"Nope," Tom said. "Chicago, Cleveland, Detroit and Grand Rapids," he said, pointing first to himself and then to Chloe, Jill and Ken.

"Detroit," Crystal said, looking at Jill. "So this will be a trip home for you."

"Well, yes and no. I actually live in Birmingham, a northern suburb about fifteen miles from the city. But I have spent a lot of time downtown, at concerts like the one we're going to, lots of outdoor weekend festivals at Hart Plaza, waterfront jazz clubs and Greektown. But if you want to walk the streets safely after dark anywhere else, you have to cross the river for Windsor, Ontario."

"What's Birmingham like?" Crystal asked.

"It's one of those upscale suburbs where families raise their kids in relative safety," Jill said. "Birmingham's top-notch theater, string of art galleries and Cranbrook Academy, where I took several classes while still in high school, helped me find my way into my majors, art photography and modern dance."

"I got my GED while in prison and came to Miami as a condition of my parole," Tom said, and they all laughed as the bus horn sounded.

"Time to head back," Chloe said, collecting the group's trash. "It was great meeting you, Crystal. I'll have to get your number before we part so I can sponsor you for admission to the BOZOs."

"Thanks, I appreciate your help. Maybe we can talk more on the ride back tomorrow."

"Great!" Chloe answered, and Tom accompanied her to a trash barrel as Jill, Ken and Crystal returned to the bus.

Droning north past Toledo, Dave shouted a call for all to show their entry visas as they crossed the state line into Michigan, and all cheered as they hoisted their drinks and an occasional joint.

The party revved into serious pre-concert gear with alcohol and weed coursing through the bus as it continued past Monroe and Flat Rock to cruise through Detroit's gray, industrial Downriver suburbs.

The gleaming Renaissance Center towers dominated the Motown skyline, and as a confused-looking Dave slowed for and then passed one exit, Jill moved forward to act as navigator.

She directed him to take the Fort Street exit, and it was a straight shot north under the Ambassador Bridge footings to Woodward Avenue, then over to Michigan Avenue and their destination.

Dave pulled the bus to a stop a block from Joe Louis Arena, and people were converging on the building from all directions.

"About fifteen minutes to showtime," Dave called as he stood at the head of the bus. "Listen up! This is important! In a minute I'm going to pull up in front of the arena and let you guys out. Fonda has your tickets and will hand them to you as you jump off. As soon as the concert is over, I'm going to catch a cab back to the bus and bring it back for you. Exactly thirty minutes after the music stops I will return to the same spot where I dropped you off to pick you up again. *Remember*, you *must* be back for the bus no more than one half hour after the concert ends. That should give you plenty of time to put away your Bic lighter, buy your T-shirts and find a spot at the curb. Otherwise, it's a very long walk back to Oxford. *Capiche?*"

Someone in the back of the bus screamed and began singing "My Generation," and the whole group joined in as Dave steered the vehicle into place before the large bronze fist statue memorializing the arena's boxing legend namesake.

Dave put on the bus flashers, swung the door open, and Fonda leaped off with the tickets.

"Don't leave anything behind that I could get busted for," Dave shouted over his shoulder. The front seats emptied quickly, with those from the back of the bus forming a conga line exit.

Crystal held a plastic cup of white wine in her left hand as she rose, swayed and almost fell. Ken helped steady her.

"Oh, man!" Crystal paused, laughing as she raised a palm over her eyes. "I hope I haven't overdone it already . . . Here," she said, shoving the cup into Ken's hands. "Drink this for me."

"Always glad to help a lady in distress," he replied, and drained its nearly full contents.

Fonda dropped Ken's ticket into his empty cup as he left the bus. He, Crystal, Jill, Tom and Chloe cheered and whirled across the large cement square, then ran up the broad, multi-tiered stairs to the arena entrance.

The cavernous gray lobby was a beehive of people checking out T-shirt and other concession booths, trying to find or reconnect with friends or making last-minute bathroom stops on the way to their seats.

"Looks like a sellout crowd," Tom said. "It's almost showtime; we'd better get inside. Dave bought our tickets in a block, so our seats should be together."

"Uh oh," Crystal said. "I'll bet we're separated. I bought my ticket myself on campus . . . Sure enough," she continued, comparing her ticket stub to theirs. "You're all in D section, and I'm over in R."

"Row R seat 22," Tom said, looking at her ticket. "Tell you what," he said as the warm-up band thundered into action behind them, "we'll ask if there's anyone near us who would be willing to swap seats with you so you can join us. If we find someone, I'll send them over to R-22. How's that sound?"

"Thanks! I appreciate it."

Jill grabbed Chloe's arm and pulled her towards a crowded booth. "We're going to look at the T-shirts and other stuff while the opening band plays," she said. "We'll be inside before The Who starts."

Tom and Ken joined several others from their group and headed for section D. Right away Tom abandoned his plan to find someone to trade seats with Crystal. D section was a prime location, in the upper deck at about two o'clock in relation to the stage. R was closer to six o'clock, at the far end of the arena. And since it was a sell-out crowd, there were no empty seats for Crystal to claim.

"This oughtta be a kickass concert," Tom shouted into Ken's ear. "I saw The Who in Cleveland when I was a junior in high school. My dad took my brothers and me. How about you?"

"No, but I've always wanted to. I love their stuff," Ken yelled back, and he hesitated as he looked at two adjoining empty seats in the row before them. "You know, Crystal could have sat with us anyway," he said. "Remember? Dave said there were two no-shows, and he already had their tickets."

"Hey, yeah! Listen, I'm sure Dave must be out front scalping those tickets, so I'll find him and get one for Crystal. Meanwhile, you go to R-22 and get her."

"No way," Ken said. "I'm afraid Jill might already think I've thrown a little too much interest Crystal's way. Why don't you send Jill or Chloe on the way out?"

"Okay, chicken," Tom said as he turned for the aisle. "We'll take care of everything, you just sit back and enjoy the music."

The obscure opening act revved into a blitzkrieg finale in their mad attempt to embed their name into the crowd's memory before vacating the stage for the group all had come to see.

The few drinks Ken had on the trip up, topped-off by the glass of wine he chugged on the way off the bus brought him a light, mild buzz. Soon a warm, soothing flush came over his face and chest.

A joint came Ken's way from somewhere behind him, so he took a hit and passed it back. Closing his eyes, he felt like an anchor plunging through dark water as the house lights dimmed.

Jill and Tom rushed back just as the stage lights went up to reveal The Who as they tore into a jump-start rendition of "Won't Be Fooled Again."

Ken joined the others as they leaped to their feet, but he felt as if he were standing on a waterbed. His hands, feet and face tingled as if filled with seltzer, and his whole body was hot and cold at the same time.

Damn! That must have been good weed, he thought as Jill took her place next to him. She explained that Tom had caught Dave before he scalped the spare tickets, and Chloe had gone for Crystal. John Entwistle's bass storm, Pete Townshend's windmill guitar strokes and Roger Daltrey's soaring voice and orbiting microphone kept the throbbing crowd on their feet.

Ken gasped as his fluttering heart slammed up to close his throat, and an icy electric flash raced up his spine, then back down into his constricted gut.

"Holy shit!" Ken heaved under his breath, and he felt the grip of panic squeeze his stomach harder as his breath and pulse raced each other out of control.

"Jesus Christ!" he said, lifting his hands over his face. He turned around to find a girl he recognized from the bus, but had not met, lighting another joint. "God *damn!*" he shouted. "What's *in* that stuff?"

"It's just weed," the pudgy redhead said, noticing his agitation. "Really . . . I've been smoking out of this bag for a couple of weeks, and it's just Mr. Natural. Why? Are you okay?"

"Yeah, sure . . . just had too much to drink on the ride up," Ken lied.

None of Ken's friends noticed his conversation with the girl, and Jill thought nothing of it when he excused himself to use the bathroom.

Taking the aisle steps two at a time, Ken felt like he was running through waist-high Jell-O. Stumbling into the men's room he lunged for a sink, grabbed it with both hands and thrust his face close to the mirror. His pupils had opened so far that there was only a thin blue circle of iris around each, and when he closed his eyes tight a few seconds and opened them again, the pupils had remained frozen open.

Ken heard a sizzling, crackling sound come from the bright fluorescent lights, and he jumped back from the sink as a flushing toilet behind him became a lion's roar.

"Oh *shit!* Oh *goddamn shit!*" he spat in panic. "Oh shit! I'm *tripping!*"

Ken had never gone beyond alcohol or pot, and didn't think he would enjoy handing his mind over completely to any drug. Now, although he didn't know how it had happened, that decision had been made for him.

He jumped again as another roar echoed through the tiled room. Then, while backing out slowly, it appeared to Ken that the row of men using urinals along a nearby wall were getting oral sex from kneeling women wearing only white wedding veils.

Stumbling back into the lobby, Ken shook his head in confusion, wondering how he had come to find himself in a subway station. Walking back the way he had come, he moved towards the D tunnel and the music that poured from it turned into a river of green and purple honeycomb patterns. He could feel them snapping and popping around him like elastic spiderwebs as he lunged back through the doorway. The arena had become the inside of a volcano, dark except for the erupting stage. Walking carefully down the stairs toward his friends, Ken bumped against a woman who lost her balance and fell into her aisle seat. But he saw that he had punctured a life-sized doll, which hissed into a crumpled heap.

The entire crowd sang and danced to The Who's "Bargain" and Jill alone noticed Ken as he stepped back into his place.

"Hey, Ken, are you okay? You look kind of out of it."

"Yeah," he said, shaking his head. "I just couldn't believe all that," he added, and Jill gave him a confused look.

"Believe what?"

"Believe it or not!" Ken answered, and he laughed uncontrollably. He hadn't consciously thought-out the response. The words were coming out on their own.

"Are you sure you're all right, Ken? What's wrong with you? What are you on?"

Jill held up her hands to feel Ken's forehead and steady his head to look into his eyes. He saw her watch melt over her wrist like in the Dali painting.

"I'm on time!" Ken said, and again laughed hysterically.

He looked out over the arena again, and now it was a scene from Dante's Inferno. As he stood on one of the outer rings of the underworld, he peered to see those who writhed in pain at the center below. Those on stage became devils who sent fire upon the heads of the damned with each laser or spotlight flash that swept the dancing crowd.

Faintly, Ken heard a familiar voice call his name. Looking back and up the aisle he saw that it came from one of the three men silhouetted in the exit doorway.

Illuminated by several of the flashes of light, Ken recognized them. Dressed in camouflage military fatigues, Dennis Truro and Paul Cody stood on either side of Walter Perry, his father. He wore a dark blue suit and tie and was barefoot.

Without realizing that he had moved, Ken found himself halfway up the steep cement steps and closing in on the trio.

Cody and Truro stood silent and expressionless as Walter Perry, eyes remaining closed, raised his right hand and extended it toward his son.

Jill thought Ken was heading back to the men's room when he bolted without a word, but she followed anyway, knowing something was wrong. When he was near the top of the stairs, Cody, Truro and his father disappeared into the lobby, and he sprinted to catch up with them, losing Jill in the crowd.

Nearly blinded by the brightly lit lobby, Ken soon found the three standing motionless as they floated down the stairs to the street below, as if on an escalator.

By the time Ken scrambled frantically down the cement steps after them, Cody, Truro and his father were already nearly a block north on Michigan Avenue.

Night had fallen, and the approaching headlights were a stream of blinding meteors, while the crimson taillights on the northbound cars became tracer bullets.

"Dad, it's me! Dad!" Ken screamed. But no matter how fast he ran, the three remained at least a block ahead of him. Even though they moved quickly along the sidewalk, Cody and Truro seemed to be marching, stiff-legged, in slow-motion, while Ken's father stood silently, staring ahead, his arms at his sides as he glided between them, bare feet suspended inches off the ground.

"GODDAMN IT, STOP! *STOP*, GODDAMN IT!" Ken screamed with all his strength, and the few street people and other pedestrians he passed all seemed unreal, as had the deflated girl in the arena. They were all mannequins, dressed in army combat gear.

A mongrel dog ran from an alley and barked at Ken's weird behavior. But Ken saw a hyena, laughing hysterically in a child's voice.

Passing the large Federal Center building on his left, Ken stayed in pursuit of all three men as they continued their somber procession. His father raised another couple of feet into the air and stretched out his arms, crucifixion style, as he continued to glide forward between the still-marching Cody and Truro.

The vacant lots and park area they passed had become a desert. A teenager on a bicycle approached, but Ken saw a pale horse bearing a parched-looking rider. The rider's cracked and dusty lips remained shut tight, then bled as he smiled at Ken. Though he said nothing, Ken heard his thoughts mock as he rode by: *Just desserts in the desert. Like father, like son. Finding just desserts in the desert.*

"If this is a desert, where's the sun?" Ken asked as he came up to a tarnished statue of a long-dead war hero.

You are his son, the statue replied, and its empty eyes rolled back into its bronze head, then melted over its cement base.

Still pursuing his father and the others, Ken saw Tiger Stadium rise as a castle overlooking the desert, which then became a sea. The headlights were now lightning strikes that razed everything around Ken in a storm so violent that he feared the bolts would strike down him or his father before they were reunited.

The black paving of Michigan Avenue and Trumbull became an inky moat separating Ken from his father, Cody and Truro as they passed the box office and glided through locked metal gates into the dark, sleeping ball park.

Ken flew across the black ice of Trumbull Avenue and smashed into the tall wrought iron grate when he tried to move through it as the others had. Rising to his feet he didn't notice the bloody gash over his left eye. Next he scaled a section of the fence that afforded him access to the main entrance rooftop. From there he was able to jump onto an entry ramp leading to the infield seats.

As he came to the box seats behind third base, the stars seemed to fall from the sky until they froze just above the field, bathing it in daylight. Then, in perfect silence, thousands of people processed in to fill every seat in the stadium. Although they seemed real they remained seated in frozen, expressionless silence.

Programs! Get your programs! a 1930s-era newsboy cried, waving a copy for Ken to take. Ken moved towards the boy, who dropped the program as he dissolved into the night. In reality the program was an old sheet of newspaper caught in a whirlwind.

Picking it up, Ken saw the word *PROGRAM* on the front, and opened it to see his father's obituary, which had run years before in the *Grand Rapids Press*. He stuffed the paper in one of his pockets and resumed his desperate search for his father.

"GODDAMN IT, DAD, WHERE *ARE* YOU?" he screamed into the silence. He wasn't sure if he heard an echo or a response.

Once again the young boy who had the programs appeared. Standing just a few feet away, he pointed toward the field and continued to sing, *Oh, say, can you see? Oh, say, can you see? Oh, say, can you see?* . . .

There, in the brilliant darkness, still wearing their army fatigues, Paul Cody stood holding a baseball on the pitcher's mound, as Dennis Truro crouched in the catcher's stance behind Ken's father, who stood directly on home plate, facing his son. Again Walt Perry levitated about two feet off the ground and extended his arms, and the program boy continued his eerie chant as Cody went into his wind-up.

"DAD! OH MY GOD, *DAD!* LOOK OUT! *WATCH OUT!*"

The force of Cody's fastball ripped a gash above his father's left eye. His head recoiled from the impact but he didn't flinch, his unblinking gaze fixed on his son.

"*Jesus Christ,* dad!" Ken bellowed as he scrambled down the aisle. Cody's second pitch found the same wound that his first throw had opened, and Ken felt a warm spray shower him. He wiped his face and saw his father's blood drip from his hand.

"DAD, IT'S *KEN!* IT'S *ME KEN!* COME *ON,* DAD!" he screamed, hurtling atop the third base line dugout. "*PLEASE,* "DAD, *PLEASE!*"

Cody's third pitch tore his father's wound yet deeper. Crimson poured over both of his eyes as they remained locked on his son.

Ken was crouched to jump onto the field when he felt a tug on his pantleg. Without letting go of his pants, the program boy looked Ken in the eye and said, smiling and matter-of-factly: *Cuz it's one, two, three strikes you're out at the old ball game.*

The boy then turned toward home plate. Ken looked to see that Truro and Cody had resumed their places on either side of his bloodied father, and all three moved toward then dissolved into the backstop behind home plate.

The boy had also disappeared as Ken turned and raced back through the seats, hoping to catch his father and the others as they left the stadium.

The phantom crowd sat staring in silence as Ken raced back up to the ramp.

"DAD! *DAD! WAIT FOR ME!*" he screamed into the night. Jumping back onto the edge of the ramp railing, Ken dove onto the entry roof and hustled to its edge, overlooking Michigan and Trumbull. Losing his balance he fell onto the top of the iron fence, and one of the bars tore through his shirt and pierced his chest. Screaming from the pain, he flopped over the fence and slid down its cold bars to collapse on the sidewalk below. Panting against the rough sidewalk, he looked up to see a Black Hawk helicopter cruising over the stadium, spraying it with machine gun fire.

Before him, Michigan Avenue had become a slowly rolling
black river. The sidewalks on either side were sandy banks, with
the stores and other buildings set inside tall palms, vines and other
jungle overgrowth.

The horizon was a 360-degree vision of madness as dozens of B-
52s rained bombs everywhere. Orange and black napalm eruptions
fed each other into a fiery tempest that engulfed the city.

Unaware that his pants were soaking up the flow of blood
from his face and chest, Ken instead felt the warm river water
rising up his legs as he stood to find his father. Turning north he
spotted him, Cody and Truro on the sidewalk about midway along
the left field wall. It was the same place where his father was gunned
down years before.

Cody and Truro turned from Ken's father and faced opposite
directions, arms at their sides.

Walter Perry again extended his arms and hovered just above
the ground, facing the rear of the stadium. There, near the end of
the block, the police helicopter that Ken had seen as an army
combat chopper rose over the wall and headed toward his father. It
had responded to a silent alarm Ken had triggered in the stadium.

Panic overloaded the acid-fueled circuitry of Ken's brain as he
saw a grimacing black machine gunner crouching in the Huey's
side door. And when the spotlight shone on his father, Cody and
Truro, Ken had no idea that in reality they were three homeless
drunks staggering their way from one Corktown bar to another.

Ken watched the low and slow-moving chopper ease towards
the three, and he couldn't make out the electronic barking that
boomed from the copter's loudspeaker.

"*RUN! DAD, RUN!*" Ken screamed, and he fell as he let go of
the wall to run to his father's aid. Nearly unconscious from blood
loss, Ken raised to all fours and finally to his feet, forced two deep
breaths and bellowed again: "*RUN,* DAD! *GODDAMN IT,* DAD,
RUN! *RUN!*"

But his father and the others stood motionless as the chopper
closed in on them. Despite the determination that overshadowed
his pain, Ken lost his race against the chopper as it bathed his
father in a million candlepower of light. The wild-eyed door gunner
sent a deafening burst of .50-caliber bullets through his father's
torso.

"*JESUS CHRIST!*" Ken cried, and his father fell to the sidewalk in a heap between the frozen Cody and Truro.

"OH, *JESUS CHRIST!* DAD! OH *MY GOD, DAD!*" Ken choked through tears. He dove to his father's side, pulled his head and shoulders over his own, then fought to stand and hoist the limp body over his back.

Oblivious to his fate, the old drunk vomited a cascade of cheap wine over Ken's back as he weaved from the sidewalk into the roiling black river that was Michigan Avenue. Ken mustered all his strength to carry his father through the thick, heavy waves toward the other side, unsuccessful in his bid to evade the copter's light.

Avoiding the white snakes that Michigan Avenue's broken center line had become, Ken and his father emerged from the hallucinated river onto its sidewalk shore.

"FREEZE! YOU ARE UNDER ARREST," a voice boomed from the copter's speaker. "This is the Detroit Metropolitan Police Department. *Stop now* and *drop to the ground.* You are *under arrest!*"

Ken looked south along the storefronts and saw an empty lot where he could escape into the jungle with his dad. While shifting him for a better grip, Ken caused the drunk to vomit again, which he saw as blood gushing from his father's bullet wounds.

Only three strides into his desperate flight, Ken's knees buckled and he fell forward onto the sidewalk, the weight of his "father" ramming his face against the cement.

More scrambled electronic commands shrieked from the sky as Ken moved from beneath the drunk, who was muttering incoherently.

Ken sat in a pool of blood and vomit and cried uncontrollably as he cradled the moaning, delirious old man in his arms.

"Don't *die,* dad! Oh, *please, God,* don't let my dad *die!* I *love you* dad! Dad . . ."

Bathed again in the hovering copter's blinding halogen spotlight, Ken never saw or heard the lights and sirens of the responding Detroit Metro police cars.

"Oh, God, *save him! Save my dad!*" he pleaded as two officers scrambled up, guns drawn. "He's my *dad! Please* don't let him *die . . .*"

Ken's consciousness flowed away with his blood, and the police pried the drunk from his arms.

CHAPTER TWELVE

Ken awoke to restraints strapped tight around his wrists and ankles. And it took him a few seconds more to realize he was lashed to a hospital bed.

Weak sunlight tried to bleed through a crack in the heavy, drawn curtains, and the only sound was the slow, steady beep from a heart monitor taped to his chest.

Trying to shift in the bed, Ken felt dried blood crack on his chest, and there was a tug from the IV needle taped into his left hand. He looked up to see a bottle of clear liquid dripping into the plastic tube grafted into his vein. Next he noticed the low buzzing in his ears. His breath came slow and with difficulty as he now found the black stitches across his lower right chest, and his whole body ached, as if his muscles had remained rigid while he slept. A wave of nausea swept Ken's attention away from the throbbing numbness in his head.

He raised as best he could to look through a large glass window next to the door and saw several women at a nurses' station. A closed circuit camera was focused on him from its perch in a ceiling corner, and soon a woman's voice came from a speaker.

"Are you awake, Mr. Perry?"

Ken could see the redhead in the nurses' station who looked back at him through the observation window as she spoke into an intercom. "How are you feeling this morning?"

"Yeah, I'm awake," he said into the empty room. "Where am I?"

After a pause the thin nurse in a blue smock and pants left the station and walked into Ken's room.

"Don't be alarmed by the restraints. They're standard operating procedure when someone's . . . disoriented. You had a pretty rough night . . . Remember any of it?"

"Some, but not everything," he said. Closing his eyes he tried to think back. "Where *am* I?"

"This is Mercy Hospital. Psychiatric wing," the nurse said, standing at the edge of the bed. "My name is Lisa Marsh and I'd just come on duty when the police brought you in last night, about 11:30. You appeared to be under the influence of some kind of psychoactive drug, and were involved in some sort of . . . disturbance that the police responded to and then brought you here for treatment. X-rays showed no apparent internal damage from your head injury," she said, brushing her fingers across the right side of her forehead. "But it took twenty-seven stitches to close the wound in your chest.

"Even so, you were lucky," she continued. "Apparently you were stabbed with or impaled by an object that entered your upper right abdomen, then traveled up and tore the right chest muscle on its way into the fleshy area between your shoulder and collarbone.

"I say you were lucky because whatever it was didn't puncture your lung or any other vital organs."

"Yeah. I feel really *lucky*," Ken groaned, not opening his eyes.

"As you wake up you'll discover an assortment of minor cuts and bruises," Nurse Marsh said as she released his wrist straps. "We drew blood, but the toxicology report's not in yet . . . Care to tell me what you took?"

Ken took a deep breath and exhaled slowly.

"Yes. I *took* a few beers and a couple of hits from a marijuana cigarette. What I was *given*, without my knowledge, appears to have been a pretty serious dose of LSD, or something like it. I was with a group of friends from school in Ohio, going to the Who concert at Joe Louis Arena last night, and one of them asked me to finish her glass of wine. That has to be where I got it," he thought aloud. "It had to be spiked. That's the only place it could have come from.

"Damn!" he said, wincing as he recalled his friends. "I was supposed to meet them after the concert for the ride back to school . . ."

"I know," the nurse interrupted. "When you didn't show they called the local police and hospitals until they found you here. A Jill Mangan told me to let you know she's stayed behind for you and can be reached at this number." She pulled a slip of paper from a pocket and sat it by a telephone next to the bed. "If you'd like, I could call to let her know you're okay."

"No, thanks. I'll do it myself."

Ken raised his right arm up and under his head. "Do you think you could open the drapes for me?"

"Sure," Nurse Marsh replied. As she moved around the bed to the drawstring, Ken spoke again.

"You said the police brought me here . . . Am I in some kind of trouble?"

"I don't know," she said. "An officer is on his way here now to talk with you. I had instructions to call him when you came to."

"Great! Just *great!*"

After releasing the ankle restraints, Nurse Marsh left and Ken picked up Jill's telephone number. He winced again as he turned to pick up the phone, but stopped when he heard a loud voice outside his door.

"Yes. Kenneth W. Perry," the man's voice boomed.

"In that room, there, to your right," someone replied, and a large, blue-uniformed Detroit Metro police officer appeared at the door.

"Good morning, Mr. Perry," the policeman said. His muscular frame almost filled the doorway. "How are we feeling this morning?"

"*We're* feeling like *road-kill,*" Ken said, returning the handset to the telephone.

"I'm Officer Joseph Petrie of Detroit Metro," the cop said, pulling a chair up to the bed. "I took you into custody and brought you here last night. Well, actually I followed the ambulance that brought you in."

"Am I under arrest?"

"No. You're in protective custody. Where we go from here depends on your answers to a few questions."

"Can I have some water?" Ken asked.

Petrie filled a Styrofoam cup from a blue plastic pitcher by the phone.

"Thanks," Ken said. He took a long drink, then held the cup in both hands as he closed his eyes to think back. "I'm a student at Miami University in Oxford, Ohio, and I came up here yesterday with a group for a concert at Joe Louis Arena."

"The Who concert?" Petrie asked, pulling a pen and pad from his shirt pocket.

"Yeah. Well, anyway, I was drinking some beers with friends on the drive up—except for the driver," he was quick to add, "and we got to the arena just before the music started. I felt fine . . . a little buzzed, but fine."

"Buzzed?"

"From the beer. That's all, nothing else. And I didn't have much of that . . . three or four, tops."

"Go on."

"Well, this one girl I met on the ride up—there was a big group of us—she asked me to finish her drink when we got off the bus. It was a cup of wine . . . and I did, without a second thought. Anyway, that had to be where the LSD or whatever I was on came from, because about a half hour later I lost my mind."

"What happened?"

"I thought I saw my father and a couple of his friends, and I followed them to Tiger Stadium. My father was killed in a drive-by shooting while leaving a game there five years ago, when I was in high school."

"What was his name, and the date?"

"Walter S. Perry . . . August 14," Ken replied, and Petrie scratched the information into his pad.

Ken took another long drink, dropped his head back on his pillow and again closed his eyes.

"What happened after I got to the stadium is all kind of jumbled and crazy." He paused. "But what I do remember, and strongly, is that I had a chance to save my dad's life. I grabbed him and tried to get him away, out of danger . . .

"Then I woke up here, all beat to shit and strapped to a mattress."

"Did you go into the stadium?"

"Yes, I think so . . . I mean, it seems like I did."

"How did you get in? And what did you do there?"

Images flashed through Ken's mind and he struggled to piece together and make sense of them.

"I'm not sure how I got in, but I remember following who I thought were my dad and his friends. I remember being in the stands, above the third base line, I think, and I saw my dad and the others come onto the infield . . . After a while I followed them back out and onto the street. That's when I hurt my chest," he said, fingering the stitches. "I remember falling from a fence or something back out and onto the sidewalk.

"Then it was chaos. The area around the stadium was like Vietnam, with planes spraying machine gun fire and dropping bombs everywhere. Michigan Avenue became a black river through a jungle, and napalm fires raged as far as I could see . . .

"Anyway, when I looked up from where I had fallen onto the sidewalk, I thought I saw my father, twenty or thirty yards away, with a helicopter gunship closing in on him. That's where he was really killed five years ago. And last night, all drugged up, I thought I could save him. So I grabbed him, well . . . someone, I don't know who . . . and I started running.

"That's all I remember."

Petrie poured himself a cup of water.

"Well let me fill in some of the blanks for you," he said, taking a drink. "It looks like you climbed a tall iron fence into and/or out of the stadium, because you left a lot of blood where you fell onto it. I didn't find any blood in the stadium, so you probably fell on it on your way out, as you remember.

"When my partner and I arrived in our patrol car you were in a police chopper's beam, cradling in your arms one Howard B. Sperlazza, age 54," Petrie read from a few pages earlier in his notes. "At that time, in a very agitated state, you indicated that he was your father, urgently pleading with responding officers to save his life.

"Mr. Sperlazza, who was himself intoxicated and unable to provide a home address, declined medical attention for what were apparently minor injuries. He was released to the care of two of his friends at the scene. While they, too, appeared to be under the influence, they agreed with Mr. Sperlazza's account that you ran up, grabbed Mr. Sperlazza, threw him over your shoulder and took off running.

"Whether it was because he was blind drunk or because he felt a 'paternal bond' with you, Mr. Sperlazza declined to press charges. Be glad," Officer Petrie said. "He could have nailed you for assault or even kidnapping, since you whisked him for a brief but unauthorized joyride.

"And as of this morning, there were no reports of theft from or damage to the ball park, and the owners have not indicated that they wish to press any charges for breaking and entering or trespassing.

"In summary," he concluded, "when we put this all together, the bad news is that you went through a night of hell."

"And the good news?" Ken interrupted. "I'd really like to go right to that, if I can."

"Don't blame you," Petrie said. "The good news is that the stadium is not pressing charges, Mr. Sperlazza is not pressing charges, and I believe your story, that your 'misadventure' came about not as willful acts, but because someone drugged you. I've done a background check on you and it came back clean.

"If you find evidence for the drugging, you can seek prosecution against whoever did that," Petrie said as he stood and threw his empty cup into a wastebasket. "I'll let them know you're free to leave the hospital whenever you're ready."

Officer Petrie moved toward the door, then paused inside its frame, just as when he arrived.

"One last thing . . . no, two," he said over his shoulder. "I'm going to check records to make sure you weren't making up that story about your father's death for sympathy. If you did, I'll be back with my own charges . . . The other thing is that you might want to reconsider your friends. I would if one of them did this to me.

"Take care of yourself," the cop advised, and he was gone.

Ken turned towards the opened drapes, but got no relief from the view. A jagged gray sky looked ready to explode in lightning, thunder and rain as it scudded low above the dull black parking lot. He watched a linen truck pull up to a service entrance. The wind gusted papers from the dashboard as the driver jumped out, and he gave chase into an adjoining alley.

Looking at the number next to his bed, Ken wondered what he would say to Jill. He reached for his water again and felt the IV needle twist in his hand. Then, closing his eyes, he thought of how, less than 24 hours earlier, he was getting ready for the fun of a road trip and concert. Now he lay battered, gashed and dazed in a hospital—a psychiatric unit, at that—fresh out of his restraints and feeling like shit.

Nurse Marsh carried in a tray with milk, raisin bran, a blueberry muffin and butter, and a silver pot of hot water with Sanka and decaffeinated tea packets on the side.

"I guess it's a good idea to make sure the psycho ward boys get decaf," Ken said as she slid the tray over his bed.

"If I could only get my husband to drink it," she said, ignoring his sarcasm.

"Can I get a TV in here or is that my only entertainment?" Ken asked, motioning toward the beeping heart monitor.

"Sorry. No TV in the 'psycho ward,' but I can get you some magazines," the nurse said, patting his good shoulder.

"Oh yeah . . . Do I need to dial anything special to get an outside line on this phone? I want to call the number you gave me."

"Local calls will go through on direct dial, but you'll need to go through the switchboard for long distance . . . Which reminds me, you should call your family to let them know you're all right. When you were admitted the telephone company gave us the number for the home address on your drivers license. They said it was listed to a Maureen Perry, so we left a message on her answering machine explaining where you are, that you were brought in for treatment and that your condition was not life-threatening."

"Wonderful," Ken said.

Just as he finished his breakfast, Nurse Marsh brought him two old issues of "Sports Illustrated," the current "Esquire" and that day's *Detroit Free Press*. As she carried the tray out she passed a thin, black, male nurse who entered and handed Ken a small paper cup with three pills and a larger one with water to wash them down. He then drew two vials of Ken's blood.

"Thanks a lot man," he said, untying the surgical tubing from Ken's arm. "You're a lot more cooperative than most we get on this floor."

"You mean the nut ward?"

"Well, that may be a little . . . *indelicate* . . . Anyway, I'll be back after you have lunch," the male nurse said, taping a cotton ball over the red dot on Ken's arm. "Chicken tetrazzini or tuna tetrachloride, something like that . . . Smells real good!"

"I can't wait."

Again alone, or alone as he could be in the windowed and electronically monitored observation room, Ken once more turned to the phone. First he would call information for his sister's new number in Chicago, then try to phone his mother there before she retrieved the hospital's message from her home answering machine. Next he would call Jill and hope she understood that the previous night's madness was not his fault.

Once more the sound of voices in the hall drew closer until Nurse Marsh appeared outside his opened door. "He's right here," she said, motioning toward Ken. "Feel free to stay as long as you like."

Jill was timid as a child as she peeked around the doorway, dropped a large paper bag and put both hands to her mouth as she began to cry.

Nurse Marsh put an arm around Jill and led her to a chair by the bed. "Don't worry, honey, he's going to be fine," she said. "You can sit here, and there's water on the table for both of you. Mr. Perry will be having his lunch soon and you can order something too . . . Maybe a sandwich or dessert?"

"No, no thank you," Jill sobbed, sitting instead on the edge of the bed. She straightened her hair and pulled a handkerchief from her jeans. "I'll be all right, thank you."

Ken raised his hand and Jill cried harder as she took it in both of hers, kissed it and held it against the tears on her cheek. Beginning to speak, she saw the empty wells of his eyes, stopped and kissed his forehead. A tear dropped onto Ken's neck as Jill's fingertips traced the cut over his eye. The shaved skin around the stitches in his chest was stained yellow-brown from antiseptic swabs, and Jill followed the taped IV and heart monitor connections to the bottle and machine above him.

"You know something, Jill?" he asked, pouring her a cup of water. "I think those Who concerts are highly overrated."

"Good God, Ken . . . What happened?"

"Well," he said, stroking her hand, "to make a long and very weird story short and very weird, I found myself running around Detroit tumbling along fence tops, sidewalks and winos, absolutely Loony-Tunes after one of our *friends* from the bus slipped me acid."

"What?" Jill gasped. "Nobody from that group would do such a thing. Are you sure it wasn't something you had in the arena?

Did you eat or drink or smoke anything out in the lobby, or from a stranger?"

"Nothing. But I agree with you," he said, motioning for a cup of water. "I don't think it was anyone from our group, either.

"Remember Crystal? The girl who joined us at the last minute? Well, my 'cosmic excursion' began not long after she asked me to finish a glass of wine for her. It was her," Ken said. "I'm sure it was.

"Hey, wait a minute!" he interjected, sitting bolt upright. "The group, the BOZO's . . . they've left. How are you getting back?"

"The same way you are. We'll catch a flight."

"I can't ask you to wait for me," Ken said, turning his face away. "I don't even know when I'll be able to leave . . . And you have classes . . ."

"Listen, I'm from a suburb about a half hour north of here, so it's no big deal," Jill explained. "Let me go over what happened with the rest of the group last night, then you can share your story with me. Fair enough?"

"All right."

"Well, first of all, just into the concert you said a couple of things to me that didn't make sense, and were acting a little strange not far into the music, then you turned and darted towards the exit. I went after you but couldn't keep up, losing you in the lobby.

"I spent the rest of the concert looking all over the arena for you. When it was over Dave parked the bus a few blocks from the arena and several of us started calling local police and hospitals. That's when we found out you were here. I called my mom in Birmingham and Dave waited until she came to get me before he took the bus away for the overnighter in Ann Arbor. This morning they left for Oxford."

Besides literally finding his own ass in a sling, Ken now felt that he had become a hassle for everyone else in the group, with Jill now his babysitter.

"What did you tell your mother?" he asked.

"I told her that a group of us came up for the Who concert, that my date was jumped and beat up afterwards, and that I needed to stay and help you."

Ken turned away in shame.

"She wasn't surprised that I wanted to stay for you, because I've already told her about you several times before, in phone calls home from school. So she knows you're important to me," Jill said, again taking his hand. "Now it's important that you know, too."

When Ken turned back toward her, a tear rolled onto his pillow.

"What happened, Ken?"

Ken recounted in detail the story he had shared earlier with Officer Petrie. He started with the appearance of his father and the other two men in the arena, and continued through the weird scenes leading up to and inside the stadium, to the bloody conclusion on the adjacent street.

Jill took a soft plaid shirt, a pair of blue jeans and underwear from the shopping bag, removed the tags and placed them in the closet. They were replacements for the torn, blood—and vomit-soaked clothes he wore when admitted.

Ken picked up the phone and called Chicago information for his sister's new number. The hospital operator put the call through, and when Marg answered, Ken found that he was successful in getting to them before his mother retrieved the message the nurse had left on her machine in Grand Rapids.

After a brief update to his sister on how he had all but completely recovered from his mugging in Detroit, he had her put their mother on the line.

"Oh *Kenny!*" she gasped. "I'm *horrified!* Are you *sure* you're all right?"

"I'm sure, mom. Besides, this gives me a good excuse for not hauling heavy furniture around for you guys. Is the move going okay?"

"Yes," she told her son. "It's going great. But I'm going to fly out immediately to come to your side."

"No, mom. I'm okay, really! In fact, they're keeping me overnight for observation, then releasing me in the morning. Then I'm going to Jill's house until our flight back to school. So don't make this bigger than it is," he begged. "Some joker just punched me when I wasn't looking and I needed a couple of stitches. It's not nearly as bad as when you took me to the hospital that time I fell out of my tree house. Remember?"

"Yes, Kenny, I remember. But . . ."

"But *nothing!*" Ken insisted. "You stay there and help Marg and Janice with the heavy lifting. I'll see you later on, probably at Thanksgiving."

"Well, all right," she conceded. "But if you need to reach me I'm going to stay here another week to help Margaret and Janice with some painting. We might put some flowers in their cute little yard, too. Why don't you and Jill come up next weekend and join us?"

"I'd love to mom, but a . . . project I'm working on is coming due. I'll be dealing with that."

"Well, if you change your mind, just call. The girls said they can probably arrange for a free flight into O'Hare."

"Okay mom. Tell them thanks, and that I'll take them up on it if I can. But I'm sure I'll have to stay at school, glued to the books. I love you, Mom."

"I love you too, Kenny, and the girls send theirs, too."

Jill remained at Ken's side throughout the long, gray and quiet Sunday broken only by lunch, dinner and his all-too-frequent blood and urine tests. She left when visiting hours ended at nine.

When Perry awoke the next morning he looked through the inside window to see Jill talking with an old doctor in the hall. Noticing that Ken was awake, they entered his room together. Jill leaned over to give him a hug and kiss, then sat on the bed.

Dr. John Strand introduced himself and bit his lip as he scanned Ken's chart. "Good news," the Einstein-haired doctor said over his clipboard. "We've decided to release you to the care of this beautiful young lady." He winked at Jill and returned to Ken.

"Your blood tests show that what was a massive dose of LSD has disappeared, and I'm going to suggest that you get a neurological workup when you return home. I doubt if you did any lasting damage to the brain, but with all that acid and the knocks you took, it's a good idea.

"The stitches in your chest will dissolve as that wound heals over the next couple of weeks, and the muscle tears and other damage to your chest and shoulder will hurt and cause limited range of motion for your right arm for a while. You didn't sever any nerves, arteries, tendons or break any bones, so time and rest should give you 100 percent recovery."

Dr. Strand shined a small penlight into both of Ken's eyes, and wrapped a blood pressure cuff around his arm. "I'm going to prescribe something for the pain, if you can promise me you'll take it as prescribed," he said, pumping-up the device.

"Listen doctor, you can keep your goddamn pain pills. I am not a drug addict. I did not *take* that LSD; It was slipped to me by a stranger. Up until Saturday night you probably had more contact with that shit through treating people on it than I ever had through my friends."

"I'm sorry. I didn't mean to . . ."

"That's all right. I don't care. I just want to get out of here and back to school."

"Of course. I can understand that," the doctor said, pulling the cuff from Ken's arm. "I didn't mean anything by that . . . But you really should take the medicine. Besides the pain killers there are antibiotics you'll have to use to allay any infection. I'll leave a prescription with the nurse, and they can fill it through the hospital pharmacy on your way out."

Dr. Strand patted Ken on his good shoulder and turned around on his way to the door. "And try to take it easy. Physical exertion could open your chest wound."

"Does that mean I can't run?"

"Not for *at least* several weeks, and then only if the healing has gone well. Anyway, your chest and shoulder trauma would probably make the upper body motion of running too painful now."

Ken heaved a long sigh.

The doctor pulled a pen from his lab coat as he walked back to Ken. "If you get discouraged, just remember," he said, tapping Ken's chest with the pen. "If that injury was one inch to the left it would have gone through a lung. And over here," he said, tapping a couple of inches farther from the stitches, "it would have skewered your heart like a shish kabob."

"People keep telling me I'm *lucky*," Ken said, reaching for water. "You know when I'll be lucky, Doc? When I find the bitch who drugged me I'll be lucky if I don't kill her and end up in prison."

"Well, that's out of my jurisdiction," Dr. Strand said, turning again to leave. "I think you should join your girlfriend here and concentrate on getting well."

Jill nodded a goodbye to the doctor, and Nurse Edwina Lyles entered the room as he left. "I'll be back for you in a few minutes after Dr. Strand signs your release papers," the stout black woman said. "Then I'll take you for any meds, patient services for billing, and finally wheel you back out into the free world."

"I am more than ready when you are," Ken replied. Jill took her place by him and kissed his cheek.

"Mom's looking forward to meeting you," she said in an upbeat tone.

"Oh sure," Ken said. "Who wouldn't be proud to have their daughter bring a recently arrested friend home from the psych ward?"

Jill rolled her eyes and walked to the closet. "None of this is your fault," she said, laying the clothes she had brought for him across the foot of the bed. "I told her you were jumped outside the arena, remember?"

"Yeah. It's just that I would prefer to meet your mother under better circumstances."

"Ken, remember, what happened was not your fault. You did nothing wrong. Someone else gave you that drug and what happened afterwards comes down to a son showing his love for his father. There's nothing wrong with that, and no one blames you for anything. Remember that Ken, please?"

Nurse Lyles returned and drew yet another vial of blood from Ken as she pulled off the heart monitor pads. His IV had been removed earlier that morning.

Jill walked to a small waiting room by the fourth floor elevators while Ken dressed. Several minutes later the squat no-nonsense nurse wheeled him into the elevator. He held a small white paper bag with his medication. When they arrived at the first floor patient services office, Jill left to get her mother's car while Ken completed his paperwork.

As soon as Nurse Lyles pushed Ken's wheelchair through the lobby and out the automatic doors into the late morning sun, he sprung to his feet, anxious to stretch his legs. After two steps he paused and wobbled. The nurse took his arm as Jill rushed around the pearl Cadillac Escalade to open the passenger's door.

"Nice ride," Ken said, and he was glad the car offered plenty of room for his beleaguered body. He reclined the seat and Jill reached behind him, brushing his chin with her breasts as she retrieved and then fastened his seat belt.

A few blocks later they were northbound on Woodward Avenue. The asphalt artery cuts a straight path through the length of the economic spectrum that begins in Detroit's gray business district and hurries past its black arson-pocked ghettos into Highland Park,

Ferndale and a couple of other blue-collar suburbs on the way to the manicured lawns of upper crust Birmingham. Jill turned the car left onto West Maple Road, past the southern edge of the trendy downtown square to Glenhurst Drive. Two long blocks later they pulled into the driveway of a stately, two-story Southern colonial home, and Jill clicked a remote control to open the garage.

"Nice digs," Ken said as the car rolled to a stop.

"Yeah, daddy did all right," Jill said, turning off the car. They sat in brief, awkward silence until Jill took Ken's hands in hers.

"Now remember, you have nothing you need to explain or be sorry for. You really *were* attacked, just not in a direct way you could defend yourself against. Okay?"

"Yeah, okay," Ken agreed.

"And I *am* looking forward to introducing you to mom," Jill continued as she opened her door. "She's a great lady and I'm sure you'll love each other."

Jill waited for Ken as he rounded the car and together they entered the kitchen, where Audra Mangan was waiting. She hugged her daughter and then smiled broadly as she reached for Ken.

"You're Ken," she said, taking his hand. "Jill has told me so many absolutely wonderful things about you. I'm so sorry to hear about the nasty incident that happened Saturday night," she said, pulling him a chair from the table. "You two have a seat and I'll bring us some pie and something to drink. Is coffee all right?"

"Sure, black," Ken said, and he winced as he sat.

"Poor thing . . . Are you okay or would you like to lie down?"

"I'm fine, Mrs. Mangan."

"No, call me Audra. I insist. When you get to my age, you don't want to be reminded of your seniority. I'm Audra, please."

"Audra it is," Ken said, and he smiled as Jill handed him a fork and napkin.

Jill's mother didn't need to worry about her age, Ken thought as he watched her pour their coffee. Her figure was every bit as lean and well-proportioned as her daughter's, and while her black hair was peppered with gray, it framed a smooth face that time hadn't tarnished. Traces of wrinkles at the corners of her eyes and mouth were born of a lifetime of laughter, crying and loving.

The smile on Jill's face as she sat beside Ken showed that she was proud of her mother.

"Well, I've found two flights out of Metro tomorrow for Cincinnati," Mrs. Mangan said, slipping on reading glasses as she reached for a pad. "One leaves at 7:45 a.m. and gets in at 8:30, and the other departs at 4 p.m. and arrives just before 5."

"I'll have to see when a ride can pick us up," Jill said. "But I imagine the 4 o'clock is the best bet."

"Okay," her mother said. "I'll leave the flight information and airline's number here. Just let me know what you decide, and I can drive you to the airport whenever. Anyway, I'll leave you two alone now. Jill will show you to the guest room, Ken, and if you need a toothbrush, medicine or anything you just let us know."

"Thanks very much, Audra. You don't know how much I appreciate everything you and Jill are doing for me."

"Don't be silly. This way I get to meet you and begin what I'm sure will be a long friendship," she said, turning for the living room. "I'm going over to the Somerset Mall for awhile with a couple of friends from St. Dunston's," a local theater company where she volunteered as a set designer. "They'll be picking me up soon, so you'll have the car if you need it. But don't eat dinner; I want to make it for us when I get back."

Jill hugged her mother as she left, and Ken looked out the kitchen window at the sprawling green lawn with several old oaks bordering a large swimming pool.

"Mom's a swimmer," Jill said, pouring them both more coffee. "As far back as I can remember she's always begun every day with an hour swim before breakfast. Here, weather permitting, and in the pool at the Birmingham Y when it doesn't."

Jill looked at her watch. "It's time for these," she said, pulling two amber bottles from the prescription bag. She fished out two blue capsules and a tiny white pill, then handed them to Ken with a bottle of water from the fridge.

"What were those for?" he asked between long, cold drinks.

"The blue ones are antibiotics, with a little white pain killer chaser."

Jill then picked up the phone, called her number at school and was happy that Chris was there to answer. Ken finished the water as Jill assured Chris that he was fine, and then asked Chris to call back when she found someone able to pick them up at Cincinnati International Airport the next day. Jill suggested going first to another resident assistant on the first floor who owed her a favor. If that failed Chris should call Dave Pung to see if he or another BOZO could come for them.

"Yeah," Ken said loud enough for Chris to hear. "Anybody but Crystal!"

"I'll explain when we see you tomorrow," Jill told her roommate, and hung up.

Jill picked a shopping bag from under the table, grabbed Ken's hand and pulled him to his feet. "This is a few things you'll need . . . toothbrush, razor and other toiletries and another change of clothes for the trip back."

She kept the bag in one hand and took Ken's with the other, leading him through the Victorian living room and up the mahogany-paneled stairs. She opened a hallway closet, pulled out a couple of towels and showed him the bathroom on the way to the small bedroom where he would spend the night. The wallpapered ceiling was arched to conform to the roof of the house, and a small, four-paned window looked out onto Glenhurst. Ken closed his eyes and took a deep breath. The earthy scent of the large cedar armoire mingled with that from a freshly placed bowl of cinnamon potpourri.

Jill opened the window as Ken dropped the bag to take her into his arms. A long kiss later he sat on the twin bed's goose down comforter and again opened his arms, welcoming his lover.

Jill put one knee next to Ken, leaned down, and her palm froze just over his chest. "I'm afraid I'll hurt you," she said.

Ken said nothing, and her fingertips traced softly over the soft flannel until he flinched. She leaned forward and kissed him again, then tugged the shirt from his pants and off over his head.

Beginning at his temple, she kissed him lightly, lips and tongue gliding like a butterfly along his mouth, cheek, neck and chest, stopping at the wide gauze patch.

Ken cupped her shiny black hair in both hands, pulled her flushed cheek against the wound, and felt her hot breath course down his stomach. She rose, moved to the foot of the bed and tugged off his shoes, socks, pants and boxers, then slid beside him and pulled up the comforter.

Ken's stirrings of passion were quickly overtaken by the freshly administered medications, and Jill let her love and strength flow into him as he fell asleep. She carefully rose, spread the contents of the bag on a shelf in the armoire and pulled a robe from one of its drawers. She draped it over a chair beneath the window, tucked the comforter under Ken's chin and again kissed his brow before leaving the room.

Jill spent the next few hours down the hall in her room, lying on her bed and reading in the quiet, her door open so she would hear if Ken stirred. After leafing through her high school yearbooks, she felt herself drifting into sleep and rose instead to go back and check on Ken. Slowly pushing open his door, she saw a shaft of bright midday sun shining through the small window and onto Ken's sleeping face. She tiptoed back to her room for a camera, hurried back and was glad that the clattering shutter didn't wake Ken as she shot several frames. She placed the camera on the chair by his robe and carefully slid under the covers and next to Ken in the spoons position, her forehead against the back of his neck, her left arm curled around him with her palm flat against his stomach.

Jill decided to ignore the phone that rang in her mother's adjacent bedroom. Then, remembering that she was expecting word from Chris, she raced to get it.

It was Chris, and she explained that Tom and Chloe would meet their afternoon flight when it arrived the next day. She added that Mrs. Caulkins—the dorm's head resident and Jill's supervisor—said there would be no problem with her being gone another day, but she would need a call put in to her if it looked like it would take any longer.

"Super!" Jill said, relieved that all was ready for their return to campus. "Please just tell Mrs. Caulkins that I'll be back tomorrow afternoon and that I appreciate her cooperation on this one. Oh, and thank Tom and Chloe, too. We're on United flight 1226," she said, referring to the paper her mother had given her, "arriving from Detroit at 4:57 p.m."

Don't worry about a thing; everything's set," Chris assured. "You and Ken just relax and be well."

"Yeah!" Kaaren yelled from the background. "You take care! It's just too bad you guys can't be here for the beer-blast toga party we're having in the dorm tonight!"

"Tell Kaaren I enjoy her delightful sense of humor," Jill said.

"Oh I'm sure she knows," Chris answered. "Don't worry. We'll see you guys tomorrow."

Jill hung up and returned to find Ken sitting awake in his bed.

"Good news," she said. "Tom and Chloe are coming to the airport for us tomorrow afternoon. So all we have to do is rest, relax and rejuvenate. We could sneak a snack before mom gets home for dinner. Anything sound good to you?"

"Yeah, shoe leather. After two days in bed I feel like I want to get up and move around more than I need another meal. Can we go for a walk?"

"I know just the place."

They reboarded the Escalade and left the garage for a sunny five-minute drive through the winding neighborhood streets to the long, straight and heavily wooded Lone Pine Road. Less than a mile later they turned into the campus of the Cranbrook Academy of Art.

"This is where I come to get away," Jill said, turning right at a fountain overlooking a small lake. The grounds of the exclusive school reminded Ken of Miami's Western Campus, and Jill pulled the car into a parking space outside the science museum, tucked amidst the school's rolling woods and meadows.

Jill took Ken's hand and they walked a short way back up the road from where they came. Then, at a break in the thick pine trees, she led him onto an earthen trail that opened overlooking a lush green valley. It was bordered on three sides by the tall firs, and extended about a quarter-mile to a narrow lake at its bottom.

"This is gorgeous," Ken said, and they stood speechless, hand-in-hand as they took in the sights and sounds of the late summer afternoon. Phys ed department canoes were pulled onto the opposite shore, near freshly abandoned field hockey equipment. Songbirds called to each other from the pine-scented heights, and a scattering of frogs answered from the muddy shores below.

The couple walked from the trees into the full afternoon sun, and Ken slowly lowered onto the warm, thick grass. He then rolled onto his back and looked at the puffy white clouds as Jill sat cross-legged beside him.

"If everyone could spend five minutes each day in a place like this there'd be no crime," he said, still gazing upward.

A little later he lowered his eyes and saw Jill looking at him.

"And no more fear?" she asked. There was a knowing, expectant look on her expressionless face.

Ken knew the time had come. He had trusted her all along. Now he had to bring her into the darkness that troubled his heart, just as she had brought him into the light of this place that warmed it.

"When I was home last, the weekend before we met, I accidentally found something my father left hidden before he died. It was something neither I nor my sister or mom knew of. And I haven't shared it with them for the same reason I haven't told anyone else. I don't understand what it *was,* what it *is,* or what consequences it could bring on myself or anyone else if I talk about it.

"I found evidence that my father was deeply involved in some sort of secret work or activity in our home, literally under our noses, without telling us a word. And that makes me ask two questions that bother me to the core . . . Was my father the man I . . . we in the family . . . knew him to be? And was his *random* killing really a planned murder, related to whatever it was he was doing on the sly?

"Making it all worse, I don't know if I can ever hope to find solid answers. And I'm afraid I'll never find peace unless I do."

Jill's eyes had stayed on him.

"It's made me feel guilty to suspect my dad's former friends and co-workers as potential suspects. But it hurts a lot more to know that we, the family, didn't have *all* of him, enough of his confidence that he could share with us all of what his life was about."

"But you know he loved you," Jill said.

"Yes. But love stands and walks on trust and honesty. They hold it up and make it real. Any lie, secret or other betrayal can erode or destroy that. One as big as I found could knock it flat on its ass."

"Regardless of what happened, what didn't happen . . . right now I love you," Jill said. "I've fallen in love with you and I hope you'll let that love be strength for you. Maybe when you want to despair from what you discovered at home, from your crippled confidence or insecurity . . . maybe then you can gain hope in what we've found in each other."

Ken pulled her atop his chest, and he imagined the sharp pain from his wound was her love, searing its way into his heart.

"I love you too, Jill."

As they lay in the gathering darkness, there was nothing else to say.

CHAPTER THIRTEEN

The drive from Birmingham to Detroit Metropolitan Airport took almost as long as the flight to Cincinnati. And Tom and Chloe were relieved to see a reasonably sound-looking, if not agile Ken emerge with Jill from the concourse.

Jill carried their only small carry-on bag with one hand as she held Ken's hand with her other, following his slow, steady gait.

Chloe's welcome home hug brought a grimace from Ken, and she cringed when she saw the pain in his face.

"Oh god, Ken, I'm sorry! Are you all right?"

"Of course he's all right," Jill said. "He's just faking it for sympathy."

"Sure," Ken said. "I *only* ran a pole halfway through my body."

"Come on, Ken," Tom said, nudging Ken. "If you keep talking like that you're going to get Chloe excited!"

During the drive back to campus Ken told Tom and Chloe about the spiked drink Crystal gave him, and the bad trip that took him through a baseball park and into a psych ward.

"But the up side of it all is that I got to meet Jill's mom and sample her *pasta il mare*," Ken said.

"And don't forget," Tom said, looking into the rearview mirror, "if those stitches in your chest don't heal just right, you'll have a shirt pocket even when you're not wearing one!"

"What I'm *really* looking forward to is finding Crystal," Ken answered, his eyes closed as Jill held his head on her lap on the back seat. "I'm going to give that bitch a piece of my mind. She sure as hell helped herself to *mine!*"

"Good luck," Chloe said as she adjusted the air conditioning. "Not only is Crystal a bitch, but she seems to be a ghost, too. She never showed up at her seat during the concert. And afterwards, she was the only one besides you not to show at the bus.

"Then, when Jill told us what Crystal did to you, we tried to find her ourselves. With no last name to go on, we couldn't check the campus or town phone books. When I called a couple of friends—a grad assistant and an assistant prof in the English Department where Crystal's supposed to be majoring—neither recognized her by name or physical description."

"Well, tomorrow I'm going to the registrar's office and find out for sure," Ken replied. "I don't care if I have to go through every *Crystal* in Ohio. I need to find out if she enjoyed the concert as much as I did."

The old Grand Prix made the gradual climb up U.S. 27 into Oxford and Tom steered left onto Spring Street. After another left onto Maple they stopped in front of Minnich Hall, where Jill kissed Ken, took the small bag and exited the car. Without speaking, Ken followed her out.

"Come on, Ken, get back in," she protested. "You need to go home and rest."

"Yeah," Tom said. "Let those stitches take hold before you go walking around any more than you need to."

"They laced up my chest, not my legs," Ken said. "So unless I crawl home on my belly I'll be okay. I need the exercise. I appreciate all your help," he told Tom and Chloe. "I owe you."

Seconds later they drove away and Ken joined Jill in Minnich's lobby. She went to the front desk, opened her mailbox and pulled out several envelopes.

"Ken, I think I need to answer some mail, get tomorrow's assignments together and just deal with some things right now."

For the first time, Ken wondered if they would weather his problems together.

"I really need some time now, okay?"

"Sure," Ken said. "Thanks for everything. You and your mom really went 'above and beyond' in all this."

After a quick kiss Jill handed Ken the bag with his clothes and medication, and he headed for the door to the courtyard.

"I'll call you!" Jill said, and hurried for the stairs.

During his walk home Ken watched the students moving to and from class. The guilt he felt at missing his own classes was now compounded by the inconvenience he was bringing upon Jill, Tom,

Chloe and others. He wondered how long Jill would put up with it.

Dragging himself along the sidewalk Ken felt dizzy from his medication. He was suddenly angered by not having a clear head to deal with his frustration.

Arriving home he pulled some junk mail from his mailbox. Without looking, he balled it up and threw it into the Dumpster.

Ken felt heavy and dull as he dropped onto his bed, and his spirits faded to gray with the creeping dusk.

Several hours later he stirred with the eerie feeling that comes with waking up at the wrong end of the day. Still fully dressed and half asleep, he left empty-handed for the library. The lights coming from student apartments and passing cars had a spooky, unreal quality in Ken's groggy, medicated state. The low hum of student activity in the library brought him the reassurance that comes with a sense of connectedness with others. He took the stairs to the second floor, found an empty table near a rear corner and fell heavily into a chair.

Here he could be surrounded by people, not alone, yet not having to speak with or listen to anyone. He needed a familiar, reassuring place to think.

Ken felt defeated. It was like he had climbed a mountain to seek answers only to find no wise man at the top. Even if he had the strength to climb higher, he was out of mountain. Any help would have to come from somewhere between the top of that mountain of questions and the dark, empty hole beneath his house.

Ken folded his arms on the cool wooden tabletop, placed his forehead on them and listened to the muted conversation of several nearby couples, punctuated by the hum of a photocopy machine.

Knuckles gently rapped the wood next to Ken's head, and he looked up at a mousy-looking woman in a sweater.

"I'm sorry, but the library is closed," she whispered. "We'll reopen in the morning at eight."

"Thanks," Ken said. He rubbed his eyes in disbelief as he scanned the empty room. It was just before midnight, and the gray-haired woman covered a gasp with one hand as Ken raised up, revealing a large blood spot on his shirt.

"I'm sorry," he said, placing a palm over the stain. "I got some stitches over the weekend and my bandage must have slipped."

Now, on top of everything else, Ken felt like a leper as he walked past other stragglers from the building. He was hungry and thirsty and the world seemed all the more unreal as he walked home, his head now pounding since the pain killer had worn off.

Halfway up the stairs to his apartment, Ken saw Jill sitting on the floor with her back against his door.

"I came to change your bandages," she said.

Ken unlocked the door, then dropped to sit beside her.

"I can't go on like this," he said. "I don't want to lose my mind and I sure don't want to lose you."

He pulled his knees up to his forehead and wrapped his arms around his legs.

"Maybe I've been too careful," he went on. "Maybe I need to be more direct. I know there's someone who has at least part of the answer I'm looking for. But I've been afraid to ask him. I've been dancing around the point and now it's time to get to it. At first I thought my imagination had blown this out of proportion. But someone's searched my apartment," he said, nodding backward. "That was soon after my dad's friend visited from back home . . . And I think my being drugged by Crystal, or whatever her name is, most likely is part of this too."

Jill listened in silence. She looked tired but focused as she stared straight ahead.

"At this point I don't know if I'm putting together pieces of a puzzle or building a castle in the sky," Ken admitted.

Jill stood, helped Ken to his feet and opened the door for both to enter. "Take off your shirt," she said, disappearing into the bathroom. She returned with medical tape, bandages and towels. Ken lay on his back, hands under his head as Jill sponged the old blood and ointment from around the black stitches. He winced as she prodded a cotton ball full of hydrogen peroxide over the wound, then applied more antiseptic cream and taped a fresh gauze pad over the stitches.

She put the supplies back in the bathroom, where she dropped his bloody shirt to soak in a sink full of cold water.

Ken was feeling more rooted in reality as he listened to Jill go about her work. She ended up in the kitchen, fixing chicken soup for Ken and sandwiches for them both. Without speaking she returned, took him by the hand and led him to their meal on the kitchen table. Then she took a candle from the living room, put it in the center of the table and lit it before flipping off the overhead light.

A full moon shone over the tangle of trees outside the window, and Jill put two blue capsules next to Ken's soup. "You're supposed to take these with food, until they're gone," she reminded. "To prevent infection."

He picked them up and then dropped his hand back onto the table, as if it was too heavy too lift.

Jill picked up the capsules, brushed his chin downward and dropped them between his parted lips. He wrapped his arms around Jill's legs as she gave him a drink of water. Then she fell to her knees, placing her head on his lap.

Rain began to fall, and they listened to the big drops slapping the elm leaves.

"I'm tired, and right now I feel defeated," Ken said. "But I'm not weak. And I won't give up. I'll find my way through this and we'll be happy. I promise," he said, stroking her hair.

There was another long silence that grew deeper with the slowing rain. The steam had stopped rising from Ken's soup.

"It was hard for me to accept the meaninglessness of my father's death," he said in a soft but strong voice. "But it was harder to deal with the anger, the hate. Whoever killed my dad had no good reason to do it, and they were never brought to justice. I never knew their names, never saw their faces, was never able to scream my hatred at them or try to forgive them. And it pained me to see my mom and sister lost in the cruel absurdity of it all. My helplessness there made me seethe all the more.

"But I dealt with it. We all dealt with it. We buried my father, mourned and moved on. Our love carried us through. And we found we could be happy again. That's what dad would have wanted for us."

Jill wrapped her arms around the small of Ken's back and pulled herself tight against his stomach.

"I thought I fought-off the faceless ghosts who killed my father, and that I had found peace. But the murderers have come back to taunt me, and now I fear I didn't really know the man we left in my father's grave."

Jill looked up at Ken, her blue eyes like those of a little girl listening to a sad story.

"When I went home the weekend before we met, I discovered a secret my father had kept from us," Ken repeated. "It had something to do with his work, and that he was involved in something we knew nothing about, something big.

"The trouble is, I don't know exactly what it was, just that it was a big part of his life, his work, and that he never shared it with any of us in the family.

"But I'm almost certain it had to do with some kind of security or intelligence work, and that's what's got me crazy," he said with a sigh. "If my father was so deeply involved in something so secret, if his work took him into another world, of darkness and shadows, could the *stranger* who killed him be from that same hidden world?

"My hatred for the killer was rekindled when I realized he might not have been a random crazy, but a calculating assassin.

"Which would be worse?" Ken asked. "A senseless death brought on by frustration and bigotry or a cold-blooded killing pulled off by someone as a business arrangement?

"And then, *if* my father was killed because of something he knew or did or might discover or do . . . then who did it? Was it the 'other side' or ours? Was he a threat? To whom? Was he a patriot? A traitor?

"Anyway, it's not the kind of thing you can forget or walk away from. No matter how hard you try."

Jill looked toward the sky. It had stopped raining.

"Would it help if you stopped trying?" she asked.

"No. No matter what I think or do, the temporary distractions offered by friends, class, running or whatever end up just that— temporary distractions. When the distraction's over, this thing always comes back into my mind the same way that lone mosquito buzzing around your head in bed keeps you awake all night. You wait for it to land, then you slap yourself in the dark, thinking you've got it. But just as you're drifting off to sleep, the damned buzzing starts again.

"That's how this has been for me," Ken said. "Most of the time I'm with you I don't think about it; I can forget about it then, and sometimes in class or in a store or wherever . . . But it always comes back, just like that damned mosquito, sucking me dry."

Jill took his soup to the stove and poured it back into a pot. Before she could turn the burner on, Ken stopped her. The rain started again, harder than before.

"I'm really not hungry," he said. When she started to protest he put his fingers over her mouth and kissed her forehead. "I'll finish the sandwich now, and I'll have a good breakfast in the morning," he promised. "It's late, and we need to get you home."

"No," she said. "You stay here. I won't have you walking that wound around in the rain." She took a large golfing umbrella from its place by the door. "I'll return this later," she said. "You just finish that sandwich and get some sleep."

It was still raining when Ken awoke the next morning, and it brought a depressing aura to his new and time-consuming ritual of bathing around and changing the dressing on his chest wound. The light but steady shower greeted him when he left the building. Jill had taken his only umbrella, so he returned to his room and pulled his poncho from the bag where it remained since his last hitchhike home.

Halfway to class a sharp, a throbbing sensation under his bandage told Ken he had forgotten to take his pain medication.

That's all right, he thought. *I'll just let that be a reminder of how much I'm looking forward to my meeting with Crystal.* He went over the tongue-lashing he intended for the vile bitch, and his building anger carried him to fantasies of punching out her boyfriend, if she had one.

Ken entered Upham Hall and then stopped as he realized the fire in his belly wouldn't let him sit still for German or anything else until he found Crystal. He wondered if there was any way he could have charges brought against her without any witnesses or evidence. He doubted that anyone saw her put the drug in his drink, and he had pitched the cup, the only material evidence, into a City of Detroit trash can.

Ken left Upham Hall. And by the time he got to the English Department offices in Bachelor Hall, he was sweat-soaked and miserable inside the poncho-turned-sauna. He went to the secretary and sat his dripping backpack on the floor before her desk.

"Excuse me," he said, handing her his student I.D. "My name is Ken Perry and this weekend I met a girl named Crystal who asked me to call her, but I lost her number and she never gave me her last name."

The bored-looking receptionist stared silently over the top of her reading glasses.

"I really need to get in touch with her," Ken went on. "She's tall, with brown eyes and straight brown hair, and a little older, in her late 20s . . . She said she was an English major."

"Listen, I'm not a matchmaker, and I don't have time . . ."

"No! Really!" Ken insisted. "I already have a girlfriend. I need to get some information from her. She said she has an uncle who's a doctor and might be able to help me with this," he said, raising his shirt to show his bandage. "Please?"

The secretary hesitated, then tapped a few strokes on her computer keyboard. "I checked the list of our declared majors and minors, and I don't find anyone named Crystal, beginning with a 'C' or a 'K'." She said she couldn't recall anyone by the description Ken offered, and suggested he try the registrar's office.

But his luck was no better in Roudebush Hall, the administration building, where a willing office assistant found several Crystals, but no Krystal, and none in the English Department. Neither were any of them from Cincinnati, and the oldest of those in the database was a 22-year-old senior in business administration, at least several years younger than the woman Ken sought.

He left Roudebush just before noon and decided to head for lunch in the Zebra Room at the Shriver Center. The rain turned into a full-fledged deluge as he walked along Patterson Avenue, and he arrived early enough to grab a booth before the lunch rush.

Well, I've managed to miss another morning of classes, Ken thought as he stretched out on the vinyl seat, his back against the wall. *And, as usual, I've accomplished nothing. Zip. Nada.*

A tuna melt and fries lay untouched before him as he sipped his iced tea and watched as lightning snaked over the reflecting pool of the adjacent Schiewetz Fine Arts Plaza. The nearly simultaneous thunder rattled the windows, and the lights flickered several times.

Ken looked at his book bag and wondered if he should even bother to study, given the amount of classtime he'd lost. And now, in addition to his battered and bruised chest and head, he was finding that the days without running were causing his muscles to tighten.

I don't know who you are, 'Miss Crystal from Cincinnati,' Ken thought as he scanned faces in the crowded cafeteria. *But if I ever find you I'm going to take a tit in each fist and drag you to campus security.*

Why the hell would anyone pull such a stunt? he asked himself. High school punks spike each other's drinks, and then there's the loser who resorts to that as an way to get laid . . . But why a seemingly friendly woman seeking entry to a new group of friends?

Caught up in the moment, had she forgot about the acid in her wine when she offered it to Ken? No, he reasoned. Something like that you don't forget.

Or maybe someone else spiked her drink, and then she unwittingly passed it on to him. That could account for her own disappearance. No again, Ken thought, watching another bolt of lightning branch across the sky. In that case, she should have been found too when Jill and the others scoured the police and hospitals looking for him.

And why wasn't she registered at Miami? Had she lied about who she was? Was she enrolled under another name and had given him and the rest on the bus an alias? Was she a student there at all?

If not, why the lies? Just for a one-way ride to a concert in Detroit?

Or was the *real* reason for her trip that of sending Ken on *his?*

He decided to go home for some bed rest before his night class. On the way, he stopped at Bonham House, and a campus security officer took a report from Ken on Crystal's description and the events surrounding the drugging. The officer told him the case was out of his jurisdiction, since it happened in Michigan. But he said he would try to track her down for questioning.

"Authorities in Detroit might pursue it," he said. "And if she is using or trafficking drugs here we'd want to know about that, too."

The officer took Ken's phone number, photocopied his driver's license and student I.D. and promised to call if anything developed. "But I wouldn't hold my breath," he said as Ken left. "I'd watch the company I keep if I were you, too."

That seems to be a developing theme, Ken thought as he threw his poncho on and headed home. He looked forward to the next few hours of listening to the rain as he dozed.

As Ken unlocked his door, Blue emerged from the apartment behind him. The left side of his face was a dark rainbow of bruises, and a bandage covered the brow over his blackened left eye.

"*Holy shit,* Heavner! What happened to *you?*"

"I was defending your castle while you were gone, Sir Leave-a-Lot," Blue said, moving his jaw painfully. "I came home from a party Saturday night at about one a.m. and I saw what looked like a flashlight beam in your living room window. I knew you were gone for the weekend so I got my bat and waited inside my door, watching through the peephole. I didn't hear anything until two guys came out of your place with what looked like a big suitcase, closed the door behind them and took off rubber gloves."

"Rubber gloves?"

"Yeah, as in *no fingerprints,*" Heavner said. "Anyway, I busted out and confronted them, asking what they were doing, and they told me the apartment manager sent them. When I asked why, they just turned to leave. The first guy was hustling the case down the stairs and I asked what was in it, thinking they might have ripped you off. The other guy put his hand in the middle of my chest and told me to butt out, that it was none of my business.

"Then I knew something was rotten and I tried to push past him to get to the case. He jumped in front of me and I faked like I was going to hit him with the bat.

"That's when the shit hit the fan. When the other guy was running out downstairs, he bashed the case against the door frame and it fell to the floor in pieces. It wasn't a suitcase at all, but some kind of electronic machine with cables and a big glass screen.

"Anyway, when I'm glancing at the guy picking up the deal on the floor down below, the other one plants a perfectly executed roundhouse kick up the side of my face. My lights went out before I hit the floor."

"God damn!" Ken said. "Thanks for the effort, Blue! I owe you. Too bad they got away."

"Oh wait, there's more," Heavner said, lighting a cigarette as he sat against the wall. "About the same time I settled in for my 'spontaneous nap,' and the one bad guy is fumbling with the doo-dad on the floor and the other is helping him, all the commotion wakes Anne and Linda. They come out and start screaming when they see my arm hanging over the stairs and the two strangers blow past them and out the door.

"In turn," Heavner continued, pausing for a drag from his cigarette, "their screams draw Blakely, who emerges with his own Louisville Slugger, and he catches up with the guys out in the parking lot as they're boarding a white van. Blakely sprints up to the van as it's backing out and tries to get the tag number, but its light is out and he can't read it. The best part is that he has the presence of mind to add an identifying touch of his own, gutting the right taillights with a good swing of his bat as the van peels out."

"*Awright Todd!*" Ken said. "That boy does have a lawyer's temperament."

"But here's where it gets *really* strange," Blue said. "As if anything so far makes sense . . . I came to in Anne's arms just before the EMTs and cops arrived from Linda's call to 911. The commotion drew the rest from the building outside, and they gathered to watch the paramedics work on me in their truck while the cops took information from Todd, Linda, Anne, and then me.

"An Oxford city cop radios dispatch a description of the van—complete with broken right taillights and two white male occupants. Less than five minutes later, while he's still interviewing us, the cop gets a call back from dispatch saying that an Ohio State Trooper was pulling the suspect vehicle over on the road to Hamilton.

"So they caught them?"

"No. And this is where it gets weirder," Blue said, flipping ash from his Marlboro. "We're all standing there like, *Yeah! They got the son of a bitch!* Then the cop gets a call back saying they got the wrong van. No further explanation, just that they pulled over the wrong guys and were going to let them go."

"So, he had the wrong van," Ken said.

"You're not *listening*," Blue answered. "This cop radioed that he was pulling over a white van with two white males inside and the rear right lights bashed out. And it was heading away from Oxford. It *had* to be the right vehicle.

"After the trooper let the guys go Blakely asked our cop to give us a copy of the van's license number, so he could have it for reference later if there was an investigation. But when the Oxford cop radioed the request to the trooper who pulled over the van, he said he hadn't bothered to write it down, since it wasn't the right guys. When we asked if we could get it off the dispatch tapes from when the trooper pulled the van over, they told us the tape wasn't rolling then."

"You're right," Ken said. "Apparently, whoever was in that van had some kind of get out of jail free card."

"And good luck finding out who the trooper was," Blue continued. "The state boys we called at the post in Hamilton said they had no record of any such incident, and that a sheriff's deputy must have pulled the van over."

"And?"

"The Hamilton County Sheriff's Office said it wasn't them, and that it must have been the State Troopers."

"So we're left with nothing."

"*Au contraire,*" Blue said. He rose, re-entered his apartment and returned with a small box. He motioned Ken into his living room and closed the door behind them. Blue then opened the box and spilled the contents onto his coffee table. They were a few shards of green glass and a couple of black knobs with white markings. One of the knobs had something that looked like a trademark, and the other the international sign for radioactivity in its center, with an indicator arrow on the rim for adjusting to some kind of settings.

"These broke off of the case the one guy smashed against the door as he was running out," Blue said, handing the knobs to Ken. "I was going to give them to the cops as evidence until they let those guys in the van go. Then I decided to hold onto them and see what I could find out myself."

Blue held out the box and Ken dropped them back inside.

"Blakely copied the insignia from the one knob and said he thinks he can find out what it means," Blue continued. "He had a class in copyright law, and in it he found out how to look up trademarks in a federal databank. If we can find out the company name and address, they can tell us what kind of device these came from," he said, shaking the box. "Then, depending on what kind of machine it is and how many there are in the area, we might be able to locate the one our friend dribbled out of our building."

"Sounds like a lot of work."

"Yeah. But I have more than a passing interest in finding these guys," Blue said, pointing to his bandaged face. "I've enjoyed wearing this so much, I'd like to give them an opportunity for a fitting."

"They're all the rage," Ken said, pulling his T-shirt up to expose the patch over his own chest. For the next half hour he shared his own misadventure in Detroit. By the time Ken settled into his place, watched the news and fixed dinner it was time to head back to campus for his Taoism class.

But he didn't go.

What had been a nagging paranoia for Ken had now turned into a very real—if not clear—and present danger. He had felt like an insect that had been neatly pinned under glass. Now it had gone beyond mere scrutiny. "They" had intruded into his apartment, violating his privacy. Beside that, they had brought physical harm to one of his neighbors and scared the hell out of several more.

And if they were behind the drugging in Detroit, then they had attacked him, too.

Ken stared out his kitchen window, but he saw Blue's bruised and bandaged face, the gash in his own chest, and the smile "Crystal" had flashed when she handed him her drink. That smile, that lying smile . . . Where had he seen it before? Was it the same one Cody wore when Ken's door opened to him the week before?

Ken noticed the low, nagging discomfort runners get in their leg muscles after several days without a workout. Not really a pain, but more of a constricted, pent-up sensation that only running can fix. He had tried morning and night stretching routines and lengthening his walking stride to compensate for not running, but they brought little relief.

Being kept from his running was yet another burden Ken had to suffer at the hands of . . . who? Crystal? Certainly she had put him in the mind-bender that brought on his wounds. Was she just a thoughtless bitch or part of a team that included whoever had invaded his apartment?

Who were the intruders who had attacked one of his friends and apparently had enough clout to keep themselves from being arrested? Was Cody's unexpected appearance at Ken's door in reality his role as a member of the 'opposition'? For that matter, anyone could be suspect . . . like Crump, the affable soldier "with a friend in intelligence." But that was impossible, Ken thought, since he had not told anyone about the secret room when Crump gave him the ride.

Still, he reasoned, anyone from that time on could and perhaps should be considered suspect. Whereas before he felt lost in a fog of confusion, now that mist was charged with a crossfire of people and events centering on him.

The sun went down and Ken sat at his kitchen table in the darkness, watching as lights pierced the branches from a couple of houses across the woods.

The frustration that had been festering inside him mingled with the sense of violation against him and his friends in the building. Now he was angry. It began as a low simmer in his gut, but steadily grew as he realized he was no longer a bystander to a silent mystery. Figures had emerged from the shadows. And although they remained faceless, they not only confirmed that there was something to Ken's secret discovery, but they had already assaulted him and his friends. Who was next? His mom? Margaret? Tom? Chloe? Jill?

Ken doubled-up the gauze and tape on his chest, slipped into his running gear and did double his usual stretches on the living room floor. If he didn't get at least a short run in, his muscles would soon be coiled as tight as his nerves already were.

A couple of blocks into a slow jog toward campus, the heaviness in Ken's legs was matched by a light, almost dreamy sensation in his head. He stopped near the sundial, afraid that if he pushed himself he would pass out onto the sidewalk. Looking towards Minnich Hall, he saw light through Jill's open window. The weight seemed to go from Ken's legs into his heart, and he walked past the dorm and sat on a bench.

Fate's phantom had stolen way too much from Ken. The time had come to turn around and rip off its mask.

Before, he had accepted that there was no more to his father's murder than a carload of frustrated, angry street kids. Since he found that secret chamber he had groped from suspicion to fear to anger. After what had already happened, what could be next?

Ken had experienced a too-coincidental visit from an old family friend, was drugged by a total stranger, his apartment had been searched and a neighbor assaulted. He wondered if Crystal, Cody and the pair in the van were all dangling from the same puppeteer.

Ken was still confused. But whatever fear had built up in him had been knocked out by a heavy dose of LSD and the kick to Blue's face. Ken's interest had been personal all along. But the assault on him and one of his best friends had just bumped it over the redline.

Ken had never run a race without a finish line as a goal. Could or would Cody provide something to put to rest the mysteries surrounding his father? Would Cody explain the secret room, or at least offer a solid lead? What would happen if, in his mother's absence, Ken led Cody directly into the basement hideaway? The old family friend could deny any knowledge of it, as he had done with the photo. Or would Cody be moved to offer a little instruction on what it meant, and why it had been important for his father to keep it from the rest of his family? Would he ask Ken to keep it secret? Could it hold some importance that had outlived his father?

But most importantly, could it point to a reason why his father had been deliberately killed?

The time had come to find out—or try to—before Ken or anyone close to him was again attacked, or worse.

Yeah, Ken thought. *It's time.*

He picked up a pebble and bounced it off Jill's window screen. Chris appeared and cupped her hands around her eyes as she peered outside.

"Who is that?" she demanded.

"It's me, Ken. Is Jill there?"

Chris stepped aside as Jill took her place at the window. She wore an oversized T-shirt and pulled her wet hair back as she leaned toward the screen. "I just got out of the shower," she said. "Give me a minute and I'll be right down."

Ken sat on the same bench they had occupied a few nights before, and listened to the music that competed for his attention from two nearby rooms. It was an unlikely duel between Ted Nugent and Harry Connick Jr.

Suddenly Ken realized he might be telling Jill goodbye. Maybe he wouldn't come back. He knew that people were silenced every day by lots of organizations all over the world. If "they" had gone to the kinds of extremes already experienced by Ken and his friends, what would keep them from escalating from harassment and assault to abduction or worse?

Was it out of the realm of possibility that Cody would have a good explanation for the secret room? Or a solid assurance that Ken's father's death was a random act? Could this whole thing blow over and allow him a normal life again?

Maybe yes. Probably not. And certainly not without a confrontation.

Ken wished with all his heart he'd never found that room.

Jill smiled as she approached from the dorm, and he rose with a drowning sadness. The thought of never seeing her again filled him like lead, leaving room for nothing else.

"Hey," she said softly, entering his arms. "You're not supposed to run yet."

Ken held her tight and took in the lavender scent from her shining black hair. It was darker than the night and seemed to reflect the stars.

"Is your chest okay?" She pulled his T-shirt free, lifted it and saw a pink dot in the center of his thick bandage. The wound had become more than an obstacle to the running Ken loved. It was a symbol of his frustration. He didn't know if he had hit bottom in Detroit or if that was yet to come. But whatever happened, things would never be the same. Not without a miracle.

"I wanted to see you again before I leave," he told Jill. She had the unapproving look of one caught between anger and tears. "Tomorrow morning I'm going back home to get together with one of my dad's old friends . . ."

They sat on the bench and Jill leaned forward, burying her face in both hands.

"Somebody's broken into my apartment a couple of times looking for something. While we were in Detroit a few of my neighbors caught somebody leaving my place, and Blue got banged up trying to stop them . . . And nobody knows anything about who Crystal is or why she slipped me that acid at the concert."

Jill remained motionless next to Ken, and he didn't know if she was angry, scared or just as frustrated as he.

"Anyway, there seems to be a lot of interest in me since all this confusion about what I found at home. So I'm going back home to find some . . . closure."

The following silence made Ken uncomfortable. He wished he had details to give reason, hope or teeth to his vague plan. But he had none. Just Cody, a few Polaroids and the basement room itself.

When Jill looked up, Ken saw that his words had left her eyes empty. They began to moisten as she stood and pulled him close.

Jill knew that whatever was happening in her new love's world was reaching critical mass. Unsure what to say, she wrapped both arms around Ken in an embrace that showed her acceptance, despite her confusion.

When they separated Jill saw tears swelling in Ken's eyes. He reminded her of a child determined to defend someone he loved from a strong enemy. And for the first time, she feared losing him.

Ken swallowed hard, looked upwards to avoid her eyes, and tears spilled from both of his.

"Look! Look at the stars!" Jill said, forcing a smile as her own tears fell. She wanted to tell him that the cold, tight feeling in the pit of her stomach warned her that if he left, he wouldn't return. She knew his love was beyond question, but she also believed he was caught in the gears of something that would not let him go until it ground him up.

"See how they shine!" Jill went on, desperate to find a point of light they could both cling to.

Instead, all the darkness in the heavens pressed hard against Ken as he saw where his love had taken this beautiful friend. He couldn't bear hurting her any more.

"I'm sorry," he said. "I need to go."

Jill's mind reeled as she frantically sought words that would keep their hearts together, no matter what happened after he left. Sobbing, she pulled Ken a few yards further into the dark courtyard.

Jill looked up and placed one hand on Ken's chin, tilting his face towards the summer night.

"Which one is ours?" she asked, almost pleading. "One of those stars is ours, but I don't know which one. I know it's there, Ken. Find it and show me. Then, while we're apart, we can find it in the sky and we can be together in it."

"Which one?" Ken groaned. "Hell! Half of them aren't even there at all. They're dead, burned out centuries or eons ago, but so far away that their light is still coming."

"Don't poison yourself, or us, with bitterness," Jill said. "Be glad the light's there. That's what we can mean to each other."

Ken looked higher and his eyes stopped on the brightest point in the sky.

"There!" he said, raising Jill's hand toward the star. "Neither of us are astronomers, but we should both be able to find that one okay."

Nodding her head, Jill cried harder and buried her face in his shoulder.

The music had stopped, and Jill's room was one of the last few with its lights still on.

"Now that we have our star, we have to make a wish on it," Ken said, stroking Jill's cheek.

"Of course," she said, and she smiled as she wiped her eyes.

Then, joining hands, they sent silent wishes towards the shimmering pinpoint.

Ken saw Jill to the lobby door, kissed her and she seemed to bear a heaviness as she watched him leave.

They didn't share what they had wished for.

CHAPTER FOURTEEN

Ken rubbed his eyes as he stopped to wait for traffic along northbound U.S. 27. Dawn had just broken and cars were sparse as he adjusted his pack that held a change of clothes, rain poncho and kit bag of toiletries with his meds and bandages. He wouldn't need any reading material on this trip. He wouldn't want any advance knowledge of his visit to Cody, either. That's why he kept to hitchhiking and hadn't bought a plane or bus ticket or rented a car. He'd also decided against asking to borrow Tom's Grand Prix, which was famous for its frequent breakdowns. No matter what would happen at home, this hitch home would appear business as usual.

Ken forgot his cardboard sign, but didn't go back for it. He had started out at dawn, and since it was a Saturday, maybe some other Miami students would be driving north for the weekend.

A green Eddie Bauer edition Ford Explorer pulled next to Ken and the passenger side window hummed downward.

"Where you headed?" the driver asked. He wore a knit shirt and khakis, and a small silver cross hung from his rearview mirror.

"Going home to Michigan, but any distance helps."

"You're in luck," the driver said, waving Ken inside. "I can take you about halfway. I'm going to Fort Wayne . . . Been standing there long?"

"No," Ken said, buckling up for the ride. "I was expecting a long wait, but I just stuck my thumb out and there you were."

Maybe a little too soon, Ken thought. He unconsciously tightened the grip on his pack and thought back to who knew he was making the trip. He had only told Jill. But had she shared that with Chris and Kaaren? Had Jill mentioned her concern for Ken to anyone else over a tapped telephone line? Was the 30-something, squeaky-clean-looking driver beside him a Good Samaritan or one of 'them' . . . a friend of Cody . . . or perhaps of Crystal? Maybe the man beside him had been one of the black baggers in the white van Todd and the others chased off.

"Where you coming from?" Ken asked.

"Cincinnati," the driver said. He lowered his visor and pulled out a pair of sunglasses. "I live there and commute to Fort Wayne two or three times each month to keep tabs on how my business there is doing. I have bookstores in both cities and I shuttle between them, doing accounting, inventory and the like." He jerked a thumb back towards about a dozen boxes stacked behind them. "Overstock I'm moving from my Cinci store."

Ken turned to see the plain, new-looking cartons, sealed with strapping tape. During his freshman year he had worked at the campus bookstore, and never saw a box without address labels, invoice pockets, scuffs, dents, scrapes or other shipping wear. Unmarked and in perfect condition, these looked like props.

"Is it all books, or do you sell T-shirts and other stuff, too?"

"All books on this run," he answered, pulling a Thermos from between the seats. "What's your story? You a Miami student?"

"Yeah," Ken said as the driver poured steaming coffee into a travel mug. "Studying philosophy and secondary ed. Probably be teaching high school in a couple years."

"I'm Buck. Buck Matthews," the driver said. He offered Ken the screw-off lid of the Thermos as a cup for coffee.

"No, thanks," Ken said. "Just had some before leaving my place. My name's Eric," he lied, responding to Buck's thrust for a handshake. "I'm Eric Sundberg and I live in Kalamazoo."

Ken's basic sense of honesty was disturbed by the lies he was telling Buck as the Explorer slowed its way through College Corner, a sleepy, ramshackle hamlet divided by the Ohio-Indiana border. But even if Buck was who he said he was, they would almost certainly never again meet anyway. And if the driver wasn't the innocent book peddler he said he was, the lies would still mean nothing, since "Buck," who had appeared all too conveniently, may have already been briefed on Ken's real name, and a lot more.

They continued in silence until wheeling into Richmond.

"I've been on the road a couple of hours now and I need to get some gas and stretch my legs," Buck said, and he pulled the Explorer up to a pump outside a combination gas station and cafe. As he turned off the ignition, he saw Ken glance at the gas gauge. It read three-quarters full.

"I like to keep her topped off," Buck explained. "I had a half tank of gas one time I got stuck in a monster traffic jam on the interstate. Before it was unclogged, I was on empty."

After filling the Explorer, Buck got in and pulled it into a parking spot next to the cafe. "Time to refill the Thermos and empty my bladder," he said. "Come on, I'll buy you a doughnut."

They exited the Explorer and Buck squawked the remote door locks as they rounded the corner and entered the coffee shop. Ken wasn't bothered by the interruption, since he knew he'd still be in Fort Wayne before noon.

Buck asked a waitress to fill his Thermos with black coffee. "When my coffee comes back, give her this," he said, handing Ken a twenty. "Tell her also to take out a cup of coffee and a bear claw for me, and whatever you want, too. I need to make a phone call."

Buck walked to a pay phone over a newspaper rack by the entrance. He then punched a few numbers and scanned the front page of the *USA Today* showing through the rack's window. The call lasted just long enough for the waitress to bring the Thermos, two cups of coffee, Buck's bear claw and an apple fritter for Ken.

"Bad news," Buck said, easing onto his stool. "I just checked in with my store in Cinci and found out a clerk loaded the wrong books into my Explorer. Now I have to turn around and get the right ones.

"I've gotta get a cellphone," he said in disgust. "I hate the damned things, but if I had one they could have called me with the mistake before I was out of Cinci. They said they caught it just after I left. At least I got you a good start, and a little breakfast to help you the rest of the way."

"I appreciate it," Ken said. But he was really grateful for the opportunity to get away from the driver. Their long ride hadn't taken any of the 'fishy' smell from Buck.

"Too bad you have to backtrack so far," Ken said.

"Well, it's early enough for me to go back and still make it to Fort Wayne before too late. And if your rides get sparse and I see you between here and there, I'll stop for you again," Buck promised.

They finished their break and Buck thumped a dollar tip on the counter. "Oh yeah," he said, "don't forget you still have your backpack in my Explorer."

"Right," Ken said, and they walked back around the building to the vehicle. Buck opened the passenger's door and pulled the pack from the seat. He handed it to Ken and they shook hands.

"Vaya con Dios, amigo!" Buck said, climbing into the Explorer. He pulled his sunglasses from his shirt pocket and pointed them towards the highway. "Good luck on your rides," he said, slipping on the shades. "If things go slow you at least know I'll be back through here in a few hours."

"No offense," Ken answered, "but I'm hoping to be in Michigan by then."

Buck gave 'Eric' a goodbye salute and turned into the southbound traffic. Ken returned to the coffee shop, used the bathroom and got a large black coffee to go. He took it outside and sat on the sidewalk, his back against the wall in the store's shade. Ken sipped the coffee, sat it next to him and pulled his pack onto his lap. He then unzipped it and removed each item, placing them one by one next to him on the cement. Everything was there—the rain poncho, map, change of clothes and overnight kit—everything.

Ken re-stuffed the pack and put on his sunglasses.

Buck is no more a bookstore owner from Cincinnati than I am Eric from Kalamazoo, Ken thought, taking another drink of coffee. To begin with, Ken recalled watching Buck as he punched numbers into the pay phone to call Cincinnati. He had only hit seven buttons, meaning it was really a local call.

Okay, Ken thought, *maybe he called a lover for a quickie before leaving Richmond. Or perhaps he had some other personal business.*

But that wouldn't explain Ken's other suspicions.

Why had Buck chosen to park his Explorer around the side of the coffee shop when there were several spaces open near the front door? And then, when he and Ken returned to the vehicle after their break, Buck simply walked up and opened the door, without using his key or remote entry system. The locks Ken heard Buck click shut as they went into the building had somehow become unlocked before their return.

And when Buck pulled Ken's pack from the Explorer, it came from the seat. Ken had left it on the floor, pushed up under the dashboard.

Just as conveniently and quietly as he had appeared, Buck was gone. But before he left he had apparently set Ken up to have his backpack searched, undoubtedly for the Polaroids. In fact, Ken theorized, the local call Buck made from the coffee shop could have been to a partner, letting him or her know the coast was clear.

Ken doubted he would see Buck later on the road. But if he did, there was no way in hell he'd take another ride from him.

Leaving the empty Styrofoam coffee cup on the sidewalk, Ken stood and walked the road's shoulder a couple of blocks before turning to face the northbound traffic.

No sooner than he had stuck out his thumb, a gray Pontiac Grand Am glided up to meet him. He walked to the passenger's side to find a white, middle-aged couple listening to National Public Radio.

"We don't usually do this, but you look like a college student," the blonde woman said, exiting the two-door to let Ken into the back seat. "My husband and I both work at Ball State," she continued as she re-entered the car and locked her door. "I'm an admissions officer and Jeff here is an assistant professor in the physics department."

The 40-something driver flashed Ken a smile over the rearview mirror as he kept both hands on the steering wheel.

"Let the poor guy get a word in, Martha," he said, switching off the radio.

"My name's Bill and I'm a student . . . a junior at Calvin College in Grand Rapids," Ken said. "My home's in Detroit, and I'm returning to school from a long weekend visiting friends at Xavier University in Cincinnati.

Small talk about Cincinnati, Ball State and Detroit kept the group busy through the sleepy Hoosier towns of Chester, Fountain City, Lynn and Deerfield. A little more than two hours after picking up Ken the car rolled upon Portland, where Ken assumed the couple would head west on State Road 26 to Ball State in Muncie.

"It was great having your company," Martha said as 26 came into view. "Too bad we couldn't take you farther."

"We can help you out at least a little more," her husband said as he drove the car past their turn. "If we take you through Portland and drop you off at the road leading north from town you'll probably get another ride quicker."

"Thanks Jeff," Ken said, and Martha beamed an approving smile.

By the time they drove through Portland, Ken still hadn't decided if it qualified as a large town or a small city. Then the surrounding neighborhoods quickly faded as the road stretched forward into flat farmland.

"We have plenty of gas, but I need to take a nature break," Jeff said, looking around intently. "Ah, there!" he said, pointing to what looked like an old, abandoned feed store. "I'll pull around back so I can take care of my business while we drop you off."

Chalk-white dust billowed behind the large car as Jeff steered it across the dirt parking lot and around the faded, boarded-up building. Martha opened her door and folded the seat forward to let Ken out.

"Well Bill, you be careful hitchhiking," she said. "I've enjoyed our time together."

"Yeah," Jeff agreed, stepping out his side of the car. "You were great company."

Ken turned to walk around the building and back to the highway when he heard a loud metallic 'ka-shak.' He turned to see Jeff holding a cocked .9 millimeter handgun.

"Raise 'em up . . . and head over to the building, slowly," Jeff said with an eerie calmness. "I want both hands flat against that wall, and spread your legs."

Ken's jaw dropped and he felt like he'd fallen through a hole in reality. His shock turned into sarcasm as he raised both hands and turned, facing the couple. "Oh come on, Jeff. I can understand the hands against the wall, but won't Martha here get jealous if you start asking every hitchhiker you pick up to spread their legs? Oh yeah, I forgot . . . You don't usually pick up hitchhikers," he continued, fear now fueling his sarcasm. "Maybe you make exceptions for the ones *Buck* recommends?"

Martha pulled a small black leather case from the glove box and walked a couple of steps behind Jeff until he shoved Ken against the wall. Fire blazed through Ken's chest, and he felt the blistered and cracked paint crumble against his face and palms as Jeff put him through a rough, police-style pat-down.

"Take off your shoes," Jeff commanded. As Ken bent over to untie his tennis shoes, he saw Martha unzip the case, remove a syringe and load it from a small vial. The smiling couple of Midwestern academics had become as cold and methodical as robots.

"What are you going to do . . . give me a shot in the foot?" Ken asked as Jeff took one of his wrists, then the other and handcuffed them behind his back. "If you do, I hope it swells up real nice," Ken sneered, "because I'm gonna plant it up old Jeff's *ass!*"

An icy stomach and hands and bear hug-tight chest were physical responses to the terror that had gripped Ken. Then, slowly and spontaneously, a primal instinct for survival deep inside began to transform that fear into aggression.

Jeff grabbed Ken by the elbows and guided him toward the front of the car. Martha followed, holding the needle upward, flicking air bubbles from the syringe.

Ken didn't know if the drug was meant to kill him or knock him out, but the fear of either brought a surge of adrenaline that made him feel he could break the cuffs. His head buzzed with a strange electrical sensation as he strained against the brass bracelets.

Jeff hoisted Ken face-down onto the hood of the car, his feet hanging over the side. Jeff then grabbed Ken's handcuffs with one hand and wrapped his other around Ken's legs to keep him from thrashing as Martha approached with the syringe.

"Don't fight this or it could get very messy," she said from somewhere behind him.

Ken went limp, as if surrendering to his fate. Then, as soon as he felt the needle touch his right shoulder, he jerked as fast and violently as he could, hoping to break the needle before it could deliver its load.

"*GOD DAMMIT!*" Martha shrieked, and she flinched hard, falling backwards onto the dirt. The stitched wound on Ken's chest seared with pain as he arched his back and kicked out as hard as he could. Jeff's grasp was no match for the leg muscles honed by a lifetime of running, and Ken felt his right heel crackle into Jeff's ribs as he snapped free. Ken knew he had only a second before Jeff regained his balance and drew his gun, so he used it as best he could, stomping the black case holding Martha's toys.

"All right, asshole," Ken snarled as Jeff drew the pistol onto him with both hands. "If you want to kill me you're going to have to do it the old fashioned way. Go ahead, *shoot.*"

What amazed Ken more than his captors was that he meant every word. The couple had churned so much adrenaline into Ken's blood, and then brought it to such a boil, that his blind rage now blotted out any fear, even of death.

"If we wanted you dead, then we wouldn't be having this conversation," Jeff answered, his own face purple with fury. "We were just trying to give you a little something for the road," he said sarcastically, and then barked for Ken to turn around.

Ken complied, and saw Martha going through the black case, liquid dripping from one corner.

"I guess I'll have to pass on that *one for the road*," Ken said with a smirk.

"Not to worry," Jeff replied, equally sarcastic. "I'll just improvise." And Ken instantly lost consciousness as Jeff brought the butt of his Taurus .9 mm down hard against the back of his skull.

When he came to, Ken found himself draped across the back seat of the car, still shoeless with both hands cuffed behind him. His ankles were tied with a nylon rope, and a jellified pool of blood from his chest matted his shirt to the seat. The sun was directly overhead, making it about noon.

"All right," Ken groaned. "What do you two want?"

Neither answered nor moved as Jeff continued to drive, eyes straight ahead. Martha sat with her back to the passenger door, the pistol on her lap and her stare fixed on Ken.

"Can I at least sit up? It might slow the bleeding from my chest," Ken said, nodding toward his shirt. "Oh, I really don't care about me," he said. "I just don't want to get your back seat all messy."

"Go ahead," Jeff said, glaring back through his rearview mirror. "But if you do anything more than just sit and breathe, Martha here will see to it that the back seat gets a lot more than messy."

"Believe it," she said, raising the business end of the handgun.

The base of Ken's skull throbbed with pain as he nudged himself up onto the middle of the seat. He was surprised to see that they were on a four-lane divided highway, and soon an I-9 marker zipped by. As they traveled past exits for Daleville and Chesterfield, Ken knew they were southbound and about an hour north of Indianapolis.

Ken closed his eyes and leaned back. Slowly and quietly, he eased off his socks, then began to stretch and flex his feet, which were directly behind Martha's seat. With a slow circular motion he worked both ankles against the rope, trying to stretch and loosen the knot. Ken saw his backpack on the floor in front of Martha, and they had thrown his shoes in the back seat with him.

Ken's wallet was gone, but he was still able to use his cuffed hands to pull his comb from his rear pocket and work it down and out from between his legs. Then, slowly working both thighs, he moved the comb to the edge of the seat and let it drop silently onto the carpeted floor. Next he pulled off his high school class ring and nudged it to the floor, making sure it didn't click against the comb as it fell.

Meanwhile, the slow gyrations of his ankles had loosened the rope a little, but not nearly enough to escape. Jeff must have been a Boy Scout, because his knot remained solid as a lock.

Ken slid the ring over behind Jeff's seat, and the comb behind Martha's. He then shifted on the seat and stretched his feet behind Jeff. Ken used the toes of one foot to grasp the ring and the other to pull down the lever on the back of the driver's seat that allows it to fold forward. After dropping the ring twice, Ken gingerly slid it over the lever, leaving it propped in the open position.

Then, after a long yawn for distraction, Ken again shifted on the seat, sliding his feet behind Martha. Again using his toes, he pulled her seat lever back and jammed the comb teeth-side-first into the hinge. Now both Jeff and Martha's seat levers were blocked in the open position.

Looking at his tennis shoes, Ken had another idea. Again using painstakingly slow moves, he propped one of the shoes below him, laces against the seat with the sole facing forward. He then began to slowly massage the knot against the sole, hoping it would work itself loose against the grip of the rubber. Pretending to stare blankly downward, Ken saw that if he could rub a certain point on the knot, it would begin to unravel. About fifteen minutes later the end of the rope slipped open. That, combined with a little more steady, hard grinding with his ankles worked the knot more and more loose until it was completely undone. But he left the loosened binding around his ankles in case Martha glanced down to check on it.

With that, the stage was set for what Ken knew would be his one and only chance to escape. He watched the distance keenly, paying close attention to each approaching overpass. He wanted one that served as a bridge going over the highway but was not connected to it by any on or off ramps.

Finally, an old cement overpass appeared at the end of a long straight-away. As the car approached, Ken saw that it supported a set of railroad tracks crossing the farm country he guessed now to be some twenty miles north of Indianapolis.

Ken again considered that he would probably have only one chance to execute his plan, and timing was critical.

Jeff was driving at about seventy miles per hour, and Ken put both feet on the transmission hump in the center of the floor. Martha followed his shift with a casual glance, the gun cradled in her lap.

Just under a quarter mile from the overpass, Ken went into a long yawn, drawing attention to his upper body as he raised his head and arched his back. Then, in a fluid move he'd been rehearsing in his head for the past hour, he separated and raised both feet, placed them flat against the backs of Jeff's and Martha's seats, and rammed them forward as fast and hard as he could.

Jeff's startled yell was squelched to a wheezing groan as Ken's left leg crushed his chest against the steering wheel, and Martha's gun discharged with a muffled pop somewhere in her lap as her face shattered the windshield. Jeff's arms flailed and he mouthed a breathless scream as the car veered off the right shoulder. His foot pinned to the accelerator, Jeff watched helplessly as the cement bridge abutment came up fast.

Her own chest pinned to the dashboard, Martha struggled to squeeze her right hand around herself to get a shot at Ken. But even if she could move the gun, she would have had to guess where to fire. Her eyes were bleeding and involuntarily clenched shut in the middle of a face that looked like hamburger studded with diamonds.

Now pushing ninety, the car sailed over the gravel shoulder and the front bumper slammed into a grassy ridge hard enough to blow out both front tires. It also exploded both airbags, blasting Jeff and Martha's seats back so hard they almost broke Ken's rigid legs.

Ken dived onto the rear floor and braced as best he could for the coming impact. The engine was revving so wildly he thought it would self-destruct if they missed the wall. But that turned out to be wishful thinking as he felt a shuddering *WHUMP,* and the car was airborne. It seemed to keep flying as Ken heard what sounded like steel tearing from the front of the car, along the bottom and out from under its trunk. There was another quick dropping sensation and the car slammed over onto its side, sending Ken's head and shoulders down hard against the door to his left. Dirt and grass grated into the car through where the driver's side windows had been. The loamy smell exhilarated Ken, if for no other reason than reminding him that he was still alive.

The car teetered on its left side as it finally slid to a stop, then dropped onto its roof.

Ken scrambled to right himself and lurched forward to grab the gun and pack from the front of the car. Still wearing the handcuffs, he placed his cheek in the curve of Martha's neck, checked for a carotid pulse, and found none. The crash was bad enough, but the airbag had probably killed her, since her upper body was pressed hard against it when it deployed.

The same would have been true for Jeff. But a splash of blood high on his right side told Ken the errant shot Martha had jerked away at the onset of the chaos probably killed her partner.

Hands still cuffed behind him, Ken couldn't reach the gun, which was jammed in the vent slot between the windshield and dashboard. He snatched the keys from the ignition, unlocked the handcuffs and stuffed them in his pocket. Less than a minute had passed, and he wanted to get away before witnesses or rescue personnel arrived. So he grabbed his pack and shoes and wriggled through where the rear windshield had been.

When free of the wreckage Ken saw that the car had left the highway to rocket headlong over the shoulder, then ricocheted up the embankment to the top of the overpass. There it had slid atop a guard rail and flipped up over the railroad tracks the overpass supported before falling to rest upside down in a field.

Barefoot and holding his shoes, socks and pack, Ken glanced down the rails in both directions and saw a farm building of some sort about a quarter mile to the west. He started running for it in the soft grass that grew alongside the crushed rock railway bed. Coming to a stand of trees, he stopped and dove into the brush to avoid those he heard shouting to each other as they scrambled up the hillside from the highway to the wreck. That was why Ken had chosen an overpass without a connecting ramp—so he might have a chance to get away before others responded to the wreck.

Satisfied that he was concealed by the thick bushes, Ken watched as several men and women and even a couple of children frantically tried to get to Jeff and Martha. As Ken put on his shoes, he heard sirens approach from the distance and then die at the foot of the embankment. Four paramedics hustled emergency equipment up the rise and moved the others back from the wreckage. One of the medics leaned in through Martha's window, excitedly waved all but the other paramedics away from the car, and called out to an approaching state trooper.

He must have found the gun and Jeff's wound, Ken thought. Minutes later there were about a dozen officers from nearly as many cars spread across the scene. Ken unlocked and quietly buried the handcuffs under the thick green sod, then lay where he could see everything.

A medical examiner's van pulled up behind the patrol cars, and a heavy-set man got out, removed his jacket and waddled up the embankment to the wreck. He leaned through the driver's window for a moment, spent the same amount of time in Martha's window, then wrote something on a paper he held against the front bumper. A police photographer snapped the car's exterior and interior from every angle before the paramedics lifted first Martha, then Jeff through the shattered windows and placed them in blue body bags on backboards for the descent to the ambulance.

Another officer used a ballpoint pen to pick the gun up by the barrel, then dropped it into a brown paper evidence bag. Several other items were bagged and Ken remembered the comb and ring he'd left in the car.

About an hour later several troopers helped a wrecker crew roll the wreck back onto its wheels. Finally, it was loaded onto the flatbed wrecker and taken away, wrapped with yellow crime scene tape, scarlet evidence stickers sealing the doors, hood and trunk.

Several officers remained another two hours, carefully sweeping the whole area for evidence and measuring the distance from the highway to the guard rail, to the railroad tracks and on to where the wreck came to rest. They took yet more photographs and videotaped the entire area.

Then, finally, the police were gone. Ken's instinct had been to emerge from the brush and tell them everything, since he had only been defending his own life. But he was afraid they would turn him over to the folks who sent Jeff and Martha—and almost certainly Buck, too. As part of the national security infrastructure, Knoblock Industries had long, invisible tentacles. They were Ken's real threat, and they had demonstrated that there would be no more subtlety in dealing with him. The gloves were off.

Ken wasn't sure what his next move should be, but he was certain he needed to stay off the road for a while. Whoever sent Jeff and Martha had probably already dispatched others to the crash scene. Ken took off his bloody Miami jersey, did his best to clean up his chest, and put on his only clean shirt. After the sun had dried the bloodstained shirt, he rolled it up, stuffed it in his pack and started walking west along the tracks.

He watched the sun sink in front of him until it melted into the long, flat horizon. Two trains had passed him along the way, one in each direction. But they were going full speed, and there was no way Ken could snag a ride. He had hidden from both as they approached so the engineers wouldn't mention him in their contact with other trains or stations. But the more Ken thought about it, the more hopping a freight made sense. If he could board one it would provide concealed, anonymous, long-distance travel.

When he was a boy, Ken and his friends used to ride their bikes to Grand Rapids' main rail yard, where they would climb atop parked boxcars and explore any with unlatched doors. One morning they came upon an old hobo who called himself Rock Island Red. The congenial old bum gave the ten-year-olds an introduction to the taste of Night Train wine and how to read boxcar tags for their contents and destination.

"After meeting me, you boys won't ever need a travel agent for the rest of your lives!" the toothless drunk beamed.

Ken didn't know it back then, but the tips Rock Island Red gave him over a decade earlier would prove invaluable.

Oh God! he thought, jerking to a stop. *They know I'm headed to Grand Rapids. They don't really need to intercept me along the way. All they have to do is park outside my house.*

Despair again shrouded Ken. He couldn't go home and he couldn't return to school. They wanted Ken with just as much earnest as he had in seeking his own answers about his father. He was playing a game they had perfected, and getting away from Jeff and Martha had surely been beginner's luck.

Ken came upon a crossing where the tracks intersected a lonely two-lane blacktop. Scatterings of trees and brush lined both sides of the tracks and roadway, and a pair of raised black and white crossing gates stood at attention, awaiting the next train. Oncoming trains would trip a switch activating flashing red lights above the X-shaped railroad crossing signs as the wooden barriers would drift down into place behind them.

The tracks stretched in a straightaway for over a mile in each direction. Ken thought about disabling the crossing gates, hoping they would signal the train to stop so he could jump aboard. But what if there was no alarm to alert trains to the disabled safety equipment? At best the train would simply cruise past the immobilized barriers. At worst it could cause an innocent motorist to be killed.

Ken decided that a clearly visible obstacle blocking the track, giving the engineer plenty of time to stop the train, would be his best bet. He went about piling tree branches atop the rails about a quarter mile from the crossing. The leafy boughs weren't big enough to derail a train, but would be sufficient to cause the engineer to stop and have the debris cleared away. That's when Ken would emerge from the bushes to hop aboard a boxcar somewhere far behind the engine.

Ken sat in the brush for nearly three hours before the faint rumbling of a freight train rose from the southeast. He hugged the ground as an electric horn sounded several short bursts and then a long, sustained wail. Bells clanged from the opposite direction and Ken turned to see red warning lights flashing as the wooden barriers lowered.

The train's wheels skidded a few seconds before it slowed enough to creep up to the leafy blockage, where the chain of boxcars shuddered and groaned to a stop. Several of the cars banged loudly as their couplings jerked in chain reaction, and air hissed from their hydraulic brakes.

An old engineer in coveralls leaned from his window and laughed as he shouted something to a younger man who was visibly pissed-off as he yanked and kicked what he thought to be a child's prank from the rails.

Meanwhile, Ken crouched and weaved to the center of the long train, hoping to elude the pair at its front.

The train was about a quarter-mile long, and Ken didn't see any open boxcar doors. The young man appeared beside the engine, then walked around to the other side to get a better look down the string of faded, rust-colored cars before he finally reboarded.

A series of about ten grain carriers were linked near the center and Ken decided to target one of them, since their design offered spaces to crouch and hide. And if one of the grain haulers were empty he could get to a hatch and let himself inside.

The train began to bump and rumble back to life, and Ken saw the engineer lean out to check Ken's side of the cars. His partner eyeballed the other side.

Then Ken made his move. Backpack over his shoulders, he ran low and fast towards a grain car. He made a jumping grab and clenched one of the iron rungs welded up the side of the tanker, and the train's building momentum jerked him from his feet. Ken climbed to the top of the tanker, dropped to his stomach and reminded himself to face forward and stay down in case the train came upon a tunnel or other overhead hazard.

As the train approached full speed, Ken crawled to the center of the tanker's roof and wrenched the hatch open. He saw that the tanker was empty, and he left the hatch open as he climbed down the rungs on the inside curve of the steel grain hauler. Ken kicked around a small pile of soybeans left in one end of the dark, echoing steel cylinder and another atop the unloading hatch in its belly, and was pleased to find they held no rats.

Ken pulled the bloody shirt from his pack, filled it with soybeans and used it as a pillow as he lay looking up through the opened hatch. The train slowed and sped up again as it made its way through a series of towns and cities. Each time the train slowed, Ken would grab his bag and climb to the hatch for a glimpse of the area.

Since the train was northbound, and held a number of empty grain cars, they were most likely headed for refilling at a grain elevator somewhere in the Midwest, and would probably be routed through a major railyard, maybe in Chicago.

Wherever the train took him, Ken would have to leave it as carefully as he had boarded. He slowly chewed a few mouthfuls of the small, tough, white soybeans, but they did nothing to allay his growing thirst. A good hard rain would remedy that.

On one of his climbs Ken saw that a fuzzy white aura had appeared on the forward horizon. As it grew increasingly brighter he realized it must be the train's destination. Information on billboards at road crossings and the looming lights of the Sears Tower told Ken he was approaching the Windy City. He thought about heading for his sister's place in the northern suburbs, but rejected that as too predictable. There was also the possibility of bringing her, his mom and Janice into harm's way.

Besides, he had an appointment to keep in Grand Rapids.

Rolling slowly through the south side ghettos of Chicago, Ken's train sailed along a track that gradually merged into several parallel sets of rails. They led into the Chicago train yard, a massive snarl of tracks peppered with signal lights and control towers watching over the sea of sleeping boxcars.

Ken strapped on his pack and climbed back atop of the grain hauler as it floated past another train parked on its left. He rose to a crouch and carefully timed his jump onto the top of one of the stopped train's cars.

Ken's timing was fine, but he overcompensated the height necessary for the leap, and landed hard on the boxcar, slamming his already throbbing chest onto its grimy brown roof. Again he lay flat, listening as the other train faded away somewhere deep into the crowded train yard.

Orienting himself from the southern entry he had made to the station, Ken climbed down and set out for its northeast corner. There, he figured, he could find a train headed for or close to Grand Rapids.

Ken stole through the dimly lit rows of boxcars, careful to avoid the guards he knew would patrol the area for bums, vandals and thieves. A series of rails branched eastward, and he followed several to a section with boxcars tagged for Michigan and Canada.

Ken jumped in quiet celebration as the third train he checked included several carloads of parts ticketed for a furniture manufacturer in Grand Rapids. The sliding doors on both sides of all of the boxcars were locked shut, and climbing atop any of them would make him too visible to traffic managers in the towers scattered around the vast expanse of yard. So Ken crawled beneath one of the cars and eased onto an axle strut, buckling his backpack straps around a metal brace. Rock Island Red had told Ken and his buddies about this precarious style of travel. The old hobo had explained that its perilously close proximity to the tracks had long ago given birth to the phrase, "riding the rails".

After taking precautions to assure that he was wedged firmly in place out of sight of guards, Ken kept his mind busy so he would be awake whenever the train lurched to a start.

Just after midnight Ken heard its diesel engine rev high and hard, and he watched several pairs of legs pass on either side of the train before it shuddered forward at 12:30.

Ken was grateful that the train crawled slowly at first, the wheels banging loudly over the rails and grinding at the long, sweeping curves. Soon the cars gathered speed, and the engine's electric horn screamed its way into the silent night.

Unable to see anything but the blur of brown wooden ties rushing beneath him, Ken had no idea what the surroundings looked like as the train sped out of Chicago, slowed to pass through some towns and stopped to drop off or pick up boxcars at others. But it didn't matter since he knew his car was destined for Grand Rapids. Despite what was now a full 24 hours without sleep, staying awake was no problem. It was absolutely prevented by the steel wheels grating sparks from the tracks, the groaning wood of the boxcar around him, and the steady wind raging from below.

Ken kept both arms and a leg locked in a numbing embrace around a frame support, his back hard against the wheel well brace.

Dawn glinted from the mirror-smooth rails and brought a rosy hue to their white rock bedding, and by full light of day the train rolled into another station. This time Ken heard a string of boxcars, including his, being uncoupled from the rest of the train. After waiting for a couple of railroad workers to leave, Ken grabbed his pack, dropped onto the tracks and rolled from beneath the car.

Looking northward, Ken saw the Sunday morning sun kissing the taller buildings of the modest Grand Rapids skyline. And although he was proud of his resourcefulness in finding a way home, he still felt and looked like a bum, covered with bloody dirt and smelling of the acrid creosote tie coating.

Ken shouldered his pack and hustled to an isolated spot where several broken-down boxcars lay forgotten by a tall chain link fence. He looked around, climbed over the barrier and headed across a grassy field for the neighborhood several hundred yards east. He then spotted an unlocked bike leaning against a garage, grabbed it and pedaled the three miles to Garfield Park, where he got off and abandoned it against a streetlight. But Ken stopped abruptly as he rounded Hoyt Street for the three-block walk home along College Avenue.

If Buck, Jeff and Martha had been sent to intercept him on his way home—and he had escaped them—wouldn't it make sense someone would be there waiting for him?

Shielding himself behind a large oak, Ken peered up College Avenue towards his house. He saw a couple of his neighbors' cars parked along the curb, and a white van from a plumbing company sat across the street and down the block from his home.

Ken hurried two more blocks over to Union Avenue, which ran parallel to College. He moved up Union until he got to the house bearing the same street number as his, then cut straight across the lawns over Union and Paris avenues and into his own backyard.

After a quick look around he crept up, unlocked the back door and hurried inside. A spookiness came over Ken as he felt like a burglar in the silent emptiness of his own house. He hoped that none of his neighbors had spotted him as he unlocked the door and slipped inside. Dropping his pack on the kitchen floor, he pulled a butcher knife from its wooden block holder and went through the house, careful to avoid windows as he made a room-by-room search for any unwelcome visitors.

Satisfied that he was alone, he returned to the kitchen and used an entire quart of orange juice to wash down a couple of hastily made sandwiches.

After a long, hot shower Ken wiped down the kitchen and bathroom, put his soiled clothes in the basement hamper and took his pack and a sleeping bag to the attic. The past day and a half without sleep, spending the night clinging to the undercarriage of a boxcar, had left him feeling drunk with drowsiness. He cleared some boxes from a wall, rolled out the bag, sat a flashlight next to it and was asleep less than a minute after zipping himself in.

Ken was lost in deep slumber from about nine a.m. until well after dark, when he rose for a toilet break, using the flashlight to find his way to and from a second floor bathroom.

On his way back he extinguished the flashlight, stopped in his mother's bedroom and peered through a crack in the curtains at the street below. The plumbing van now faced the house from about the same distance in the opposite direction. He decided against further investigation as to whether it belonged to a failed lookout or legitimate laborer.

Ken unplugged the refrigerator so the light would stay off when he opened the door for a glass of grape juice and another sandwich. Then, after closing it and plugging it back in, Ken had a thought as he crept back up the stairs in the dark.

His corner spot in the windowless attic was out of view, but not nearly as concealed as what should have been his first choice as a hideout—the hidden room off the basement.

Ken finished his snack, grabbed the flashlight and dragged his sleeping bag down to the basement. Then, finding the right spot on the panel, he held up the magnet to trip the latch.

Nothing. No response at all. Ken backed away and counted the panels. Certain he had the right one, he tried again, with no luck.

"Dammit!" he whispered, and yanked a keychain from his pocket. He picked out the longest, sturdiest looking key and pried at the seam of the woodgrain wall panel. It wouldn't budge, even slightly. Ken got a knife from the behind the bar and jammed its tip between the panel seams where he had discovered the edge of the metal door. The blade broke at the handle, and Ken went upstairs for some heavier tools.

He returned to fit a chisel blade in the small gouge the knife had made in the edge of the panel, then tapped it with a hammer until a fist-sized piece broke away.

Ken switched on and stuck the back of the small flashlight in his mouth so he could use both hands to work at the panel. His eyes narrowed as he moved the beam onto where the piece of panel had broken off. Instead of a gray metal door, the light showed rough, sand-colored cement block.

He had picked the wrong panel.

"No, it's the right one, dammit!" he muttered under his breath. A desperate feeling swept him as he backed against the pool table and again ran his eyes along the full length of the basement wall. Another careful survey of the wall confirmed what Ken hadn't doubted when he first returned to the where the doorway panel should have been. He *knew* he had the right panel. Even if he had been in doubt as to its exact location—which he wasn't—the small dark 'peephole' knothole he saw near the center confirmed it.

Wiping his face on his shirt, Ken stepped back and guided the chisel bit inside the break in the paneling. He brought the hammer down hard and separated the bottom right quarter of the panel from the adhesive that held it to the wall. Dropping his tools, he fell to his knees and grabbed the loosened panel with both hands. His heart pounded as he firmed up his grip and yanked hard, breaking off nearly the entire bottom half of the panel.

Ken was in disbelief. There was no door, no entryway, no secret room. Just a plain cement block wall, snaked with the dried black adhesive compound builders commonly use to attach wall paneling.

He backed away in slack-jawed amazement. What the hell had happened to the hidden room? It was *gone!* Had it been a *dream?* A *hallucination?* Did the trauma of losing his father lay dormant in Ken's psyche until some unknown event or emotion triggered a delusion of denial, complete with a hallucinated secret chamber? Had the drama of Ken's recurrent dream played itself out in some kind of pathological fantasy?

"Oh shit!" Ken moaned. "Holy *shit!*"

He sat on the floor in stunned silence for what seemed an hour before rising and picking up the tools. He fitted the chisel under the next panel to the right and struck free a small corner, then compared the exposed area with that from behind the first panel.

At first they looked identical. But then Ken noticed that the bricks where the concealed door should have been were lighter in color than those behind the adjacent panel. And the dried adhesive behind the second panel was silver-colored, not black.

Was it possible? had someone walled-off the hidden room? Ken's heart sank yet deeper as he realized that the only thing that would sound crazier than trying to explain the discovery of a secret chamber in his own home would be that it had then disappeared. Taking a hammer to the bricks didn't seem any saner.

But hope rose inside him as he remembered the envelope he had taped under the desk in King Library. *Delusions don't take nearly that well to film,* he thought with a smile.

He gathered his tools, flashlight and pieces of panel, stuck them in a corner of the laundry room and returned to the attic.

After placing a change of clothes next to his bedroll, Ken set the alarm function on his wristwatch for five a.m. He would slip away from the house before dawn, and the only item on his agenda was an unannounced call on Paul Cody.

CHAPTER FIFTEEN

Ken rose, showered, changed his bandage and dressed in the dark. Next he loaded his pack with extra bandages and another change of clothes and peeked outside to see a plain blue Chevy van where the plumbing van had been the day before. He packed but did not take his meds, since he would need to remain totally alert. On his way to the back door he unloaded $47 from a cookie jar in the kitchen, then left the house as he had entered, stealing through the yards across Paris to Union Avenue. Then it was just three blocks to Eastern Avenue, where he boarded a bus for downtown.

It was crowded with Monday morning commuters, and Ken jumped off at Butterworth Hospital, where he entered and went to the main cafeteria. He knew the way from numerous visits to sick or injured friends and family he had visited there while growing up. He had his tonsils out there when he was eight.

Shouldering his pack, Ken grabbed a gray plastic tray and loaded it with ham and scrambled eggs, toast, a bagel and cream cheese, milk, orange juice and black coffee. He needed to carefully plan this day, and he didn't know when he would be able to eat again.

After a long, slow breakfast, Ken picked up his bag, got change from the cashier and went to a pay phone in the lobby.

He took it for granted that calls he made to friends or family would be monitored and traced. He yanked the battered White Pages from where it was chained beneath he phone, opened it and found the number for Ellis Q. Bilby. Ellis Quentin Bilby had been dead for over ten years, but his wife and the Perrys' neighbor, whom Ken had always known only as Mrs. Bilby, continued to list the phone in his name for added security. Or maybe, he thought, it was her way of keeping his memory that much more alive.

"Hello? Mrs. Bilby? This is Ken, from next door. How are you this morning?"

"Oh, I'm doing good, Kenny. I didn't know you were home."

"I'm not. I'm at school in Ohio. The reason I'm calling is that I know the house is empty while mom's in Chicago with Margaret, and I just wanted to know if you'd keep an eye on the place . . . in case mom hadn't asked you already. One of my friends lost everything to burglars a couple of nights ago and maybe that's got me a little paranoid."

Ken was confident that he had provided a credible smoke screen for his call.

"Oh, you know me, Kenny," the old lady replied. "I *always* watch out for my neighbors.

"There was quite a bit of activity at your house last Sunday," she continued, the pitch of her voice raising with a gossip's enthusiasm. "City trucks and workers were tearing up your backyard and had the whole area enclosed with a tall canvas barricade to make sure no children or animals got hurt."

"What?" Ken asked. "Not hurt by what? What were they doing?"

"Well, I went over to the barricade and talked with a nice young man from the city who said he was in charge of the whole operation," Mrs. Bilby went on. "His name was Michael and he said there was a water main break behind your house, and that when they went to fix it they found a really old septic tank from back before the sewer lines were run out this way.

"Anyway, Michael said the septic tank had to be dug out because it was too close to and threatened the water main.

"I couldn't believe how fast they did the job," she went on. "They began digging before I went to church in the morning and by the time I got home they had broken up and dug out that old septic tank. One truck hauled it away while another brought in fill dirt and dumped it into the hole. They were done by dark, and on a *Sunday!*" Mrs. Bilby concluded, obviously impressed. "They even put the sod back in place so nicely you'd never know they were there."

I sure didn't, Ken thought, biting his lip.

"Michael said he tried to call your mother but no one was home. They went ahead anyway since that nasty old septic tank was a public health threat. He was so nice he said the city wouldn't charge anything for the work. I told him I'd call your mother as soon as she gets home."

"Thanks so much, Mrs. Bilby. It's great having a neighbor like you. You've been a big help."

Before hanging up, Ken asked one more question.

"How long was your water turned off?"

"When?" Mrs. Bilby asked.

"When the city crew was working on the water main. You said they were fixing a break in it, right?"

"They must not have needed to turn off the water," she said. "Ours never was."

Ken knew that if there had been work on the water main before the "septic tank" removal, his nosy neighbor would have seen it, too. And it would definitely have meant a water shutoff.

By the end of his conversation with Mrs. Bilby, Ken still didn't know the function of the secret room, but now he knew where it had disappeared to—the city landfill—under the undignified guise of an abandoned septic tank.

Besides the Polaroids, now Ken had an eyewitness to describe whoever it was that had scooped the mysterious chamber from the earth. And there was no way the septic tank ruse would stand close investigation. It would not explain the patchwork in the basement wall, since a septic tank would never be placed that close to a house.

If the lot never had a septic tank, building records would reflect that. And if it ever did, it would still be in the ground, since that was not what "Michael" and his "city" crew ripped out and hauled away.

Next Ken wanted to phone Blue for a follow-up on the break-in at his apartment. But he couldn't risk calling him at his place, so he thought of an alternative. Ken knew that Blue joined Black and his ROTC friends for lunch most days at a corner table they had claimed in the Zebra Room.

It was just after nine a.m., meaning he had several hours to pass before trying to call Blue during lunch. So he took his pack, grabbed an abandoned copy of that day's *Grand Rapids Press* from a nearby table and left the hospital. He crossed a side street into a public park and lay under a tree, well away from street and sidewalk traffic.

Time seemed to move slow as a glacier as he read every word in the newspaper before finally returning to the hospital lobby at 12:15.

Information gave Ken the number for the Shriver Center. His call to the switchboard was then transferred to a cashier in the Zebra Room, where Ken asked to speak with Blue.

"Yeah, his name's Jim Heavner, but he goes by Blue . . . He usually joins his roommate, Brian Resnick, and a bunch of their buddies for lunch at the ROTC table," Ken said. "Could you please check for me? It's kind of an emergency."

"Sure, I guess so," the black female voice replied. "I know those guys. Hang on."

A minute later Blue picked up the phone with an unsure "Hello?"

"Hey Blue, this is Ken. I'm glad I found you!"

"Where are you?" Blue replied. "Nobody's seen you for a couple of days . . . And after that incident with the two jokers in the van we were starting to wonder if they came back after you."

"I'm all right," Ken assured. "I had to return home to deal with some family business. I should be back in a day or two."

Ken didn't care if Blue knew where he was. This line was almost certainly not being monitored. And even if it was, Ken didn't plan to return to his house before leaving town. The only stop he had left in Grand Rapids was his meeting with Cody.

"Did Blakely figure out what kind of machine those parts you showed me came from?"

"Yeah," Blue said, his voice lowering against the cafeteria chatter. "He ran them through the trademark and copyright databases, and it turns out they came from a portable X-ray machine," he said in disbelief. "He told me they're used to scan walls, doors, furniture, anyplace you want to look for something without tearing the place up. They're generally used to find hidden money or other items a metal detector or dog can't locate.

"You don't have the haul from the Great Train Robbery or a shrink-wrapped Jimmy Hoffa in your walls, do you?"

"Relax," Ken said. "You know me, Blue. I'm just a garden-variety student whose been targeted for whatever reason by some pretty exotic creeps . . . Maybe they've got the wrong guy. Maybe they were really after you and Black. God only knows what you two have secreted in *your* walls."

"Are you *sure* you're okay, man?"

"Absolutely," Ken lied. "And would you do me one other favor?"

"Name it."

"I'd appreciate it if you'd go over to Jill's and tell her we talked and that I'm okay, and that I'll see her soon."

"Sure. Glad to."

"But be sure to go see her," Ken emphasized. It's important that you tell her in person."

"And less likely to be overheard by a phone tap?" Blue said.

"Uh, yeah," Ken admitted with a sigh.

"Well don't worry, old buddy. I'll take care of it," Blue assured. "Meanwhile, if you need to reach me over this line I'll be here weekdays for lunch from now on, until I see you. And then I can't wait to hear what this cloak and dagger shit's all about."

"It's going to be a real six-pack explanation," Ken said.

"I'll keep them on ice," Blue promised.

The two exchanged good-bys and good luck, then hung up.

It was 12:30, and Ken was less than a mile from Knoblock Systems' building on Monroe Avenue. He decided to try to intercept Cody when he returned from lunch, since going inside the building to look for him would be too risky, even if he could manage to bypass security. At ten minutes to one, Ken arrived at the seven story building, windowless except for the first floor lobby and top floor executive offices.

He positioned himself at a bus stop across the street where he could clearly see Knoblock's front entrance and the gate where drivers had to swipe an ID through a slot for admittance to the basement parking garage.

"Fancy meeting you here!"

Ken's heart stopped as he spun around to the mystery voice. His panicked response caused the tall brunette speaker to jump, then giggle into her hand.

"Brenda! My god! Don't *ever* do that! Where did you come from?"

Brenda Stone was a Central Catholic classmate Ken hadn't seen since their graduation.

"I'm on my lunch hour," she said, raising a large Styrofoam cup with a lipstick-smudged straw sticking out the top. "I'm an intern over at Saunders, Subko and Thomson, training to be a paralegal. I heard you went away to school somewhere."

"Yeah, Miami of Ohio," he said, shifting his eyes between Brenda and the building across the street. "I'm going into education . . . and I just came home for a while to take care of some stuff."

Brenda asked if Ken was still going with Terri Schmitzer. While he was explaining that he wasn't, he spotted Cody in a group of four men walking up the block.

"Listen Brenda, I need a quick favor . . . You see those guys?" Ken asked, his back to the group approaching the Knoblock building.

"Yeah," she answered, looking over his shoulder.

"See the bald one wearing the green tie?"

"Uh-huh," she answered, taking a sip from the straw.

"Well I'd really appreciate it if you'd go over and ask him if he's Paul Cody. When he says yes, tell him you have someone you'd like to introduce him to. Then bring him back here and I'll surprise him from behind the bus stop."

Brenda groaned and said she could never walk up to a complete stranger on such an assignment.

"Come on, Brenda. He's an old friend of my family and I want to surprise him. He'll be thrilled, honest. Please?"

"Oh, all right," she conceded. "But you have to promise to call me for dinner the next time you're in town."

"You're on!" he agreed, and the pretty blonde's long curls bounced as she trotted her high heels over to the men, her soda still in hand.

Stepping behind the bus stop billboard, Ken hoped Cody would take the bait, and that he would come over without any of his friends.

Watching their reflection in a nearby store window, Ken saw Brenda beaming with a smile as an amused looking Cody followed her across the street. One of Cody's buddies shouted that he wanted her to come and get him next time, then he and the other two laughed as they went inside the Knoblock building.

Brenda walked Cody past the bus stop and stopped as Ken turned to face him.

"*Tah-dah!*" Brenda sang with a broad smile and flourish. Her expression morphed from enthusiasm to confusion as she saw Cody's jaw drop before a stone-faced Ken.

"Thanks honey," Ken said, kissing Brenda's cheek. "I'll look forward to that dinner . . . just as soon as I'm back in town."

Brenda nodded a frightened smile, stumbled and regained her footing as she backed away from the pair.

"I enjoyed you dropping in on me in Ohio so much that I thought I'd return the favor," Ken told Cody. "I would have been here sooner, but a couple of strangers dramatically altered my itinerary."

Ken said a lot more with the long, cold stare he shot into Cody's unblinking eyes.

Cody finally turned for his friends across the street, but they were gone.

"Oh that's okay," Ken told him. "I wanted this to be a private discussion anyway, just you and me."

Cody brought a cellphone from inside his jacket, and Ken responded by clumsily grabbing a small handgun from his bag. He had taken it from his father's things before leaving the house. After showing the weapon, he held it back inside the bag and pointed it at Cody.

"So it's come to *this?*" Cody asked. "Do you actually believe you could *shoot* me? I knew your parents before you were born. I was your father's best friend."

"Let's take those one at a time," Ken answered as calmly as he could while taking Cody's phone. "Yeah, it *has* come to this, and given the fact that people I believe are also your friends have beaten, chained and held me at gunpoint, I think a little extra *caution* on my part is wise. And regarding you as my dad's best friend . . . I think that calls for further discussion," Ken said. "I have just the place."

Ken walked a couple of paces behind as he directed Cody several blocks to a parkside bench overlooking the Grand River. Cody sat in the middle, but Ken motioned him to one end as he lowered on the other, the bag on his lap and his hand gripping the gun inside.

"For God's sake, this is fucking *ridiculous!*" Cody said in disgust. "Stop this *crazy bullshit* right now and I'll forget any of it happened."

"Seems like you're good at forgetting things," Ken answered. "You couldn't remember the room in those pictures I showed you. And I know you recognized it. It was very important to my father, and so of course you would be in on it, I mean since you were his best friend and all.

"And if you *really* didn't recognize it, then you wouldn't have told your people. And they wouldn't have sent a crew of goons over to rip it out of the ground and fill in the hole."

Cody was incredulous.

"Ken, I'd like to indulge you in these delusions, hallucinations or whatever you want to call this insanity. But you aren't making a damned bit of sense, and I have work to do."

Cody moved to get up and Ken rammed the gun barrel hard between his ribs.

"Listen, *friend*," Ken seethed, lips drawn white against his flushed face, "this isn't just about some goddamn broom closet I found in my basement. When I found out my father had a secret that big, in the same house he shared with his wife and two children, it got me to thinking. First I wondered what the hell it was for, and why we weren't told about it. I always knew—and so did mom and my sister—that dad worked on sensitive government projects. So it's a logical deduction that the hidden room was for some kind of secret homework.

"Continuing that line of reasoning, I can understand why he would even have to keep its existence secret from his own family. After all, mom, Marg and I had long ago accepted that dad couldn't tell us much about his work, even if we could have understood it."

Cody suddenly winced as if Ken were going to shoot, and the move startled Ken for the split second that passed before a pair of arms flashed over him from behind. One clamped Ken into a headlock as the other tore the bag and gun from his hand.

"You won't have any trouble understanding *us*," a voice boomed. Ken was flung face-down on the grass, then frisked and handcuffed by one man in a plain blue suit while another trained an automatic pistol on him with both hands.

The first man yanked the dumbfounded Cody to his feet, snatched the pack from the ground and motioned a waiting car forward. He then hustled Ken into the back seat as the other man holstered his gun and opened the front passenger door for Cody.

Ken couldn't quite make out what the other two said as Cody entered, and the one who had jumped him got behind the wheel. Minutes later the car descended into the fluorescent cave of Knoblock

Systems' parking garage and stopped by an elevator door. Cody seemed like a bystander as he got out and watched the other two silently and methodically pull Ken from the car, add ankle bracelets to the handcuffs he already wore and shoved him into the elevator. One of them motioned Cody inside, too, and the doors closed.

The elevator dropped one level and they exited into a sub-basement with a long, narrow hallway. They stopped before a gray steel door and the man who had sat in the back seat with Ken placed his hand flat on a glass pad. A laser scan of his palm granted them access.

The driver went into another office as the man in charge led Cody and Ken to a simple table and chairs in the center of the otherwise empty room. Cody watched as the fourth man returned with a pitcher of water and two glasses, placed them on the table beside Ken's pack, closed the door and freed Ken's hands and feet.

"Do not mistake my courtesy for weakness," he warned, taking a seat across from Ken.

"Don't worry," Ken said. "I'll continue to think of you as an asshole."

Cody shook his head and sank into his chair.

"*GOOD GOD!*" he shouted. "Why, after all these years, are you going *nuts* on us?"

"When I found that hidden room it made me rethink the nature of my father's business and the type of people he worked with," Ken said. "People like *you*, who wouldn't acknowledge the truth of something I brought to you, or respect my integrity with some kind of real answers.

"And people like you," Ken continued, turning to the bull-like man sitting between him and Cody. "You don't seem much like a systems analyst. You look like you'd associate with more *exotic* types. You wouldn't happen to know who killed my father, would you? Or maybe you're just a rent-a-cop with a good tailor?"

"My name's Michael. And yes, I suppose I am a sort of high-priced security guard," he said. "But if you want to look at degrees of competence, remember who brought you here in shackles . . . Didn't you think we were expecting you?"

"Well, after Buck turned me over to Jeff and Martha I figured maybe you'd lost interest in me. I guess that was hoping for too much . . ."

"I don't know who you're talking about. Friends of yours?"

"Friends of yours," Ken answered. "Or Buck is, anyway. Seems Jeff and Martha met with the reaper while in the process of kidnapping me."

Michael leaned back and put a finger against his mouth as he gazed thoughtfully at the ceiling. "No, wait . . . It's coming back to me," he said. "Yes, I did see something in the paper about a couple in Indiana—a Jeff and Martha—who were robbed and killed by someone who fled the scene. Looks like authorities will get the guy though, since he was stupid enough to leave his high school class ring and a DNA-bearing comb in the car.

"Martha's prints were all over the gun that killed Jeff," Ken said. "And she died from trauma in the crash. I'll have no trouble shining the truth all over that blundered abduction."

"A jury might buy that," Michael said, pausing to sip his water. "But I think poor Martha accidentally shot her husband while trying to defend themselves from you. After all, you've exhibited the most irrational, and even dangerous behavior for a while now."

"That's bullshit," Ken said calmly. "I can show that anything I've done or said that may have seemed extreme was only in response to an unusual or threatening situation."

"Really?" Michael replied. He pulled his chair back a little, crossed his legs and leaned on one elbow, his serpent-like stare fixed between Ken's eyes. "I understand that for the past couple of weeks you've been raving to Paul here and others about some phantom, here-again, gone-again 'Bat Cave' in your basement. And now you're not only blaming us for that hallucination, but you're somehow connecting it, and us, with your father's death."

"With his murder," Ken corrected him.

"Apparently your instability from the original trauma of losing your father has worsened and found expression in these delusions," Michael continued without pause. "That may also explain your drug abuse, including the recent *situation* in Detroit. Seems you dropped a massive dose of LSD and ran screaming through the city, stopping only to break into Tiger Stadium and carry off a street drunk police say you thought was your father.

"Your professors will testify that you've attended nearly no classes this semester. And your paranoia finally took a deadly turn when you killed an innocent couple who picked you up hitchhiking.

"According to friends who know about these things, you're almost certainly in the later and more dangerous stages of schizophrenic paranoia.

"Were there any voices in that basement chamber, Mr. Perry?"

Ken was seething as he returned Michael's cold, arrogant stare.

"Is this your *coup de grace?*" Michael asked, waving his hand toward Cody. "Using a concealed handgun to kidnap a longtime family friend, on a busy city street, in broad daylight?"

Cody remained silent, his eyes closed in an expression of pity and disgust.

Michael poured another glass of water and slid it across the table to Ken.

"Federal security laws prohibit me from going into detail about the nature of your father's work or the room you say you found," Michael said, obtusely confirming its existence. "It *must* suffice to say that your father rendered exemplary and vital service to his country and his company. The room you described would allow him to do what any other systems analyst does—to take his work home with him.

"Your father's work was classified, demanding his work space to be secure, as well. It also afforded him direct and immediate contact with us here and elsewhere.

"Believe me," he stressed, "your father wasn't the only person to work under such conditions. Sustained security demands sustained vigilance for those who maintain it. If you or anyone else were to go public with such details about their work, it would compromise that level of security, for them and the whole country they help protect.

"And we will *not allow* that, at *any* cost, *without question.*"

Ken left his water untouched.

"All I want to know is who killed my father," he insisted. "You can twist, fabricate and orchestrate any number of ways to make me look like a psycho, druggie or killer, but in the end you can't discredit me," he sneered. "The truth is on my side. My friends will attest to what really happened in Detroit, and I suspect Crystal worked for you just as much as did the guys who broke into my apartment. My neighbors didn't imagine chasing that pair away, and even if the cops don't have their description, we do . . . and some physical evidence they left when they smashed their X-ray machine."

Michael looked up at the guard by the door, as if he were angry no one had told him about the dropped hardware.

"I've got the license number from *Buck's* Explorer, and the evidence will show only Martha's fingerprints on the gun that killed Jeff," Ken repeated. "But we've already been over that, haven't we Paul?"

Cody said nothing.

"Investigators will also have found the smashed goodie bag dripping with whatever that nasty stuff was Martha tried to inject me with, too."

Michael shook his head in pathetic amusement.

"Since the couple in question died in a case regarding national security, the final investigation was conducted by those at a higher level, who understand, shall I say, the *subtleties* of the situation."

"Would they be the same people who investigated my father's murder?"

Cody shook his head and groaned as he turned his tired gaze towards the ceiling.

After a moment, Michael pushed his chair back and stood.

"Mr. Perry, I'm going to step out for a few minutes so you can continue the discussion you came here to have with Paul. When you're finished, I'll be outside."

Michael motioned for the other guard to follow him as he left, and the heavy door closed behind them with a solid locking sound.

Ken nodded towards a surveillance camera in a corner of the ceiling. "I guess it's still just the four of us," he said, finally taking a drink of water.

"Ken, do you really think . . . do you really *believe* I or any of us here had anything to do with your father's death?"

Cody looked sincerely incredulous, even exasperated by the thought.

"Your father was involved in extremely sensitive work, work that only a handful of mostly co-workers will ever know about," he said. "But it was and remains a vital element in keeping each and every one of us free and safe.

"Ken, not everyone involved in top secret work is a spy, being chased around by assassins. Your father wasn't a spy, he was an engineer. And even though his death would have been a loss to

this country as a security asset—and desirable to our enemies—
they don't use black teenagers as their enforcers.

"Your father, and my best friend, was not killed by an ideology
or a conspiracy," he concluded. "Frustration and hate pulled the
trigger. And the victim could just as easily have been myself or any
of the other thousands of people leaving the stadium that day."

Ken was silent. Not out of defiance or contempt, but simply
because he could find no words. Despair and doubt began to fill
the void in his heart.

Cody rose slowly, went to the door and banged it twice with
his fist.

Michael re-entered with a manila folder and joined Cody in
returning to their places at the table.

"Given your father's dedicated service to his country and to
Knoblock, and the difficulties his death brought upon you, and
the additional . . . confusion . . . your recent discovery imposed
upon you, we are prepared to absolve you of any transgressions up
to this point," Michael said, "including the situation with Jeff and
Martha Tonrey, *if* you will accept the following conditions . . ."

He opened the folder and placed a paper before Ken.

"First you must sign this document explaining that you
understand and will not divulge to anyone, in any form, the
classified nature of your father's work, of Knoblock Systems in
general, and in particular of the subterranean room you found at
your home. You must swear that you will never reveal to anyone
your discovery of that room.

"And finally, you must submit to us immediately any and all
photographs or other evidence pertaining to that room."

Michael clicked a pen, then slid it across the table to Ken.

"And if I don't?"

"Then the wrath of God will fall on you."

"So now you're God, too, and not just the defender of the Free
World?"

"I am to you," Michael hissed through clenched teeth. "Starting
right now, daylight could become the scarcest commodity in your
life.

"There is a special court established to hear cases such as yours,
involving classified information. Those who know about it like to

call it the Star Chamber. There are no TV cameras, no reporters, no family or college pals watching from the gallery—because there is none. Just seven Federal judges who were hand-picked by a U.S. Supreme Court Justice to hear *special* cases, like yours. They convene in the Justice Department building in D.C., but you won't find it in any government or court directory. It exists only for those for whom it was conceived.

"However, for you, Mr. Perry, it could become a stepping stone to prison for the rest of your life, in a cell that would make this room look like a suite at the Hilton."

"You know, Michael," Ken said, leaning back, "just when I'm beginning to like you, you turn into an even bigger asshole. It's most disappointing."

"Ken," Cody pleaded. "What can we do to convince you we had nothing to do with your father's death? Tell me, how do you *prove* something like that? Am I supposed to find some nonexistent document explaining that Knoblock and/or other parties got together and agreed to have nothing to do with his unforeseen, random killing?"

Michael reached for the paper and pen and Cody stopped him.

"I don't know if it will make any difference," Cody said, "but there is one thing I never told you because I never fully understood it myself, and thought it may have just been senseless rambling as your father was losing his fight for life.

"While Truro ran for a cop, I held your father. First he told me he didn't want to die, that he loved you, your mother and sister . . . I told you all that right after his death.

"Then, as he was losing consciousness he said, 'The road never ends'. He passed out and died moments later. I didn't mention it to you or your family because I thought it was delirious nonsense."

Ken fought back tears. "It's from something we'd say after every race," he explained. "Mom would have water or Gatorade for us at the finish, and we'd share a toast. I'd say 'The race is over,' and dad would answer 'But the road never ends'.

"It was a celebration of the race we'd just finished, and in anticipation of those to come."

Ken looked at Cody with contempt.

"If you didn't understand that, what else did you miss?"

"Without malice I could turn that question around," Cody answered, with forced understanding in his voice. "If your father didn't see fit to tell you about his hidden room, if he chose to remain true to his vows of service, then why would you come to me, to us here, for an explanation of what he dutifully reserved to himself?"

Michael looked at his watch and pushed his chair from the table. "Gentlemen, I've had enough of these diplomatic negotiations," he said. "It's time to make a decision, Mr. Perry."

"If I sign, what then?"

"You'll be detained for further investigation of the Tonrey deaths and other aspects of your case. Once exonerated, you'll be debriefed and released. If not, justice will be served."

"So I could end up going to prison for the deaths of two people who attacked and kidnapped me while I was innocently seeking answers about my father's murder?"

Michael placed both hands flat on the table and leaned towards Ken.

"As I said, son, you are riding a fine line between prison and a quickly evaporating opportunity for you to return to a semblance of normal, free life. If you are deemed a security threat, meaning that you will not or cannot be trusted to remain silent on certain matters, you will be incarcerated, indefinitely."

"Intimidation won't silence me," Ken assured. "All I need is the answer. Who killed my father?"

"*FOR CHRIST'S SAKE, KEN!*" Cody railed, finally losing his composure. "What do you want us to do, go out and comb the black ghettos of Detroit until we find the crackhead that picked your father out of a crowd at random, five years ago?

"I saw it with my own eyes, Ken. A black kid no older than you were at the time leaned out of an old car window and just fired into the crowd. If you want to be pissed-off at someone because the killer was never caught, go to the Detroit Police Department. It was their jurisdiction, their investigation, and *not* an act of espionage."

Michael put on his jacket and picked up the handcuffs and ankle bracelets.

"Time's up," he said. He cuffed Ken's hands behind his back, then clamped on the leg shackles.

"We're taking you to a cell where you'll have a night to reconsider signing that paper, and just how badly you want to remain incarcerated," Michael said. "If you decide to sign the agreement, and hand over the photographs in your possession, then perhaps we can trust you to remain silent on this whole matter."

"What about Jeff and Martha?" Ken asked.

"Your personal items from their car will be returned to you, removed from the evidence list and you will not be implicated in their 'accident'. The remaining evidence would point to some sort of personal squabble culminating in their mutual demise."

Michael turned to Cody and told him he could return to his job upstairs. He also instructed him to join them in that same interrogation room first thing the following morning for their next meeting with Ken.

Cody left without any goodbyes, and Michael returned the paper to its folder and snapped it shut.

"Come on," he said, taking Ken's elbow with his free hand. "Stand up. It's time to get you to a nice little room where you can think overnight."

Ken started to rise, then leaned back in his chair and smiled at Michael.

"Play any sports in school, Michael?"

"Some . . . Why?"

"Oh, I was just thinking about my old high school soccer days," Ken said, again leaning forward. "I played two full seasons and scored only one goal, with a header," he continued, starting to rise. "Just like *this!*"

Shooting to his feet, Ken rammed his upper forehead against the bottom of Michael's chin. A grinding snap from Michael's teeth was the only sound he made before thumping face-first and unconscious onto the wooden table.

Eyes closed, a whimpering groan issued from Michael's half-open mouth as his head rolled onto one side, showing a splash of blood where his nose hit the table.

Ken bit the edge of Michael's right trouser pocket and tore it open with his teeth, spilling change and keys and a money clip onto the floor.

Ken dropped to the floor, grabbed the keys and unlocked his cuffs and shackles. As quickly as he could he then used them to bind Michael to a water pipe that hung low against the rear wall. He then stuffed Michael's socks into his mouth and used his belt to cinch them in place.

Frantically, Ken grabbed his pack, cracked the door and peered into the hall. He heard a radio from the open doorway at the far end of the hallway and made his move for the elevator at the other end.

Ken silently raced the few steps to the elevator, punched the button, backed into a corner and waited. After an eternity, a bell signaled its arrival. Ken leaped in, punched the button for the garage and saw Michael's partner fly from the far room.

"HEY! HEY! WHAT ARE YOU DOING?!?" he screamed, dropping a newspaper. His sprint to the elevator was a fraction of a second late, and he rammed against the doors as they bumped shut.

Ken hadn't seen any stairs next to the elevator, so he assumed they would be at the other end of the hallway. He prayed that would give him time to get away.

The doors hissed open in the parking garage and Ken bolted for the car he had arrived in. He had Michael's keys, and one opened the Crown Victoria. The slamming open of a steel fire door and the guard's shouts ricocheted through the garage as Ken wrenched shut and locked his car door.

"STOP OR I'LL SHOOT!" the frantic guard screamed over and over as he ran toward the car, his pistol aimed at Ken through the rear windshield.

In one motion, Ken tweaked the ignition, threw the car into reverse and gunned the accelerator. The rear bumper hit the guard at the knees and belly-flopped him onto the trunk, sending his gun through the rear windshield.

Ken yanked the transmission into drive and floored it. The wheels smoked the car into a fishtail swipe for the exit ramp, sending the guard flying into the side of a parked van.

Halfway up the ramp Ken heard gunshots that sent slugs punching through the trunk and tires. One hit the rearview mirror and exploded it out through the front windshield.

Ken gritted his teeth as the large car splintered the wooden gate. Steel spikes that would have retracted into the pavement when the gate opened gashed the front tires which had been spared the hail of gunfire that had claimed the rear two.

Ken clenched his eyes as the mangled vehicle rocketed blindly up the exit ramp to launch onto Monroe Avenue. The front end crashed down onto the trunk of a passing Lexus, and traffic skidded to a stop from both directions. A teenage boy jumped from his motorcycle, removed his helmet and ran forward to offer help. Ken tumbled from the car, dashed past the boy and strapped on his pack as he kicked the cycle to life and sped off. He thundered up the sidewalk past the fast-clogging traffic, then wove through a few other cars and onto Ottawa Avenue, where he went against the one-way traffic and up the exit onto I-96.

Ken sped west to Garfield Avenue, then followed it south to its end near the Grand River. He kept going across a wide grassy field, cut the engine, looked around for witnesses and dumped the bike into the river. Ken paused, again checked to make sure no one was watching, then threw his father's gun as hard and far as he could into the waves. He knew the weapon would present more of a threat than it was worth. If he had to go through a metal detector somewhere, or he accidentally let someone notice it, he was caught. Besides, a pistol would be no match for just about any situation the opposition would throw at Ken, if they found him. So until he came up with a better plan, he would simply do his best to avoid capture.

Carrying his pack, Ken walked back north the few blocks to John Ball Zoo, bought a ticket and walked inside. He ducked into a rest room and changed into the clothes from his pack so he wouldn't match his description from the escape. The blue pack itself was another possible give-away, so he shoved it under paper towels in the bathroom trash can.

Back in the early afternoon sunshine, Ken bought a bag of popcorn and found a quiet spot on the grounds where he could feed it to the ducks. When it was gone the ducks waddled away for other prospects, and Ken lay on the grass feeling defeated. He had escaped his captors twice, but it had only brought him to a dead end.

The meeting with Cody was a disaster. He couldn't go back to school, he couldn't go home, and he hadn't the money or other resources to get away for safe haven abroad—even if he did have the right contacts.

What can I do? Ken thought. Should he have signed Michael's paper? Should he have let them lead him to that overnight cell? Had his violent escape from Knoblock burned his last bridge to a way out of his mess? Would he ever be free? Or find peace?

Surely Ken could be set up to take blame for the deaths of Jeff and Martha, and Michael had laid out in detail how a case for mental instability and irrational, even dangerous behavior could be built against him. And now he'd stolen a bicycle and motorcycle, and crashed a car he grabbed for a getaway from authorities, fueling the crazed, fleeing head-case profile.

Several adults led a small group of children past Ken on what looked like a school field trip to the zoo. The infinite emotional space between him and the care-free, laughing children stung the heart under his stitched, infected chest. A constant low-grade fever and throbbing headache aggravated his emotional pain.

It's not fair, Ken thought, rolling over on the grass to face the sky. *I haven't done anything wrong. I found something that demanded explanation, set out to find it and had to defend myself against people who attacked me.*

Certainly he was justified in fighting Jeff and Martha; they had tried to inject him with God knows what, bound and beat him and took him away against his will. And since they never identified themselves as part of any law enforcement or security organization, their actions constituted nothing less than kidnapping. Ken was certain the couple were free-lance operatives Knoblock's people had hired to bring him in.

But what about Ken's head-butting, gun-blazing, tire-shredding, Lexus-smashing escape from Knoblock? As far as he could recall, Michael nor his partner ever identified themselves as law enforcement officers. And if they were private security for Knoblock, they had no legal right to apprehend him on public property away from the concern they protected. Ken was never read his rights nor allowed a phone call to legal counsel, friends or family.

Ken realized that security protocol surrounding restricted areas or classified information or agencies was probably extensively different from that of the average corporate security guard. But that made it all the more crucial that Ken stay in the free light of day and away from the peculiar darkness of their basement interrogation rooms and holding cells.

No, Ken thought. *You've done the right thing, every step of the way.* And it would all hold up in a legitimate, open court of law, depending on how skillfully Michael and his people could fabricate or manipulate motives, witnesses and evidence.

Ken assumed that any connection between Jeff and Martha and Knoblock Systems and any other corporation or agency could be sanitized, making his abductors seem like a typical pair of middle-aged, middle-class, Midwestern Good Samaritans who were killed by a deranged hitchhiker.

That and the recent acid incident in Detroit could be used to build a mental instability case against Ken that Michael's people could allege culminated with Ken abducting Cody. It could also be a pretty convincing explanation to a jury for Ken's paranoid ranting about a nonexistent secret chamber in his own home.

Except for one thing. Ken had photos of that room. And while he could not prove they were sent by Knoblock, the city of Grand Rapids would not have any record of any of its crews working on his family's property the day of the alleged septic tank removal.

The difference in the fill dirt, patched masonry wall and panel adhesive wouldn't prove that they masked where the secret room had been. But combined with the photos, they could. Polaroids are more credible than conventional film or digital photos, since there are no negatives to be doctored, no opportunity for digital enhancement.

That's why Michael had made them the main bargaining chip in negotiating Ken's freedom.

Ken finally settled down enough to realize he was thirsty, so he bought a soda from a vendor. Sipping it before the bear cages, he contemplated his next move. Ken had to get those Polaroids to a secure place. The spot under Tatro's desk was good enough for now, but what if a janitor spotted them while cleaning the study carrel, or if Tatro bent down for a dropped a pen or something else and found them himself? The desk itself could disappear if the library figured it was time to move or replace it. And a more unlikely but not impossible threat was that of a fire, tornado or other disaster striking the building.

Should he phone Tatro, Tom or someone else he trusted to safeguard the photos? Calls to Jill and other friends were out of the question. They were certainly being tapped. And his pursuers might be watching Ken's study group friends or other classmates.

Ken quickly discarded the idea of calling anyone except for Tom, per the lunchtime connection they had established in the Zebra Room.

But eavesdropping wasn't the only threat to Ken's freedom. Without doubt, there was a small army of human beings actively searching for him from Knoblock Systems to Miami University and all points between. And he doubted that the next time they got their hands on him he would have enough luck left for another escape.

How would he get to those Polaroids? And when he did, what would he do with them? Take them to a newspaper or television station? Hire a private investigator to hold them while building a case for Ken's innocence?

A security guard was strolling a little too close for comfort, and as Ken turned to move away, he saw a sign indicating that the zoo would close in just two hours.

The saying that you can never go home again had turned into more than a cliché for Ken. He was sure to be caught if he went anywhere near his home, back to Oxford or his sister's place in Chicago. He had nowhere to turn, and the reality crashed upon him that he had also lost any hope for a normal, safe life. All he could do now is run, with only a matter of time until he was caught, prosecuted for any number of charges Knoblock's people could trump up against him, and grow old in prison.

The only weapon Ken had to snap that chain of events was the Polaroids. They would not only help prove the existence of the room, but show that Ken had become the victim of attack by those trying to keep him silent—in Detroit, Oxford, and on the highways of Indiana. The photos would help exonerate him from the deaths of Jeff and Martha, as well as damages from his havoc-wrought flight from Knoblock Systems earlier that day.

The plan snapped focus and resolve into Ken's despairing mind. He would have to get those photos, reproduce them if possible,

see to it that the originals were secured, and get the copies to
someone able to use them in his defense.

The next time he fought, he wanted it to be alongside allies in
a court or newsroom, and not behind a deserted roadhouse or
chained in a corporate basement.

But how to get to the photos? Surely Oxford was under close
watch. How would he get there, anyway? All air, bus, rental car
and passenger trains would be monitored, and hitchhiking was
out of the question.

He could steal a car or another motorcycle, but the theft could
be quickly reported, making him a hot target. And any vehicles he
discarded would leave a trail for others to follow.

The freight train connection had worked to get Ken home
undetected. Maybe it was his best chance to get back to Oxford.

Ken walked to the zoo gift shop, bought a stuffed giraffe doll
and several bags of trail mix which the cashier placed in a plastic
bag. He then returned to the bathroom barrel where he had buried
the pack and tossed in the giraffe. Next he fished out the pack, slid
it into the gift shop bag with the trail mix and headed for the zoo
exit.

He stopped when he noticed an unlocked bicycle leaning
against what looked like a zoo employees' building. The 12-speed
mountain bike had a radio clipped to the handlebars, and twin
nylon panniers mounted on either side of the rear wheel. It was
obviously a means of transportation for one of the zoo staff. And
apparently he or she believed it was safe from theft while inside
the park gates.

Ken was grateful.

He knew he would probably be caught if he just tried to push
the bike along the sidewalk and out the exit. Instead he quickly
mounted it, pedaled behind the building and through some brush
to the zoo's fence. Then, hoping he wouldn't damage it beyond
use, he heaved the bike up and over the six-foot-tall chain link
separation between the zoo and adjoining John Ball Park. He then
tossed the bag across before himself climbing over.

It was only a couple of miles to the train yard, and Ken made
the whole ride along back roads, keeping away from busier streets
patrolled by police.

Ken pedaled to the end of Whiting Street at Burlingame Avenue, jumped off the bike and concealed it within a cluster of bushes and trees in the grassy acreage surrounding the train yard.

He lay low under the trees until dark, then made his way to the rows of silent, still boxcars. Frequently stopping to look beneath the parked cars for the telltale legs of patrolling security guards, Ken hustled along looking at the tags to find a load headed near his destination. He almost settled for a boxcar tagged for Columbus before he found another bound for Cincinnati.

Ken knew his chances of being discovered were too great if he climbed aboard then, so he made a note of the car's exact location and description and sneaked back to where he had concealed the bike, about a quarter mile across the field.

While Ken waited for his train to stir to life, he dug the zoo bag from the brush concealing the bike. He pulled out his backpack, put the trail mix inside and discarded the plastic bag back under the branches. Next he got some bandages from the pack and tended to his inflamed chest wound.

The boxcar Ken planned to hop was empty and tagged for return to some company in Cincinnati, so its doors would probably be left open.

When darkness finally fell, he slapped on his pack, pulled the bike from the branches and ran it under a pale sliver of moon to another thicket only steps from the rails, just south of the train yard. He again secreted the bike and pack under pine boughs and waited.

The train wasn't far enough away to gather much speed before reaching Ken's spot. His plan was to throw the bike and backpack through the selected boxcar's open door, then dive aboard himself. Grand Rapids police would be looking for the stolen bike, but the search wouldn't extend anywhere near Indiana or Ohio, where it would come in handy when Ken jumped off the train.

But now he had to make sure he would make a clean boarding of the train, because if he was caught, police would find they had something much more interesting that a hobo with a stolen bike.

Ken heard several trains groan, bang and lurch their way out along tracks heading north and east, and another raucously shuddered by him on the southbound rails. He didn't know if the train he was awaiting would leave in five minutes, five hours or five days, but he was determined to be on it when it did.

Despite his best efforts to stay awake, Ken drifted in and out of a restless sleep. He was roused for the last time just before midnight by the sweeping, million-candlepower headlight and grating wheels of an approaching train. A quick check confirmed that it was the one he was waiting for, so he rose to a low crouch, uncovered the bike, shouldered his backpack and poised to strike.

The darkness was sufficient cover against anyone who might be watching from the engine, and when his boxcar was still a couple hundred feet away Ken made his move.

Guiding the handlebars with both hands, he trotted up to and alongside the rumbling train. It slowly gathered speed as his targeted boxcar wobbled and banged up from behind. Just before it arrived Ken picked the bike up by the frame and took aim for a one-chance throw.

Holding the heavy bike just off the ground, he swung it in a long arc and let it fly. The front wheel banged the side of the doorway, but took a lucky bounce that carried the bike through the opening.

Running alongside the car, Ken whipped off his pack and lofted it inside. He had to sprint to keep up with the accelerating freight car, thought about grabbing its ladder, but then decided to make a jump directly into the doorway. He leaped, slapped both hands against the car's wood plank floor and thrust his body upwards, gaining a foothold that allowed him to spring inside.

Ken rolled onto his back and heaved a sigh of relief, and the steel wheels radiated strong, steady and wonderfully soothing vibrations through his limp body.

The watery thin clanging of railroad crossing bells sounded in the distance and Ken stood, pulled the bike into a corner away from the doorway and lay with his backpack as a pillow.

Headlights from stopped traffic flashed into the boxcar as it passed the railroad crossing, and its bells rang deeper as they faded behind him.

Lying in the rumbling car, Ken reflected on how his life was like those bells, how coming up on them and leaving them distorted their sound. Their true tone could only be heard while present to them, and not while approaching or leaving.

Ken thought of how his crisis had been brought on by obsessing about an unknowable past that grew more distant with every passing second.

And now he lay in the dark, shuddering limbo of the fugitive, struggling to grope towards a secure future.

But the present finally asserted itself, and closed Ken's eyes in sleep.

CHAPTER SIXTEEN

A sharp jolt woke Ken to a pearly pre-dawn glow on the horizon east of the boxcar. The car then rolled slowly backwards until it banged into union with another, their steel handshake sending another shock through the wooden floor and into Ken.

He crawled over to the door on the dark side of the train and peered out. His was one of about a dozen empty cars being transferred to another train, probably so the one they were originally attached to could continue westward. Ken didn't know where he was, but it wasn't Chicago. This rail yard was much smaller, and the city it skirted was about a fraction its size. He guessed it was South Bend or Fort Wayne, Indiana.

Regardless, he would be about halfway to where the train would eventually either go through or pass near Oxford on its way to Cincinnati. He wondered if he was lucky enough for the train to use the same set of rails that came within a few blocks of his apartment as they sliced through the center of Oxford. The realization that he would most likely be there in a matter of hours moved him to plan what he would do when he arrived.

Ken heard the train that had cut his car loose rev its engines and roar off to the west. Then, after the shouted commands of a couple of yard workers, the twin diesels at the head of the train his car had joined thundered to life and yanked its cars southward.

Enough sun had risen to cast a strong shaft of light into Ken's boxcar, and he opened a bag of trail mix for breakfast. After eating he decided to check out the contents of the bike's panniers, and was pleased to discover a bag of granola and several Power Bars in one. The other held an empty Thermos, a crumpled brown bag that had probably contained that day's lunch for the owner, and a large can of chemical spray tear gas, most likely a defense against aggressive dogs.

Satisfied that the train had reached cruising speed on its way through rural Indiana, Ken moved to the doorway on the eastern side and sat cross-legged in the sun. The cobalt blue sky and scent of freshly cut hay from the passing golden fields brought an exhilaration that lulled his thoughts from those of escape or capture, lying or being lied to, freedom or punishment. He almost forgot to ease back into a dark corner when the train slowed to glide past a grain elevator and small cluster of stores and the one sole pickup truck stopped at the next pair of clanging crossing guards.

Soon billboards and other signs told Ken the train was entering Goshen, and he tried to recall just where in Indiana that was. Signs for New Paris, Milford and other ride-bys offered even less of a clue. Then, coming up on Warsaw, Ken finally had his bearings. He knew it was about an hour northwest of Fort Wayne.

The train's ear-splitting electric horn blasted twice as it snaked through neighborhoods, the downtown district and back out across more residential streets.

The horn issued several more long screams as the engine slowly regained speed, pulling the train toward field and pasture.

Halfway back to his place at the doorway, Ken was nearly hit by a dirty nylon bag that sailed through the opening. Another zipped past, then two men belly-flopped onto the planks and heaved and flailed their way into the boxcar.

Ken froze with surprise, and the two derelicts didn't notice him until they'd brushed themselves off and turned for their bags.

"*Holy shit, Croaker,*" the shorter of the pair said through broken black teeth. "Looks like we got us a *roommate!*"

The other bum removed a baseball cap so filthy that the team logo was no longer identifiable, and he bowed from the waist. "Please excuse our hasty entrance," he rasped in a voice belying some sort of past throat injury or surgery. "We almost missed the train when we got all tied up at the ticket office . . . This *is* first class, isn't it?"

Ken's gut told him these were evil, dangerous men. They bore the bitter sarcasm and accumulated grime of those who cared nothing for themselves, and even less for others.

"Just like home," Ken answered. He backed to where the bike lay, then sat leaning against it. His right hand was folded behind him so he could slip it into the saddlebag for the Mace, if necessary.

Allow me to introduce ourselves," the taller man said. "I'm Croaker, and this here is Captain Carl. Who would ye be?"

"My name's Hank," Ken said. "I jumped on at the last stop before Warsaw, and I'm getting off at the next."

Ken was more intimidated by the pair of degenerates than the hassle of finding another train or alternate means of travel to Oxford.

Croaker removed his hat that looked as if it had been used to filter crank case oil, and Captain Carl wore a faded red bandanna tied over his head like a pirate. Both wore blue jeans and T-shirts, and Ken guessed that they had got their shoes free at a mission or stole them somewhere, because neither pair fit. He guessed that their long, greasy hair and beards had seen neither comb nor razor in at least a year.

"Hank," Carl said, sitting close enough to make Ken nervous. "You're getting off at the next stop, right? Just where exactly would that be?"

"Yeah," Croaker grunted. He slid his back down the wall until he fell to his seat opposite his friend, with Ken in the middle. "We wouldn't want you to miss your stop, would we Carl?"

"Absolutely not," Carl said. He untied the bandanna from his head, wiped the sweat of the train chase from his face and neck, and returned it to his matted brown hair. "But you're gonna have to do one thing before you leave us at your next stop. You see, me and Croaker been under a lot of stress lately and we need some *release*," he said, pulling a six-inch hunting knife from his grubby bag.

"Do you know how to *suck?*" he asked, and a malicious laugh rumbled from Croaker as he pulled his own butcher knife from his boot.

The terror gripping Ken made him long for the holding cell in Grand Rapids.

"Or maybe we should teach him how to squeal like a smooth, pink piggy," Croaker said, rubbing his crotch.

The cool can of Mace felt awfully light to Ken, and he prayed it wasn't empty.

"Oh, looky Carl. You got Hank all tensed up . . . Don't you worry, Mr. Hank. We'll see to it that you make your next stop all right. We'll be sure to toss your squeaky clean ass out right on target," he sneered, "just as soon as we're done with it."

Carl held the dull, nicked blade close and edged towards Ken as Croaker slipped his knife back in his boot and unzipped his jeans.

Ken's grip tensed on the frame of the bicycle behind him, and he moved to stand.

"Just stay put right there!" Carl growled. Ken let go of the bike with his left hand and eased into a low crouch. Then, like a tripped spring, he shot to his feet, whirled the bike around and rammed the handlebars into Carl's gut. His knife blade strummed across the spokes of the front wheel as Ken lunged hard, shoving Carl off balance. A second jolt from the handlebars sent Carl backwards out the doorway and onto the speed-blurred gravel of the rail bed.

Ken dropped the bike and kicked Croaker hard in the chest as he bent for the knife in his boot. Croaker slammed hard against the wall, and Ken grabbed the Mace from the bike and fired a blinding stream into his eyes.

"*YOU GODDAMN MOTHER FUCKER!*" Croaker screamed, grinding balled fists into his searing eyes. Blinded, Croaker scurried backwards and fell on his ass, a stream of tears and saliva flowing from his chin.

Ken put a foot hard against Croaker's crotch, pulled off his boot and picked up the knife that fell out. He kept the Mace in his left hand and the knife in his right as he backed away from the whimpering transient.

"Stand up!" Ken commanded.

Croaker rose and stood rigid with fear as he felt the tip of his own knife against the middle of his back.

"Oh *shit,* man! We wasn't gonna hurt you, man . . . We was just *kidding,*" a desperate Croaker stammered. "Come on, man! *Honest!* We wouldn't do you nothin' like that! *Honest!*"

"Nothin' like *what?*" Ken seethed into his ear.

"You know, like we was talking about doin' . . . *jokin'* about doin' . . . It was all a big *joke!*" Croaker said between machine gun breaths. "I'm sorry! Hey man, you gotta believe me!" he pleaded. "*Honest!*"

The derelict's panic was so severe that Ken could no longer tell if his tears came from the chemical spray or if he was actually crying.

"First I want you to repeat the question your friend asked me before I 'helped' him out of the car," Ken said.

"I d-d-don't recall."

"Sure you do, Croaker," Ken said. "He asked me if I knew how to do something with my mouth."

"He asked do you know how to suck . . . But it was just a joke, only a joke!" Croaker repeated desperately, wringing his hat with both hands.

"Well let's say it was just a joke,' Ken conceded, the calmness of his voice scaring the tramp yet further. "I want to ask a question of my own, now that our situation has taken something of a . . . turn."

"Sure! Yeah! Go ahead! Anything!"

"Move!" Ken barked, and he jabbed the knife point behind Croaker's heart as he edged him to the doorway.

"I want you to take a close, long look out there and answer me this one question," Ken said as an Indiana cornfield reeled by. Croaker said nothing, but just waited for what he knew would certainly demand much more from him than a simple yes or no.

"The question, my greasy, filthy, in-bred, shit-eating, rat-bastard friend, is this," Ken paused and put his right knee firmly against Croaker's back, just below the blade.

Leaning into Croaker's left ear, he whispered: "Can you fly?" and kneed him hard through the opening. The bum screamed with all the anticipation of a mortal stab wound as his flailing body soared from the speeding boxcar. Ken leaned out fast to see Croaker slam face-down into bushes alongside the tracks, then bounce high before rolling to what had to be a bone-breaking stop.

Ken tossed the knife into the passing blur and turned to check the bike for damage. Then he went through Croaker and Carl's bags and found nothing he could use, so he waited until the train came to a bridge, and tossed both into a stream.

Pulling a bottle of water from his own pack, Ken's heart rate returned to normal as he took stock of his situation. Croaker and Carl had undoubtedly spent all their lives on the wrong side of the law, and probably wouldn't report Ken to the police.

Still, he didn't want to risk even the slightest chance that cops would search the train for him at the next stop, or maybe at one of the next small towns or even a country road crossing.

Regardless, Ken thought, propping the bike next to the door Croaker had exited, the train had already taken him much closer to his destination. About fifteen minutes later it slowed to enter the outskirts of Marion, and Ken peered out the west side of the boxcar. A man in an engineer's cap and bib overalls leaned from the engine to view the length of the train, so Ken took the bike to the opposite side door, again checked for a witness, saw none and pitched the bike onto the trackside grass. He then grabbed his pack, crouched at the edge of the doorway and hopped to a rolling landing in the deep grass. The strong, sweet smell of the grass rose from where his elbows and knees had bruised it, and he remained unnoticed as the train glided onward.

As the string of cars faded away, Ken was able to hear the bells of the crossing the train had slowed for about a half mile up the track.

The bright sun was warm and welcome after the dusty, dank boxcar, and it was good to feel firm ground replace the pitching vibrations of its wooden floor. And after the steady roar of the rails, the birds, animals and insects of the Indiana farm country took on a musical quality.

The bicycle had fared well for its punishing odyssey. Other than numerous scratches and one broken spoke, it was fine.

Ken stuffed his pack in one of the bike panniers and began walking it along the tracks toward the two-lane county blacktop the train had slowed for. Once there he boarded the bike and rode due east, using residential streets to skirt downtown Marion, where police would be more apt to spot him.

Within minutes Ken left the last of the wood frame houses and tree-lined sidewalks behind as he pedaled out of Marion, the sun on his back as he rode east on State Road 18. The two-lane blacktop was flat and straight as an arrow for the next twenty miles to Route 1, another lightly traveled two-lane that would take him south almost all the way to the Ohio border, near Oxford.

The heavy mountain bike moved well along the edge of the shoulder, and Ken quickly nursed it into twelfth gear. Coming up on the farm town of Montpelier, he decided against turning south on Route 3, since it went directly through Muncie and would therefore mean more traffic. Instead he continued another ten miles to Route 1 at the town of Fiat. The ride took Ken just over an hour, and he stopped at a gas station convenience store as the burning orange sun fell behind the cornfields he had just passed.

An overweight teenage boy sucked a Slurpee as he sat behind the counter, and Ken's entrance roused him from a vacant stare.

"You look like you been ridin' hard," the boy said without taking the straw from his mouth. "You on one of those cross-country bike trips?"

Good, Ken thought. Either word wasn't out to report someone matching Ken's description or, if it was, junior here hadn't heard.

"Yeah," Ken answered, moving to the cooler. "I started out in Terre Haute, and I'm taking country roads all the way to Cleveland," he said, picking the cities at random. "I'm on vacation from my job for two weeks and so I thought it would be fun to pedal up there, visit a few friends and ride back."

"How long you figure it's gonna take you to get there?"

"I left this morning, just before dawn," Ken said, placing his purchase on the counter. "So I suppose it'll take me another two days to get to Shaker Heights, where they live."

The clerk never sat his drink down as his free hand slowly rang up Ken's pint of white milk, a 1.5-liter bottle of water, several small bags of trail mix and a fistful of beef jerky.

"You must be an awfully good packer to get everything you need in them two saddlebags," the teen said, finally parting with his cup long enough to make change for Ken and bag the items.

"You have to travel light in biking," Ken said. "Just a few changes of clothes and the bare essentials."

"Where you stay at night? Can't have a tent and sleeping bag in there."

"Motels," Ken answered. "I'm more interested in riding than camping. I'd rather drive over the dirt than sleep in it," he finished, forcing a chuckle.

Actually, Ken was growing more nervous with each passing moment. Even if a police officer didn't come in before he left, he was sure the clerk would tell someone about the bike rider who came for food on his way to Cleveland. So Ken decided to waste no more time in heading out.

The clerk wished him good luck as he left the store, stashed the food and drink in the bike panniers and added a few pounds of air to both tires. When he jumped on and pedaled from the parking lot there was just enough moonlight to see the road clearly. As soon as he was out of sight of the store, Ken lay the bike behind a large tree on the edge of a field. He pulled the milk and some jerky from his stash, then lay down in the grass and enjoyed his dinner, well out of the headlights of the occasional passing car or pickup truck.

Staying at a motel was out of the question. Not only would it put him in a place where he could easily be found, but even a cheap room would drain him of the $30 he had left. And even if he had a credit card—which he didn't—he couldn't use if for the same reason he couldn't use the ATM card he did have . . . It would be an instant homing beacon for those seeking him, who were certainly monitoring his credit and banking accounts.

No, his only option was to keep on riding and find shelter wherever he could. It made more sense to ride at night anyway. There would be less traffic, and while headlights were still way off in the distance, he could drop away from the shoulder for cover in fields or trees until they passed. It would be much easier than trying to explain to a cop what he was doing pedaling a bike along a country road in the middle of nowhere in the dead of night, especially if Croaker or Carl had gone to the police.

And if the police—or anyone else—were looking for him they would probably expect him to move in daylight. So Ken jammed his crushed milk carton and wrappers in a pannier, walked the bike back to the road and took off. He would ride through the night, and at fifteen to twenty miles per hour, by dawn he should make it to a country road leading the short distance across the Ohio border and into Oxford.

But before that final leg of his ride he would hole up in a barn or abandoned farm building somewhere to sleep during the next day. He also needed to figure out how to get into Oxford, grab the photos and leave without being spotted.

Then what? he thought.

Ken had been so single-minded in his focus to get back to Miami for the Polaroids that only now, wheels humming along what was becoming an unseasonably cool night, did he consider what he would do in Oxford . . . or beyond.

"That's okay," he reassured himself. "One step at a time."

A lonely flashing red stop sign welcomed Ken as he rolled up
to the junction of State Roads 18 and 1, and he went into a steep
bank on his right turn to head south. About an hour later he came
up on Redkey. When he got to the edge of the sleeping burg he
turned onto a secondary road so he wouldn't have to pedal along
its main drag. The passing was uneventful except for a couple of
barking dogs that reminded Ken he should keep the Mace at hand.
Safely south of Redkey he stopped, fished the Mace from a pannier
and stuck it in a rear pocket.

As he resumed pedaling a pair of headlights blinked over the
ridge behind him, but he figured it was all right, since the distant
roar told him it was a mufflerless pickup truck and therefore not a
police car.

The driver hit his brights and gunned the engine as he raced
up on Ken, who jerked the bike across the dirt shoulder until it
bumped along in the tangled grass.

"HAVE A BEER, *PEDAL PUSSY!*" one of several men in the
truck bed bellowed, and they all whooped and cheered as a bottle
shattered against Ken's left elbow. Ken felt like he'd been stung by
a hundred-pound bee, and the force of the blow sent him crashing
to the ground.

The driver dropped the truck a gear, squealed the tires and left
Ken more pissed-off than hurt. He hadn't broken anything on
himself or the bike, and other than some momentary numbness
and a small cut, his elbow was all right, too. He just hoped the
assholes wouldn't come back.

"You know Lord," Ken said aloud, catching his breath, "we
haven't talked much in the past few years, but I could sure use a
little help here."

He sighed, made a Sign of the Cross, brushed himself off and
got back on the bike. It was near midnight, and the lights of the
already sparse traffic gave way to that of the farms he passed. By
now most farm families were long asleep, leaving outside lights to
stand guard over lonely barns and other buildings.

Virtually every farm has at least several dogs, but most were
set far enough from the road that they never heard Ken cycle past,
or by the time they did, he'd passed too far to chase.

Ken's bike had no lights, but he wouldn't have used them if it
had. The slit of moon gave enough light for him to see the shiny

asphalt road clearly enough to spot any bumps or debris well before he got to them. He steered wide of what looked like a raccoon or possum as it hustled across the pavement, and not long later he downshifted for the climb up a long, steep hill. He was pedaling fast in first gear as the bike neared the crest of the hill, where a porch light shone from a big farmhouse.

Reaching the top winded and covered with sweat, Ken coasted by the white, two-story house. The furious scratching of paws against pavement came from nowhere, and Ken jumped off the bike and braced himself behind it. A charging Rottweiler stopped just short of the barrier, lowered his head, fixed his eyes on Ken and growled from deep in its throat.

Ken had been around enough dogs to know that the ones that bark usually don't bite. But a wild-eyed growl like this one was always a prelude to attack. And this dog was bred to fight, with jaws able to crush bone. His best hope was for the owner to call off the animal. But with no barking to alert him, the dog would probably have Ken half digested before anyone would wake and respond to his screams.

His only other option was the Mace. But if he moved for the canister, the dog would attack. Even if he could grab it in time, would it be enough to stop a crazed Rottweiler, or only stoke its rage?

Ken remembered something a hunter friend once told him about defense against wild animals. "Make yourself look as big as you can," he advised, "and let out with the loudest scream, whistle or yell you can." The theory was that the animal would equate the volume of the noise with power and retreat. At least it had worked for his friend when a bison had charged him in Yellowstone . . . Or so he had claimed.

It was time for Ken to find out for himself. He slowly filled his lungs with as much air as they would hold. Then, after licking his dry lips he blew the loudest, shrillest whistle he'd ever managed. The dog dropped to the pavement and scuttled backwards as Ken grabbed the Mace. By the time he could aim and fire, the dog had sprung for him.

Ken jerked the handlebars with one hand to block the dog's lunge while spraying a stream of Mace from the other.

The lights of a passing car shone on the muscular dog as it howled, writhed and thumped on the road. The front door of the farm house exploded open and Ken saw the owner running towards him with a flashlight and shotgun.

"*WHAT THE FUCK ARE YOU DOING?*" the farmer screamed, clad only in undershorts and eyeglasses. "*WHAT THE FUCK ARE YOU DOING WITH MY DOG?*"

The fat, bald man dropped to his knees and grabbed the dog, which bit him in all the confusion.

"*MOTHER FUCK! GOD DAMN!*" he bellowed, clutching his bloody forearm. He jumped back, picked the shotgun from the ground where he'd dropped it and aimed it at Ken's chest.

"God *dammit,* you *fucker!* What the *hell* did you do to *my dog?*"

"I'm *sorry,* man! I'm *sorry!*" Ken pleaded, both hands thrust high as the bike rested against him. "I was just riding by and it *attacked* me. I just sprayed a little bit of Mace at him so I could get away. It'll wear off! He'll be fine, *really!*"

"Listen you *asshole,* you get *up there* while I call the *cops,*" the farmer seethed, waving the twin gun barrels toward his house. "Otherwise I'll shoot your ass *right here* in the *road!*"

"All right! Okay!" Ken said, keeping the Mace in his left hand as he lifted them higher overhead. "But first we have to get your dog out of the road," he urged. "I don't want you to blame me if he gets hit by traffic."

Calmed some by the easing effect of the spray and what he now recognized as his owner's voice, the dog whimpered and rubbed its eyes with its front paws.

Still fuming, the farmer tossed the flashlight onto his lawn and kept his right hand on the shotgun triggers as he slid his free arm under the dog. Straining to lift the writhing animal from the pavement, the farmer's glasses slid to the end of his nose and the gun barrels waved as he fought for balance.

Seizing the opportunity, Ken fired the Mace point blank into the farmer's face and both shotgun barrels discharged, sending a lightning-flash and roar skyward as the farmer and dog tumbled backwards onto the grass.

The farmer was so frenzied with rage and pain that Ken couldn't make out what he was screaming as Ken grabbed the bike, jumped on and pedaled as hard as he could. Coming upon another farm about a quarter mile away, Ken pulled onto a dirt trace going back into a fallow cornfield, and he rode on the grassy shoulder, careful not to leave tracks in the dirt. He knew the enraged farmer would reload his weapon and come for him as soon as his eyes cleared. So finding cover was priority one.

Ken came to a cluster of tall trees around a spring-fed pool he assumed was there to irrigate the field. He lay down and covered the bike in a tangle of high grass, then climbed deep into one of the oaks.

A couple of cars cruised by on the highway before a new red GMC truck roared from the farm where the altercation took place. The illuminated over-the-cab lights and bright headlights bathed everything before the truck for a half mile in near daylight as the farmer floored it looking for Ken.

The farmer would soon realize that Ken had gone off the highway. Then he was sure to search along the side roads, including the one where Ken was hiding. But he was satisfied that both he and the bike were well enough hidden, and braced himself to wait it out.

But that could take awhile. The exchange of Mace and gunfire between Ken and the farmer, combined with whatever heavily biased account of same the farmer would give the police almost assured that they would continue to search for him throughout the night . . . Maybe the next day, too.

Ken thought about leaving the bike and taking off across the fields on foot, when he heard a familiar sound far behind him. Pushing apart some branches he saw a brilliant light low in the southern sky. Within seconds the choppy roar of a helicopter became clear, and its searchlight made a wide sweep over the fields on either side of State Road 1 as it zoomed north, just above the telephone poles.

As it passed, the searchlight didn't swing wide enough to hit Ken's hideout. But he knew that—like the farmer—the plain black chopper would come back for a more thorough search of the side roads after its initial sweep along the blacktop. The familiar grip of fear again bit Ken's gut as he realized the copter would have night vision. The infra-red scope could read the heat given off by Ken's body, making him clearly visible although concealed by branches.

They would be back in minutes, Ken thought, watching as the distant aircraft moved west along a side road. If he was still in that tree when the copter thundered along the road he'd chosen, his hot, excited body would glow like a flare in the night vision. The bike was no problem, since it would give off no heat and therefore remain hidden under the grass.

Near panic as the copter weaved southward along the dirt roads, Ken desperately looked for a hiding place. He thought about slipping in the pond, but he would still show up in the night vision, since he would be warmer than the water being chilled by what was becoming a brisk cold front. The closest structure was a barn about three-quarters of a mile away on the other side of the highway. But crossing it now, even if he had time to make it that far, was too risky because of the copter, farmer, police and other road traffic.

Less than a quarter-mile away, not far from the pond, Ken saw what looked like a small group of shrubs. But when one of them moved, he realized they were a cluster of cows, left to graze in the crisp, pre-autumnal night.

Ken dropped from the tree and moved toward the animals, quickly at first, then slowing so he wouldn't spook them.

Even so, several of the cows shied away as Ken drew near. Several remained clustered around a cow that lay on her side to expose a swollen, pregnant belly. Cooing softly to soothe the animals, Ken was able to move inside the small grouping. He softly stroked the expectant cow, then carefully lowered himself beside her. Now his main concern was that the cows remain calm and not run off, leaving him sitting on the grass like a fool for those in the chopper or anyone else to see.

But he would know soon, because the helicopter was traversing the last roadway parallel to the one he had taken. His area would be the next one covered by the chopper in its classic, grid-pattern search.

Molding his body to fit the curve of the pregnant cow's form, Ken felt his heart pounding against the sweat-dampened animal, and he buried his face between her belly and the crusty brown earth.

The cattle shifted but remained huddled as the copter drew closer until thumps of air pressure accompanied the pounding pulse of its huge propeller.

It may have been that hammering wind, or maybe it was the light canon that blazed from the hovering monster, but something edged Ken's panic to trigger a flashback from the acid he'd been given in Detroit.

Normal perception left Ken as a disorienting wave swept through his skull, front to back. He became a tree, roots flowing from his skin and twisting into the manure-scented soil. The blinding light of the chopper was now a sun that coaxed neon green leaves and slithering vines from his glowing skin, and the deafening helicopter engine became a chorus of angels, the hymn of the universe, the sound of ecstasy.

Fortunately for the fugitive, the acid-driven visions riveted him into motionless wonder inside the cluster of cows which were equally transfixed by the consuming light.

The plain black copter only hesitated over the scene before continuing on its way, methodically scouring the fields in a checkerboard pattern.

With the searchlight gone and the rotor noise fading, Ken slowly came back to his senses, his moans driving the remaining cattle away. He shook his head, fell onto his back and sorted out what had just happened.

It seemed everyone, everything and every situation had gone against him. Was his mind the next to defect? Would he lose *everything?*

He sat up and looked around. The chopper was already a half mile away and fading, but he didn't know if it would return. And several police cars had been cruising along the highway and side roads searching the adjacent fields with their own spotlights. He wondered if the helicopter, police cars and farmer wouldn't quit until they found him.

If Ken stayed where he was, he would eventually be spotted. If he took the bike back to the main road, he was certain to be grabbed. And he had no idea where the overgrown dirt road he had followed into the field led.

Ken decided to wait another hour to let the initial excitement of the farmer and local law enforcement officers subside. Then he would hustle the bike along the dirt road deeper into the farmland, or wherever it went. He was sure it must extend to another paved road somewhere on the perimeter of the farm, hopefully one parallel or adjacent to State Road 1.

Returning to the bike, Ken pulled it from the grass and dug some water and trail mix from one of its side bags. Back up the tree, he took his time eating and watched the helicopter almost disappear to the south before working its way back northward on the opposite side of the highway. Police cars with local, county and state markings cruised the roads, spotlights darting in all directions. A sheriff's cruiser passed beneath Ken, but saw neither him nor his concealed bike. They also took their search into the several farmhouses, barns and outbuildings Ken could see from his perch.

That damn farmer must have told the cops I tried to kill his fucking dog and him, Ken thought.

Or maybe the farmer's call to police alerted them to Ken as someone wanted by authorities for more serious misadventures.

Regardless, Knoblock's people could now add throwing two hobos from a moving train and attacking an innocent farmer and his dog to their trumped-up charges against Ken.

He was stricken by the glimmering spray of stars in the black country sky. But he felt as if the universe was collapsing upon him, pinning him to that spot and crushing from him any hope for freedom.

Freedom, Ken thought. *Will I ever be able to walk to class again? To laugh and talk with my friends? To find a future with Jill?* Was there any way Ken could find his way back to freedom across the bridge he'd set ablaze when he confronted Cody in Michigan?

The original question of who killed his father had faded to black as Ken now fought to save his own skin.

Careful to make sure no one was watching from the roadway or adjacent farms, he hoisted the bike, mounted it and followed what was little more than twin tire ruts further back into the sleeping fields.

The darkness forced him to peddle slowly, since the rutted, uneven road offered little reflection from the scant moonlight. Within minutes he came to an intersection with a paved road like the one he had been traveling earlier. He made a right turn southbound and kept riding for about a mile, where he arrived at another two-lane blacktop. If he turned right it would lead back to State Road 1, probably about a mile east. He didn't know what lay to the west. Given the topsy-turvy logic that prevailed in his situation, that made west the obvious choice. The authorities would expect him to return to State Road 1, and by now any route into Oxford had most likely been put under a microscope.

Ken's plan was simple and immediate—to head west and pedal as fast as he could, turning south at the next available road, trail or cow path.

He managed less than several minutes before he had to stop and dive into some bushes to avoid an oncoming pair of headlights that turned out to be an Indiana State Police car. It's spotlight glinted off of the bike's handlebars, but went unnoticed as the car continued eastward.

Ken performed several such bail-outs before coming to an unmarked dirt road. He was again careful to stay on the grassy edge as he took the road south, so as to leave no tell-tale tracks in the chocolate brown dirt roadbed.

He saw a weak light on the crest of a far-off rise, and soon determined that it came from a small building. Whether a gas station, farmhouse, cafe or whatever, Ken decided he would leave the road as he approached the structure in order to make a wide pass through the fields around it.

Still a half-mile away, Ken could make it out as a restaurant or bar, a lone light glowing morosely over a vehicle-strewn parking lot.

Cruising yet nearer, Ken saw that the cinder block building sat at the intersection of another anonymous, lonely dirt road. He considered a western turn there to take him farther away from any route authorities might expect him to follow towards Ohio.

Ken slowed to scan the old wire fence along the field to his right. He was looking for a break in the barrier so he could make a 45-degree cut through the corner of the pasture and onto the other road without having to pass directly by the lighted building.

As he slowed to lift the bike over the sagging, rusted fence another weak sound eclipsed the whisper of his tires against the grass.

Ken's heart shot into his knotted throat as he saw the helicopter. Although it was still far behind him, Ken knew he had been spotted, because it was making an accelerated beeline for him.

Ken twitched the front tire onto the packed dirt roadway and instinctively bolted for the roadside building. He feared the pedals would snap from the pressure of his violent strokes, and the chopper's searchlight locked onto him about a quarter-mile from his destination.

The prop-wash nearly knocked Ken over as the chopper roared overhead, just clearing the power lines strung next to the road. It made a tight turn and hovered over the road as Ken shot beneath it, catching a glimpse of at least two figures leaning on struts outside either side of the aircraft. He looked back and saw ropes snake the twenty feet or so to the ground, and the men stood ready to slide down at their first chance.

Keeping close to the side of the road with the utility poles, Ken strained every muscle in his body against the rotating pedals, and he nearly overshot the entrance to the gravel parking lot. An unlighted, faded sign with the words "Beer & Wine" overlooked the parking lot's few cars and long row of motorcycles.

Hitting the driveway at full speed, Ken's tires shot outward and the bike tumbled wildly into the parking lot. He was half-laying across the bike as it slid and bounced along the rocky surface, spraying gravel until Ken's head and shoulders slammed to a stop against a Harley Davidson engine block. The motorcycle teetered and finally fell opposite Ken and his mangled 12-speed.

The copter's searchlight eclipsed the one weak parking lot lamp, and then circled the building as if sizing up its prey.

Ken frantically kicked himself free of the wreckage and hoped his numb left arm wasn't broken as he struggled to his feet. The helicopter landed a couple of hundred yards away in a cornfield, and Ken sprinted for the dilapidated bar as two men in black with rifles jumped from the craft.

Pumped with adrenaline, Ken felt no pain from his numerous scrapes, bruises and reopened chest wound, and he nearly fell on the loose gravel as he raced to the door in the front of the windowless, gray building. A metal clasp used to padlock the entry from the outside nearly hit Ken's face as he tore the door open. Without slowing, he passed a pay phone and cigarette machine on his way through a small foyer and exploded through another door into the bar.

Humble Pie's "30 Days in the Hole" continued its pounding beat from the juke box as Ken jerked to a stop in the shadowy, smoke-blurred room. His chest heaved for breath, and the stale smell of sweat, beer, tobacco and marijuana was thick as bus fumes as it burned his lungs.

Ken's eyes were wild and wide-open as he scanned his surroundings. About forty bikers stared back in a mix of disbelief and anger. Some had been playing pool or pinball, while the rest stood at the bar or played cards at tables and booths.

A short, toothless man built like a fire hydrant slid from a barstool and carried his beer bottle slowly towards Ken. He stopped about a foot away from the gasping, bloody intruder and lowered his arms to his sides as if making it obvious he was ready to do something.

"I hope you rode in here on a bike, son," he sneered.

"Yeah! Yeah I did!" Ken panted, motioning toward the lot. "I need to find a back door or hide or something," he said, desperation radiating from him just as much as his sense of being totally out of place. "These guys are after me and I have to get away!"

A tattoo of the name "Bull" stretched taut over the biker's left bicep as he crossed his arms and smiled approval.

"So who's after you? State boys? Sheriff?"

"No! I mean yeah! Both of them . . . and others, too . . . But I think the ones outside are more like Federal."

"*All right!*" a voice cheered from a booth. "Give that man a beer!"

Bull reached up and offered his half-empty longneck, and Ken guzzled it.

"In about two seconds some guys in swat gear from a helicopter are going to come in here to take me away," Ken half-yelled, pointing the longneck Bud towards the door. "Please, either get me out of here or hide me."

Bull edged to the entryway, disappeared into it for a second and reappeared with a howl.

"*Shit fire!*" he yelled, "there's guys running over here from a helicopter in the field, just like he said! I don't know what you did, son, but let me shake your hand!"

After a quick handshake, the short man who was apparently the motorcycle gang's leader shouted a battle plan.

"All right everybody, we got no time to screw around . . . We're gonna do a fade-away," he instructed. "K-Whopper, you take the ball."

A tall woman in the same denim and leather outfit worn by the rest of those in the bar left a booth and grabbed Ken's arm. She hustled him back to the booth and slid him over against the wall. Then she and several men took the rest of the bench space in the booth, providing cover.

"What kind of bike you drive?" the tattooed, long-haired man next to him asked. "Harley?"

"No," Ken replied. "Huffy."

The bikers gave each other a confused look.

"Not too fancy," Ken offered, "but *damned* dependable."

The song's last notes faded from the juke box and the acrid air of the bar seemed more piercing in the tense silence.

Ken felt the same squeeze in the pit of his stomach that had come with the slam of the car door when, as a child, his father would come home at his mother's request to give him a spanking.

The bar's outer door was wrenched open, causing a vacuum to suck open the inside door just before the two men in riot gear burst through it. The first made a low, wide sweep of the bar with his automatic rifle as his ninja-hooded partner did the same from a full standing position. One stayed by the door as the other moved behind the bar and caught sight of the kitchen and back door.

By now the bikers had pushed Ken beneath their table. They dropped him a leather jacket, bandanna, sunglasses and a helmet and he did his best to put them on as fast as he could.

"All hands up, *NOW!*" the guard by the door screamed. His command was like the barking snarl of a Marine drill sergeant, and the knit masks he and his partner wore under their helmets heightened their anonymous intimidation.

No one moved.

"I said *ALL* hands up, *NOW!*" the intruder by the door shrieked louder. He chambered a round in his rifle, and his partner in the back room did the same.

Bull walked over to the man by the entrance and stood before him much the same way as he had before Ken.

"We're sitting here peacefully enjoying some beers, and you come in here threatening to shoot us?!? For what? What have we done?"

"We want the man who ran in here," he answered. "We're law officers and he's wanted for murder, assault and other charges."

"No shit?!?" Bull exclaimed. "Well, you must be mistaken, man, because there's nobody here but us Trauma Kings. Right y'all?"

The crowd nodded.

"We *SAW* him come in here and we *WILL* take him *OUT,*" the guard growled. "His bicycle is out there in your parking lot."

"Oh, that's mine," Bull said with a smile. "I did my paper route on the way here.

"Anyway, since we've broken no laws and you need to get this bad ol' bicycle gangster, we'll just get out of your way and let you do your thing.

"Come on folks!" Bull called over his shoulder, pushing past the guard to the door. "Let's go find us a church so we can pray for the poor misguided soul these fellas are looking for."

The group rose to their feet and Ken was jockeyed to the center of the cluster as the bikers calmly separated into two lines. One filed out the front door and the other through the kitchen and out the back.

"*YOU WILL HALT!*" both guards bellowed, and the one by the front door fired a short burst into the ceiling. But the bikers knew the pair wouldn't open fire on them, nor could they physically stop them from leaving the building.

Carrying the black helmet, Ken's mirrored shades and bandanna-covered hair combined with the leather jacket to blend him in with the others.

"Stay with me," K-Whopper mumbled to Ken as they left through the kitchen. And Ken watched as the pair in black grabbed the crashed bicycle and hauled it with them aboard the idling helicopter. It then swirled a brown tornado of dirt and dead corn husks as it rose from the field to float low over the parking lot.

Ken climbed behind K-Whopper on his chopped Harley and the parking lot thundered to life with the roar of nearly two dozen motorcycles, their headlights cutting the prop-driven dirt and debris. The helicopter's searchlight switched on to rain daylight onto the parking lot as those inside scanned the brown cyclone for Ken.

Bull raised one arm and the choppers formed two columns behind him, then banked out the driveway onto the dirt road.

The helicopter floated just above and in front of the columns, flying in reverse so all inside could continue to look for Ken.

The bikes turned left onto the first blacktop road, then drove several miles to State Road 3. There one column took the north turn and the other went south, leaving the frustrated helicopter pilot with a 50-50 decision.

While the pilot didn't realize it, he lucked out, as Ken was on one of the southbound motorcycles the copter now followed.

Then, at the small, sleeping town of Deerfield, the cycles made a four-way split. Half of them branched off east and west on State Road 28 while the other half continued south on or U-turned northbound on 27.

The helicopter rose to about two thousand feet to watch as many of the motorcycles as it could for as long as possible, until all finally faded away in different directions.

K-Whopper knew all police for at least a hundred miles in each direction would stop every motorcycle they saw, so he had to get his passenger to cover soon.

Without speaking, he took a roundabout route back to State Road 1, then made a series of turns along desolate dirt roads. K-Whopper then eased back on the throttle as they glided into a tiny, dozing farm town. But a police car switched on its lights and siren as they approached its brief strip of downtown.

"Hang on!" K-Whopper barked over his shoulder, and Ken clamped both hands under the seat frame.

The police cruiser's tires screamed louder than its siren as it chased the bike around several corners, and with each steep bank Ken was certain K-Whopper would dump the Harley.

K-Whopper jumped the bike over a curb and steered it between several houses in the darkness. As quickly as the cop had appeared he was gone, and K-Whopper turned off the motorcycle's lights as they roared beyond the village limits.

He left the lights off for what seemed like twenty or more miles. Then they finally bumped from the pavement onto a dirt road that wound into heavy woods.

The Harley's exhaust echoed even louder against the dense foliage that flew past the re-ignited headlight beam. The road narrowed to two tire ruts along a green grass forest bed, and K-Whopper slowed the bike, his feet skimming the ground as he looked for something.

A small trail opening on either side of the ruts turned out to be a footpath, and K-Whopper stopped the motorcycle and killed its lights and engine.

Ken's ears rang in the silence.

"Okay man, this is gonna be your best shot," the biker said, motioning for Ken to dismount. He raised an arm from the handle grips and pointed into the darkness.

"Follow that trail about a half mile and you'll come to a big place surrounded by a stone wall. Inside there are some good folks; they'll help you," K-Whopper assured. "Tell 'em Kerwin sent you."

Ken handed the helmet and sunglasses back to K-Whopper, now with a better understanding of where his nickname had come from. After all, what self-respecting Trauma King would go by Kerwin?

"You can keep the bandanna, but I gotta have my colors back, man,"

Ken wasn't necessarily trying to keep the denim jacket with the gang's insignia, but it would go a long way in keeping away the damp chill settling over the woods.

"Here," K-Whopper said, digging into a saddlebag. "You can have this flannel work shirt . . . And this is all I have to offer you for your breakfast," he added, handing Ken a Snickers bar and a pint of Jack Daniels.

"Ask for Adrian," the biker said, backing the Harley up to turn for the way they had come. "And remember, tell him Kerwin sent you."

Before Ken could thank him, K-Whopper kicked the Harley back to life, switched on its single bright eye, and disappeared like a comet through the green tunnel of overgrowth.

A heavy pall of desperation fell over Ken as he stood in the darkness holding the shirt, candy bar and bottle. The low canopy of oaks, elms and vines blocked what little light issued from the moon and stars. It was replaced by a jet black chorus of crickets and frogs, punctuated by the hoot of a distant owl.

Ken started down the trail, moving slower after banging his head on a low branch. When he felt he was out of sight and earshot of the dirt road, he stopped, removed his T-shirt and sat against a large oak. He broke the paper seal on the Jack Daniels bottle and took a long, hard gulp that moved down his throat like a drill bit. But the piercing burn quickly gave way to a warmth that melted deep into his gut, then spread throughout his aching body.

Next Ken tore his T-shirt into long strips, folded one into a pad and soaked it with whiskey. He winced as he used it to swab clean his freshly opened chest wound, then applied more to the cloth to disinfect the rest of his cuts and scrapes from the bike crash. The feeling had come back to his left arm while in the bar, and he figured the temporary numbness must have been from a pinched nerve.

He tied several of the cloth strips together and wrapped them around his chest to hold the alcohol-soaked pad over the oozing wound, then put on the long-sleeved flannel shirt. The soft cotton was warm against his skin, and he thought about curling into a ball and sleeping there under the tree. But even in the dense woods, travel was safest at night.

Tucking the excess bandages, candy bar and pint into various pockets, Ken rose and cautiously made his way along the pitch-dark trail. He was glad for the long sleeves. Besides the warmth they provided, he also had no way of knowing how much poison oak or ivy he was brushing as he shuffled along the leafy path.

The croaking frogs got louder until their chorus blended with the sound of moving water, and starlight from a break in the trees glittered on a narrow brook. The croaking stopped as Ken tested the wooden planks of a small, rail-less foot bridge, and he made it across in two steps.

The croaking resumed and then faded away as Ken continued along the path. Within fifteen minutes, about a half mile from the dirt road, just as K-Whopper had predicted, the trail opened onto a narrow grassy border along a stone wall. It was about eight feet tall and made of large cemented granite blocks, probably from one of Indiana's many stone quarries.

Ken looked at his watch and saw a fractured crystal with the hands frozen at 12:22. "Well, now I know what time I spilled the bike," Ken said aloud. He estimated that would put the present time somewhere between two and three a.m. "Probably not the best time to knock on the castle gate," he again said out loud, unconsciously reassured by the sound of his own voice.

The idea of relishing the gift candy bar and remaining half-pint of whiskey seemed especially enticing now that he'd reached his destination.

He lay on the grass near the base of the wall and savored the candy, then reopened the bottle.

Looking upwards, Ken shifted, peered between the wall and branches and smiled. The star he and Jill had claimed was there, clear and bright. It gave precious little light to the darkest night of Ken's life.

But it was enough.

CHAPTER SEVENTEEN

The empty whiskey bottle shot from Ken's chest as he jerked upright from a deep, if not restful sleep.

The heavy, leaden peals of bells sent dull waves of thunder over him from just across the wall. Ken retreated fast into the tree line, then crouched behind a gnarled oak.

By the time he spotted the low, square bell tower, the old iron instruments had swung to a stop.

It was not yet light, but enough predawn sun glowed from the east for Ken to make out a large church building with wings extending from both sides to wrap around a central courtyard. The buildings were made of the same roughly hewn granite and mortar as the wall that surrounded them.

"It's a freakin' *monastery!*" Ken said in disbelief.

He stood, brushed the dirt and leaves from himself, and realized that the smell of the whiskey on his wounds and breath made him something less than a credible pilgrim. So he backtracked to the brook he'd crossed earlier that night, and as dawn broke he stripped, washed his clothes and hung them across branches to dry as he bathed. He left the water for a break in the trees, where he stood and dried in a shaft of sunlight. A deep sorrow came over him as his shivering nakedness drove home how he had been stripped of his freedom, his security—everything.

Ken had been chased into a medieval, granite-block corner, where he was unsure if or how he would be accepted. If the monks did take him in what real help could he expect, except for perhaps some brief sanctuary behind their stone walls?

If they turned him away (since a biker, he thought, wouldn't be the most compelling reference for entry into the cloister), he would again be on the run. And now he was on foot, with less than $30 in his pocket.

The flannel and denim seemed to take forever to dry in the humid woods, and his jeans were still damp when he slipped them back on.

When he returned to the clearing by the wall, the full light of day showed a large barn and several other buildings on the far side of the monastery. Several brown-robed monks moved around them, and one drove an old green tractor into an adjacent field. He bounced on the spring seat as he proceeded to disc the brown stubble remains of a harvested wheat field back into the rich, black earth. There it would become compost to fuel the next year's planting.

Ken climbed a tree to get a better look over the wall into the monastery. Dozens of cows grazed in a lush pasture beyond the hayfield, and several rows of small white crosses marked the ground just over the wall from where he had slept. Beyond the monastery graveyard was one of the three-story wings that flanked the church. To his right, directly across the courtyard from the church, a small gatehouse opened onto a gravel parking lot. About a dozen cars were parked just outside the pair of green wooden doors that served as the main entrance through the foot-thick stone wall. The side door of the gatehouse was propped open, and Ken saw a monk reading at a table. He was ready to welcome anyone who would call, either at the gate or over the telephone near his elbow.

All right, Ken thought, dropping from the tree. *It's time to meet Adrian.*

He followed the wall closely around to the front and saw the words *Deus Solus* chiseled in the granite over the windowless green doors.

"God alone," Ken translated aloud. He remembered standing naked at the brook moments earlier. *If I can find God in there, I'll have that much more than nothing,* he thought, and yanked hard twice on the rope hanging by the doors.

A tinny-sounding bell roused the monk from his book, and he pulled one of the doors open. He was middle-aged, clean-shaven and, except for the robe, could have passed for an accountant or real estate agent.

"Peace to you, brother," he said, and beckoned Ken forward with a smile.

Ken accepted the invitation and found himself looking at a perfectly manicured courtyard as the door swung shut behind him. Sidewalks extended all the way around the courtyard and two intersected in the middle, where benches ringed a life-size statue of Mary holding the Infant Jesus. Several monks read the *Lectio Divina* as they moved about the walkways, and another busied himself on a ladder pruning one of several dogwood trees.

"I am Brother Brian," the gatekeeper said. "What brings you to us this morning?"

"I was sent by a friend who said I should ask for Adrian."

"Yes. He is our guest master," Brother Brian said. "If you'd like to sit, I'll call him."

He motioned towards a bench outside the gatehouse, and Ken sat as the monk picked up the old, black telephone. A few seconds later he hung up, looked at Ken through the doorway and said Father Adrian was on his way.

Soon, a bald man wearing wire-rimmed glasses came out of the building on the right and breezed down its stairs and across the courtyard towards the gatehouse. He was little more than five feet tall but had the jaw and hands of a prizefighter.

"Good morning," he called, offering a smile and handshake. "I'm Father Adrian. What can I do for you?"

Ken instantly liked and trusted Father Adrian. His hazel eyes showed a blend of wisdom, compassion and humor.

"Kerwin sent me," Ken said.

"Really?"

"We met when I was kind of in a . . . jam, and he brought me here . . . on his motorcycle . . . and said to ask for you."

"All right," the monk nodded, his smile unchanged. He pulled several envelopes from inside his robe, dropped them in a basket marked "Mail," and walked a few steps from the gate. "Come on," he said. "Let's go over to the guest house. We can talk there."

They crossed the courtyard to the building from which the monk had come, climbed its cement steps and walked down the first floor hallway into what looked like a small study.

"Have a seat," Father Adrian said. He drew the thin white curtains for a view of the sunny courtyard, then dropped into a chair opposite where Ken had sat on a couch. Ken was again struck by the peace, confidence and acceptance radiating from the monk, who looked to be in his fifties.

By contrast, Ken knew he looked like an animal who'd just escaped the hunt. Indeed, the monk read fear, despair and fatigue in Ken's dull eyes and the heaviness with which he moved.

"Are you Catholic?" Father Adrian asked.

"Well, yeah . . . But that's not really why I came here. You see, I . . ."

"Oh, you don't have to be Catholic to be welcomed here. And it's certainly not a prerequisite for us to help someone in need," Father Adrian explained. "It's just that if you are Catholic, and you come to me for confession, I am bound not only by my word of honor as a man, but also by an oath to my God to keep all that we share in confidence."

Ken paused, then looked forward, facing the floor. This priest was wise.

"Bless me father, for I have sinned. It hasn't been that long since my last confession," Ken began, looking up as if to stress that he wasn't really a bad person. "But a lot of stuff has happened since then. I've been involved in some serious trouble, but I don't know how much of it was my fault. I mean, I was trying to do something I believed was right, and I hurt others who tried to stop me."

The monk leaned forward too, and was patiently intent as Ken went through the convoluted odyssey which had led him there. Ken hoped he wouldn't lose credibility as it wound from discovering the secret room to the drugging in Detroit, the apartment break-ins, the deaths he caused during his abduction, his escape from Cody and the others in Grand Rapids, the bums he'd thrown from the speeding train, and the farmer he'd Maced. Ken unbuttoned his shirt to reveal his makeshift bandaging, and wrapped up the surreal chronology by sharing how the bikers had got him out of his last jam, ending with Kerwin dropping him in the forest outside the monastery.

When he finally stopped, Ken saw by a clock on the wall that he'd been talking for nearly an hour.

"Anything else?" Father Adrian asked, his expression unchanged.

"Yeah, one thing," Ken said, looking up. "How do you know Kerwin? I mean, of all the places to be brought by a biker . . ."

"Kerwin has family here."

"What? You mean he has a brother or cousin or somebody who's a monk?"

"An older brother," Father Adrian said. "Me."

The monk's smile became laughter as he watched Ken's stunned reaction.

"It's a long story, even longer than yours," the monk continued. "I'll just say that Kerwin followed me into that motorcycle gang when I was much younger, and that I pray every day that he'll eventually follow me here . . . Or at least out of the gang.

"But this is your confession, not mine," Father Adrian said. "And it's not an easy one. You've been involved in everything from bicycle theft to assault and even the taking of two lives," he said matter-of-factly. "But as best I can tell, little to none of it may be sin—at least on your part—since you were motivated by self-defense rather than selfishness.

"Regardless, I believe you've made a good confession, that you've been truthful and contrite for what are as well as what may not be your sins.

"Now for your penance," the priest concluded. "I want you to take a couple of days off to think about everything you've been through and prayerfully seek where you'll go from here. If you want to do it here, I'll see to it that you have someone to help you with spiritual direction. Your concerns are serious and demand serious reflection, with prayer and wise counsel," Father Adrian continued. "Given your place in the eye of the storm, no matter how smart, wise or lucky you are you can't expect to see it all clearly, in context."

"Could you be my director for this 'retreat'," Ken asked.

"I'm a guest master. That calls more for hospitality and discernment than actual spiritual direction," Father Adrian said. "Besides, I think I know someone who can help you a great deal. We were in seminary formation together a number of years ago, and he's since gone to another of our monasteries out west. But given the gravity of your situation, I think we can get permission from our superior for him to guide you."

"You'd do that for me?" Ken asked.

"Our work as Benedictines is to seek the face of God in prayer and work—*Ora et Labora*. We welcome all who come to us seeking God, salvation, peace."

Ken wondered if he should entertain the glimmer of hope the monk had sparked in him.

"So what should I do?" he asked.

"When we leave here I'll tell my abbot that we have another retreatant, who may be with us awhile," Father Adrian hesitated. "Meanwhile, you can take lunch in the refectory. By the time you're done I'll have your room assignment. You'll stay upstairs in this wing, which is our retreat center. The rest of the monastery is enclosure, and open to the monks only. You can attend Mass and prayer in the chapel loft, which is just off the second floor of the retreat wing and overlooks the main church.

"We monks here have taken a vow of silence, so if you run into any of us while on the grounds or in the halls, you can smile, nod or just pass by. We can speak to answer a question or for any necessary reason, but any other talk is discouraged. Silence is important in seeking God, which is what brought us all here.

"We monks maintain silence among ourselves. We always have a number of lay people like yourself who are here as guests, and therefore some of us speak as necessary, such as in my role as guest master, and retreat leaders who guide and counsel those here on silent retreats. And while the retreatants have taken no vow of silence, they have chosen to come here for a silent retreat. So conversation with them must be avoided, too.

"Then again," Father Adrian said, "given the *popularity* that drove you here, you may want to avoid others entirely."

Ken nodded.

"So the penance is appropriate?"

"More than appropriate," Ken replied. "It brings hope to me in that storm you were talking about, kind of like a lifeboat."

"Let's hope it carries you to safe harbor," the priest concluded.

Ken murmured a low Act of Contrition as Father Adrian signaled his absolution with a high, wide Sign of the Cross.

Both then leaned forward in their seats.

"Lunch is in 45 minutes," Father Adrian said. "The refectory or dining room is on the right, just past the main entrance. Afterwards I'll show you to your room. Meanwhile you're welcome to rest here or go for a walk."

"Thanks," Ken said. "I'll just sit here awhile."

Father Adrian opened the door and paused.

"How's Kerwin doing?"

"Well, our meeting was brief and rather chaotic," Ken said. "But he seemed to be okay. I know his heart's in the right place . . . I mean, he sure helped me."

The priest smiled and nodded. "I'll see to it that you have some medical supplies and a fresh change of clothes or two in your room waiting for you," he said, and then left.

Ken stretched out on the couch and watched the second hand in its orbit around the face of the wall clock. A little after noon he walked to the dining room, served himself from the sandwiches and soup spread out on a counter by the kitchen door, poured himself a glass of milk and sat alone at a table overlooking the courtyard. The other men on retreat offered nods and smiles to acknowledge his presence, then found their own places to eat in silence.

A bulletin board over the coffee urn held snapshots of groups of men or women with several of the monks, and Ken figured the retreats alternated for both sexes.

The turkey and Swiss cheese sandwiches and French onion soup were sumptuous despite their simplicity, and Ken went back for thirds. He would later learn that the variety of savory cheeses he would enjoy there, along with donations from retreatants, provided for the monastery's financial needs.

Ken had just drawn a cup of coffee from the large aluminum urn when Father Adrian ducked into the room and motioned him into the hall. Ken put his dirty dishes on a counter, then grabbed his coffee and picked an apple from a bowl of fruit on his way out.

"I'll show you to your room, if you're ready?"

"Sure, of course," Ken said, and he suddenly felt self-conscious carrying the food and drink from the dining area.

Not spilling the coffee became a test of skill as Ken tried to keep up with the monk. He half-ran up two flights of stairs and to the far end of a long, dimly lit but clean hallway. The smell of freshly laundered linens and Pine-Sol hung in the air over the polished wood floor.

They stopped at the last room on the right and Ken followed Father Adrian through the already open door. The small room held a twin bed, simple wooden table and chair, small chest of drawers and nightstand.

"This goes to your door," Father Adrian said, placing a key on the table. "Although you'll find that locking your room isn't necessary. The people here are quite trustworthy.

He motioned toward a roll of gauze, tape, scissors, a tube of antiseptic cream and bottle of aspirins spread across the top of the dresser. "Inside the drawers there are a couple of modest changes of clothing," he went on, then picked a small folder from the desktop. "This is a guide for retreatants," Father Adrian explained, replacing it on the desk. "It has the daily schedule of the monastery and suggestions on how to make a good retreat.

"We're Cistercian monks, or a reform of the Benedictine Order which follows the strict observance of the rule our founder, St. Benedict, lay down for monasteries," he explained. "We observe all seven daily times of prayer in the Liturgy of the Hours, and you're welcome to join us for any of them, but they're not mandatory.

"Matins, or morning prayer, is at 3 a.m. The last daily prayer is compline, at 8 p.m. Then we observe the Grand Silence from just after compline through morning prayer, meaning the rule of silence should be especially observed then, and we ask you to respect that. As I said, if you have good reason you may approach any of us here, at any time, and you are welcome to move about the retreat wing, the courtyard and surrounding acreage, as you wish. But remember, the enclosure is open to monks only. And the gate is locked overnight, from compline to matins, so if you lose track of time during an evening walk you could end up spending another night sleeping in the woods."

Father Adrian showed Ken the way to the community bathroom and showers down the hall. They then went down to the second floor for a look at the library, and the entrance to the chapel loft at the end of the hall.

When they returned to Ken's room Father Adrian told him he had called his friend, Father Cassian, who would arrive to see Ken "as soon as he can make it."

"Meanwhile," Father Adrian advised, "try to get some rest and enter into the spirit of your retreat. We have a former medical doctor among our number, should you need his attention. Otherwise, you need to settle down to see things more clearly. With that and prayer, you'll find your way.

"I've told the abbot only that there were some rather 'extraordinary' circumstances surrounding your path here, and he's all right with allowing you to stay awhile. If anyone should come looking for you I'll be honest in my response that we have only registered retreatants, since that is now what you are."

"Thanks," Ken said.

"One last thing," Father Adrian added, picking the apple from atop the nightstand. "You are welcome to all you can eat in the dining room, but no food up here, please. We don't extend the same hospitality to mice that we do our human guests."

The monk offered one last smile of encouragement and left. Ken turned to the window, opened it and smelled the sun-warmed earth of the freshly plowed field. He also caught traces of muskiness drifting from the wooded hills, where lush foliage had begun to flush crimson and gold on its way to the parchment brown of autumn.

The green tractor reappeared, with its robed driver now piloting a trailer full of freshly baled hay towards a barn. Three other monks sat high atop the stacks, their sandal-clad feet swinging with the trailer's rocks and bumps.

Ken turned and looked over his room, then laughed aloud at a sudden realization. A monk's room is called a cell, just as is a prisoner's. And while Ken had recently feared he was destined for a cell, he could never have dreamed it would be one like this.

Several modest changes of clothing lay folded in the dresser, and Ken threw on a set after a long, steamy shower in the community washroom.

After using the sink in the corner of his room to wash and then rebandage his chest, he felt like taking a walk. But he thought showing his face anywhere just yet would be unwise, considering how a car or helicopter could zoom up. Instead he went to the library, scanned the shelves and finally decided on "The Seven Storey Mountain." Ken had always intended to read something by its author, Thomas Merton, who had belonged to the same religious order as the monastery where he now hid. Writing from his monastery in nearby Kentucky, the prodigious Merton had churned out scores of books ranging from Church history to spirituality to social activism and interfaith dialogue. He died of accidental electrocution during a Christian-Buddhist conference in Bangkok in the 1960s.

Ken took the book to his room, read the first chapter by the light coming through his window, then lay on his bed to digest what had happened that morning.

There was a light rap at the door, and before Ken could rise a stately monk leaned inside. His expressionless face was framed by a closely trimmed, gray beard.

"Mind if I empty the trash?"

"No, of course not," Ken replied. "But I don't think I've been here long enough to produce much."

The monk picked up the basket by the desk and asked if Ken found the room to his satisfaction.

"Oh yes, absolutely," he answered, standing by the window.

"The weather's been fine. You chose the perfect time for a retreat, don't you think?"

"Couldn't ask for better," Ken said, and he wondered if all the monks there took their vow of silence so casually. He smiled appreciatively, hoping the monk would take the cue to leave.

The Benedictine smiled back, returned the basket to its place, then remained inside as he eased the door shut.

An lightning bolt of panic shot through Ken as the monk again turned to face him, and he wondered if a gun and silencer would come from under the brown robe. Ken edged to the desk, ready to grab the lamp as the only weapon at hand.

"Relax," the monk said, dropping both hands to his sides. "I'm Father Cassian . . . the man Father Adrian said he would send. Is this a good time to talk, or should I come back?"

"Sure, sure . . . I mean *no!*" a relieved Ken stammered, his heart pounding as he fell onto the edge of the bed. "I mean *no*, you don't need to leave, and *sure*, we can talk now. Right now is fine . . . perfect."

The lone wooden chair creaked as Father Cassian sat, then remained quiet. Ken wondered if he was praying, preparing to speak, or waiting for Ken to do so.

"*Relax*," the monk repeated. "Adrian told me all that he could, which was not much, since he was under the seal of confession. All I know is that you're in some kind of crisis he feels I can help you with. And given my background, I think I can assume what that may involve."

"What's your background?" Ken asked.

"Well, a Benedictine monk for the past twelve years," he said casually. "And counter-intelligence for about 25 before that."

Ken sat a little straighter and cleared his throat. "Who did you work for?"

"In intelligence, one never asks who one worked *for*," the blue-eyed monk explained with a wry smile. "One asks who they worked *against*."

The humor put Ken a little more at ease. But he decided that asking Father Cassian who he had worked against would elicit just as sly a response as his first, so he just returned the monk's smile and waited for him to continue.

"I guess I went into the 'family business,'" Father Cassian said. "I finished studies at the same schools as did my father, then took the same civil service path as he, ending up in the same well-known intelligence organization."

Father Cassian sat bolt upright, yet aristocratically casual in the plain brown robe and sandals of his vocation. He made direct eye contact throughout his conversation, which was matter-of-fact in a way that conveyed not arrogance, but authority.

"It didn't take you long to get here," Ken said.

"I live here," the monk replied.

"But I thought Father Adrian said you were teaching at another monastery."

"I think Father Adrian harbors a fear that some 'bad guys' from my days as a spook may come back to find me. So he was a little evasive until I could check you out myself. He did tell me he was actually quite certain you were sincere in your reasons for coming here. And that was easy for me to determine when I arrived.

"So," he concluded, "do you still want to talk?"

"Yes," Ken said. "I need to."

Father Cassian pulled his chair from the desk and sat near the window. Ken remained rigidly on the edge of the bed and fidgeted with the corner of its pillow.

After an uncomfortable silence, the monk spoke.

"Why don't we go for a walk," he said. "It might do us both some good."

They left the building and Father Cassian led them onto the walkway that lined the courtyard. For the next 90 minutes they walked, sat on a cement bench and walked some more while the monk listened to what had consumed Ken's life for the past month. Father Cassian kept the same expressionless expression throughout most of Ken's long, desperate narrative, offering occasional nods of understanding and speaking only to have Ken clarify or elaborate on something or to ask a brief question.

By the time the birds filtered out of the brisk sunset, Ken had told Father Cassian everything. And he hoped against hope that the priest had something or someone from his past to offer him help.

"So what do you think?" Ken concluded. "What should I do? Is there anything I can *do* to get my life back to *normal?* Or have I hung myself."

"That would be *hanged* yourself," Father Cassian corrected him. "Anyway, you've given me a lot to digest. Right now it's time for evening prayer and the Grand Silence. If you wish to join us for compline you will find space with the other retreatants in the church loft. We begin in fifteen minutes," he said without looking at his watch. "Then get a good night's sleep and we'll talk again tomorrow, after lunch," Father Cassian said as they re-entered the guest house. "I'll come by for you in the refectory at one, sharp."

Without goodbyes, Father Cassian turned for a doorway into the monastic enclosure and Ken took the stairs to his room. He had no idea how much hope he should put in the priest, whose last name he didn't even know. At least he had a history in intelligence, and he did project a strong, quiet confidence.

Ken washed up, combed his hair and walked to the loft at the rear of the long, high-vaulted granite church. About a dozen other men were scattered about the small grouping of pews, and they were bathed in the soft light from the ceiling lamps that cast a glow over the rest of the church.

The monks sang a cappella as they filed in below and took their places in choir stalls facing each other from both sides of the sanctuary. Drawn brown hoods covered their heads and faces, and Ken couldn't determine which were Fathers Adrian and Cassian.

Ken thought about how he had come to the monastery to escape pursuers, and wondered what had motivated the career spy to choose to fully and permanently dissolve into its life of self-denial.

While those around Ken echoed the ancient prayers and responses of the monks below, he recalled the goal chiseled into the gateway arch: *God alone.*

I guess I'm halfway there, he reflected. Because even though he had found others willing to help him, he still felt hauntingly alone.

CHAPTER EIGHTEEN

The soft knock at the door to another retreatant's room at the other end of the hall was enough to rouse Ken from sleep. He thought about how the past few weeks, and especially the past several days, had sharpened his senses into hypervigilance. The wake-up knocks got louder as the monk moved from door to door until he finally reached Ken's. Its brass doorknob and hinges rattled lightly with each rap, and the monk's footsteps again faded down the hallway as several men stirred towards the showers.

Ken sat on the edge of his bed, rubbed his face and pulled open the curtains. The sky was still black, with dawn edging over the eastern horizon like a thin purple blanket.

He grabbed a towel, showered with the rest of the men in the communal bathroom and returned to his room, where he shaved in its sink.

After dressing he left for morning prayer. Along the way he wondered if the blue jeans and pullover shirt he wore were perhaps castoffs from a man who had surrendered them, along with the rest of his life, when he took the medieval robes of the Benedictines. Or perhaps they'd been left by a retreatant—someone who, like Ken, may have come to find the way to peace from his own demons.

Ken took a prayer book from the stack at the loft entrance and sat on a pew behind the others. As the monks processed in below, Ken stood with the rest of the men in the loft and thought that none of his fellow guests looked particularly troubled. *Lucky to be on a simple religious retreat,* he thought. But then again, Ken considered, he probably looked no different to them either, despite the fact that he had found the place while literally running for his life. That realization brought back the words of his high school religion teacher: "Be kind to all you meet," she had exhorted, "for they are fighting a terrible battle."

An anonymous monk, eyes shrouded by his drawn hood, stood to offer the first Scripture reading. Ken was further humbled when it came to him that this place into which he had blundered was a chosen refuge for those around him who were using their vacation time to seek God rather than taking a cruise, or sightseeing from a five-star hotel.

An old, long-haired man wearing a large wooden cross around his neck could have been deeply religious or simply fanatical. The disheveled sweat suit and sandals of a guy not much older than Ken made it impossible to determine whether he was a grocery store clerk or a bank president.

And the remaining mostly middle-aged men of various shapes and sizes also wore casual attire making it difficult to determine their stations in life or income levels. Some wore blue jeans and T-shirts, others khakis and knit sport shirts. Despite the fact that no two of them seemed alike, and that they would spend their time together with almost no conversation, Ken sensed a nearly palpable bond between them all. They had each come for their own reasons, and for the same reason—to go deeper than what they found in their daily roles as car salesmen or teachers, plumbers or doctors—to cultivate and carry back a deeper faith to their everyday lives.

They were drawing from a well in which Ken, so far, had found only a hiding place.

Ken knew about monastic life from his reading of Aquinas, Luther, Augustine and other religious thinkers, including the Buddha and the sages of Taoism and Zen. He had once spent a day with his high school religion class on a field trip to a Ramakrishna sect Hindu ashram near Grand Rapids, and he had also heard missionary monks make appeals from the pulpit for contributions during Masses at his home church.

But Ken had never lived the daily routine of a monastery. Christian monasticism didn't offer him the spiritual allure that fascinated him in Eastern mysticism or the abstract hypotheses of his library full of philosophers.

But this went beyond the hypothetical and theoretical. These were men immersed in something beyond theory, speculation or curiosity. They had found and tasted God.

And as the leaves fell from the trees around the monastery, and nearby farmers mowed their hay, this group sought to empty the million and one everyday concerns from their hearts and minds in order to enter the mystery each carried at his center.

Everything Ken had ever read, studied or heard about transcendence, the holy, God, began to slide into sharper focus.

Or was his desperate situation urging him to feelings of profound reassurance the same way one lost in the desert hallucinates an oasis?

He pushed the rationalizations away and concentrated on reciting that morning's psalm with the rest of the monks and laymen.

When the prayer time was over and the last of the monks had disappeared from the church, Ken followed the rest of the retreatants into the hallway, then down to the dining room for breakfast. He fixed a large bowl of cereal, grabbed a glass of milk and took a seat. The homemade, oven-roasted granola turned the milk a malty brown, and the nutty mixture was the best Ken had ever eaten.

When he was finished he drew coffee from the urn and took the steaming cup out into the courtyard. Birds combed the dew-covered grass for worms as he eased onto a bench. The sun was up but had yet to breach the monastery wall, and Ken wondered what he should do until his one p.m. meeting with Father Cassian.

Several of the men on retreat exited the building, walked across the courtyard and left through the gatehouse. Then a couple more followed. A few carried books or notebooks, but none had luggage, so Ken figured they must just be going for a walk. He carried his coffee to the gatehouse, where another monk sat reading.

"Excuse me," Ken said. "I'm new here and I noticed several men leaving with notebooks and stuff. Where are they going?"

"There are several trails through the woods around the monastery and behind the hayfield across the road," he answered. "The trail behind the field leads to an old Forestry Service observation tower," the monk continued. "That's a nice spot for prayer and reflection, along with a great view of the surrounding area."

"Thanks," Ken said. He returned his cup to the dining room and headed for the tower trail.

The golden bristles of mown hay crackled under Ken's shoes until he reached the earthen trail leading into the dense woods. It was similar to the one that had led him to the monastery, except it was well worn and obviously much more traveled.

After several hundred yards it opened to a small clearing with a split log bench next to a bronze, life-size statue of St. Francis of Assisi, his arms raised in frozen adoration.

Ken kept following the trail up a couple of bumpy hills and over a stream he assumed to be the same one he had bathed in the previous morning. Then, after following the path across and up a broad, sweeping rise, he again stepped out of the trees. The sun warmed his face as he stopped at the edge of a wide, grassy hilltop with a rusty steel-frame tower at its center. It looked about fifty feet tall, with a simple steel stairway crisscrossing inside the frame to a faded green watchpost at the top.

A hollow metal drumming sounded with each step Ken took on the long climb. When he reached the top he pushed open the trap door above his head and took the final three steps up through the floor of a ten-by-ten-foot observation room. Glassless, steel-framed windows from waist to ceiling provided an unobstructed view of the countryside for miles in every direction. The room was empty but clean, and a knot of wires sticking from one wall told him where the rangers' phone or radio had been.

Ironically, even though it was lined with windows and loomed some five stories above a broad Indiana forest, the outpost reminded Ken of the room he had found in his family's basement. Both were small, deserted, scoured of what had once made them useful, and remained anonymous shells of what they had been.

With no place to sit but the floor, Ken went several steps back down the ladder. He rested there so he could look out over the color-dappled trees of the rolling forest, the bronze stubble of the hay field, and the monastery's bell tower.

Ken wasn't sure if he was talking to himself or praying, but he spoke aloud as he pondered what had happened to him, where he now found himself, and what he could or should do next.

"As hideouts go, I couldn't have done much better than this if I'd tried," he said. "But where do I go from here? I'll never be able to go back to school or home, or have any kind of normal life until I deal with dad's company, or the people who control them.

"I didn't kill that man and woman in the car," he told a hawk circling the grassy area beneath him. "But that doesn't mean I can't be prosecuted for causing their deaths when I escaped. All I knew was that a couple who offered me a ride turned around and kidnapped me at gunpoint. Who wouldn't fight to escape? Who could blame or prosecute anyone for that?"

Several deer crept into the clearing below to graze on the thick green grass. Ken's murmurings had not carried down to the animals, and his scent was high above them, too. He watched as their white tails twitched as they ate, and the scene soothed him.

The monastery bells came to life in the distance, signaling that it was noon. The stairway creaked as Ken jerked to his feet, and the deer bolted back into the brush.

Losing track of the time meant Ken would miss lunch and could be late for his one o'clock meeting with Father Cassian, if he didn't hustle. He hadn't timed his slow trek to the tower, but it seemed to take about a half hour. So he double-timed it back to the monastery, spooking yet another pair of deer from the path on his hurried descent.

Ken managed the trip in just over twenty minutes, and the gatekeeper smiled and waved him back inside. He then went to his room, washed his face and hands and returned downstairs for his appointment with the priest.

Even though Ken was ten minutes early, Father Cassian sat waiting on a chair in the hallway.

"Have a good morning?" he asked.

"Yes. I went up to the watchtower and had a great view of the area while I thought things over."

"Have any revelations?" the monk asked, rising from his seat.

"Not in the biblical sense," Ken said. "But I think it did help me to settle down and see some things more clearly, things relevant to my . . . situation."

"Ah, yes," Father Cassian said, motioning him to the courtyard door, "your *situation*. I've been giving that some thought as well."

They reached the far end of the chapel's outside wall, then walked around the building to the cross-dotted burial ground Ken saw when he first arrived. Father Cassian sat on a bench, and Ken lowered against a large elm between it and the monastery wall.

"So what do you think?" Ken asked as the monk watched a bird, squirrel or something else stir in the branches above. "Was I wrong in questioning my father's death? Or his motivation behind the hidden room? Or for causing two people to die while defending myself? Can I reason my way out of this? I've done no premeditated harm to anyone or anything.

"Or am I destroyed. Fated to prison, or worse?"

Father Cassian sat in silence, knowing the desperate stranger wasn't finished.

"All I want is to be able to live my life again," Ken said. Then, drawing his knees to his forehead, he began to cry. "All I want is to go back to school, to see my mom again, to hold my girlfriend . . .

"I didn't mean to hurt anyone or get out of line with . . . God knows who. All I wanted was to make sure that if someone had gotten away with murdering my father they should be dragged out of the shadows and brought to justice."

Ken's weeping gave way to a long, desperate sigh. "That's all I wanted," he finished. "Justice."

Father Cassian leaned forward on the bench and made lines in the dirt with a stick.

"Your motivation is completely understandable, even noble," Father Cassian said. "But I'm afraid that motivation, combined with an overactive imagination and more than a little naiveté about how covert organizations work, have all blended you into a nasty stew."

The thoroughly dejected Ken sat motionless.

"But not to despair," Father Cassian added matter-of-factly. "Let's take this on, point by point."

Ken looked up.

"Well then," the priest continued, "first of all, there's the hidden room you described. Actually, those aren't unheard of among those in certain types of intelligence work. Most embassies and consulates worldwide have at least one, and I understand they're also used here in the U.S., depending on the organization and level of operation.

"They're simply a way of keeping work secret, sometimes from those in the same company and, apparently, from family members as well.

"They're also a safeguard against intruders," he continued. "If an enemy gains access to the property by break-in or other means of stealth, he or she may ransack the open areas, leaving the black room undiscovered and unviolated."

"But in a private home, among family?"

"I have heard of it," Father Cassian said. "It would really be no different than the others I told you about. Black rooms are havens of secrecy, and if their existence becomes known, their usefulness is compromised and they're worthless.

"Standard operating procedure for any such 'black' station, platform or facility is that no one beneath the level of the primary user is ever allowed knowledge of its existence. And if discovered, as in your case, they are immediately sanitized, then abandoned or destroyed.

"Apparently your father was in a position that was either sensitive or critical enough to his company's mission that his work demanded placement of such a room. Perhaps he had to be available at a moment's notice, or constant contact and quick response were crucial to his role in the organization.

"Or maybe he never used the room at all," the monk continued. "Maybe it was there for him in the event of some emergency or other contingency.

"In any event, what it all comes to, and the point of view that would probably give you most comfort, is that your father wasn't nefariously holding a dirty secret from you and your family. He was most likely simply doing his job. Like thousands of other men and women, he was bringing his work home with him. And while the degree of secrecy may present an affront to your personal pride, it looks to me nothing more than your father following a matter of professional procedure."

He saw Ken's grudging acceptance.

"You apparently missed it, or perhaps you were too young to notice," Father Cassian went on, "but several years ago—maybe ten or fifteen—the media carried a brief news item about an American woman in London whose husband, an executive for some U.S. corporation, suddenly disappeared. He just left the dinner table of their flat, went into the study while his wife busied herself with the dishes or something, and *poof!* he was gone.

"Well, when the night passed and he never materialized, his wife reported his disappearance to the authorities. He wasn't expected at work for a few days and she thought perhaps he was taking time to ponder some personal problem or something like that.

"Several days later the police still had no luck finding him. Then the woman noticed a foul smell in their study and thought perhaps a rodent had died in a wall. She called the building maintenance man who broke into the wall and, like you, discovered a hidden room. The poor lady's husband was slumped over dead in a chair, papers from his 'real' job spread over the desk before him."

"That's it!" Ken said, jerking upright in the grass. "I heard pieces of that story from an army guy who picked me up hitchhiking awhile back . . . So it *did* happen!"

"And the only reason it made the news was because the custodian ran off to call a television reporter before the dead man's people had a chance to take care of the situation."

Ken felt reassured. He and his family weren't the only ones who had lived a wall away from a secret world. And it appeared to have been a necessary secret, for a good reason.

But none of that solved Ken's other mystery, the one that had catapulted him through the looking-glass and into hiding in a monastery.

"Well what about my father's murder?" Ken asked, hoping the old monk would be able to help put that question to rest as well.

"Again, as with the hidden room, I think you should accept and do your best to understand and be at peace with the reality of that, too."

"What do you mean?"

"I believe what happened to your father is probably what you've always thought happened, that he was the innocent victim of random violence."

"You don't think the 'unusual nature of his work' put him at greater risk of assassination?" Ken asked. "I mean, if he was some kind of spy, doing God knows what in a secret room, and in his office downtown, and in his travels, doesn't that put him in the type of company where murder is an occupational hazard?"

"Perhaps," Father Cassian conceded, "depending on what his specific work was. But certainly not in such a way as you described happening to your father."

"Why not?"

"Those in the intelligence community don't entrust something as weighty as the termination of a threat or enemy to a carload of teenagers. They dispatch in-house or contracted professionals who know how to do their work with speed, precision and, in most cases, a method leaving the death to appear due to an accident, natural causes, suicide, a botched robbery or such."

"Or a random act of violence?" Ken proposed.

"Not per the scenario you described," the priest said. "First of all there is positively no way a carload of black teenagers would be recruited for such an operation. Secondly, the shooter, in a moving car, would have had to be a marksman unlike the world's ever seen in order to pick out and hit a moving target in a thick crowd.

"A crowd can be a good setting for an assassination," the monk conceded. "But then the killer almost always shoots, stabs or injects the target at close range, usually while walking past. As the body falls, the assassin keeps walking, blends into the crowd, and leaves unnoticed."

The matter-of-fact, businesslike tone of the priest's voice as he described the obscene act of 'pickpocketing' another human life was drawing Ken's ire, and Father Cassian sensed it.

"I don't blame you for being disgusted," the priest continued. "It's a thoroughly repulsive act, killing someone."

"So have you killed anyone?"

"Directly, no," Father Cassian answered. "I mean I never pulled a trigger, planted a bomb or set a poison . . . But I'm sure I was instrumental in seeing that plans were assembled, relayed or carried out for others to do so.

"I'm not proud of that," he quickly added. "It's a big part of the reason I'm here," he said, the tone of his voice lowering for the first time in their discussion. "You see, Ken, spies are nasty people, very nasty people. Most are real patriots, with blind allegiance to their country . . . But the combination of patriotic zeal, the conviction that the end justifies the means, and participation in a 'privileged' profession are a heady and dangerous combination.

"In espionage few know who you *really* are and what you are *really* doing—and fewer yet care about how that gets done. Then the lines can blur, and evil becomes good, or at least acceptable, if it helps you meet your objective.

"The Cold War was raging when I served," Father Cassian mused, his stare unfocused over the rows of white crosses before them. "That's how we justified such things. And there's no doubt in my mind that many of our people were spared and freedom was safeguarded through our work.

"Still," he concluded, "I've confessed, prayed for and, hopefully, atoned for whatever violence I committed or supported along the way."

There was a long pause, and Ken felt as if he had just heard the old priest's confession.

"It's a muddy, murky, messy business, espionage," Father Cassian said. "At first the road's nothing but excitement as you're trained in whatever area of the business for which you've been selected. And that alone, being chosen to enter the 'black' world, is quite an ego-inflator.

"Then, along the way you begin to lose so much, doing or being party to things you would never have dreamed possible in your former life.

"But when you see yourself as a member of the initiated, the inner-circle, the chosen few, the rules are dispensable . . . You've risen above them.

"You lose . . . no . . . you give away so much, so much humanity. I was prepared to end my own life, if need be," he said, again too casually for Ken's liking. "I was issued what we called an 'L-pill,' as in L for lethal . . . to be taken if I was subjected to torture, so I wouldn't talk. It wasn't a pill at all," he went on, still as casually as if talking about the weather. "It was a common pocket item, impregnated with something that would cause immediate death if I were to pop it in my mouth."

He again saw disgust welling up in Ken.

"I know it's completely amoral, and not to be taken lightly," Father Cassian said. "But there's a point to be made here . . . an important one for you, especially, having had a father in 'the business'.

"That business can be dirty, and it changes people. But it sounds to me that your father was in a more technical area, removed from some of the more distasteful aspects of the work.

"He probably regretted not being able to tell you more about his work and the secret room just as much as you wish he had— maybe more. Love means sharing all that you have and are, and secrecy carries a terrible loneliness."

Ken crossed his legs on the ground and pulled a handful of grass to twist in his hands.

"So how did a civil servant, or spy or whatever you were come to a life of monastic silence in the Indiana hinterlands?"

"I guess I thought I was telling you," Father Cassian replied. "Ultimately, 'spooks' deal with communication, information, secrets. But in intelligence, true communication is hardly possible. There's never complete trust, no room for complete faith in another. The ensuing isolation is unconsciously projected onto others who are then seen as subservient to *the cause*, expendable if they get in the way. That isolation dries up your connectedness with humanity until others seem unreal, of no individual value or consequence. Then, before you realize what's happened, you're alone, hollow.

"I became so absorbed in myself that I was alone even among my most blindly loyal peers. Others had become a projection of the shell I'd become, devoid of any ultimate truth to hold onto or meaning to guide me.

"Perhaps your father knew the pain of living with secrets—maybe even living a secret—knowing only parts of information he would pass along to the next level without ever being entrusted with the whole story on anything.

"Eaten away slowly by the isolation of my work, my life, and the feeling that I was not held to the conventions defining the rest of society, my soul was slipping away," Father Cassian said. "Then I joined others in seeking comfort in the pleasures of power and privilege that only further distance one from what is real."

"So you came here to not be lonely?" Ken asked. "To a place where you live in silence?"

Father Cassian just smiled.

"What is *real*?" Ken said.

"I've only glimpsed it, but it's what brought me here," the priest answered. He went on to tell how he had been put up in a Buddhist monastery for a year while doing surveillance work at an outpost in the jungles of Laos in the 1960s.

"There were only several of us and we paid the monks rather handsomely for accommodations that made the hay barn here look like a palace," he said with a reminiscent grin. "But I found something there that opened the floodgates to all the meaning and love that had slowly bled from me.

"I was befriended by an old monk who taught the younger ones, and true to the tradition of the guru, he read me like a book. He knew my heart, and I didn't realize it at first, but his friendship became a spiritual boot camp for me. Within hours of our meeting he began teaching me to meditate, giving me a mantra from the Christian Bible. He said one should never leave the tradition in which they were raised, and I respected him all the more for not attempting to recruit me into the sangha.

"That's what the Buddhists call life as a monk," he said in response to Ken's questioning look.

"Anyway," Father Cassian continued, "I immediately found the meditation emptying me of something while I entered into what I can only describe as a silent, infinite source, home, reality . . . God. That old, toothless and nearly blind monk read my bankrupt heart and hooked me up to an endless wellspring of truth.

"For the first time I knew the reality of Christ's words: *Behold, I make all things new,* because I truly *experienced* reality for the first time. All was as it always had been, but I saw it anew, through eyes opened on the stone floor of a Buddhist temple.

"Soon I found meaning rushing back into my life. And my teacher told me that as I continued to meditate, and join that to my faith tradition, God would restore wholeness to my being. I came here because this is where I was led.

"I've seen what 'it' is that makes up God . . . God is the love that literally makes up and holds together all of reality. I see that more clearly every day as my vision is cleared by the love I find in silent prayer and in the people and life around me. It's a divine, cosmic adventure."

"Right about now I'm not even sure what my middle name is," Ken said with another sigh.

"It's Walter," Father Cassian said, rather offhandedly.

Ken was shocked.

"How did you know that?"

"It just came to me," the monk answered, a hint of amused bewilderment on his face. "Happens every now and again . . . You could call it clairvoyance, ESP, a coincidence or even a lucky guess, but I believe it's a by-product of meditation.

"The Holy Spirit gives each member of the church at least one *charism,* or gift for the benefit of the faithful. One of them is called the word of knowledge, or having unknown information revealed through the working of the Spirit," Father Cassian continued. "Deep prayer or meditation, or other openness to God cultivates those gifts, and they can then be used to bless or build up others.

The Hindus have a similar concept they call *siddhis,* or powers that come with various stages of meditation."

Ken was skeptical, and the suspicion darted into his mind that the priest had checked into his background through friends on the outside who were still in "the business".

"I assure you it's completely natural," Father Cassian said of his supernatural twitch. "Just about anyone you talk with who has been serious about meditation for any length of time will tell you they've had varying degrees of similar experiences . . . like knowing something without being told, 'hearing' other people's thoughts, even levitation, some say, although God's never cleared me for take-off."

Ken smiled. "Impressive," he said, not so much because he was impressed as that he didn't know what else to say.

"Those of us here aren't overly impressed by such things either," Father Cassian said. "In fact, without a good teacher to keep you focused they can be a serious distraction to the true work of meditation. I suppose if I wanted to impress people I would've joined a circus, not a monastery."

They talked awhile longer into the sunny afternoon, their words blending with the earthy scent of a forest surrendering its leaves to the leading edge of autumn.

Ken spoke of wanting to bring his life back to some semblance of normalcy. And the old monk told of saints and patriots, how one moves closer to the God and the other to a monument-topped grave.

"But it does seem that you might glean some further information from this Paul Cody, and his other friend, too . . ."

"Truro," Ken said.

"Yes, him as well," Father Cassian continued. "I mean, from what you said, they certainly spent a good deal of time together on and off the job."

"Yeah, I'm sure Judas was Jesus' friend, too," Ken said. He spat out the words with suspicious sarcasm. "That friendship didn't mean much when Judas handed him over to his enemies on Good Friday."

"Actually it was Wednesday," the priest corrected him.

"It's now kind of faded into obscurity, but when I was a boy you heard folks refer to 'Spy Wednesday' as the middle day of

Holy Week, followed by Maundy Thursday, Good Friday, Holy Saturday and Easter Sunday.

"It's called Spy Wednesday because Judas was a 'double agent' of sorts, betraying Christ to the Romans on that day. Based on that information they arrested him the next night."

Father Cassian shifted on the bench and leaned forward.

"I've paid serious attention to your situation, what you've told me and how you've told it, what you've done and what you believe about your past, present and future," he said.

He paused and locked his knowing, sky-blue eyes onto Ken's.

"I believe that the most important thing you can learn is how to be betrayed," Father Cassian said.

Ken was confused.

"One day when I was a young boy my parents announced that they were going to take me to the theater," Father Cassian continued. "I loved plays, and I was dressing for a night of lights and music and a magical story with characters in all sorts of fantastic costumes, when a knock came at our door.

"My father answered and it was a friend of the family who hadn't been around for ages and had arrived unexpected.

"I peeked around a corner just in time to hear my father explain that we were on our way to the show, and I couldn't believe my ears when he offered my ticket to his friend.

"'Why don't you join us?'" my father urged. 'We were only going to bring Patrick.' Patrick was my name before I took Cassian upon entering the monastery," he explained.

"You see, my father only meant well. But in offering the opportunity to his longtime friend, he didn't realize the crushing disappointment it would bring me.

"Betrayal is like that," Father Cassian said. "It's always a selfish act, but not always consciously so. It may be a seemingly benign decision made without taking into consideration how it will affect others. At worst, it disregards or even sacrifices others for one's own benefit.

"I suppose your father's keeping the secret room in your house could be seen as betrayal," the monk continued. "But I think he probably believed it was for the greater good, and that since the secret would never come to light, it would not hurt or be of concern to you and the rest of your family.

"Now," he went on, "regarding your current plight, I'm sorry to say that I see only two viable options."

He paused as if to signal Ken that he would give advice only if asked.

"And?" Ken responded.

"Well, the first and, I think you will agree, very unwise option would be an attempt to keep running, to assume a false identity and start your life over. That would be an extremely difficult undertaking even for someone with a background in deception. For you . . . You'd be caught in weeks, a month or two at best."

"And the other option?" Ken asked.

"The only other option I see is to turn yourself in."

Ken's head sagged.

"No . . . Don't despair!" Father Cassian said. "It seems to me that any violence or other infraction you committed was done either in self-defense or while being pursued by others."

"But they were the *law,*" Ken countered.

"Are you sure? Did you ever see a badge or any other valid I.D.? Did anyone ever identify him or herself as a representative of an agency empowered to abduct, incarcerate or threaten you?"

Ken's eyes narrowed.

"No," Ken answered. "*Never.* Except for the security team at Knoblock."

"Since when do security guards have any of those powers?" Father Cassian asked. "And the filling-in of that secret room is material evidence of a quite *literal* cover-up, if it can be connected to them."

"I don't get it," Ken said. "You mean if I went to the proper authorities they could just excuse me for the whole thing?"

"First of all we don't know for sure who *they*—those who grabbed you on the road and at Knoblock—*are.* They may be Knoblock's own security personnel, or maybe they work for . . . someone else.

"But we do know what they want—silence," the priest said. "They don't want you telling anyone about that room you found, or sharing pictures of it. And they may be afraid you'll talk about something else, like the real nature of Knoblock's work—whatever it is—or something else of which you're probably not even aware."

There was another long pause and Ken watched a flyspeck airliner make its slow crawl across the sky, leaving a soft white scratch in the blue void.

"What it comes down to is this," the monk concluded, "are those on your trail the good guys or bad guys? If they are the *good* guys, carrying the authority and sanctioning of the U.S. government, you are in trouble. Period.

"And if they're the *bad* guys?"

"You're still in trouble, but the consequences could be more immediate, and final. Based on your response to their efforts to force silence upon you earlier, they could decide to forego any such inconvenience in the future and simply eliminate you.

"Either way, I wouldn't turn myself in to *them*," Father Cassian advised. "I'd go to the FBI, since they would have access to information and the ability to protect you. It's their jurisdiction anyway, since your odyssey covers several state lines."

Ken didn't know what he had expected the priest to say, or what kind of a solution he could have hoped for, but surrender had been the farthest thing from his mind.

"I've never felt this powerless before in my whole life," he said.

"Powerless isn't necessarily bad," Father Cassian said. "When bad weather approaches it's a good idea to lower your sails, so the wind doesn't tear them apart. You can raise them again after riding out the storm."

Ken thought about how this storm was going to cost him at best an entire semester of college, and at worst a long prison term.

"You know, there is one thing that could help me to stay sane through all this," Ken said. "Before all this happened I was training for a marathon. It's two months away and if I could spend some time on that each day it would be a big help."

Father Cassian said he would be glad to get him a pair of running shoes and the necessary clothing.

"I'm no athletic trainer, but if you'd like I could put you on a spiritual regimen which would toughen you up on the inside," he offered. "You might even find some of the answers you've been chasing in your philosophy studies."

"And maybe how to read minds, levitate and pick stocks and lottery numbers?" Ken asked with a smile.

"Look to running marathons for excitement," Father Cassian said. "I'll show you the way to peace."

CHAPTER NINETEEN

Jill made one last try to call Ken in his room, got yet another steady ring and threw her phone back onto its hook.

It was Thursday, and Ken should have been back sometime Monday. She had called his mother's place in Grand Rapids too, but only got her answering machine with each try. Jill left no message because she didn't want to worry Ken's mother. But she had to do something, beside herself that Ken may have been assaulted, abducted or killed by some crazy on the road. Or maybe he got sick along the way, was shot or beaten by thieves or a gang.

Jill grabbed a sweater as she prepared to meet the early cold front that had crept over Oxford. She was afraid a telephone call would be too easy for campus security to brush off, so she made the five-minute walk to Bonham House herself.

A lean, middle-aged man sat behind the front desk and looked up from his paperwork as Jill entered.

"Morning. What can I do for you?"

"I'm kind of afraid a friend of mine might be in trouble," Jill said, forgetting the explanation she had tried to memorize during her hurried, nervous walk there.

"His name is Ken Perry. He's a junior here and he hitched home like he sometimes does—to Michigan—and he was due back three days ago and he's still gone. He's not at his home in Grand Rapids, either, and I'm afraid . . ."

"Whoa!" the officer interrupted her sputtering. "You say he was hitchhiking? And he does that a lot?"

"Yeah, but he's never had any problems before, and he's not naive or stupid. He's sharp enough to steer clear of anyone who'd be dangerous."

"But you're obviously afraid something's happened to him."

"Yes," Jill confessed. "I'm sure something has. Something was bothering him before he left, and he was going home to deal with some kind of problem."

"Was he going after someone?"

"No! He's not like that, not mean or vengeful. I think it was more a personal problem he was looking to fix."

"Well, I'll start by having you fill this out," the officer said, handing Jill a missing persons form. "I'm Officer Chuck Turner, and I'll call around and see what I can find out. Just try to settle down. Hang on."

"I'm Jill Mangan. Thanks," she said, then sat in one of the lobby's old plastic chairs. She completed the form as the officer retrieved Ken's school and home addresses and phone numbers from a computer. Like Jill, Officer Turner got no answer at Ken's apartment. He then called Grand Rapids, got Mrs. Perry's answering machine and Jill rose with uneasiness as he left a message.

"Mrs. Perry, this is Officer Charles Turner of Miami University security. I'm trying to locate your son Ken and I'd appreciate it if either he or you would give me a call."

Jill's stomach churned as he left the campus police number, and it only heightened her sense that something was terribly wrong. She returned the missing persons form to Officer Turner as he went back to working the computer keyboard.

"I'm sending an alert to law enforcement agencies between here and Grand Rapids," he said. "And I'm also running a check to see if he's received emergency medical treatment or been admitted to any hospitals between here and there."

Jill bit her lower lip and gave him a frightened look.

"Listen," he reassured, "I don't think you should be too worried, at least not yet. You wouldn't believe how many of our kids disappear for a few days, only to reappear with tall tales of high adventure and severe hangovers . . . Or maybe he's spending a couple days with whoever it was he needed to work something out with.

"Regardless, we'll soon know if he's been admitted to a hospital or jail, or is being sought for anything."

Jill hadn't considered the last two possibilities.

Officer Turner tapped out a couple of sentences, hit the send command and waited in silence. Another screen scrolled down and the officer typed a few more strokes, hit a key and waited for paper to reel from his printer.

Jill started to speak, but the officer held up a hand signaling her to wait as he went to another site on the computer. After a little more typing and waiting he gathered several sheets from the printer, pulled reading glasses from his shirt pocket and quickly scanned them.

"Why don't you step back here, miss?" he said, holding open a swinging gate for Jill to move behind the counter. "I'd like to go over some things with you."

Turner called another officer from a back room to take the front desk as he and Jill went into an office, where they sat at a table behind a closed door.

She told the officer about Ken's change in mood leading up to his disappearance, and how he had been drugged in Detroit, and of the melee between Ken's neighbors and the pair who fled in the van. But none of it was making any sense as part of a connected series of events. Ken just seemed to be in the middle of a whirlwind of bizarre incidents.

"Well," Officer Turner said, scanning the papers before him, "I can't find anything here about a Ken Perry or anyone matching his description. He hasn't been treated or admitted at any of the hospitals or clinics in Ohio, Indiana or Michigan, and he comes up clean for any arrests or warrants, too."

Jill could almost feel the loud electrical buzz that came from the phone on the desk.

"Yeah," Officer Turner answered. He listened briefly then told Jill Ken's mother had returned their call. He hit a switch activating the speakerphone, hung up and punched its lone flashing button.

"Hello? Mrs. Perry? I'm glad you returned our call," the officer said. "I have a friend of Ken's here and she said your son hasn't returned from a trip home. Have you seen him?"

"I just got home from Chicago," she answered. "I just now checked my messages and got your call. I haven't been here for over a week. Is something wrong with Kenny?" her voice rose. "You say he's *missing?!?*

"Oh my *God*," she gasped, "I told him a million times I didn't want him hitchhiking! What do you think happened to him? He hasn't called Jill, either?"

"I'm sure everything's fine, Mrs. Perry," the officer reassured as her panic snowballed. "We just haven't heard from Ken since he left, and he's a little late returning. But it's like I was telling his girlfriend here, these college kids take off for their own adventures all the time, and they nearly always come back safe and sound. He's probably with old friends he went to see or new ones he's made along the way."

"It's me, Jill," Ken's girlfriend said as she leaned towards the phone. "I just got a little worried . . . Ken said he needed to go home for a couple of days and when he didn't return yesterday and wasn't there for my calls to your house, I got nervous."

Jill didn't know whether she should feel silly for worrying, be ashamed for scaring Ken's mother, or if she was right in following her fear that Ken was in trouble.

"The officer's right," Jill said in an apologetic tone. "I'm sure Ken's fine. You know him much better than I, and I know he can take care of himself."

All three—both women and the security officer—were thinking about the sheer foolishness of hitchhiking, but none mentioned their fears aloud.

"You know," Mrs. Perry said, her voice hollow over the speaker, "I did find one strange thing when I got home, and now it troubles me all the more."

"What's that?" officer Turner asked.

"I went down to the basement to do laundry from the trip to Chicago and there's a big piece of wood paneling torn from a basement wall," she said. "Nothing was stolen, no windows or doors were broken, nothing else out of the ordinary, just part of that panel broken from the wall.

"Did you file a police report?" Officer Turner asked.

"I called them," she said. "But they just said I should report it to my insurance company, make sure I keep my doors and windows locked and that they would keep a closer watch on the place for a few days."

"You be careful," Officer Turner advised. "Meanwhile, if you hear from Ken let me know. We'll have him call you when he turns up here, as I'm sure he will, safe and sound."

None of them believed it.

"All right," Mrs. Perry said. "I'm going to call Ken's sister in Chicago. Maybe he was going there . . . I'll call everyone I know."

"That's a good idea," Officer Turner said. "Thanks for your quick return call, ma'am. Try not to worry, okay?"

He and Jill gave Mrs. Perry their phone numbers before hanging up. Jill left a few minutes later, and a breeze cascaded rusty gold leaves over her as she wondered how she could sit through that afternoon's classes.

Meanwhile, several hundred yards down the same street, a phone rang in the Zebra Room, and a cafeteria worker found Blue at the table where the caller said he'd be. Blue's friends had no idea what was up as he left to take the call.

"Blue here."

"Good to hear a familiar voice," Ken said. "You wouldn't believe what I've been through."

"*Holy shit,* Ken!" Blue blurted. "Is that *you?!?* Where the hell *are you,* man? And what the hell's *going on,* anyway? You've got us all *crazy!*"

"What have you heard?" Ken asked. "Has there been anything in the news?"

"Jesus Christ, Ken! The *news?!?* What the hell have you been up to? I mean, *Jesus,* Ken . . ."

"Listen Blue, the shit *has* hit the fan, but I need to know where I stand in relation to the rotors. Hang with me here Heavner, okay?"

"Yeah, of course I will. But I mean . . . Jesus, Ken!"

"I know we don't have long to talk, so just tell me what, if anything, you've heard about what's been going on with me."

"Nothing, man," he answered. "I mean, among us friends of yours there's been a lot of concern and confusion, but I haven't seen or heard anything over the TV or radio. There was a police report in *The Oxford Press* about the incident where Todd and Black chased off the guys who sneaked into your place. But so far that's all.

"Why?" Blue asked. "Should we know more?"

"No. Not much more to know . . . Just tell the gang I'm okay and I'll see you all when I can."

"When?"

"For certain, I don't know," Ken said. "But it shouldn't be long."

Ken then left Blue with several instructions to pass on to Tom Porter. He was careful to go over each in detail, including a request that Tom write an anonymous letter to Ken's mother explaining that Ken was okay and would surface soon.

"Have him mail it from Cincinnati."

"God damn it, Ken! What else can I do? What can we do to help you? What's *going on, man?*"

"Just follow through on what I asked you to do for me," Ken said. "Keep this line our little secret and keep eating your lunches in the Zebra Room."

"Will do, bro," Blue said with a deep sigh. "I guess it's a good thing for both of us that I like greasy cafeteria food."

After their final nervous laugh, Blue returned to his friends at their corner table, and Ken turned from the gas station pay phone to head back down the lonely dirt road to the monastery. Along the way he reflected on how the damp, cold air, dying leaves and gray dusk melded to create a totally depressing atmosphere. He hoped the parting instructions he'd left with Tom would help him find his way out of his mess. And the fact that Ken's status as a fugitive had not made it into the news was also encouraging.

When he returned to his room Ken found a new pair of Brooks Beast running shoes, socks, plain red cotton athletic shorts and a Georgetown Hoyas sweatshirt neatly placed atop his desk. There was also a cheap plastic sports watch with a stopwatch function.

"The clothes and watch were left by a retreatant years ago," Father Cassian said from the open doorway. "And several of us chipped in for the shoes."

Ken felt like he was ready to run back-to-back marathons as he tried on the shoes, and he couldn't remember when he'd ever felt more gratitude.

"You don't know how much this means to me," he said.

"Tell me about this marathon you're training for," Father Cassian said, closing the door behind him.

"Well, I've run it several years now, but this year it's taken added importance for me," Ken said, sitting on the desktop. "This year I want to win it. And I think I can if I train well enough."

"But I thought you'd lost hope for any kind of normal life," the monk replied.

"I pretty much have. But that's why I need to win this race and not just run in it. I'm thinking of a plan . . . ," Ken's voice trailed off. "And besides, the past several years this guy named Don Hogan has won it, and he's the most arrogant bastard on the face of the earth.

"Er, sorry," Ken said in response to the monk's raised eyebrow. "Anyhow, not only is this Don guy full of himself, but he thinks he's some kind of god. While he's approaching the finish line he'll yell *Show me your tits!* and throw a thumbs-up signal for the girls along the sidelines to flash him their breasts. And he's gained something of a following of schoolgirls and bimbos only too pleased to oblige.

"I'd love to break that tape ahead of him and put him in his place."

"Sounds like a good plan to me," Father Cassian said, picking up and inspecting one of the running shoes. "The fellow at the shoe store said these would be sturdy and offer good support. I suggest you keep your training to the paths in the woods and fields around the monastery. You might be spotted by someone on the roads.

"And for the time being, keeping you here in the retreat center may be too risky, as well," he continued. "We have a small hermitage set back in the woods, and I think you'd better stay there. You'll have no visitors and we won't have to worry about another guest making you as a fugitive. It might be kind of lonely at first, but as I pointed out earlier, I think you need time for serious reflection anyway."

Ken agreed, and less than an hour later he and the priest were carrying two boxes of clothing, toiletries and food along a trail behind the monastery. It took over a half hour to get to the small opening holding the unpainted gray cement block cabin. An old water pump stood in the ground near the covered front porch, which extended the full twenty-foot length of the cabin. A weather-beaten wooden rocking chair sat next to the door, and an outhouse stood near the tree line behind the building.

"It's rather Spartan, but it was built as a hermitage, and generally hermits aren't too demanding," Father Cassian said, opening the unlocked door. "I'd give you the key, but it's been long lost. You can put the hook latch on while you sleep, if you'd like. But we've never had any trouble with break-ins, theft, vandalism or anything like that."

"Okay," Ken replied, and he put his clothes in a dresser by the simple twin bed. The only other furniture was a small kitchen table with two wooden chairs, and a bench and upholstered chair before a soot-darkened fireplace. There were windows on each of the four walls, including one between the pair of kitchen cupboards above a faucetless sink.

"You may have to work the pump outside for a while to get the rust out of its pipes, but when you do you'll find its water better than champagne," Father Cassian assured. "And you have enough bread, fruit and cheese here for a couple of days. I'll bring more as you need it. There's no electricity," he continued, "so you'll have to live by the sun, candles and fireplace."

Despite the lack of creature comforts, or perhaps because of their absence, Ken felt a strong peace in the tiny cabin. It was the purest, freshest air he'd ever breathed inside a building.

"If you see anyone, remember that if they're not in robes they're probably on retreat, and neither would expect you to speak, so you'll be fine with a wave and a smile," Father Cassian said. "Other than that, your only company up here should be of the animal or spiritual categories."

"I certainly hope so," Ken said.

On the way out Father Cassian showed Ken where the firewood was stacked and gave him a refresher on the route back to the monastery through the maze of trails around its vast acreage. Standing on the porch, Ken also had the priest sketch out a running course of about five miles through the monastery property, including a long loop around its good-sized lake.

"And of course if you need anything you can come down and get me at the monastery," Father Cassian said, handing Ken the map. "Meanwhile, enjoy your training. I wouldn't mind hearing that you had beaten this 'Show me your tits' fellow."

"I'll do my best," Ken said. "But before you leave," he hesitated, "you mentioned you'd be willing to be my spiritual coach. What exactly would that mean?"

"You've been seeking answers for a long time, trying to find answers to both the great mysteries of the universe in philosophy books and those surrounding your father's death," the priest said.

"I can show you a way that may, or may not, help you find an answer or two. But if you give it the same energy that you put into your running, it will bring you to a true, deep peace. And whether or not you find the answers to the questions you've been asking, you'll understand and draw strength from what it is that moves you to ask them."

"When do we start?"

Father Cassian walked into the cabin and returned to the clearing with two blankets. He handed one to Ken, folded his own double-thick and used it as a cushion as he sat cross-legged on the ground.

"I don't know what you understand of meditation, but the less the better," the priest said. "All you need to know is the following: You can sit like this, on the ground, or in a chair, against a wall or tree—any way you're comfortable—as long as your back is straight. You can fold your hands in your lap or place them on your knees," he went on. "Form isn't really important, except that your spine must be erect. And that's not for any esoteric reason," he explained. "It's so you won't fall asleep.

"Next you close your eyes, breathe deeply and silently repeat your word—*maranatha.*"

"*Maranatha?*" Ken asked.

"That's right. It's Aramaic, the language Jesus spoke. It's pronounced with soft a's in all four, equally emphasized syllables, and means 'Come, Lord'.

"But you aren't to think of the word or its meaning while you meditate," Father Cassian instructed. "You simply listen to it silently as you repeat it, using it to free your mind of distractions."

"Then what?" Ken asked.

"That's it," Father Cassian said. "Do that for a half hour each morning and night. You'll find it's very simple in theory but difficult in practice . . . for the first ten or twenty years, anyway.

"But if you remain faithful to the practice things will happen, insights will come, and you'll understand. Want to give it a try?"

"Sure," Ken said. "Why not?"

Silence fell as Ken assumed the position and closed his eyes. The next half hour was like a psychotic newsreel as disjointed images cascaded across the screen of Ken's mind, sometimes seducing and sometimes jerking him from his silent word. His mind jumped from images of those hunting for him, to what he would have for dinner, to Jill's smile, scenes from a long-ago Christmas at home, to his father's death, Rochelle's white breasts, and on and on and on, stealing his attention from the word he repeated silently.

At first the exercise seemed to drag on forever. Then, as if he had moved forward in time, Ken was called from a dreamlike state as Father Cassian began the Lord's Prayer aloud. Ken joined in, then together they stood.

"Remember," Father Cassian said. "Another half hour tonight, and again each morning and night. There's a wind-up alarm clock in there somewhere," he said, motioning towards the cabin. "You can use it to time yourself."

Over the next eight weeks Ken adapted his life to the rhythm of the sun, the prayer times he continued to join in the chapel loft, and the running and meditation that punctuated each day. His chest had completely healed after several weeks, and his trips to the monastery kept him in fresh fruit and vegetables, milk, granola, pungent wedges of just-packed cheese and warm loaves of coarsely ground bread.

Ken's long and winding runs along the trails around the monastery also took on a prayer-like quality. Feelings of solitude gave way to a sense of nearly mystical union with nature as he observed the cycle of life around him. And something else was stirring somewhere deep inside, too, as he treaded the silence of the mantra.

When he wasn't praying, running or carrying wood or water, Ken would work at piecing together a bridge to carry him back to the everyday world he had been forced to flee. It had been a long road from the carefree college parties to a silent monastic life in the woods. Ken wasn't sure what to tackle first—how to find his way back, or if that was even possible.

But the answers would come, Father Cassian had assured. "Just say your word and go about the work at hand."

And so it was, as Ken ran and prayed and thought and meditated and ran and prayed and thought and meditated yet more until gradually, the rhythm took on its own life and began to change him.

The mental chaos slowly settled as Ken sat in meditation, and he found a silent well of strength that calmed his spirit and brought him the peace Father Cassian had promised.

His running along the rocky, log-strewn paths sharpened his agility and reflexes as the uphill trails honed his strength and the winding downhills stoked his speed. Ken soon knew every inch of the lakeside trail by heart, and the surrounding honeycomb of wooded paths gave him countless route combinations, so he never got bored.

Far from it, he wondered why he had never run trails before. The scenery, smells, sounds and challenges of the terrain made the whole experience so much more sharp and vivid. And it was paying off. Wherever the rest of his life was taking him, his summer of trail training had put him in the best shape of his life.

About six weeks into his stay, Ken waited for sunset and walked to a stretch of isolated road he'd found along the western border of the monastery property. Using old rusted highway mile markers as a guide, Ken set his stopwatch, did a full set of stretches and took his mark.

The night was cold but calm, and Ken lowered his head, took another deep breath and punched the stopwatch button as he pushed off with his right leg. The road was flat, smooth and dry, and Ken heard only his own heaving breaths and the slapping stabs of his feet against the pavement as he raced through the darkness.

He was in the zone. After all the weeks of trail training, his strides against the unyielding blacktop seemed nearly effortless, as if he had been shot from a cannon over greased glass. The corroded, bent mile marker came up fast and Ken ticked his watch as his body broke its plane.

He pushed another button and the dial lighted to show the time: 4:22.

"*YEAH!*" he shouted, jumping like a schoolboy. "OH, *HELL YEAH!*"

It was the first time he had ever done the mile in under five minutes, shaving over a half-minute from his previous personal best for that distance. He was ecstatic.

I'll have to tell Father Cassian he's a better running coach than he realizes, Ken thought. He smiled and belly-flopped onto the roadside grass.

As monumental as his running breakthrough had been, it would soon be overshadowed by one much more profound. Ken found that his times of meditation brought a peace that went beyond what he had previously understood that word or concept to mean. With each sitting he went deeper, farther still to a place that was nowhere and everywhere, an eternal presence that didn't so much blot out the past or future as to show them irrelevant when compared to the eternal now. All knowledge was no knowledge, falling before the silence that holds and loves all.

Each time Ken sat the half hour grew shorter as he surrendered to, became lost in and one with the silence. And when the inevitable distractions intruded, he patiently swept them away with the word assigned by Father Cassian.

Phases of the state resembled his LSD experience, with time, space and logic blurred, distorted or lost completely. But the meditation eventually brought a clarity and sense of mystical union that had been missing in the pandemonium of the acid trip.

Ken thought of how breakthroughs—whether in running, meditation, scientific research or personal relationships—are rarely planned or foreseen.

One afternoon he sat cross-legged on a thick cushion of pine needles under a fir near the cabin. As he entered silence, he noticed that the forest sounds had quieted as the crickets, frogs and other creatures had apparently begun to settle in for the coming winter.

Closing his eyes, Ken slowed his long, deep breaths and his pulse followed as he repeated his word in silence.

It had now been two months since he found himself hiding in the monastery—working, praying, running and meditating. The daily routine had given him at least a temporarily normal life again, as he had finally found himself going about his days without looking over his shoulders, or jumping at sounds in the night.

He enjoyed his simple chores, such as cleaning the cow barns, helping the monks stack hay and washing windows back at the monastery. He had also found a new appreciation for Mass and the traditional prayers of the Church, although he couldn't say how much of that fervor was an emotional response to overwhelming crisis.

But that didn't matter, Father Cassian was quick to assure him, pointing out that genuine spiritual growth is often born of darkness and pain. "Don't second-guess yourself," the priest exhorted. "Commit yourself to the way you choose. Be single-hearted and persevere."

Ken found himself treading further and deeper into the silent, dark mystery of meditation. Sometimes mental images, forest sounds, physical itches and other distractions would hound him for the entire thirty minutes. Other times he would settle into repeating his word, then hear the alarm clock sound after what seemed only moments, rousing him from what he would have thought to have been dreamless sleep, had he not remained sitting erect.

Ken hadn't noticed that the forest sounds had faded away, or that he wasn't conscious of his breathing and was aware of his continuing mantra only in a detached, almost unconscious way. He had found this place maybe a dozen times as he grew in meditation, and soon an utterly black and empty silence held an incredible presence he could not describe. It was much more profound than the vivid, vision-like flashes that also came, as Father Cassian said they would.

"Whether sacred or profane, just let them go and patiently return to your word," the priest had advised. "Gently return to saying your word."

But what Ken experienced on this fall night would make that difficult.

Balanced on a cushion at the edge of infinity, in dark, timeless silence, an image pierced Ken's mind like a razor-tipped arrow. In a vision as brief as it was vivid, Ken saw his mother and father in an embrace of deep love, as were their parents, grandparents and each of the countless unions which had led to his own birth. In what seemed like a millisecond Ken glimpsed and knew in a mystical way the myriad succession of intimate, ecstatic unions which had culminated in *him,* and now left him awestruck.

When the experience ended, Ken realized his mouth was still open from the gasp the revelation had punched into him. He looked down at his palms, and the whorls of his fingertips reminded him of the unique person all those past unions had melded to create.

Ken knew he would never again see himself or anyone else as a solitary soul, and he hoped someday he would take Jill in such an embrace to plant a child in her womb, securing their place in the chain of creation.

Ken then closed his eyes and went back to repeating his word, doing his best to follow Father Cassian' instruction.

Later that night he sought out the priest after evening prayer and shared what had happened during that afternoon's meditation.

Father Cassian said it had shown Ken two important things: The first, he said, was the "gift" or realization the vision itself had left with him.

The second and perhaps more important thing, he said, was that Ken had faithfully returned to repeating his word.

"No matter how deep or profound the interruption may be," he said, "if you are doing or thinking about anything else, you are no longer meditating."

Ken also told Father Cassian about how well his running was going, and about his personal best in the mile.

"I'm not sure where I'm going with things in the bigger picture, regarding the problems that brought me here," Ken said. "But I have a plan, and a big part of it involves running that marathon in Detroit, and humiliating 'Mr. Show-Me-Your-Tits' in the bargain."

"Well Ken, I'm sure you'll do what you need to do to resolve your situation," the monk answered. "And I think it would be a damned fine thing if you were to win that race, and perhaps help this other fellow to find a little more . . . humility."

"But beyond all that—the meditation, the race, my plans— something's happening," Ken insisted, his eyes narrowing. "I can *feel* it in my gut . . . kind of a coiled feeling . . ."

"Pay attention to that, Ken," the priest advised. "Spies, soldiers, policemen, anyone who regularly puts his life on the line, for any reason, will tell you that's the first and most important thing they learn.

"One of my teachers in my 'previous life' always said I should learn to think fifty percent with my head and the other fifty with my gut—and always give my gut priority."

"But what if it's just paranoia?" Ken asked.

"Paranoia comes from the head, from an imagination out of control," Father Cassian replied. "Gut feelings are intuitive, and carry a wisdom that speaks truth."

Ken rose to leave for his cabin. "You know, Father Cassian, if I could not have had the father I grew up with, I would have wanted someone like you."

"Nonsense!" Father Cassian replied. "Even if I hadn't taken a vow of chastity, the only female we have here is a cow . . . And besides, your father sounds like he was an outstanding man. The person you are, including the part that appreciates whatever I've taught you, was brought forth through him."

With those words Ken's mind shot back to his vision, and the chain of unions that began with God's breathing into Adam and led to his father's impregnation of his mother just over twenty years earlier.

"Sleep well, Ken . . . And say your word!" the monk called out.

Ken turned, smiled, nodded and left. But the anxious feeling continued to gnaw at his gut, as if he were being stalked. As he returned to his tiny, dark cabin he wondered what had brought it on, and what, if anything, he should do about it.

Ken thought about building a fire in the fireplace, but then decided it was too close to bedtime and opted instead for the light of a large candle on the mantle. He looked at his bed and wondered if a good night's sleep was all he needed to uncoil his tension. He coaxed a glass of icy water from the outside pump, returned to sit in the candle's glow and digested all that had taken place that day.

Several hours later, just before the monks would stir for their morning prayer, a faint chopping sound grew closer from above the trees to the north of the cabin.

It quickly grew into a shrill roar as prop-jet engines and helicopter rotors raged it low over the clearing, then bumped and hovered to a standstill directly over the cabin, the prop-wash scattering its split-wood shingles. The high-intensity searchlight bathed the tiny building in a blistering white circle that remained frozen on the structure as the chopper then floated to and from the edge of the woods. Ropes dropped from the doors on either side of the copter, and four men in swat gear and night vision goggles slid through a whirlwind of dirt and leaves to the ground below.

Sprinting towards the cabin, one dropped to his stomach and trained his automatic rifle on its door and windows as the other three dashed forward. One of them leaped onto the porch and took aim through its window, covering the remaining two as they exploded through the ramshackle wooden door.

The man on the lawn and the other at the window then scrambled to join the others inside. One stood in the center of the cabin, his weapon lowered, as the others tore open cupboards and drawers, looked up the fireplace and under the bed.

It had not been slept in, and Ken was gone.

CHAPTER TWENTY

A burly man with a thick, black, shoulder-length braid and one silver earring stepped up to a runners' packet pick-up table under a predawn Detroit sky.

"Perry," he snarled, exposing a front tooth made of gold. "Ken Perry."

"Yes Mr. Perry. Here it is, right here," said the lady in the official volunteer T-shirt. A steady breeze from across the Detroit River sent a chill through them and the rest of the throng gathered outside Cobo Hall preparing for the annual running of the Detroit Free Press International Marathon. The volunteer smiled as she handed the rough-looking man the envelope containing his race number and safety pins to secure it.

Unnoticed and only a few feet away, a man wearing sunglasses and a nylon running suit spoke into a cellphone as he watched the braided man carry away the envelope.

Neither did anyone notice another man who wore sunglasses, running sweats and a baseball cap as he approached the D-F pickup table to receive his packet. With a slight smile, "Harley Davidson" signed the register and took his manila envelope.

Another man with binoculars watched from a nearby rooftop as the person who was obviously not Ken boarded one of the buses waiting to shuttle the runners to the starting line across the border in Windsor, Ontario.

Yet another man stood near the idling buses, wearing the same running suit and sunglasses as his two partners. All three were locked onto the impostor who had picked up Ken's number. They had hoped to follow Ken from the table, jab him with a sedative-loaded syringe and whisk him away unnoticed through the bustling crowd. But now the fact that the man holding Ken's credentials, and most likely his location, would soon be spirited across the

border into Canada worked the trio into a frantic visual sweep of
the ocean of runners for the real Ken Perry.

The two on the ground moved into positions in relation to
their partner on the roof to enclose the plaza full of runners in a
triangle, maximizing the efficiency of their search. Even though all
three were using binoculars they didn't attract any attention since
they blended in with the legion of security and race officials. All
three trained their gaze on the chunky, long-haired man as he
carried Ken's packet onto a bus. The trio then made long, slow
sweeps from their points on the triangle deep into the crowd and
back again, methodically covering the sea of men and women
preparing for the race.

'Harley Davidson' looked much like any of the hundreds of
other runners in his age division, and he had not attracted the
attention of any of the watchers as he climbed the black rubber
steps into a warm, crowded bus.

By the time the buses shuttled the real and fake Perrys over to
the Canadian side of the border, a rosy sun was beginning to chase
away the fall morning chill. A score of police and media helicopters
swarmed over the several thousand runners as they staked out places
behind the starting line on the road leading from Windsor's
MacArthur Park.

One of those choppers, bearing fake markings, wasn't there for
the race. Its crew combed the crowd for one man—Ken Perry—
and as the eight a.m. race time loomed nearer they had been just
as unsuccessful as their earthbound counterparts.

That trio had made their way through customs and had now
joined the search for Ken on the ground in the park.

But there were also three friendly faces that Ken would have
welcomed. Jill, Tom and Chloe stood among the rest of the
spectators crowded along the starting area as they scanned the
runners for Ken. Shielding their eyes against a now bright sun,
they figured their chances of spotting Ken before the race were
slim. And they were right, because he would see to it that no one
found him until the race was on. Ken had complete trust in his
friends, but there was too much of a chance that they too were
being watched by the others. Besides, the instructions Ken relayed
to Tom through his Zebra Room phone call to Blue called for
them to meet him at the finish line.

Meanwhile, the three watchers from the Detroit side now triangulated themselves around the runners in the park. They remained in radio contact with each other and the helicopter.

"Setter One in position," one of them radioed from his place on the crest of the roadway behind and above the runners.

"Setter Two in position," came the message from the spotter atop a van parked immediately west of the starting line.

"Setter Three, ready," called the third, standing atop a park bench on the east side of the runners.

"Father sees his children," came the response to all three from the helicopter, which hovered, circled, rose and lowered among the rest of the choppers vying for position over the crowded field of runners.

No one had spotted Ken nor his unlikely stand-in as they approached each other near the long line of yellow portable toilets. Passing each other, they exchanged packets in a fluid motion, without stopping.

"Thanks, K-Whopper," Ken said without turning.

"*Kick ass,* man," the biker growled.

Kerwin dropped his packet into a trash can and Ken stepped into a portable toilet to pin on his number and suck down three of the Power Gel packs his friend had stuffed into the envelope. He pulled seven more from the packet and tucked them into his socks and waistband.

Ken left his sweats in the portable but kept the stocking cap pulled low above his sunglasses as he walked, head down, towards the starting line.

On the way he stopped at an aid table and washed the carbohydrate-loaded gel down with two paper cups of water. He carried another with him to drink while waiting for the starting gun.

Loudspeakers blared the call for all runners to take position, with five minutes to race time. It also boomed a reminder that runners should place themselves according to their expected pace. Signs were spaced from near the starting line and back about a hundred yards for those ranging from six-minute-mile veterans back to the ten-minute-mile first-timers.

Ken knew placement was crucial, as being stuck in a herd of slow starters could crimp his hopes for a win. And if he took a place up front the watchers would spot him immediately.

But did that matter now? Ken had gotten past any possibility of being snatched before the race. Now all they could do is jump him during the race, or perhaps kill him with a sniper's bullet, if that's what it had all come to.

No, Ken thought. *They'll make their move at the finish.*

And he had plans in place for that.

Wading into the pack at about the seven-minute mile marker, Ken stopped and looked for spaces that would allow him to weave closer to the front. Edging forward, he lightly bumped a man who spun around, his eyes round with panic.

"Hey man, it's *all right!* I'm *sorry,* okay?"

The middle-aged man heaved a sigh, as if he'd just survived a close call. Then he dropped his head, and wrinkles creased his face in an expression of embarrassment.

"Sorry, man," he said. "But I wish we'd get on with this thing . . . I'm a Vietnam vet, and the sound of all those choppers so low has me in a bad place."

"Yeah, I know," Ken said. "They make me pretty nervous, too."

Ken finished his water as the Canadian national anthem thundered over the speakers. He then crumpled the cup and threw it onto the grass beside the road as the American anthem sounded.

Without hesitation the starting canon thundered, and from his place about three rows back, Ken took his first strides in the 26.2-mile race.

"YEAH, *KEN! RUN YOU SON OF A BITCH!*" Tom screamed, as Jill and Chloe then located their friend. All three had him in full view and cheered him on as he pushed out just behind the front-runners.

Ken slipped off his hat and glasses as he and a cluster of about a hundred elite runners quickly pulled from the thundering herd.

He was now totally unmindful of those he had worried about only moments before. The control room of Ken's brain was now consumed with the measure of his strides in relation to the speed given each, and to the cadence and depth of each breath. The greatest danger Ken now sensed was the temptation to surrender to the starting-gun flush of adrenaline and run too hard. Everyone knows marathoners are in top shape, but the best ones know that good physical condition means nothing without smart running. The exuberance of the fans lining the streets of downtown Windsor made it all the more difficult for Ken to rein it in as he sailed by on the leading edge of the shrinking cluster of leaders.

Ken had become expert at swigging down cups of water at a full run, and he hit the first water station at the one-mile mark in just over six minutes. He recognized several of the runners around him, including Don "Show Me Your Tits" Hogan, who was tightly grouped with three other runners several strides ahead of Ken.

At the two-mile mark, just before the Canadian Customs gateway to the Detroit-Windsor Tunnel, the runners again took water, as they would at each mile marker to avoid dehydration. Ken wasn't sure if it was accidental or intended, but Hogan flipped his empty paper cup so that it glanced off Ken's neck.

The runners left the 50-degree Canadian sunshine to descend into the long, sagging womb of the Windsor tunnel—which gives the Detroit marathon the distinction of having the only "underwater mile" in the centuries-old sport.

Maybe it's the child each runner may hold a little more closely inside, or perhaps it's an unspoken runners' tradition, but when the harriers reached the center of the tunnel, each let out a growling scream that rumbled through the full length of the ceramic-tiled tube. The howls rallied the throng of spectators who waited for them on the American side, and they broke into cheers as the runners erupted from the mouth of the tunnel into Detroit.

The grade from the tunnel up onto Michigan Avenue was steep enough for Ken to notice as his stride shortened to compensate for the climb. A Dixieland band played on a corner where Ken and the others turned left for the roughly ten-mile run west along Michigan Avenue. They would then make a U-turn back along the same straightaway and through downtown to the finish line in Hart Plaza.

Several miles now behind him, Ken sucked down a couple more Sports Gels while coming up on another water station, and he fixed his eyes on an arch of balloons several miles in the distance as an immediate goal. Ken had found that he always did better in long races if he kept a goal in sight.

It could have been the expression on a spectator's face, or perhaps a smell in the air, or it may have just come to him the way more

and more things seemed to as he had begun meditating, but Ken's
mind went back to a man who had been on retreat at the monastery.
They had made eye contact in a hallway one morning while Ken
was looking for Father Cassian. Ken didn't know whether this
retreatant was unaware of or simply overlooking the rule of silence
when he had tried to engage him in idle chat, asking where Ken
was from, and if this was his first retreat.

Before politely reminding the man of the mandatory silence,
Ken replied that his name was Mark, that he was a car salesman
from Chicago, and that this was his first visit. After a quick apology
for the breach of monastic discipline, the man shook Ken's hand
and gave him a smile along with a long look before they parted.

By the time Ken found Father Cassian he had brushed the
encounter from his mind—from his conscious mind, anyway.
Because soon the anxious stirrings hit Ken, and later that night he
fled the cabin hours before it was raided.

The marathon had now brought Ken to literally retrace the
steps he had taken on the night of his acid trip outside the Who
concert. Spectators stood several deep before Joe Louis Arena on
the sidewalk where Crystal had given him the laced drink. And
both sides of the street were shoulder-to-shoulder with cheering
crowds as Ken ran past the Federal Building and on towards the
faded blue facade of Tiger Stadium.

Coming up on the ball park, Ken pulled another gel pack
from his waistband and crushed the contents into his mouth. He
didn't need the infusion of carbohydrates so much as the distraction
he sought from the choppers watching from above and the strobing
lights of the police cars blocking traffic to Michigan at Trumbull.
They had become a demonic reminder of the last time he ran that
stretch of pavement.

He jumped onto the sidewalk, dropped to one knee and pressed
a palm against the sun-warmed cement.

"For you, Dad."

This time I win, he told himself as he rose, and he took water
in both hands at the next station, pouring one down his throat
and the other over his sweat-matted hair.

Still thinking about the chaotic night of his acid trip, Ken
wondered if Crystal lived in Detroit. Was she there now, joining

others in setting yet another snare for him? Probably not, he thought, since the next attempt would almost certainly be a direct confrontation.

It didn't matter, Ken thought, and he steeled himself for whatever awaited him at the finish line. "I'm ready for you," he growled. A runner a pace ahead of Ken glanced backwards, thinking the remark was directed at him.

The next seven miles from Tiger Stadium to the turnaround point at the I-94 overpass went quickly, with Ken hovering around a six-minute pace as he entered the heart of the race. The turnaround was a big psychological boost which was compounded as Ken saw the five glass towers of the Renaissance Center marking the finish line in the hazy distance.

Hogan kept exchanging the lead with two other men as they remained clustered several paces ahead of Ken. Occasionally, while in the lead, Hogan would flick both thumbs up and offer his trademark "Show me Your Tits" to clusters of giggling girls along the route. Some would offer an unsolicited "Hey Donnie!" yank up their tops and jiggle with glee.

Ken didn't know if it was disciplined training, the right genetics or plain good luck, but he had never run up against the infamous "wall" notorious for hammering marathon runners around the twenty-mile point.

Fortunately, today would be no different. Ken still felt strong, fluid and focused through the buildup of lactic acid and depleting fuel and oxygen reserves that sent many others into the cramps, dizziness and nausea of the wall.

Ken squirted another gel pack into his mouth as he ran up on the twenty-mile water station to his right. As he splash-snatched a cup of water from a volunteer, Ken noticed a black woman in a full-length fur coat just ahead on his left. When he approached, she stepped forward from a small group of amused bystanders and flung open her coat, exposing a string bikini straining against her ample but curvy ebony frame.

"How'd you like to hit *this wall,* baby?" she cooed with a broad smile.

Ken replied with the okay sign and his own exhausted grin, grateful for the comic relief.

With 6.2 miles to go, Ken told himself it was just ten more kilometers, the equivalent of a good, hard, morning wake-up run. Then it would be over.

But looking several strides ahead at Hogan and the other two lead runners, Ken was reminded that this was not the solitaire of a training run; it was the chess match of competition. The physical element is only half of a marathon. The other fifty percent is a mental mix of monitoring water, oxygen and fuel intake, positioning yourself in the pack, and pacing wisely enough to overcome your opponents capabilities without exceeding your own. It does no good to be trapped in a cluster and unable to pass, to fire your guns early and sag into the pavement short of the goal, or to lead an entire race only to be passed at the finish.

The old clapboard homes of Corktown told Ken he was coming up on his return run past Tiger Stadium. As he passed the left field wall, Ken realized he was running the same stretch of Michigan Avenue where he had fallen with the street bum on the night of his trip. A helicopter zoomed up low from behind and sent a shiver down his spine. The TV chopper had come to follow the leaders to the finish, now only five miles away.

It might have been a muscle cramp from dehydration, or an old injury returning to haunt him, but whatever the reason, one of the three front-runners threw a grimace skyward, fell away and collapsed by the curb. Medics reached the fallen runner just as the pair he had left, with Ken close behind, came up on mile twenty-three.

Hogan was now in his glory, turning an occasional labored exhale into an abbreviated bark of "*Show me!*"

Scatterings of teens, 20-something girls and horny housewives responded from both sides of the street on sidewalks now jammed with spectators as the finish drew near.

"Hey Donnie!" a group of girls screamed in unison, and Ken looked just in time to see several teens hike their Southfield High School Lady Harrier sweatshirts over their white, ripening breasts.

"Oh *YES!*" Hogan yelled in return, and he took off his sunglasses and tossed them towards the girls. Hogan's libido-fueled generosity broke his focus and his stride just long enough for Ken to come up on his right. The third runner stayed on Hogan's left shoulder.

A scowl came to Hogan as he saw he was being challenged by yet another runner. And since he was in the middle, he knew he wouldn't be able to pass on a left or right turn.

So he pushed forward in an attempt to pull ahead of Ken and the other runner, who had gone into hoarse bellows as his lactose-poisoned muscles screamed for oxygen. A shaking in the legs began to accompany the growing rasp of the ailing runner, and finally he surrendered to the rubber-legged stumble of the dropout.

"*SHOW ME!*" Hogan roared, the smell of victory stoking his ego.

Near mile twenty-five Ken and Hogan were neck-and-neck as they ran past the last water station.

The helicopter that had stayed just ahead of them zoomed ahead to the finish line at Hart Plaza, and now both runners could hear the motorcycle that carried yet another TV cameraman behind them. It came up wide to their left, and the cameraman on the rear was frustrated that he had to keep the shots tight on the runners in order to avoid the flurries of bared breasts they passed along the way.

With about a mile to go, Hogan lowered his chin and began his closing strategy. Always a strong finisher, his plan was to quickly pull away from and discourage his competition at mile twenty-five, saving just enough for a hard sprint for the last two-tenths of a mile at mile twenty-six, if necessary. And he kept getting plenty of emotional encouragement, as cheers from the crowd were mingled with a liberal sprinkling of bared, quivering breasts.

Ken felt strong and stayed shoulder-to-shoulder with Hogan as they came up on mile twenty-six, and he pulled the remaining gel packs from his waistband and threw them to the pavement. Hogan shot a sidelong sneer that asked Ken *Who do you think you are?* and said emphatically that *This is* my *race.* His ego was further grated by the wide smile that creased Ken's glistening face.

"Hey Donnie," Ken huffed. "*Show me your tits!*" And Ken strained to dredge everything he had left for a flat-out, lung-burning sprint.

The incensed Hogan was forced to throw himself so absolutely into his response that he ignored the sets of breasts popping up like doe tails in the crowd.

But Hogan had spent too much in his early kick. He had underestimated his competition and now Ken capitalized on the miscalculation, turning his energy reserves into a frenzy of stabbing kicks. Less than a full stride behind, Hogan felt oxygen deprivation begin to shut down his legs, and the best he could manage was a futile headlong dive for the finish line as Ken leaned his chest through the tape.

The clock read two hours, sixteen minutes and forty-two seconds, and Ken couldn't have been happier even if he had been able to shave off the several minutes it would have taken for a course record. In the minute or so it took for Ken's mind to refocus from his marathon trance, race officials draped the gold medal over his neck and thrust a sponsor's sports drink into his hands. They then backed off to make room for the photographers, TV cameras and reporters who swarmed Ken, giving him just enough room for an unsteady pace to stretch his spent muscles.

Jill, Tom and Chloe hadn't stopped screaming since catching sight of Ken on his approach to the finish. Ken spotted them as they were being held with the rest of the crowd behind a barricade, and he called out for the guards to let them inside. "They're my friends," Ken yelled. "It's okay! They're with me!"

A woman wearing a yellow race volunteer shirt bearing the American and Canadian flag logo of the marathon opened a gate to let the three pass. A chorus of shutters snapped as Jill ran into Ken's waiting arms, crying as she grabbed and kissed him long and hard.

"Oh my *God*, Ken! Oh my *God!*" she sobbed, holding his face in both hands. Another race volunteer smiled as she gently but firmly separated the two so race organizers, sponsors and other officials could have their photos taken with Ken. A few minutes later when it was time for group pictures of the top finishers, Hogan was nowhere to be found.

"How's it feel to win this race?" a reporter shouted.

"Three times better than coming in third and a million times better than coming in second," Ken answered.

"Where's Don Hogan?" another reporter asked.

"I think he's having a mammogram!" someone yelled, and laughter swept the crowd.

Most of the photographers hurried back to the finish line to get shots of the first women and wheelchair finishers, and officials watched proudly over Ken as reporters asked the standard questions.

"How did you feel during the race?"

"Great!" Ken replied, hugging Jill.

"Did you have a particular strategy in mind before the race?" asked another. "And did you stick with it or change along the course?"

"I planned to win," Ken answered. "And no, I didn't alter that goal anywhere along the way."

Detroit Free Press sports columnist Paul Rabiteau asked Ken for a private interview, and he said he'd be glad to oblige sometime before the awards ceremony, scheduled several hours later. First, Ken said, he wanted to catch his breath, clean up and spend a little time with his friends.

"Great, Ken," answered a man in a race official shirt. "If you'll come with us we'll show you to the winners' suite in the Westin, where you can clean up."

Jill, Tom and Chloe followed Ken and the pair of officials leading Ken to the hotel housed in the tall center column of the five-towered Renaissance Center.

"I'm sorry," one of the officials said, turning toward Ken's friends. "The winners' suite is open only to race winners, officials and credentialed press. Ken's just going to shower, grab a quick drink and come right back out. We also have to take care of a routine drug test and some quick paperwork for the prizes. We'll see you back here in less than an hour, okay?"

"Come on!" Ken protested. "You don't know how long we've . . ."

Jill hugged Ken tight and kissed his cheek.

"It's okay, Ken," she said. "Just hurry up! We'll be right here."

Walking securely between the pair of officials, Ken wondered when and where his hunters would make their next move. He had successfully eluded them before the race, but now they were surely watching him, from somewhere close. He considered that he was probably safe as long as he stayed in the public eye. But what would happen when he, the TV cameras and reporters parted ways after the awards ceremony? Would accepting his trophy be his last act as a free man? Or would they wait for him to return to school?

Just as Ken and the officials crossed Hart Plaza for the adjacent Renaissance Center an elderly female official called out and stopped them. One hand kept her wide-brimmed straw hat in place as she hustled towards the trio.

"Where are you taking our winner?" she gasped with a grin, obviously not a runner herself.

"To the winners' suite," the official on Ken's right answered, and the other took her aside to explain. The woman smiled, congratulated Ken and waved as she returned to her place near the finish line.

But a sickly, poisonous feeling flooded Ken's gut, and it intensified as he and the others entered the Westin. There were no other race officials in sight, nor any of the other finishers. Ken's legs froze midway through the lobby.

The men took Ken's arms from either side with a vice-like grip and whisked him into a service hallway to a freight elevator.

"We're on seventy," one said to the other, and the churning in Ken's stomach was flushed away by the icy grip of panic.

"I wondered when you guys would show up," Ken said. "Do you really think you're going to get away with me this easily?" he half shouted, his anxiety barely restrained. "I just won an *international marathon,* and in a few hours I'm supposed to pick up a trophy next door in front of the *whole world!*"

Ken's pleas were swallowed by the carpeted walls of the elevator, and his captors said nothing as they quickly cuffed his hands behind him, then watched the numbers flash above the door.

Ken was exhausted and he knew a fight now, especially against these two, was out of the question.

The elevator hissed open and the pair tightened the grip they had never eased on Ken as they half carried him into the hall. They stopped at the first room on their right, and Ken's heart pounded faster and harder than at any point in the race he had just finished.

The man to Ken's left knocked on the door twice. "It's Hudson," he said. The door quickly swung open and he hustled Ken inside while his partner stood guard outside.

As the door closed behind him, Ken saw another man facing him from the center of the living room of a luxury suite. It was

Michael from the Knoblock interrogation in Grand Rapids, now standing before a large picture window overlooking the Detroit River and Windsor. The guard entered from the hall to join Hudson, and both looked deadly serious as Michael uncrossed his arms, walked across the room and met Ken toe-to-toe.

The hiss of air conditioning offered no comfort against the tension-charged silence of the room. Finally, a slow, broad smile crossed Michael's face and he rammed his knee into Ken's groin with a grunt.

Dropping to the floor, Ken vomited what little water, sport gel and bile the race hadn't wrung from his stomach, and the blinding pain coiled him into a fetal ball.

"Just a little something I learned in high school football," Michael leered. "We didn't play very fair, I'm afraid."

He signaled for the others to pick Ken up, and his legs buckled under him again as the two silent "race officials" yanked him to his feet. The fierce blow so soon after the marathon had temporarily shut down Ken's whole system, and his body was rigid as one of the men dropped him onto a couch.

"Looks like you still don't play fair," Ken said, wiping his mouth on a cushion. "I'm surprised my father could be associated with an outfit that would use the likes of you." He struggled to sit as the pain vibrated through his crotch and cuff-bruised wrists. "I mean, he had integrity, brains, *substance* . . . He was a *real* man.

"You," he looked at Michael, "you're nothing but a glorified *security guard.* Maybe you'd be nicer to me if I had a doughnut or two to toss your way, *eh?*"

"So that's what you think I am?" Michael asked, no change in his mildly annoyed expression. "I have more military and security commendations than you could bench press, you *piss-ant.* I hold *advanced* degrees in military science, intelligence and law enforcement. I hold black belts of the *highest degree* in Tae Kwon Do and aikido and am *decorated* in advanced weaponry.

"Plus," he sneered, "my salary's *twice* what your father's was."

The boil that had set to Ken's blood flushed him with more than enough hatred-generated adrenaline to purge him of any marathon or kick-induced pain. He had never felt more like an animal, wanting nothing more than to rip Michael into a bloody mess.

"Well you might be the biggest, baddest *asshole* alive," Ken said. "But you don't work for the FBI, CIA, NSA, State Police, Grand Rapids PD or even the US Forest Service," he continued. "Barney Fife was a *real* cop. You work for a private corporation, making you a security guard, a *rent-a-cop.*

"You know, when I crossed the finish line at the marathon today it proved something I'd only recently figured out. When I came through that winner's tape to a race official with a medal instead of a law enforcement officer with handcuffs, I knew I was free. When all the cops stayed on crowd control and the only ones waiting for me after the race were officials, the press and my friends, I knew I wasn't a fugitive from *justice.* I was a fugitive from *Knoblock Systems.* And since Knoblock Systems hadn't reported me to any other law enforcement organizations, I knew that meant you were operating on your own, a rogue operation working outside legitimate security or law enforcement organizations.

"You hold some marginal authority on Knoblock's property, but out here in the world you're just another decorated and highly trained *asshole.* And if word gets out about your precious secret rooms, I suppose that could have serious repercussions with the government agencies you work for . . . I mean if a college student can blunder into one of your little hideaways, maybe that would give them second thoughts about the confidence they put in you for their top secret, overpaid contract work . . .

"And as head of security, your 'impressive' reputation would be on the line, too. Must've looked pretty bad for you when I knocked you out, locked you to that pipe and split in your car."

Michael's expression remained the same, although Ken knew his slow burn now had to be nearly uncontrollable.

"But the *real* crime was that you weren't trying to protect a corporation or national security," Ken continued. "You were going after an *innocent private citizen.* You had no just cause to detain me. And even if you had, you would have had to call the proper authorities, since I was on public property and not that of your employer.

"More simply put, despite your *superhuman* accomplishments, you don't have simple police powers," Ken went on. "You're a bunch of security guards, trying to keep a private citizen quiet about something he found in his own home.

"If I was wanted by the law for the deaths of those two who grabbed me in Indiana I would have been arrested at the marathon finish. If I were wanted for the wreck outside Knoblock or stealing the motorcycle for my escape, I would have been arrested at the finish line. If I was wanted for anything else I've had to do to keep myself free while you assholes were after me, I would have been arrested by someone.

"But I *wasn't*," Ken seethed, "because if you had reported the crimes, I would have had to testify in court, and the discovery of your precious hidden room would have been exposed. So you came after me yourselves.

"And since you aren't turning me over to authorities, and you are *legally impotent* to detain or imprison me, I have only to assume that kick in the balls was just the beginning of some kind of *final solution* you have for the problem of my existence."

Michael remained frozen by the window, eyes burning, arms crossed and jaw set. "The *problem* never was your existence," he said. "The *problem* was, and *is,* the existence of some Polaroid photos we need, and that you seem hell-bent to use to damage interests vital to the security of this country."

"Now you're going to wrap yourself in the *flag?!?*" Ken said in disbelief. "You just don't get it, do you? Knoblock Systems, no matter what it *does,* is *still Knoblock Systems* . . . If I were a threat to national security, someone from a sanctioned agency would have been there to scoop me up after the race. You can't legally hold or charge me any more than could the cop in the Village People."

Ken leaned back and locked eyes with Michael.

"But then you don't have to worry about any annoying legal formalities if you just quietly remove the problem, right?"

Michael said nothing.

"You know, Michael, I think I finally understand. It never was about that hidden room I found in our basement. That was just a wake-up call for me to look more closely at what had happened to my dad. It made me ask myself the question: *Was my father involved in something so secret that others would take his life to protect it?* Then other questions followed: *Did he know his company was above the law? Did he see how it treated innocent people?* Because I'm sure I'm not the first 'squeaky wheel' you've gone after. Did your arrogance bother him? Did you fear his conscience might cost Knoblock its 'golden child' status by sharing some of its dirty secrets with its 'godparents' in Washington?

"Apparently, in asking the questions I'm finding the answer," Ken said. "Were you involved?" he asked, still staring Michael in the eyes. "Were you with Knoblock when my father was murdered, or were you still earning merit badges at Camp Hardass?"

There was silence, and Ken went on.

"Did you set it up? Help carry it out? Were Cody and Truro in on it?"

Michael sat on the edge of an overstuffed leather chair, placed his palms together and rested his chin on his fingertips.

"Your father made some very . . . unreasonable demands," he said calmly. "He became much too . . . difficult . . . to work with, and he knew too much to let go in his . . . confused . . . frame of mind.

"Ironically, the fact that your father had to keep that hidden room and other secrets from you and the rest of his family was not a matter of concern," Michael continued, casually leaning back in the chair. "Seems he had some fundamental problems with one or two of the company's *projects*.

"Yes," Michael said, "the fact is that we were forced to silence him."

The pair of fake race officials who had brought Ken to the hotel exchanged uncomfortable looks.

"It *wasn't* the carload of black teenagers," Michael continued. "If you look at the police report you'll see that Cody and Truro were the only ones who saw the shooter.

"The shots came from one of our men in a van across the street from the stadium. As Cody, Truro and your father left the game they positioned your father in the middle. When a car of loud, rowdy kids approached Truro signaled and the shooter acted as the distracting car passed. Cody and Truro both said they saw the black teenage trigger-man and gave an intentionally inaccurate description of his vehicle. If police couldn't find it, neither could they question its occupants, leaving their identity and motives a mystery."

"So you got away with murder," Ken said. "For awhile, anyway."

Undeterred, Michael concluded.

"As far as the confused bystanders on the street were concerned, once Cody and Truro planted the black drive-by suggestion in them, more than a few said they'd seen the shooting, too."

Ken's chained fury was agonizing, and rivaled only by the frustration and irony that he was now captive to men who were part of the machine that had killed his father.

"That's defending *national interests?*" Ken hissed. "That's *justice?!?* Is that what my father *deserved?*"

"You can ask him yourself soon enough," Michael said, rising from his chair.

"The irony here is that you've already avenged your father's death, and you didn't even know it."

"What are you talking about?" Ken replied, curiosity now mixed with his contempt.

"Remember the couple you killed in that wreck in Indiana?" Michael asked. "Well the driver was the one who shot your f[ather."

"I didn't kill him," Ken corrected him, repulsed at being lumped in with the likes of Michael's people. "The bullet his partner shot him with came from a gun that had been pointed at me . . . Apparently the folks you use aren't as *highly trained* as yourself.

"You'd goddamn better kill me," Ken seethed. "Because if you don't I'll take you out myself, no matter how many Bruce Lee movies you've watched." Ken spat the words like a cobra shooting venom.

"If I have to come back from the grave I'll see to it that the *Detroit Free Press, New York Times,* ABC, CBS, NBC, CNN, every goddamned-body gets the whole story on how you murdered my father, and tried to silence me."

"Well, Mr. Perry, I'm afraid it's a moot point, since you've drawn your last free breath. But even if you were to find your way to the hallowed halls of the Fourth Estate, who would believe you? I mean, your credibility's shot! Who would listen to a man who had taken a huge dose of LSD and run around the streets of Detroit, breaking into a stadium and hauling off a street bum he thought was his father? You are a known partyer at your university, dropped out of the school without notice to go live in a hut with a bunch of monks, harassed us at Knoblock, stole and wrecked a company car, and a bystander's motorcycle.

"You may have just won a marathon," Michael went on, "but you've also attacked an innocent farmer and his dog, thrown two men from a moving train, and caused the death of a couple who were kind enough to offer you a ride while hitchhiking. And through it all you've continued to rave about a fantasy room hidden behind a wall in your *basement.*

"Do you seriously think anyone will believe you?"

"Give me a few hours with some professional investigators and I can prove it all," Ken said. "But when you filled in that secret room you gave me more help than I could have hoped for. With a little engineering and materials analysis, it will be easy to show that fill dirt and building materials were used to erase the former room's existence. And I still have the Polaroids showing what was there.

"I wonder," Ken said. "Are there other rooms like it in Cody's and Truro's basements? How about yours?"

Michael bristled. "That's exactly why we brought you in," he hissed. "You tell us where the photos are and maybe, just maybe we can come to an agreement."

Ken laughed hard enough to bring a spasm to his lower gut and groin. "Come on!" he groaned. "I'm supposed to believe I can have a shot at getting out of this if I give you the Polaroids? After you just explained how I've used up all my fresh air as a free man?"

"No matter," Michael said. "We'll get it out of you in Grand Rapids."

"Oh, hey! No need to mess up the body before the funeral," Ken said. "You want to see the photos? Get in your car, jump onto Woodward Avenue, head north to Birmingham and look for Gallery Troyat. You missed the opening by a few days, but they're all there . . . somewhat artistically embellished, framed and hung for public display . . . nine-to-five, Monday through Friday, with groups or special showings by appointment."

"What are you talking about?" Michael growled.

"My girlfriend's something of an artist, and I had a friend show her the Polaroids," Ken said. "I wondered if she'd share my appreciation for their, shall I say, *haunting* qualities."

Michael looked angrier than ever.

"Anyway, she did!" Ken said in mock surprise. "So much so, in fact, that she went to work on a special project in which she photographed the original Polaroids, then got creative with the negatives and reprints. After a little dodging and burning and other darkroom magic she turned those Polaroids into about a dozen works of art. The exhibit's titled "A Stillborn Secret," and you can get more information on it from the favorable review it got in the arts section of last Sunday's *Free Press*.

"Oh, don't worry," Ken assured Michael. "There is no indication at all as to where the photos were taken, nor what they're about . . . Just a series of artistic renderings of photos of a dark, lonely room.

"And while neither Jill nor I have the Polaroids in our possession, they're quite safe," Ken concluded.

"Do you really think a handful of Polaroid snapshots can save your *sorry ass?!?*" Michael bellowed.

"Not by themselves," Ken said. "But they do show where investigators can find evidence of where the hidden room was. That, along with my hunch that there are others like it in Cody's, Truro's or other Knoblock employees' homes might bolster my credibility considerably.

"And now that I know who killed my father, and why, I can get the ball rolling on some justice there, too."

One of the men with a radio told Michael their helicopter was on its way and they should get Ken ready to leave.

"I don't think that's a good idea, Michael," Ken insisted. "Several thousand friends and a small army of media are expecting me to pick up a trophy and prize money down there in a couple of hours."

"That's why we're leaving now," Michael said. "By the time they start looking, you'll be long gone."

Long gone. Ken didn't know exactly what Michael meant, but he wasn't about to ask. And he wasn't about to wait to find out.

"Can I at least stop in the bathroom to get rid of what little you didn't kick out of me?"

"Of course," Michael replied sarcastically. "Wouldn't want you to be uncomfortable during your flight."

Ken had a glimpse of hope when Michael reached behind his back and unlocked his handcuffs. But the encouragement drained from Ken's heart as Michael grabbed his left wrist, then his right and cuffed them together before him.

"This gives you the needed *freedom of motion* while keeping you immobile enough for any *motion for freedom,*" Michael said, smiling at his otherwise unappreciated turn of the phrase.

The larger of the other two men helped Ken to his feet, and his grip cut off the circulation in Ken's arm as he steered him to the bathroom. The guard held the door open as Ken tried to pull it shut behind him.

"Don't worry son, I won't look."

"Go ahead," Ken replied. "Judging from your face, I'd probably be the best-looking person you'd ever seen with their pants off."

"I have a feeling that real soon you're going to wish you were a lot nicer to me," the thug sneered, and he turned away as Ken fumbled through toileting while handcuffed.

"I understand that's how Houdini got his start," Michael yelled from his chair, and he and the others laughed hard while Ken wondered what the hell to do.

Even if the door were closed there was no bathroom window nor a ventilator duct large enough for him to escape through, even if he had the privacy and time to try. All he saw on the bathroom counter was a couple of plastic-wrapped glasses, several tiny soaps and shampoos and a wall-mounted hair dryer. No aerosols to turn into makeshift flame-throwers, as a TV spy might do in such a spot.

Exasperated, Ken reeled off some toilet paper, fumbled back to his feet and pulled up his shorts. He looked around and neglected to flush the toilet, as if the guard might not return until he heard the sound.

But a two-way radio crackled to life on the coffee table, and one guard picked it up as the other returned for Ken.

"Oscar says the bird's refueled and he's en route," the man with the radio said. "Should be here in fifteen minutes."

Michael nodded approval and turned to Ken and the other guard. "Don't bother changing him into street clothes," Michael said. "We don't have time. Let's move."

Ken wondered why their room was so high on the building. At first he thought they might toss him from it. Then it became obvious that none of them would be returning to the ground, not in Detroit, anyway.

Rather, they would have to go up only three floors to the helicopter pad on the hotel's roof. The approaching chopper would then fly the group over any witnesses or other problems they might otherwise encounter in trying to extract Ken from the scene.

Michael watched Ken as the other two made a sweep of the suite, making sure they took out everything they had brought. The pair of guards then resumed what had now become their familiar tourniquet grip on both of Ken's arms and whisked him into the hall.

Michael led the group to a heavy steel fire door at the far end of the hall, opened it, made sure no one was in the stairwell and motioned the others inside. Ken felt as if he were being led to a gallows as they hustled him up the stairs, and their footsteps pounded a continuous echo from the stark cement walls.

For Ken, the three flights of steps seemed to take an eternity since he feared what would come at the top. Would they really take him to Grand Rapids? Or fling him from the roof before taking off themselves? And if he was loaded into the helicopter, what hell awaited him in Grand Rapids, or *wherever* they were going?

But the climb also seemed to flash by as Ken was running out of time for escape. Once in the helicopter, there would be nowhere to run.

At the top of the stairs there was another gray fire door. Michael led them through it to another flight of stairs leading up to yet another fire door. Black stenciled letters announced ROOF ACCESS—OFFICIAL USE ONLY.

Ken's heart pounded against the lump in his throat, and he looked at the door as if it were the gate to hell. Michael sensed his fear and smiled. "Don't worry, Ken," he said. "We're not going to throw you off."

After unlocking the door, Michael went through and held it open for Ken and the others. The pair of heavies hauled Ken through the opening into the glaring sunlight from an all-too-close deep blue yonder.

"Nice day for flying," one of the guards said to no one in particular.

"Sure is," the other answered. "And here comes Oscar, right on schedule."

The panic-driven adrenaline soared Ken into hair-trigger hypersensitivity. It pulled into focus the faint sounds of the wind, distant birds, almost imperceptible street noise and the gut-dicing chop of the approaching helicopter. Acrid traces of bile remained in his dried mouth, and he smelled his own race and panic-driven sweat, the thick cologne of one of the guards, and some chemical odor. Glancing upwind he saw a parked window washers' platform with a bucket that held the source of the smell. A couple of squeegees and a box of sponges and rags also lay about the dormant scaffold, and an opened toolbox on the roof next to it suggested the platform was out of service for maintenance or repair.

The chopper approached the white, thirty-foot circle marking the helicopter pad, and Ken tried to recall if the stairwell door had locked behind them or if he could still get through it if he was able to break free. He managed a slight smile as he realized that other than the handcuffs, he was wearing the perfect outfit for a running escape.

Then, in a flash ignited by sheer desperation, Ken's mind delivered a plan he must have contrived in his subconscious, because his surface thought was consumed with fear.

The helicopter closed in slowly from a hundred yards out, weaving and bobbing like a giant moth, and Ken saw his chance. He knew all eyes would be on the bird as it eased down onto the painted white target of the heliport, and he would strike then.

Making sure he wasn't noticed, Ken glanced at the toolbox about three good steps away. Before looking back towards the oncoming copter, he burned into his mind the position of the toolbox and its contents.

The guard to Ken's right nodded an okay to the other, who then released Ken and went to the edge of the heliport to guide the pilot in.

Michael and the remaining guard watched as the third man raised his arms high to signal that the chopper was on the mark as the pilot closed in from about fifty feet above.

"I've always wanted to do this," Ken said to Michael.

"Go for a helicopter ride?" an amused Michael replied, one hand shielding his eyes from the growing prop-wash.

"No, silly!" Ken answered. "This!" he shouted, and jerked free of the guard and lunged for the toolbox. He fell heavy onto the box, grabbed a two-foot-long, twenty-pound adjustable wrench in a baseball bat grip and heaved it toward the blades of the nearly landed helicopter.

All four dove for the roof as the missile snapped one of the long, aluminum blades with a ringing electric ping. The impact was followed by a humming zip as the severed blade shot over their heads like a twenty-foot arrow.

The chopper's engines revved out of control as the pilot fought in vain to steady the wounded bird. Its remaining, off-center rotor blades hacked at the air and rocked the aircraft before crashing headlong onto the roof, about twenty feet off target.

The pilot screamed and shielded himself as the Plexiglas nose of the copter hit first, then crushed under the weight of the craft. The crippled blades hacked at the roof, spraying Ken and the others with its tar and gravel coating. The tail section wheeled crazily as its smaller rear rotor continued to whirl. The guard who had been directing the pilot was running away when the crippled rotor swung into him, sheared his arm at the elbow and slammed him to the roof.

By the time Michael and the other guard drew their guns, Ken had yanked open the door to the stairwell and did more falling than running as he tumbled to the top floor of suites.

Michael and his partner scrambled after Ken, who bashed a fire alarm and screamed "Fire! Everybody out!" as he tore along the hallway.

Ken kept up the screams as he ran, and pushed his way into the first door that opened in response. A small man was shouting something in French, and Ken shoved him back inside and locked the door behind them as the others hammered it wildly from the outside.

"*Excusez-moi, Monsieur,*" Ken said, and a briefcase and stack of papers flew from the coffee table he hoisted and hurled through the plate glass window.

Leaning through the ruptured window frame Ken saw that there was no balcony, ledge or other means of escape up or down the smooth glass and steel building.

A pair of shots cracked from the hall and parts of the lock, latch and splintered door sprayed the room as Ken swung himself out through the jagged window frame.

Stoked into wide-eyed panic, Ken frantically looked for anything he could grab onto as he hung from the window, its glass shards slicing into his still cuffed hands. Just as he was losing his grip on the blood-slickened window frame he noticed one of the small vertical steel rails used as a track for the window washing scaffold. But it was only about an inch in diameter, and some six feet from the window, making it too far for Ken to reach even if he weren't handcuffed.

Ken looked back through the window and saw Michael and the other man, guns drawn, pushing past the Frenchman on their way to the window. Just as they lunged for Ken, he took aim, jumped and caught the scaffold rail with both hands. The handcuff chain rattled over the tempered steel railing as the momentum from the leap pitched Ken's legs up and nearly even with his head before dropping to rest against his reflection on the glass and steel wall. Ken's bloody palms slid down the smooth steel rail some ten feet before stopping against an anchoring bolt.

Michael and his partner looked out at Ken in astonishment, and Ken was paralyzed with a new kind of fear as he saw no hand or foothold other than the thin railing that extended below him for some seven hundred feet. Fire trucks, ambulances and police cars were already converging at the hotel entrance below in response to the fire alarm. And the news and police helicopters first attracted by the copter crash on the hotel roof were now zeroing in on Ken as he clung to the tower.

Ken forced himself to look only where his hands were grasping the rail, and after a few deep breaths he was able to think straight. He decided to try the several-story climb to the roof rather than a seventy-floor descent along the rail. He found that his rubber-soled running shoes took a firm grip against the smooth steel frames of the windows, and he was able to push strongly enough with them to facilitate his awkward hand-over-hand climb up the railing, cuffs and chain rattling the whole time.

Michael kept low to the floor and far enough from the window so he wouldn't be spotted by those in the choppers, but he had to shoot fast before Ken would climb out of his sight. He took a two-handed aim and quickly squeezed off three shots while Ken was midway between the seventy-third floor and the roof. The first slug only grazed Ken's right shoe. But the second exploded through the fleshy part of his right thigh, and the third entered just above the small of his back and shattered his ribs.

The initial ripping, burning sensation the bullets gave as they tore into Ken quickly faded into the numbness of body and mind that come with trauma-induced shock. But just as a nearly unconscious runner knows to keep on towards the finish line, Ken knew he had to hold on, to keep climbing.

Ten feet to go, then six, and Ken heard someone shouting from above. "Hang on! Hang on, buddy! You can make it!"

You can make it, Mr. Perry!

Was his father there? Ken shook his head and turned toward the voice, his searching, vacant stare that of one lost in shock. The blood flowing down his bare legs became his father's warm embrace, easing him up the cold, smooth wall.

Ken looked at the paramedics calling from the edge of the roof, but they could tell he saw right through them, and his eyes began to roll back into his head.

"*HEY, MAN! WE'RE COMING!*" one of them screamed as another clamped his harness to a rope.

The shouts, the vision of his father, a gust of wind or something else rallied Ken's senses and strength enough for him to claw his way a couple more feet up the wall. But he stopped just short of the rescuers above.

Browning out from the loss of blood, Ken was on the edge of inevitable unconsciousness when he felt the top bolt of the rail he'd been climbing. He placed his right hand over the end of the rail and reached his left up towards those calling to him. But the handcuffs kept him inches out of reach.

Just as the paramedic in the harness swung his legs over the edge to lower himself, Ken lost his grip.

The thousands watching from the foot of the building or via helicopter-mounted TV cameras gasped as Ken's body went limp and dropped. But it jerked to a halt as his handcuff chain hooked the end of the window washer railing.

Smoke and fire rose from the crashed helicopter on the roof as Ken's blood flowed down the tower's mirrored skin. In seconds the paramedic lowered to clamp a cable over the handcuff chain that had saved Ken. Those on the roof hoisted the paramedic and Ken together, and when Ken's hands cleared the railing, the paramedic gathered him in a bear hug for the short ride to the roof.

The front of the paramedic's blue uniform was a glistening crimson as he released Ken's limp body to his partners on the roof.

A medevac helicopter had landed as far as it could from the smoldering wreckage of the Knoblock machine, and Ken was lashed to a backboard and slid into the idling bird's belly.

One medic jammed a transfusion IV into Ken's arm to counter the severe bleeding which another was feverishly trying to stop. And in the time it took for the one-mile flight to the hospital, Ken's condition was diagnosed as critical.

They had stopped the bleeding, and Ken's vital signs were weak but steady as he was off-loaded on the hospital roof. Now the full resources of its trauma unit would be brought to bear in assessing his internal injuries and fight the onset of shock, which replaced blood loss as the imminent threat to Ken's life.

Ken's mind rested in the merciful arms of morphine and shock, his face half-obscured by an oxygen mask as a turquoise-gowned crew engulfed his gurney and ran it into the emergency room.

They finally lifted Ken from the cart onto an examining table, and the compress over his thigh tore open, splashing blood over the table's green paper liner.

Ken moaned and opened his eyes briefly before they again fluttered closed, and he snapped into a head-banging fit as his arms and legs stiffened and shook.

"He seized!" someone screamed, and a couple of muscular male orderlies restrained Ken's limbs, then pulled tight a nylon strap across his forehead.

A doctor cut straight up Ken's T-shirt and through its blood-slickened race number to expose his lower chest, where the shot to his back had exited.

"Couldn't you cut around that number, Doc," Ken gasped, his limbs knotted in spasms. "It's a souvenir!"

"Must've been one hell of a marathon!" the doctor said. He worked frantically without looking up, but was amazed that his patient was even semi-rational.

"The marathon was a breeze," Ken panted, wincing as the doctor lifted his back to look at the entry wound. "But that bed race on the way in here . . . Now *that* was a bitch!"

Ken again lost his feeble grasp on consciousness as he fell into a slumber squirted into him through a needle he never felt.

Pulling the shirt back over Ken's shoulders, the ER doctor saw the recently healed stitches on the left side of his chest.

"I remember you," he told his unconscious patient. "I sure wish you'd learn to outrun your demons, Mr. Marathon.

"I'm tired of patching up their claw marks."

CHAPTER TWENTY-ONE

Jill, Tom and Chloe had arrived at the hospital minutes after Ken, and they kept an overnight vigil as he first went through several hours of emergency surgery before his placement in the intensive care unit.

The twenty-four-hour police guard had no problem keeping watch over Ken through the glass panels of his room in the ICU. And the family-only policy for visitors was strictly enforced by both hospital and police.

Mrs. Perry joined Ken's friends in a waiting room immediately upon her late-night arrival from Grand Rapids. She was successful in convincing officials that Jill should be allowed to join her in visiting Ken, since they were engaged to be married and Jill was several months pregnant with his child.

"It's not a lie," Mrs. Perry whispered to Jill as they followed a nurse to Ken's room. "It's a prediction."

A Detroit police officer rose from her chair as the pair approached and saw Ken through the glass. Jill gasped and started to cry as she sought shelter in Ken's mother's arms. Maternal instinct steeled Mrs. Perry's nerves and resolve to see her son through whatever had come, and she half-carried the sobbing Jill inside his room.

Ken was hooked up to two IV bags and a respirator, and a tube taped to his left side drained blood from his lung into a bottle on the floor. The ribs around the tube were heavily taped and seemed to strain as Ken's chest raised and fell with each slow, labored breath. A monitor beeped in time with Ken's heartbeat.

A man with "Dr. Dieterich" sewn on the chest pocket of his lab coat turned from one of the machines and greeted the women.

"I'm Dr. Christopher Dieterich, and as head of the emergency physician staff I'm personally looking after your son, Mrs. Perry . . . and your husband, Mrs. Perry," he said, turning to Jill.

Jill smiled at Ken's mother as both heard the title used for Jill for the first time.

"I'm sure you know he's had a pretty tough go of it, and he's not out of the woods yet," the doctor continued. "But he is strong and showing good signs for recovery."

The women went to either side of the bed and each took one of Ken's hands, stroking them and his hair, face and shoulders.

"I'll have to remind both of you to be very careful not to disturb any of Mr. Perry's wounds or dressings," Dr. Dieterich said. "I think hand-holding and a kiss or two are safe."

The doctor then went over Ken's injuries with the women and told them how the flesh wound to Ken's thigh had done little muscle damage and none, apparently, to bones, nerves or major blood vessels. It would probably heal to or near one hundred percent, in time.

"The wound to the torso is another story," he said. "Other than the lung, there is no apparent vital organ damage. But X-rays show that the bullets devastated part of the second and much of the third and fourth ribs on the left side, spraying bullet and bone fragments throughout that area. Consequently, the left lung was punctured, collapsed and then filled with the blood we're now draining.

"The best thoracic surgeon in Detroit spent nearly six hours extracting the fragments, checking things out and sewing things up. And Mr. Perry took nearly thirty pints of blood through it all. Even so, his upper body recovery looks good, too, with work.

"And if you two can keep him out of trouble," he said, looking at the pair, "you could all have a long, healthy life together."

"That's good to know, doc," Ken murmured, jolting his mother and Jill with surprise.

"Ken! Kenny! I'm here! I love you!" his mother exclaimed, smashing his cheek with a kiss.

"Oh *God*, Ken! You don't know what kind of *hell* it's been!" Jill sobbed. She held his hand tight in hers. "I've been so scared for you!"

"I'll leave you three alone," the doctor said, heading for the door. "Behave yourselves," he commanded. "Lots of love, but *little* touching!"

The love Ken felt flowing through the women's hands seemed to lift him out of his battle-ravaged body. But Ken's mother's reddened eyes betrayed long tears that had preceded their reunion.

"Kenny, *dear God!*" she sobbed, "what's this all *about?* All this seems to have a connection to daddy's company," she went on, "and this morning they found Paul Cody. He *hanged himself* sometime last night in his garage. Poor Jeanette found him and they took her to the hospital in shock."

Ken wondered who had found the original Judas after his neck-breaking fall from grace.

"And Dennis Truro has *disappeared,*" Mrs. Perry sputtered. "The police are looking for him."

For the next two hours Ken told his mother and Jill of the secret room he had found in his family's basement nearly three months earlier. He spoke of his quest to resolve the doubts about who and what had caused his father's death, and the series of misadventures that had carried him through several abductions, escapes, blood, darkness, death, a biker bar and a monastery. And he told them about the old monk who showed him how to look within for the answers that he had sought in vain just about everywhere else.

Ken's mother and Jill told him that news accounts had been sketchy. But it appeared that at least two men had been arrested and charged with attempted murder in connection with the after-race attack on Ken, and that they had also been connected to the wrecked helicopter atop the Renaissance Center. All were linked to Knoblock, and the investigation would be ongoing.

Will it? Ken asked himself.

He wondered just how much clout Knoblock's status as a cog in the national security wheel would afford it special consideration by the legal system. Would they be able to get off by pleading that the whole matter dealt with classified information?

The men arrested at the Westin were to be arraigned sometime that morning, Mrs. Perry said.

"I need to make a call," Ken said, and all three looked in vain for a telephone. Jill went to the nurses' station and asked if one could be brought into Ken's room.

"I'm sorry," the head nurse said. "It was removed by the police for security reasons."

Jill returned with the news, and Ken asked for the guard outside the door to come inside and explain why.

"We've been told the judge is going to impose a gag ruling on this case," the policewoman said. "So it was taken out as a precaution."

Ken's mother offered her best maternal consolations that everything would be all right. But Ken fumed at the prospect that the whole bloody mess, especially his father's murder, could be quietly wrapped in a shroud of "national security" and slid into oblivion, as had been the hidden room.

The guard returned to her chair outside the door, and the twinkle in Mrs. Perry's eyes tipped Ken off that she was with him in this fight.

"I don't know if you're allowed to eat this, but I got it for you at the gift shop downstairs," she said, pulling a bag of red licorice, his favorite candy, from her purse.

She sat on the edge of the bed, kissed her son and pulled his hand to her side. He felt a small cellphone beneath the plastic bag she placed on his palm.

"Battery's fully charged," she whispered.

A nurse ducked in and told the women they would have to leave so Ken could get some rest.

"Fine," Mrs. Perry said, and Jill nodded.

"Don't worry, Kenny, we're staying right here until you're better," his mother assured. "We'll be in the waiting room or cafeteria."

Jill took her turn for a long, deep kiss and Ken thanked God for them both as they disappeared into the hall.

Ken sat the candy beside him, rolled onto his side away from the glass window and held the phone between his ear and the pillow. He first dialed information for the *Detroit Free Press* newsroom, then punched in that number for a connection to Paul Rabiteau. Ken spent the entire life of the cellphone battery recounting every detail that had taken him from the discovery of the secret room in his basement up to and including his waking up in the hospital where he was denied a telephone, despite the absence of any kind of court order restraining his freedom of speech.

Ken also told the reporter about Jill's art show in Birmingham, and that the original Polaroids were safe and available for scrutiny, if necessary.

"I'm a sports writer," Rabiteau said. "But it looks like the best story of my career so far is going to involve a lot more than fun and games . . . I'm on it," he assured. "Stay well and keep me updated."

The writer gave Ken his cell and home numbers, and Ken promised to stay in touch.

Several days later, after painstaking investigation, fact-checking and basic, coffee-fueled keyboard pounding, Rabiteau finished a five-part series on Ken's odyssey. The first installment appeared on page A1 of a Sunday morning edition, above the fold.

Running to Justice the headline read, with the kicker:

> *Marathon is home stretch*
> *in avenging father's murder*

Prosecutors for the Federal Court in Detroit continued to hand down indictments surrounding not only crimes committed against Ken Perry, but others related to the reopened investigation of his father's murder, as well.

Upon his release from the hospital Ken returned to Oxford, not so much for school—since he had to drop all that semester's courses—but to be with Jill. That Christmas they would be married in Kumler Chapel by a priest named Cassian, with a tuxedo-clad biker named Kerwin as a groomsman.

As Ken's strength returned he eased back into running the frozen streets to and from a snowy, deserted Hueston Woods.

Yes, he thought as the plow-compacted snow crunched beneath him, *the road does go on forever.*

But his last race for his father was finally done.

Printed in the United States
65365LVS00003B/86